A Promise Land of Plenty

by

B. P. Laz

authorHOUSE®

AuthorHouse™
1663 Liberty Drive, Suite 200
Bloomington, IN 47403
www.authorhouse.com
Phone: 1-800-839-8640

This book is a work of fiction. People, places, events, and situations are the product of the author's imagination. Any resemblance to actual persons, living or dead, or historical events, is purely coincidental.

© 2007 B. P. Laz. All rights reserved.

No part of this book may be reproduced, stored in a retrieval system, or transmitted by any means without the written permission of the author.

First published by AuthorHouse   12/31/2007

ISBN: 978-1-4343-3355-1 (sc)
ISBN: 978-1-4343-5979-7 (hc)

Library of Congress Control Number: 2007906138

Printed in the United States of America
Bloomington, Indiana

This book is printed on acid-free paper.

DEDICATED TO FRIENDS

Acknowledgments

It took four years to create, write, publish, and place this work of fiction into the hands of a reader. Without help, there would never have been such an event in my life. My thanks go out to my special friends Jeannie and Donna who were there from day one, and to those friends at tennis, golf, and my breakfast club. They all suffered through my constant updates and rewrites. Thank you to Bonnie and Howard for providing their computer skills and to Gina for all the years that she encouraged me. My very special 'thank you', the one with the star of patience, belongs to my husband for his support on this project.

Prologue

Brooklyn

At 10:30 on the last Friday night of May, temperatures were still spring-like and the sweltering days of summer had not yet appeared on local weather maps. Within a five-mile radius of Middle Street, small shops, grocery stores, and family-owned restaurants had already closed and locked their doors. Almost everything and everybody had settled in for the evening.

Light-hearted sounds of innocent laughter drifted down the otherwise quiet and deserted street as a trio of high school boys joked and romped their way home from graduation practice.

This was the eve of their last days of high school and they were preoccupied with talk of summer jobs and hot dates with cute girls. Carefree as teenagers of eighteen often are, they had only the one assignment of keeping spotless their black caps and gowns, the last explicit instruction from their homeroom teacher Miss Sarah Johnson.

A lively threesome, they had been friends and desk mates since the first day of grade school in old Miss Wesley's classroom. All about their neighborhood they were known as the ethnic trio: Samuel Abraham Steinberg, Lewis Angelo Capalo and Hubert Franz Berman.

But this night would soon change the course of their lives when suddenly, and without warning, an unmarked panel truck careened around the corner, streaking past them at an excessive rate of speed.

Tires squealed! BAM!

The speeding truck struck the concrete curb and, like a flying missal, it blasted high into the night sky. As if momentarily suspended by steel wires, it seemed to linger in mid-air. Then brutally, it spiraled downward, pounding with a loud, hard force onto the dry pavement of the street below!

The wrecked vehicle was now on its side, spinning and scooting down Middle Street. Blistering hot sparks, with electric colors of blinding yellows and sizzling reds, flamed out into the surrounding darkness. The robust and chaotic motion finally propelled the battered bulk into a lamppost, promptly knocking it backwards ten-solid feet from its base.

Savage sounds of the wreckage gave way to a pronounced slow hiss that seeped into the air as the truck's radiator water spewed steadily onto its hot engine. Vital fluids of gas and oil sneaked out in little streams down along the carnage, from bumper to bumper.

The rear doors had popped open, expelling the interior payload, an upright 3-ft long x 2-ft high, metal box mounted on four, ball-bearing wheels.

This strange cargo was rolling freely towards the direction of the three boys who had not moved from their stunned position on the sidewalk. The traveling contraption gained speed, jerking awkwardly to the left and bouncing up onto the curb. It teetered, jerked back to the right and jumped off the curb, abruptly stopping when its wheels lodged in a drainage grate.

As if destiny had designed the bizarre event, that had lasted no more than a few minutes, the mysterious box sat no more than fifteen feet from where the boys stood.

The loud commotions aroused the curious. Along both sides of the street, porch lights clicked on; people threw open their windows, leaning out to see what had happened.

The bravest of the lot rushed to their doorways and out onto the street where they were drawn closer to the gruesome sight of the driver's bloody head, protruding through the broken windshield; his eyes wide-open in a dead stare.

With due attention centered on the wreckage, the three boys ran, unnoticed, towards the trapped cargo. It was then that they first saw a few hundred-dollar bills, lying haphazardly about the pavement.

Without hesitation, Lewis Capalo scooped them up, sneakily stuffing them into his front pockets.

As the three of them finally reached the damaged box, they discovered a jagged opening at one corner. Peering inside, they saw money; **lots** of money, band-wrapped and erratically tossed about in the dented, metal container.

Quickly, the three boys rocked the box back and forth, freeing the wheels from the grate. In a spontaneous reflex, Hubert Berman threw his graduation gown over the thing, completely covering it. He grabbed the front end. Steinberg and Capalo hung onto the rear. Like thieves in the night, they greedily pushed their draped treasure into an adjoining alley.

"That's a ton of money," rattled Steinberg!

"Shh! Shut up, Samuel, somebody will hear you," Capalo whispered. "We've got to think! Shit, just shut up! Think, guys, think."

On the heels of their dilemma, a deafening boom rattled windows! Fiery flames shot high into the air and the pungent smell of heavy smoke drifted into the alley.

"Shit! What the hell?" Capalo's head whipped around for a better view of the alley's entrance.

"It blew! That truck just blew up," exclaimed Steinberg!

"We've got to get out of here," Capalo pleaded.

"I've got an idea. My grandmother died last week. We'll go to her grave and bury this money. Let's go now!" Berman promptly suggested.

"Dumb. That's dumb," snorted Capalo. "We can't go now. There's a hot, fire ball on that street and people, lots of people, are everywhere!"

"So? We go the other way. Hubert is right," Steinberg remarked. "We can easily bury the box in his grandmother's fresh grave. Get it, stupid, in the easy-to-dig dirt."

"Man, somebody is going to be looking for this money. Who does it belong to? I'm telling you two, we got to think," Capalo argued.

"Shut up, Lewis. Shut up! That guy out there burned up. He's dead meat. We've gotta hide this box and do it **now**," Steinberg said.

"Wait, you guys, I bet I know who had all this money. Yesterday my dad told me that the bookie Bruno Botello was killed outside the pool hall. I bet it is his dough." Capalo was shaking like a wet puppy.

"That's even better," Steinberg said with delight! "If that driver is dead and that guy Botello is dead and the truck is burning up, who will ever know about this money?"

"That's right," Berman agreed. "Let's go. Once the box is buried, no one will ever suspect that we have the money. We are just kids to them. They would never suspect we could be so smart."

With sirens wailing in the distance, the three of them were more than ready to go. They took off in a steady jog! And, without further planning, they spontaneously guided their loot through deserted alleys and into the murky shadows of buildings.

When they reached the cemetery's entrance, the two massive gates were wide-open. In contrast, a six-foot, iron fence marched from the entrance, encasing the full acreage. Along this barrier, a pointed-leaf vine grew in abundance. Its old, meandering branches had crawled onto the gate posts, wrapping tightly around their rusted hinges, obstructing, for many years, all possible movement.

The three boys were caught by surprise with the inky blackness and the spooky emptiness of the place. They hesitated, shaken by what lay ahead; each one not quite sure that he was up to the task.

Then, with Berman's nudging, they slowly made their way through the open gates and down a path leading to the center of the cemetery, the familiar route that he knew from the recent funeral procession for his grandmother.

Capalo's eyes darted about; eerie sights of imaginary creatures were capturing his attention. *I'm scared,* he thought over and over, praying in intensity that the others would not notice his shaking hands as they pushed the box down the pavement and across rocks and grass until they reached the grave site.

At first, six hands plowed into the digging and tossing of the cool dirt. But when Berman unexpectedly caught sight of a nearby maintenance shed, they used the rake, shovel, and a stack of boards found behind the locked building.

With their discovered tools, they frantically etched out a crude, roughly-measured hole. Steinberg arranged two boards like a ramp and they guided the metal treasure down into its dirty, hiding place.

They shoveled, kicked, and pushed the soil back into place and then, hurriedly, raked back and forth, smoothing out any rounded clots.

Steinberg had the clever idea to spread leaves and small sticks about the surface so that the dig didn't look too fresh. They returned the tools to the shed and gathered once again at the grave.

"That money is going to be trouble," Capalo sighed.

"You are a chicken, Lewis. You read too many comic books. It won't be like that. Hubert knows best."

"Well, I do know that we can't touch the money for a long time and then only in small amounts, at least until we discover a way to get that box out of here. Until then, we do nothing."

"Yea, that's right," Steinberg responded without giving Capalo time to say anything. "At first we do nothing. Then, somehow, we will meet and take out what we want to spend. Right? Isn't that right, Hubert?"

"That's right. But I think we need more. We need to take an oath not to tell anybody about this. We have got to trust each other."

"I'm not cutting my finger and drawing blood. No oath is that important to me. I'm telling you guys, let's go," Capalo said, his stubbornness like that of a mule.

Then, without warning, he jerked upright as the sensation of warm urine drained onto his leg, leaving yellowish wet spots seeping into his dirt-smudged pants. Terrorized by the whole unsavory evening, it had finally come to this humiliating calamity; at eighteen, his own pee was uncontrollably running down his left leg.

Unaware of his friend's soiled breeches, Steinberg spoke up. "Lewis, sometimes you are so stupid. We don't even have a knife. We are men now, men of honor. All that kid stuff is behind us."

"Yea, stupid, it takes one to know one! Wait a second! Hey… wait a second! I just realized that the money will get us girls. And if we are men now, we can get the older girls for the rest of our lives. Yea, I like that idea! Yea, man, I'm in! Go for it Hubert, make up the oath."

The three teenagers zipped up their graduation gowns and bowed their heads as their secret ceremony began to take root. Surrounded by the decaying remains that lay silent about their deed, they sealed their futures with their clandestine oath.

"We, the three members of the Honor Guard Secret Society, promise to keep our secret from all other friends and from all our

family members. We are bound together for life in this secret, like blood brothers, one to the other. Each member is dependent on the other two. We are therefore one."

1

Sixty- two years later
Boston

"Did you hear the one about the two nuns waiting in a long line to see Saint Peter at the Golden Gate? The first nun, Mother Superior Mary Margaret said – I pray that I get into Heaven. I have tried to live a spiritual life, do good deeds, and confess my sins. So, Sister Mary Michael, what have you done to prepare for Heaven? The other nun, old and wrinkled, replied – I bought a bingo card. WHAT? A BINGO CARD? The righteous Mother Superior yelled out! The wise little nun, with a twinkle in her Irish eyes, smiled and said, – I bought it from Saint Peter!"

Laughter erupted in the small, smoked-filled room and Patrick O'Reilly had struck again, feeding the jokes and getting the slapstick attention. Normally O'Reilly was a quiet man but, when he stood in front of an audience, he blossomed into a carnival carny, barking out one-liners and reciting a practiced litany of Catholic jokes. Years ago he had quit a boring bookkeeping job to devote full time to his comic career. Fortunately, good times came to him and he could support himself and his immigrant mother by working the nightspots in the Irish section of Boston.

"What an audience, I gotta tell you, you guys have been great," said O'Reilly as he finished out his set. "Now it is my pleasure to introduce our talented star performer. The dame you came to see. Here, on our stage at Mac's Bar; right here, TONIGHT, I give you our playgirl, banging out your favorite tunes on those pearly keys. LADIES and GENTLEMEN, please welcome the banger, the bombshell, the blond and beautiful BRANDY!"

Dirty curtains swept across the low stage and Brandy, seated behind a well-worn black-lacquered piano, hit the keys and began to sing the club's most requested song - *Diamonds Are a Girl's Best Friend*.

The crowd whistled and clapped!

For Brandy it was more than a song. It was her dream, her special dream to have such diamonds, to be a woman of wealth, enjoying an easy life. Yet, dreams for Brandy were not reality; those precious stones were never seen around her neck or found in her cheap, little jewelry box.

As she belted out the show tune, her puffed-up blond hair bobbed left to right, her red lips flashed wider, and her lusty voice was like a siren's call. The provocative v-neck dress did its job too, dipping as it did, conveniently revealing her bountiful cleavage.

The unruly fans, mostly cigarette smoking and beer drinking men, went wild!

The few women, those who came on regular occasions, paid little attention to the bombshell. They had their own agendas, either hanging tight-armed onto their current boyfriends or fanning out into the crowd, picking up new ones.

Soupy smoke drifted upward in curlicues, blending into the rays of the hot spotlight. If one noticed or even cared, the later the hour the more the thick smoke swirled and cascaded. The sticky layers of hair spray on Brandy's hair attracted the mix and it sat upon her head like a crown.

She had quit the nasty habit of smoking, but this was the price that she paid for the job. A job being what most would call it. But to Brandy, it was a passion. She had a natural, musical ability, a God-given talent as she would describe it in her modest, sincere ways.

Music carried her to places far removed from what she was and from what she had left behind.

It was three in the morning when Brandy unlocked her apartment door and flopped down on her queen-size bed. She kicked off her shoes and dutifully rubbed her swollen, achy feet. Within minutes, sleep was a welcomed visitor. It took charge way before she could remove her heavy makeup or her suffocating 40 double-D bra, the one that best uplifted her full breasts.

A single lamp on the bedside table stayed lit the rest of the night. While, across the street, a neon sign blinked off and on, advertising the vacancies at the Lamar Hotel. The blended lighting gave the room a rosy hue, but without a rosy feel. What did it matter or to whom? Without spouse or boyfriend, she slept alone in the small apartment.

By noon, the bells at St. Matthew Catholic Church loudly pealed out their call. Brandy heard them, but didn't care. Long ago, she had abandoned her family ritual for Sunday mass and, now, her Sunday mornings simply meant mugs of strong, black coffee and the Boston Globe.

She tried to stay in bed, covering her head with her favorite blanket. But the alarm clock, just beyond her reach on the nightstand, soon started its irritating BUZZ. It buzzed and buzzed, until Brandy loudly cursed the noisy morning and sent the clock sailing across the room.

She was up, but she was gritty!

Still fully clothed, Brandy walked slowly into the bathroom, her bare feet shuffling across a cold, unfriendly floor. At the mirror, the harsh reality of the morning-after jumped up and kicked her. Hair strands of bleached blond were sticking out, twisted about in all directions like a maze of Chinese noodles. Dull roots, the graying kind that women hate, were desperately crying out for immediate attention.

She studied the reflection of her fat face with its puffy bags and tired eyes; not to mention, nor did she want to, the tell-all age lines that crinkled in the hollows of her cheeks and dug deeply into the pale area at the tip of her eyebrows.

"Damn. I'm old, wrinkled, and plump," she moaned aloud as she walked from the sink, dropping her dress, stockings, panties, and bra into a messy lump on the bathroom floor.

Even the pulsating spray of the shower did little to lift her spirits. But when she began to sing, even if it was in the privacy of her shower, the music filled the spaces of her mind, pushing away all bad thoughts. At first she hummed, and then her voice lifted into a spirited hymn, a song she could never sing at Mac's Bar.

The pay at the bar did support her, barely though she would constantly lament whenever she asked for a raise. Yet, when she did need extra cash, she would flick her false eyelashes and, with a hardy laugh, throw back her shoulders in a timely launch of her 40 double-Ds. The guys loved it and if she did it JUST RIGHT, they would gladly fill her tip jar with dollar bills!

Brandy wrapped a robe about her clean, spent body; found her purse and counted her money. She tossed the loose change into a piggy bank and rolled up the bills, hiding the small wad in a coffee can. The rest of the afternoon she did absolutely nothing that required any energy.

That evening, after climbing four flights of stairs dimly lit by cheap light bulbs, Patrick O'Reilly wiped his brow, puffed and then knocked on Brandy's door. It was around 7:30 p.m. and he knew that she would be home.

Where else would she go? Mac's Bar was always closed on Sunday, the only day of the week that lonely boozers were not in the bar, putting out money and loading up on cheap beer.

"It's me, Brandy. Patrick," he shouted through the hall door.

"Coming," she answered as she flipped two, bolt locks and lifted the chain. "What are you doing out on a Sunday night?"

"Came to see you," he smiled and said.

"Well, it's certainly a nice treat!"

Closing the door behind him, she turned towards the couch, patting her hair into place and pulling her robe a little tighter. But why bother, heck, O'Reilly had already seen her in the nude. Three years ago he had put her to bed, dead-drunk she was, after one of her boyfriends had given her a black eye before he high-tailed it out of Boston.

O'Reilly handed her a 6-inch, yellow envelope. "Happy Birthday to you and best wishes for another year," he proclaimed.

"I'm trying to forget this one. But it is sweet of you to remember," she replied before breaking into hysterics over the silly message in the card.

"That's better," he said. "I like to hear you laugh. And just remember that you haven't reached your second thirties yet. Being fifty-nine is a nice odd number."

"You can say that because you are not fifty-nine. Just you wait."

"I also have a deal to offer you," he replied, giving her the newspaper he had been carrying under his arm. "I read an ad that a piano player is needed for a chartered 8-day cruise. The local musicians are not picking up on it because it is not a union job."

"How do you know this? When did you ever go on a cruise?" She laughed and winked at her trusted friend.

"I'm serious," he said. "I got it straight from my cousin. He's in the union. Look, the address is there in the ad section and it says to ask for a Stanley Fizer. He's the guy lining up the entertainment."

"Do you know the details? What about Mac? He'll cuss until the cows come home if I'm flake out and not show up at the bar."

"I don't know too much about the arrangements, but I do know that they need a piano player. See this guy Fizer at 9:00 tomorrow morning. After that, tell Mac that he owes you some time off. Brandy, you really need it. Oh…… I mean, you deserve it."

"You are thoughtful, Patrick. You always seem to have the right words. Most guys I know would come right out and say, Brandy you look like shit."

She had always referred to him as her best friend and her private confessor. He knew exactly where he fit into her life; knew that nothing more would ever come of it. But just the fact that she cared was the highest compliment to him.

She looked over the ad that he had circled and it appeared to be a very, legitimate offer. Since she had no spare money to pay for a vacation, the idea of eight days on a cruise ship was way too tempting to ignore. And, if Patrick O'Reilly had given it his blessings, what more proof was needed?

She offered him a steaming mug of aged coffee and asked him to stay around for dessert so that they could discuss the trip.

"No," he said. "I've got to go and right now. Mama is home and you know how she is. If I'm not there by 9:00, she starts calling Father Murphy over at St. Matthew's."

"Right, I remember."

Brandy had heard that same sentence so many, many times before; but not once, in all the years that she had known her wonderful friend, had he not been home before his mother could make that phone call.

2

It was 8:30 a.m. and Brandy was early. She rechecked the newspaper for the fourth time, reciting the name Stanley Fizer and verifying his address on the busy street of Commonwealth.

GALA ENTERPRISES was etched on two, eight-foot glass doors. The words halted her for a long moment and when she stepped into the foyer she was flustered for a second or two more as she walked across an oriental rug to a fancy, imported-looking desk.

Not once in her musical career had she ever left her resume at such an establishment. There was also the strong possibility that she had never once been in such an office with this very expensive decor.

No one sat at the reception desk; no one to welcome her or to stop her. And, when she heard a man's angry voice in the next room, the main office she presumed, she pushed open the door just wide enough to see in.

A slender man, with rolled-up sleeves, was pacing the floor and shouting into a speakerphone, positioned at a perfect angle on a massive but very organized desk.

"Who are you?' Fizer yelled when he saw her.

"Huh? Oh, I'm Brandy. I sing and play the piano."

"Who let you in? And which agency sent you here? Never mind," he blurted out. "Never mind, come in and let's hear what you can do."

Brandy sat down at a small upright in the corner of his office and she nervously started to play her favorite, *Diamonds Are A Girl's Best*

Friend. As she grew calmer, she displayed her full range of talent by smoothly shifting from show tunes to blues and into love ballads. And, with no cigarette smoke curling about her head and irritating her vocal chords, her voice, on this day, was in quality form.

Not missing a note, even when she turned to smile at Fizer, there was no lack of confidence in her playing ability. Yet, she began to worry over her selection of the low-cut, black dress that might soon be tagged as a bad decision for this particular occasion.

Fizer sat behind his desk, his body posture like that of a conservative judge, listening somberly to the evidence and contemplating with due diligence his final ruling. He gave no outward clues as to whether he approved of her choices in music or in her flirtatious outfit.

Brandy was sweating, but she hoped that he could not tell it from his posed distance across from the piano.

"You are hired," he quickly announced when she finished playing and turned to face him. "Get your suitcase packed with some decent clothes and be at the airport at 8:15 on Friday morning."

"That's it? Can I have a little more information?"

"Read this," he said as he handed her a manila envelope containing all the pertinent facts about the chartered flight, the cruise, the dates, and most importantly, the pay.

He opened the office door for her departure. By now his secretary had set up shop at the reception desk and she gave Brandy a raised eyebrow as the twosome walked out of Fizer's private office.

"Gigi, prepare the appropriate forms with all of Brandy's information. She's going aboard The Lily Pad for that scheduled party. I've hired her as the piano player for the lounge," he barked out his orders to the petite woman with a suspicious look still plastered on her face.

Then, with his same stern approach, he placed a quick pat on Brandy's shoulder, said no good-byes and turned towards his office door. "By the way, do you know anyone who plays the harp? I need someone for the dinner hour on the cruise."

"You might call Father Murphy at St. Matthew's Catholic Church. I've been told there's a lady in his parish that plays the harp for all the weddings and the funerals. She's the only one that I know of."

"Thanks. Gigi, got that? Check it out."

With Fizer back in his office, Gigi was rigid and abrupt as her computer gobbled up all of Brandy's information. She slid the contract towards Brandy and motioned for her to sign on the bottom line. With her signature in place, Gigi popped a copy of it into the packed envelope. And, that was all there was to it. Brandy was officially hired and cleared for boarding.

She left Gigi at her fancy desk and gladly made her way back to the more friendly surroundings of her own neighborhood.

While dressing for work, Brandy read through the various pages in the envelope, delighting over the details of the adventure that she was about to embark on.

In her overwhelming excitement about the paragraph that began with the words - THE TOTAL AMOUNT OF WAGES, that one, she circled with a red Bic pen. A wholesome monetary amount, it represented the largest paycheck that she had ever been offered for one week's performance.

When she got to the bar, she found Mac in the storeroom, moving dirty wine boxes and swearing at a frightened mouse that was darting in and out of the shelves.

"Eight nights? You said EIGHT nights," Mac boomed at her! "And what exactly am I suppose to do for eight nights?"

"I need a break, Mac. I need some good, clean air." She pleaded to the back of his head because he had stubbornly turned away from her and was pouring himself a double shot of Jack Daniels.

"Crap! The customers will drop away like flies without some music and a bouncy dame up on that stage."

"Okay, Mac. Let your niece Marsha fill in, she's always asking you for a job. So, give her a chance while I am gone. I'll call her tonight and she can come by tomorrow. I'll show her the ropes. You know she is good, you've heard her play."

"Damn, my sister Ruth will kill me if she knew that I let Marsha in this bar. Damn! Damn, Brandy, I bet you knew that Ruth was seeing about her sickly mother-in-law up there in Salem."

"No, Mac. I don't know anything about where your sister is. This offer just came up and it is a good offer. It's a chance at some vacation time for me. Besides, I can sure use the extra money."

With a grumpy attitude Mac shook his head, wiped his nose, slugged down another double shot and looked hard at her. "Marsha ain't got no boobs. Damn! You listen to me. Marsha gets your paycheck. I ain't paying twice for no woman. And, get to work! I ain't paying for you to be standing there yakking like one of my ex-wives."

She hated his grisly exterior but she respected the man for the way he protected her in the bar. He could talk rough and back it up. She knew that he would take a baseball bat to any patron who dared to sweet-talk her or tried to place a hand anywhere on her body. She was, as he often told her, a guarded piece of property that produced a profit for his till.

Later, the bar was packed the way Mac liked it. His cash register was singing with money from a group of welders who had come straight from their union hall. With such a rowdy crowd, Brandy cleverly used her 40 double-Ds to their best purpose. After all, her tip jar sorely needed the extra dough.

Patrick O'Reilly was just excited as Brandy when he learned the news that she had gotten the job on the cruise. "I'm working on a new line of jokes," he told her. "Mind if I mention you? It would be good to keep your name fresh in the minds of the customers."

"Thanks. I don't mind at all. Just don't let Mac give you any suggestions," she laughed with a wink.

By Tuesday afternoon she had purchased two after-fives at The Twice Around Shop. One dress, black and tightly fitted, had an expensive label but a very reasonable price tag. The other was a jade-green little number, not too sassy but flattering to her full-figured body. Combined with the long, black skirt and four shimmering tops in her closet, she hoped that these stage outfits would be right for the trip.

Fizer had said to pack some decent clothes but, as she figured it, what was decent to him might just be too matronly to the people at a party. So she stuck with her selections; bought a garment case and packed the outfits, along with a few casual things, including her fuzzy slippers and a robe.

By Thursday at 1:00, as she did every Thursday, she was sitting under the hair dryer at Daisy's, a combination hair and nail salon. Mildred Brown was on the stool in front of the dryer, layering red polish on Brandy's long, finely-filed nails.

"Mildred, I tell you, it was like a dream the way Patrick O'Reilly said you go see this man about the job. And it worked out. Just like a dream, it worked out," Brandy shouted over the annoying sound of the dryer. "I got the job. And the money for the cruise is more than I would make at Mac's in two months."

"I'm glad for you," Mildred sadly replied. "I dream about things like that, but even if I won a lottery I could never go on a trip. Mama would pray me into hell and my husband Wilford would just starve. He can't boil water."

"How is Wilford these days?" Brandy asked, though she knew the answer, having listened Thursday after Thursday after Thursday to the miserable details of Mildred's sour marriage.

"Oh, he's the same. Works hard he does down at the appliance store. But he never does anything else, just stares at that TV in our living room. Of course, mind you, I'm glad he works. I just dream of doing something really exciting, just once in my life. Not likely to happen though, since my Wilford is as dull as the dried-up wood on our coffee table."

"Men," smirked Brandy.

"Yeah," Mildred replied with a gloomy expression, "Yeah, men."

3

Mildred Jones Brown, thirty-two, lived in her parent's walkup in south Boston, a three-story structure on West 5th Street; it served as a church and as a house for two families. This had been the location for most, if not all, the phases in her controlled and lackluster life.

Born and raised on the second floor, Mildred had accepted Jesus and married Wilford Woodrow Brown on the first floor. And, to this date, her restricted life was continuing in a cramped apartment on the third floor.

In these mundane surroundings of family and church members, her persona projected a plain, simpleminded and unimaginative woman. But, at her six-days-a-week job in Daisy's Beauty Shop, she was viewed as a dependable worker and as a polite and friendly person. Though not one of the patrons would call her beautiful or mildly attractive, still, those caring folks judged her not by her looks.

It was there, in that friendly environment, that she had first enjoyed laughter. From her clients, she had learned to smile and was even known to giggle uncontrollably at their funniest jokes or their soap opera gossip.

Her father, who would never approve of such frivolous behavior, was the self-acclaimed Reverend Jerico Jones, founder and pastor of the Disciple's Holy Word Church. A fiery preacher of the Lord's word, he was a strict father and a withdrawn, domineering husband.

Her mother Martha Gibson Jones, void of joy, was an overly devout, born-again Christian who was so frigid, and brutally harsh, that no love was ever once extended towards Mildred, her only child.

Throughout her religiously controlled youth, Mildred obediently followed her father's dictates of reading the bible every morning and reciting her prayers, morning, noon, and night. Early on, she had also learned that her mother's sensitive temperament tolerated little noise.

No fun. No friends.

Literally, no happiness reigned in their household.

Even at school, Mildred was a sad and lonely little girl who didn't know how to play. Her classmates were cruel and insensitive.

Often they sang: *"Mousy Millie is plump and plain. Mousy Millie can't play our games."* And Mildred, weak little Mildred trying so hard not to cry, would scurry away.

By the age of twenty she was briefly courted and, without much ceremony, betrothed to Wilford Brown, a cheerless thirty-five-year-old man who had single-handily cared for his dying mother. There was no genuine romance to their ring-less engagement, only a verbal, monetary contract between her oppressive father and the shy groom.

Since their date of marriage, twelve uneventful years had slowly passed and, now, the forty-seven-year-old husband had settled into a boring contentment, bolstered only by a service technician's job at the ABC New and Used Appliance Store in a low income district.

As it had been for all those years, his meager earnings had been eaten up by the cable connection, rent, phone bills, utilities, and the Disciple's Holy Word Church. What was left was but a paltry portion for his daily lunches and the bus fares for his commutes back and forth to his repair cubical in the store.

Mildred's pay from Daisy's Beauty Shop provided the groceries, including Wilford's daily ration of beer. Her birth control pills, an absolute necessity in her view, though sex was rare, were always bought first before the milk or the bread. And when, though on very few occasions, there was enough money left for clothing, only church or work clothes were allowed.

It had turned colder on that particular Thursday evening when she unlocked the door to the dingy apartment. Even with the fresh news of Brandy's forthcoming cruise, Mildred could do no more than moan a big sigh as she entered her apartment.

Wilford, as always, was sitting on their well-worn couch, totally consumed by a weekly sports program.

"What's for dinner," he shouted over the volume of the 27-inch TV.

She cared little to make a response, simply hanging up her black, seven-year-old coat and going straight into the kitchen to begin the drudgery of cooking a large evening meal for the meat and potato man.

Like a robot on a track of habitual repetitions, she peppered the beans simmering in the pot, mashed the potatoes, and turned the frying pork chops. Endless time drug by and, in boredom, she stirred and she fried.

By 9:00 p.m., after devouring three portions of the heavy meal, stuffed Wilford fell asleep on the couch. Mildred closed her magazine, commandeered the TV remote, lowered the volume and left the room.

Her favorite place was the bedroom, though it could not be described as enjoyable or much-loved. It was merely the room were she escaped from the labors of the kitchen and from the boredom with her husband.

Behind two shoeboxes in the top of her closet, she kept a box with the wording - **Wedding Shoes,** hand printed in black lettering. The wedding shoes, purchased for her at a second-hand store by her mother, had long been discarded as a third-hand gift to another disinterested bride.

She kept her secret treasure stored in that cardboard box, the vault where she placed her private dreams in the form of tip money from her patrons at the beauty shop.

To her knowledge no one knew of this secret, certainly not her mother who rarely climbed the stairs to the third floor. Nor her father, who remained long hours in his church, sometimes even sleeping in the front pew.

As for Wilford, poor preoccupied Wilford, he had no clue that his quiet spouse was, at night, a cheating wife.

But cheating she had been doing for these past, long years. In the nightly seclusion of the bedroom, she had squirreled away the extra money for her future.

Hopefully, she deemed, an exciting future without him.

Yes, even in spite of him.

True to her bedtime routine, she said her prayers as her father constantly dictated. But only the Lord knew that these petitions were not for the church downstairs or the street missions or the soup kitchens.

They were prayers for her own special need, the need of courage, the courage to do something, big or little; just something very special with the tip money.

Falling asleep was a treat for Mildred because the dreams, that usually followed, were exciting scenes of far away places with tropical beauty and endless, happy days.

In that dreamland she roamed freely, uninhibited by high-collared dresses and her father's rigid rules. She went barefoot and the tint of her skin was a golden tan.

In this paradise she was held in the warm embrace of a handsome man. His kisses so delightful, so exciting!

She longed for all these things and if prayers helped, she would keep on praying.

4

Friday morning at Boston's Logan International, Brandy was weaving through the heavy pedestrian traffic. Dressed in a snowy white suit, her three-inch heels clicked on the hard, concrete surface. She had reading materials in one hand and a heavy carry-on in the other. Her black handbag, hanging on a long strap, swung back and forth on her shoulder while, with a great deal of skill, she balanced a black hat on her blond head as she hurried to the concourse from which all chartered jets departed.

Stanley Fizer was impatiently sitting at the gate. He had Gigi on his cell phone and a stack of papers balanced on his left knee. As Brandy rushed towards him, he nodded and penciled a mark by her name.

The harpist Mrs. Angela Cloud was noticeably late and puffing when she arrived. It had taken her more than an hour trying to get the large, harp case properly wrapped for protection.

A chef and his staff of three, loaded with cookbooks and already checked in by Fizer, were clustered together in a private conversation of the culinary type. Roberto Spezza, a very popular chef on the TV circuits, had been hired to prepare his northern Italian cuisine. The cookbooks' recipes were his original creations and his large following of readers had put him on the best seller list.

Brandy wasn't aware of his immense popularity but she could easily recognize his profession by the white chef's coat he insisted on wearing. She nodded to him as if to acknowledge that she understood his message, but he looked away, nose tilted.

When the co-pilot signaled for the group to board the flight for New York, Fizer ushered his troupe into a line and headed them towards the chartered plane. With an impatient eye, he lingered behind near the gate and waited for two more members whose names were still to be checked – Jonathan and Joseph Nickels.

Finally, the two men strolled up and not the least bit fazed about being late. They were identical twins; handsome lads and dapper dressers, they much preferred to set their own schedules. Fizer fumed over their tardiness, roughly drug his pencil across their two names and then hastily pushed them towards the plane's ramp.

When the six-foot brothers boarded, Brandy followed their masculine stride all the way to 6A and 6B, only a few seats down the aisle from her.

"Wow! What will be their jobs?" she wondered as the chartered jet took flight for New York.

Airport arrivals can be hectic and when you are ushering around a cast of eight, there can be chaos, especially in the Big Apple! But Fizer had it all planned and everything went like clockwork. The people and the luggage were accounted for, including the large harp case.

Like ducks in a row, Fizer led his group to a chartered bus for their trip out to the harbor where The Lily Pad was waiting. Her gangplank was flush to the dock and crewmembers stood by to assist the group's arrival and their transfer to the boat. A welcoming session had been scheduled for them and they were immediately directed to the main salon.

"Good afternoon ladies and gentlemen, I am Captain Norman Dover. I, along with my crew, welcome you aboard The Lily Pad. We will sail Saturday at noon. Each of you should settle into your quarters and become acquainted with the layout of this custom yacht, your temporary home for the next week."

Nodding their heads in recognition of what the uniformed Captain was saying, every one of them tried hard to pay attention. But with the humdrum level of the Captain's voice and the rays of bright sunlight, beaming in through open portholes, it was a difficult task.

At one point, Chef Roberto Spezza dozed off and actually let out an elongated, deep-throated snore. Brandy, seated beside him, quickly leaned over and gently shook his arm, rousing him back to some hazy awareness of what was going on.

"I understand," she whispered, "I did the same thing except for the loud snore."

"Thanks," the chef replied, directing his droopy eyes back to the speaker.

"Now that I have given you **all** that information," the Captain droned on. "I remind you, again, that beginning tomorrow you are restricted to the crew's mess hall, your assigned sleeping quarters, and the area where you are scheduled to work."

It didn't take a calculator to tally up a list of those who would travel on The Lily Pad. Starting with Fizer, the eight hired entertainers and food staff, the captain and his crew of seventeen, and adding in the twenty guests, the three hosts and their families, still to arrive, the final count would be fifty-seven in all.

That number and the well-designed layout of the ship safely met the standards of published codes.

On Saturday morning, ten minutes after ten, Stanley Fizer stood on deck in a light morning haze. His worried look eased when two limos arrived at the dock, delivering the three hosts, along with their families.

He was waiting more impatiently until, thirty minutes after the scheduled noon departure, the final guests whipped in, arriving in a shuttle bus with an ample collection of luggage, enough to supply an extended European tour.

Nine, cackling females emerged with wine bottles in tow.

Their liquid jubilation had begun hours earlier and, from all appearances, they were setting a fast party-pace for the rest of the week. Loose-lip gossip about their reputations had preceded the late arrival of these wealthy women and, unquestionably, their cheery behavior more than confirmed that gossip.

Fizer, a man who held a great disdain regarding tardiness and boisterous behavior, hid his true feelings behind an invisible mask. As a pro at fake politeness, he quickly and graciously welcomed them aboard.

Every detail of his pre-arrangements had been programmed, yet they had failed. Complications, including a flat tire on the party bus, had pushed the actual departure back to 3:00 p.m., an incident that grossly irritated him. Yet, his authority stopped at the Captain's helm and he had absolutely no control over the management of the 272-foot, floating palace.

Ultimately, and without further delays, lines were cast and Captain Dover and his sea-worthy crew performed their duties with flawless efficiency. The grandiose vessel was finally underway.

The passengers, invigorated by the salt air, remained for a long time along the railings, celebrating the good fortune of being invited to such a cruise. Then, at sunset, the bright golden sun slowly dropped like a large orange ball, providing them with a breathtaking and marvelous backdrop for their photographic moments at sea.

The party of nine women, hamming it up for the cameras, captured the limelight as shot after shot was snapped of this sassy bunch of socialites.

When it grew increasingly darker, dinner was announced and the first of Chef Roberto's culinary feasts was served. No extra seating was allowed at the reserved table for the nine, though the other guests held no resentment for they had witnessed enough spirited behavior.

But these hell cats didn't care; nor did they trim their festivities.

When Mrs. Cloud, the parishioner of St. Matthew's Catholic Church, finally struck the last chord on her holy harp, all the diners leisurely strolled out onto the decks or moved more rapidly to the entertainment salons.

Five of the men went to The Humidor for after-dinner cigars, smoking the illegal Cuban ones that could not officially be listed on the ship's inventory.

Some of the more fashionable ladies went directly to their cabins for fear that the night-air would ruin their expensive coiffures. Sondra Smithe Cartier and Rini Jenkins, queens of the rowdy bunch of nine, cared little about their hair and preferred to focus on poker chips in the Casino.

Bloomie Bartow, a famous author of several best sellers, led four of the cackling hens into the Piano Lounge where the alluring sounds of Brandy's music had already attracted other guests.

The dimly-lit room, of burgundy leather and polished mahogany, had a serene and composed atmosphere until Greta Donna Cupani, the loudest rebel rouser in the pack, obnoxiously broke the mood.

"DO KARAOKE SO WE CAN SING," she rudely shouted out from her seat to the left of the bar. She stood, walked to the piano and stuffed a crisp, fifty-dollar bill into the tip jar. Brandy had to think fast; she could not rebuff such a generous offering.

"We don't have the equipment for Karaoke, but we sure can do a happy sing-along," Brandy promptly suggested. "I'll play and you sing."

Unrehearsed and entirely way off-key, the hens cackled, clapped their hands and stomped their feet. Brandy led them through a series of oldies and then finally, to the mercy of the others in the bar, the ladies' nightcaps took charge and the rollicking amateur hour was over.

Tarzana Sueana Timber, an appointed member of a federal court, should have known better; but in her intoxicated state, she held onto another member of the singing birdies, BJ Turner, a lawyer of some esteem.

Such familiarity would not sit well in their professional arena; but, here in a bar, it seemed okay. The twosome locked arms in an attempt to steady their bodies and then, with one foot in front of the other, they went slowly, very slowly, towards the neon exit.

"Nighty, nighty night," they chanted in girlish voices as they pushed open the door.

Their exasperated waiter flipped his hand in a quick wave to the struggling duo and then turned to offer another alcohol round to the remaining drinking buddies, who had provided very little assistance to the departure of the judge and the lawyer. Staying a safe distance from the partying women, he kept a watchful eye on their butt-pinching fingers.

"My dear young man, we have reached our peak for this night," Greta Donna Cupani sputtered to him as she gripped the edge of the table.

"We are drunk, ladies," Arnet Lincoln blubbered in support.

Not glamorous, not pretty, their departure was like a comedy show, goofy and slap-stick to the other patrons of the bar. While their snickers and applause happily escorted the rowdies out the door, Brandy sang a peppy version of - *Good Night Irene, Good Night Irene.*

Not aware of the earlier ruckus created by their friends, Barbie Beige and Mindy Morningstar ambled into the bar looking for them.

"Champagne for two," Barbie called out with a wink to the cute waiter, who was already battled-weary from a night of dodging the groping hands of their friends. Preparing for the worst, he repositioned himself into a safety zone just beyond arm's reach.

On cue, the bartender signaled that the floor show was about to begin, and Brandy routinely switched from the requested songs to the rehearsed, dance music. The debonair twins entered the room from an employee doorway.

They were even more handsome than she had remembered from her first view of them at the airport. And, with the murmurings from the crowd, it was evident, that every other woman also appreciated their good looks.

Sharply dressed in white gloves, black bow ties and tails, the twins slow strutted over to the two, champagne ladies.

Jonathan reeked of professionalism as he escorted Mindy to the dance floor and held her trembling body in an effortless embrace. The pair literally floated, their feet lightly touching down.

Charismatic Joseph extended his hand to Barbie and they in turn stepped onto the small, dance floor. Smoothly, they dipped and twirled. Fred Astaire and Ginger Rodgers could not have put on a better show.

Though Barbie and Mindy tried to dominate most of the dancers' time, these fantastic studs did not ignore one lady in the lounge. Mirrored like clones, the twins were luscious idols in the fantasy of all the female clientele and not a single one of them wanted their turn to end.

As midnight struck, the last call from the bartender ended the party as the weary women reluctantly headed for their cabins. The mysterious twins disappeared through the employee door, just as silently as they had entered, several dancing hours earlier.

The lounge was all but deserted.

Brandy was ready to retire herself. But, one patron was still at the bar, an older gentleman with white hair and bushy, shaggy eyebrows.

He picked up his wine glass and came over to her. Leaning against her piano, he was courteous in his brief request.

"I am Hubert Berman. Will you play one last song for me?'

Though the hour was late and Brandy was dead-tired, she nodded in agreement. Maybe she was not in her best voice, yet he intently listened. He smiled a warm but serious smile. And, when she finished, he softly said, "thank you."

"You are welcome," she replied, not doing her normal pose, flicking her eyelashes and pushing up her 40 double-Ds. This time, she merely gave a smile with the simple hope that it would encourage more conversation.

"Those two fellows were quite the dancers," he continued. "I envy such youth and vitality. Fun to watch though, don't you think?"

"That's Jonathan and Joseph Nickels. When I first met them I didn't know what they were hired to do. But you are right, they sure can dance."

"And you, my dear lady, most assuredly can play!"

"May I play another one for you?" Brandy asked.

"You choose, my dear, after all you are the very talented professional." His hand went up to the tip jar and he dropped a hundred dollars into her little, nest egg.

"Okay," was the single word of her reply. Though, in fact, she should have added more words, expressing sincere gratitude about such a tip. But silence seemed to come much easier and she simply left it at that.

The waiters, finished with the cleaning of the tables, had quietly completed other chores, checking tickets and blowing out candles. Even as the darkness closed in, the two of them never noticed the emptiness of the room.

Brandy's music simply captivated the area encircling the piano.

And when she would briefly stop, this stranger would fill the void with conversations on various topics. She was literally hooked on the mere sound of his words and her face glowed in admiration of so knowledgeable a man.

There was no clear way that she knew precisely what he was thinking about her. Yet, she measured his polite mannerism and she studied the directness of his eyes. Those signs, she determined, indicated that his compliments were honest and sincere.

Finally, in the wee hours before dawn when her yawns became quite apparent, they politely parted, each going to their separate cabins in different sections of the ship.

Down in her tiny cell on the employee level, Brandy found her best sleep thus far. It came as a satisfying and relaxing sleep, inviting the sweetness of good dreams. And she had no difficulties, dreaming in vivid details about her first evening with Hubert Franz Berman.

5

The Lily Pad, correctly positioned in regulation mileage from the shore to be classified as a ship at sea, continued her chartered path along the eastern seaboard. It was the second evening of the cruise and the brilliance of a full moon lifted on the clear horizon; its light shimmered and danced like fireflies across the calm water. Hubert, having little interest in the moon, came into the lounge early with his interest solely on Brandy.

He had planned an early arrival, hoping to find her alone. In his hand was a small box, beautifully wrapped by the clerk in the ship's Gift Shop. Nervous as a schoolboy, he had practiced how to present the gift to her and had, at one point, almost decided it too inappropriate to do so. That uncertainty was dispelled, however, when he saw her at the piano, wearing a jade-green outfit.

Green was his favorite color. *Had he told her or did she already know him so well,* he thoughtfully questioned?

His heart pounded loudly, erratically beating against his chest. An uncontrollable redness, spotty on his face, announced the balmy rush of emotion he was trying to hide. He hesitated before moving, so as to collect his wits before he could walk over to where she was seated.

She smiled at him, making his approach all the easier. And when she pulled the wrappings from the small box, she gasped at the Mont Blanc pen, resting regally on the blue velvet lining of the white box.

"Thank you. I'm not sure why such a present is for me? But to tell the truth, I have never had a pen like this and I am overwhelmed. Thank you! You are too kind."

"You are welcome and kindness was not my intent. I wanted to express my gratitude for your wonderful music last night," he nodded, completely satisfied at his careful selection of the pen as his first gift; one not too suggestive but one with class.

As he had hoped for that night, only a small group gathered in the lounge, leaving Brandy freer to shower more attention his way; which, of course, she did much to his delight.

Most of the other guests were in the casino or in the privacy of their state rooms, complaining of callous corns or achy, dance-worn feet. The twins, also experts in foot massages, were on duty for these cabin-calls; and, as would be expected, the nine cackling hens pecked and clucked at each other, demanding to be first on their list.

Far removed from the petty squabbling and much happier to be alone, Hubert and Brandy enjoyed what precious time they could steal together. She played less music, preferring to talk with him. And he, closely watching her impromptu mannerisms, was totally absorbed by every one of her womanly moves. She faked nothing and completely exposed her real personality, not the stage persona she saved for the bar patrons.

To him she was a pleasurable delight, like a tasty dessert.

"I'm eighty-years-old. But spry! I stay rather busy and keep myself in good shape." He confessed this, though he wasn't exactly sure which particular nerve drew these comments from him.

In a more serious tone, he was composed enough to explain that he was a CPA and a private investor, Chairman of the Board at Berman and Rothchild in Boston, and an active member of the President's Council on Securities and Banking Conduct.

"I'm a widower and the father of two grown daughters," he finally remarked as he exposed more intimate details about his personal life. "And, well the truth is, I am a wealthy man who spends too much time with money."

"What is it like to have money? When I finish playing a favorite song, I feel contentment. I guess, perhaps, I even feel rather joyful. Is making money like that?"

It might have been foolish of her to approach such a personal matter; but, for Brandy, it was the first time she had ever known anyone who could answer such a question.

"Now that's an interesting inquiry. Earning money can be a challenging job, but, if you do it right, you can afford to do everything else. There is a powerful addiction to the drive for money and, when one finally wins it all, the emotion that is left is not like that of your music. No, I would say that a person might feel empty and discouraged."

"Hmm," she said, "that's interesting."

Brandy could think of nothing intelligent to add since that type of an emotional drive was not of her world. Not even close to it. She was but a single woman of fifty-nine, who played the piano at Mac's Bar. What else could she possibly say about earning money that would hold the interest of this worldly man?

She was wrong though, for as she played the piano he grew more interested in her. Between songs they talked of Boston, old movies, food, and the pains of being lonely. As a couple they began to blend into a comfort zone. By 2:00 a.m. a wonderful flair had ignited between them and love's hot rays had scorched their hearts!

Captain Dover had labeled the planned sea voyage - the Loop. A term he coined as a fair description of their slow trek southward along the eastern seaboard, climaxing with a wide sweep in a northern retreat back to port.

Stanley Fizer privately termed the whole thing as an expensive slumber party with a price tag that didn't bother his bosses.

In the broadest sense, both men were right!

The Lily Pad peacefully sailed along Dover's charted sea lanes and, as days passed, her passengers found their own activities in various ways. The men, preferring solitude, played cards on Deck B, drinking their liquor and smoking their Cuban cigars.

Practically all of the ladies elected to gather around the pool, where the accommodating twins were their playful mates and their attentive lifeguards.

Five of the cackling hens, ruffling the feathers of the other members of their tribal flock, soon took complete control of the shipboard activities and commandeered the best positions around the pool.

Mindy was taking tango lessons at 9:30 in the mornings with Jonathan and salsa lessons at 4:30 every afternoon with Joseph. Greta Donna, who constantly complained of muscle spasms, required the massage attention of Jonathan's special hands.

Barbie, who could swim like a fish but would not tell of it, took beginner's swimming lessons from Joseph, while Rini and Arnet asked that their tanning lotions be reapplied with every shift of the sun.

Chef Roberto, a man of ethnic appearance, chiseled nose and dark complexion, lured four of the spicy socialites into his kitchen on the pretense of sampling wines. Bloomie, Tarzana Sueana, BJ, and Sondra unofficially proclaimed themselves certified wine-tasters of the highest caliber.

The chef's sexy, off-colored approaches were false flattery to these four jet-setters who had been around the world a few times and knew well the antics of flirtatious men who dished out audacious compliments.

Still, they drank his wine, cooed about his cooking, and flashed their sexy smiles. The Italian stud, a savvy appassionato of love, had the delusion that these were signals of adoration. This back and forth flirting was a jockeying game between consenting adults, each thinking that the victory was their's to claim.

When not on duty Brandy caught wind of the cruise's grapevine, Crewmembers had told her that Hubert was a host and that Mr. Samuel Steinberg of New York and Dr. Lewis Capalo of Washington, D.C. were the other two. She had not met either of them.

However, in the lounge, she had noticed the matronly-dressed Mrs. Capalo, along with her daughter and son-in-law. A rather lifeless trio, they never danced or applauded her music.

As to Mrs. Steinberg, that was a different matter. She was a very fashionable and attractive woman, even though she was confined to a wheelchair. A uniformed attendant was always at hand, often playing bridge with the Steinberg's two daughters or tapping her toe to the music.

But for Brandy, they were merely part of the guest list to be entertained, while her familiarity with Hubert Franz Berman was not listed on the job description. That developing relationship was becoming a sensitive matter all together.

Every evening, he had happily continued the surprises from the Gift Shop; his ego soaring over his choices that so pleased her. There were Christian Roth sunglasses and Cole Hann beach sandals, even a string of pearls, the foreign name of which Brandy did not recognize nor could she pronounce.

Was it French? Perhaps it was Asian? She chose not to ask.

The clock had chimed in Friday's breaking morning when Hubert and Brandy were completely alone in the lounge. He lit up a Zino Platinum Cigar, sat back in a chair and drew in three long puffs.

There was an aroma of comfort surrounding him and Brandy was equally as content, simply focusing on the ash at the end of his chubby cigar. First it had a silvery sheen and, with each breath that he drew in, the crimson embers glowed bright and red-hot!

To her, here was a man exhibiting total self-confidence. Stately erect, groomed properly, calm, intelligent, polite and friendly - what more could she deem rewarding about this man of breeding? Certainly, there was nothing that was detrimental in her brief association with him.

"Brandy," he spoke with a serious overtone. "This has not been a casual courtship between a man and a woman. I have been analyzing our current relationship and there is a harmony flowing between you and me."

She nodded in agreement. It was all true for she had felt the same. She shifted her position, moving closer to him, intently listening.

"The body's aging technique works on its own, breaking down the body, aging all the working parts. But the heart and the mind are still capable to pump in love."

She nodded again, realizing how amazed she was at herself that she had even understood what he was saying, especially the descriptive way he had captured their relationship.

"Hubert, I can only talk to you the way we do in south Boston. I see honesty in your eyes. I feel love for you, but I believe that you have already discovered my secret."

"My dear Brandy, you are right again. I'll say my intentions in the south Boston way. Will you marry me?" And, with that, he held up a small, open box.

Brandy could see the ring he was offering and she saw again the sincerity in his eyes, but she froze and could not answer his proposal.

"I know this is not an appropriate engagement ring; it's more like a dinner ring with these small diamonds. But it was the best I could purchase from the limited selection in the Gift Shop."

"No, Hubert. It's absolutely beautiful! I hesitated only because I'm totally overwhelmed."

"I'll take that as a yes," he smiled at her as he removed the ring from its box, placing it on her left hand. "I have arranged with the Captain for a small ceremony later today, while we are still at sea."

"You've already arranged a ceremony with the Captain? You did all that for me? Oh, I can't believe it!"

Hubert, a man accustomed to details and results, not only had the Captain reserved, he had also made preparations with Chef Roberto for an elaborate party on deck following the wedding service.

The grapevine aboard ship had long vines that reached to all the cabins and, by breakfast, every guest had heard the news of the wedding and the party. The beauty salon was heavily booked; the bartender and the clerk in the Gift Shop were fast restocking their supplies.

And, in the kitchen, Chef Roberto was singing while his bakery chef was happily creating, sugary decorations for the third tier to a white chocolate, two-tier cake. Up on deck, potted palms were moved to form a semi-circle, folded chairs were lined up, and Mrs. Cloud delicately placed her ornate harp in a sheltered spot.

When it was time for the wedding, the nine cackling ladies, each wearing a wide-brimmed straw hat, paraded in like a bunch of costumed marchers at an Easter Parade. They nosily charged towards reserved chairs on the bride's side. They shuffled and fluttered about each other, trying to commandeer the first chair on the aisle.

The Capalo and Steinberg families, including the uniformed attendant, quietly sat in the front row on the groom's side, while the other guests took seats on both sides of the aisle. The members of the crew watched from doorways and along the open spaces on the deck.

When the processional strands filled the air, Mrs. Cloud nodded to the six-foot twins and they walked forward, side-by-side, to the semicircle of the potted palms. Handsome to behold in their white ties and black tails, they stood as witnesses for the couple.

Hubert, his white hair freshly trimmed, wore his best dinner jacket with a white carnation in its lapel. And, if he was nervous, it didn't show.

Brandy wore her long black skirt and her green top; well aware of Hubert's passion for the color green. Around her neck were the satin-sheen pearls that he had recently given to her as one of his lavish gifts.

Slowly, they walked forward hand-in-hand, taking their special place in front of Captain Dover. Holding a black bible, he read several appropriate passages and then briefly added his personal comments about marriage before getting to the official part of the service.

"From whatever backgrounds we have come or for whatever reasons we are here on this cruise, today, we are joined as one body, for these few moments, to honor this couple's wish that they should marry. Does anyone here have a reason as to why they should not? Please speak now or forever withhold your objection."

Not one objection was brought to light.

"Brandy, do you take Hubert for your lawful husband?"

"Irma Lou," she mumbled. "It is Irma Lou Delaney, not Brandy."

Hubert grabbed her trembling hands, reassured her with his look and then nodded to the Captain to continue.

"Do you, Irma Lou Delaney, take this man, Hubert Franz Berman, as your lawful husband?"

"I do"

And, just as quickly, Hubert rang out, "I do, too!"

"Very well, I'll accept that," Dover said. "By the authority vested in me, I now pronounce you husband and wife. Hubert, you may kiss your lovely bride."

The guests congregated around the happy couple, showering them with congratulations. Yet, even in this moment of celebration, Stanley Fizer lingered well to the back. As it was with all his appearances, he was double checking the finite details.

The tables were loaded with an abundance of food and an ample supply of various wines. The party festively rolled on through the afternoon and well past the dinner hour.

Late into the evening Brandy played in the Piano Lounge, graciously doing the requests of every guest. Hubert, ever so proud, sat by her on the piano stool.

6

Captain Dover slowed The Lily Pad's return to port, giving everyone longer hours to sleep before he would dock the boat in the New York harbor. It was late afternoon when the cruise finally ended with the last, official task of lowering the sturdy gangplank.

Brandy and Hubert were the first to go ashore and were as quickly whisked away by private car, headed for the bustle of Manhattan. Seated comfortably on the plush rear seat, the newlyweds were oblivious to the city's chaotic noises.

While they cooed and kissed, brief apologies surfaced about the weariness of their bodies on their first night as husband and wife. Though they had not sealed the bonds of their marriage that night, there was no rush, they agreed, for at their age, the when and where was not that important.

"We have time, my love," Brandy said, reassuring her groom.

When they arrived in front of the Ritz Carlton, he tipped the driver, the doorman, and the bellhop, carrying the luggage. The manager, a suave gentleman Hubert had known for many years, personally escorted the couple to their spacious, expensive suite, overlooking the park.

Routinely, as he had done so many times, Hubert flashed a fifty to the receptive manager and exchanged those courteous pleasantries – 'this will do fine' and 'thank you, as always, for your personal attention'.

Brandy was in a haze; this not being one of her routine customs.

She arranged her cosmetics on the dressing table and then she began to unpack what few clothes she had from the cruise. They took up little space in the large closet on her side of the fancy dressing room. Without being too obvious, she tried to shield her embarrassment from Hubert.

"We'll fix that," he stated as he watched her hang up the small collection of clothing. "Tomorrow we'll go shopping for whatever you need. Right now, let's order some champagne to celebrate. What else would you like? Perhaps some appetizers like fresh shrimp cocktails or crepes; or, maybe, you might prefer a little caviar?"

"Thank you, but nothing so exotic for me. Just an old fashion hamburger would settle my nerves."

"Darling, that's a great idea! After a trip, an old fashion hamburger is the perfect welcome back. What simplicity of needs you have."

"Food may be a necessity, but being nervous makes me very hungry."

At bedtime, that evening, they were both a little uncomfortable, even a little flustered at their lack of how to proceed with intimacy. They again complained of being too busy, too excited, or just plain too tired.

Brandy feared that he was concerned about his age and she, in honesty, was too worried at the prospects of her own performance.

But desires had escalated to a level, requiring some type of response. So she took the lead, making it easy for Hubert by hugging him with affection and suggesting that they cuddle for this night.

"After all, let's not abuse our energies. One big blast might do us in," she said with her wonderful, hardy laugh!

Hubert not accustomed to the art of teasing, truly enjoyed the wit of this funny lady and, with every second that past, he knew that his love for her was growing deeper and deeper. Nothing would rob him of these wonderful, new-found feelings. Nothing, he promised himself.

In their darken room, without pressure nor embarrassment, she lay nude beside him and when his aged and wrinkled hand reached to touch one of the 40 double-Ds, she did not flinch but positioned herself closer, relishing in the comfort of his warm body.

"There will be better nights," he said.

At morning light they were still holding each other, neither of them wanting to move or to break their embrace. Warmth and stillness had molded them together, encasing them in that protective place, shielding them from the outside world.

The noise of a waiter's hard raps on the door ended that peace. "Room service," he shouted!

Hubert robed his naked body and opened the door, instructing the uniformed waiter to place the breakfast tray near to the side of the bed where Brandy lay. She felt no embarrassment at her own hidden nudity, even though the young waiter cast a suspicious eye toward the form of her body, covered only by thin linens.

When they were alone again, Hubert took a single, red rose from the silver vase on the tray and delicately placed the sweet, smelling flower across her covered breasts.

"My dear, my rose, you are a natural beauty to me. Maybe those are not the words of Keats, but I'm trying," he greeted her.

Adoringly, she rewarded his poetic efforts. She lifted her head, the sheet dropping from her breast; her moist, tender lips rushed to his. Her loving hands moved inside his robe, finding his bare chest. With a smooth circular stroke, she expressed more than words would have done.

When Brandy could no longer control her sexual desires, rising to the apex, she moved her hands all about his receptive body, gently, with soft strokes. Normal exploration ensued and, if there was a tiny hint of expertise on her part, it only added to the pleasure.

Delicious passions heightened to true need. She raised herself from the bed and straddled his body. He matched her ardent kisses with a charged energy that he had not known in years.

"I love you. I love you," she whispered into his ear. "You are the one for me, all that I need."

Hubert's deep breaths grew louder and Brandy's moans were explicit as to the level of her ecstasy. Her cheeks were red and faint traces of perspiration collected on the nape of her neck. He, a vessel of determination with no impediment of age, gyrated with competence and release.

Exhausted, but with much satisfaction, she relaxed her body and rested her head on his chest. Her lover, beneath her spent body, was drained of all masculine energy, yet he found a vein of strength to caress her in his appreciative arms.

Like lovers of ageless Edens, they lay intertwined.

Napped out and freshly showered, they dressed and headed to 5th Avenue. Hubert would buy her the moon if she would but ask, but she would not. Her love for him did not require that kind of attention; a trait in a woman he had never witnessed before.

"My dear, you are in my territory now. Buying things for you and making you happy is the number one item on my agenda today." He grinned, disregarding her faint objections.

In his familiar shops they used no cash, ATM machines or credit cards; he simply signed his name on the sales tickets. He selected her clothes, shoes, handbags, and even a few delicate items, the expensive lacy type that Brandy would never have purchased on her own.

When they reached Saks, he encouraged her to sign the sales ticket. It was the first time that she had officially written the words - **Mrs. Hubert F. Berman**. It felt good, as if she truly belonged to him.

"Please come in anytime, Mrs. Berman," the helpful clerk said. "You are one of our VIP customers."

"An important VIP customer, are you?" Hubert said as they left the store.

"Stop it," she giggled.

The next morning, instead of being tired from all their previous, busy schedules, Hubert was preoccupied and started the day with numerous telephone calls. Most were private business calls that he made in the living room. When he came and sat on the bed by Brandy, she whimpered in a girlish pout. With lips puckered and head playfully cocked, she wrinkled her nose and traced her finger tips playfully across the back of his neck.

"Business for this morning, my rose, and you for the afternoon, I promise. Meet me for lunch at the Tavern on the Green," he immediately suggested.

"Yes sir," she said with a charming expression that boosted his ego to the new level!

When he left for a business meeting, she was alone for the first time in their marriage and the opportunity gave her ample time to prepare a list of things to do. Without hesitation, she jotted down two important telephone calls that needed to be made.

Of the two, the one to Mac would prove to be the most difficult.

"YOU DID WHAT," he screamed into the telephone!

Holding onto the other end of the line, Brandy could visualize his thick, broad neck; its large veins, protruding and throbbing. She could see his tense check bones, clinched tightly, on his ruddy, unshaven face.

"I got married," she quickly repeated.

"I don't care if you married Prince Charles, when are you coming back? Marsha stinks on the piano!" He snorted loudly, while inserting a barrage of his favorite words, the ones that Brandy delicately shielded from her ears.

"Stop screaming and listen Mac. I'm not coming back. Well, I am coming back to Boston to live, but I won't have a need for the job at the bar; in fact, I won't need a job at all."

"Oh, Miss High and Mighty. You won't be **needing** a job! That's it, huh? You've gone and found yourself some sugar daddy and he is going to pay the rent. Is that it? And, I'm expected to sit around, waiting until that sweet-talking stiff runs off and you come crying back to me. Is that it, Brandy?"

"No, Mac. That's not it. I love my new husband and he is a very kind man," she tried to explain.

"Yea, well that's what all the broads claim. I think I know men better than you. He'll be gone when the sex gets old. Face it baby, you are a push-over and no different than the rest of them broads. And he's no different than me."

Clearly, Brandy was shooting her news into the wind as she tried to reasonably explain her new situation. But Mac, a crude and obnoxious man, had no reasonable traits. And, as she had felt before, he could cuss until the cows came home and still never accept anything beyond his limited scope.

"Maybe you don't understand today. Maybe later on you might get a chance to meet my husband then you will see it differently."

"No need for that, he'll take off before you get here. You just tell that hustler husband of your's that Mac ain't going to pay no more. I told you once before that I ain't paying. You better be sure that your new guy understands that. Here's my message to him and you can deliver it. The old piano player just got fired. You got that - FIRED!"

He slammed down the receiver. And that was it. After all the years of committed loyalty, Mac's concern was about his precious bar and not about her. She might have cried; but, what good the tears? That seedy part of her life was definitely over. She had found a new ladder and intended to climb upward.

When she placed the second phone call, it was better received. Daisy was excited to hear from her even though she was canceling, for the next three weeks, her standing hair and nail appointments. But it was Mildred who could not be contained; she grabbed the phone from under Daisy's chin and left her patron with three unpainted nails.

"Oh, Brandy, I am so happy for you! Who is he? Where did you meet him? What does he look like? When did you get married? Oh, I'm just so thrilled and I have so many questions."

"Mildred, slow down. I'll tell you all about it in three weeks. That's when we will be back in Boston after our New York honeymoon."

"NEW YORK! Wow, Brandy. NEW YORK! That's something special! On our honeymoon we had just one night at the nearest Economy Motel. Wilford said we couldn't spend much money because he had to pay my daddy the first tithing. Oh, Brandy! I'm so happy for you!"

"Thanks, Mildred. It means so much to have a friend like you. Listen, Hubert is meeting me for lunch and I need to dress. When I get back to Boston, I'll tell you everything. Okay? I'll talk to you then."

After the two calls, Brandy shifted between the sadness of the loss of the old and the joy of a new beginning. Not looking back, she had made the decision to keep going.

"Good morning, Mrs. Berman. Your car is ready for you. Have a nice day," the doorman said, greeting her with a tip of his hat as a limo pulled to the curb.

The driver, equally as polite, promptly turned to face her. "Good morning, Mrs. Berman. I have instructions from Mr. Berman to drive you to the Tavern on the Green. Shall I take the perimeter route, adding a little guided tour? Mr. Berman said that I should leave that choice to you."

"Okay, if you think that best. Excuse me, I meant to say **yes**. I have decided that it would be nice to see more of New York," she responded.

Her shaky nerves had given it away and the driver drove on with a pleasant appreciation for her assertiveness, recognizing that she was one from his own class. What a lucky dame that she was fortunate enough to move up in this world!

The slow drive around the boundaries of the park was an added delight and it gave Brandy an extra amount of time to prepare for her first visit to the famous restaurant. She checked her make-up with her compact mirror, straightened her skirt, and went in.

Hubert was seated with chilled champagne at a reserved table for two. With beaming pleasure, he stood to greet her, as the waiter pulled out a chair, seating her with a windowed view of the large trees just beyond.

"Nice day for being in the park," Hubert remarked, his broad smile broadcasting how pleased he was to be showing off his new bride in yet another public place.

"It is a very nice day. Thank you for the luncheon invitation, dear sir," Brandy cooed lightly, placing a wifely peck on his cheek.

"My style of a picnic with no ants, flies, dogs, or those jogging, sweaty people," he laughed.

"Hubert, I believe you have told me your first joke," she giggled.

While they waited for the service of the appetizers, he withdrew a ring from the pocket of his navy blazer. "This, my darling, is what I wanted from the beginning."

"My, God," she responded in surprise! "Oh, Hubert, this is too expensive for me to wear. Shouldn't it be locked in a safe?"

"No, it was made to be enjoyed. Wear it for me everyday," he said, removing the smaller wedding ring from her left hand and placing the newer one onto its proper place.

"It is just so big! What size is this diamond?"

"Five carats."

"Five? Five!" She gulped aloud.

The stone had a brilliant sparkle about it. When it reflected the rays of the sunshine filtering through the window, the expensive gem flashed tiny, white spots across the table top as she turned her hand back and forth, admiring the ring.

He watched her in her playful trance with his latest gift while he slid the smaller, duller, cheaper ring into his pocket.

"I'm excited about this, and don't think that I don't really appreciate your thoughtfulness," she whispered, leaning in towards him. "But, may I please keep the other one? It was my first wedding ring."

"Why am I not surprise to hear you say that? Of course you may," he said, placing the original ring on the third finger of her right hand. "With these two rings, I give you endless days of excitement, just as exciting as our wedding day."

Time seemed to be of no importance to them as their honeymoon week at the Ritz Carlton easily passed with daily lunches and numerous shopping sprees.

But when they made their move from the hotel to Hubert's high-rise apartment on Park Avenue, it was a shocker for which Brandy was not quite prepared.

She was wide-eyed over his fourteenth floor apartment, a spacious and custom-decorated unit, taking up the entire floor. An extensive art collection and the spectacular view from his balcony literally took her breath away.

"This is our little home when we come to New York. But the honeymoon is not over because we are here."

"WOW," she uttered, still spell-bound!

His attentive arms drew her closer. "I've always been comfortable here," he said. "But I can't ever remember enjoying this city as much as I have with you. As your personal guide, I'll show you everything."

They happily flittered from one activity to another. By day New York was their playground and, each and every night, the twinkling lights of the big city cradled them in their high-rise dwelling.

With each passing night, their sexual desires peaked quite often. And, if their performances were to be posted on some scale with ratings from one to ten, their sex would have ranked no more than a high three to a low four; maybe classified as OK or ALRIGHT.

Yet, in spite of Hubert's advanced age and physical limitations, they fondly created their own personal adjustments.

Sex was enjoyable! It was emotional!

It was an outward, receptive display of their love for each other! There was no concern or lamenting that they could not have measured up to any national standard. On their personal scale, they rated every evening as a perfect TEN.

7

The pilot landed the Cessna Citation X at Logan International, gradually reducing the speed and then veering off the long runway to a shorter one, leading to a cluster of hangers safely remote from the main terminal.

The flight had been jet smooth, with clear weather between New York and Boston. Though Hubert lacked knowledge of the complicated issues of aviation, he spent the time talking about the expense benefits and wise decisions of his fractional ownership in the plane.

In the contract with him, he explained with spread sheet data, were four others – his business partner Victor Rothchild, Dr. Lewis Capalo, Samuel Steinberg and law partner Isaac Leftwich. These were all men of wealthy means who could easily support their personal flights between Washington D.C., New York, and Boston; the routes most often used by the individuals of the group.

Hubert told her about his own business trips, but he never elaborated on the various clandestine twosomes for which Capalo had reserved the plane, paying the pilots off in cash not to discuss his female companions.

He knew of these hush-hush trips and, whether the other partners were aware of them or not, he had never discussed those private outings with anyone and especially not now with Brandy. With his own closet, chuck full of ghosts, it would not have been wise to reveal the hidden ghosts of others.

She had absolutely no idea of the cost for this trip between New York and Boston and, quite likely, she could not have tallied it up, even with the accounting information summarized by her educated husband. Enthralled as she was with the private jet, calculating the rate per hour or jet fuel costs would have sent her mind into a mathematical nose dive. In fact, she had barely completed the twelfth grade with a weak C in Algebra II.

So accustomed to the frequency of his own travels, Hubert never thought to ask when or where she might have flown before. And since he never approached the subject, neither did she offer the details of her two experiences in the air; the cheap group tour she once took to Philadelphia and the other one recently arranged by Fizer out of Boston to New York for the chartered cruise.

When the aircraft finally coasted to a full stop in front of hanger 3, Shields Mason, Hubert's personal driver, was patiently waiting just outside. And, as Brandy and Hubert deplaned and stepped onto solid ground, Shields was already at work, gathering their luggage and transferring it to the trunk of a long, black limousine.

"Shields," Hubert stated, shaking the driver's hand, "this is Mrs. Berman."

"Welcome, Mrs. Berman," he graciously replied with a smile.

That smile, as Brandy determined, was casually pleasant but his body posture in contrast was erect and stiff as if military training had imposed a lasting discipline. With a snap of authority, he opened the rear doors for them and then he took his proper place in the front seat. He eased the long automobile away from the hanger and proceeded towards Sumner Tunnel and into downtown Boston.

There was some conversation between the three of them then Hubert started shuffling papers from his briefcase and flipped open his small cell phone for a business call to a Miss Borden, whom Brandy assumed was his secretary.

While Hubert talked, Brandy silently studied the back of Shields' head. *A fresh, neat haircut* – she thought, perhaps done by a military barber. The starched stiffness of his blue collar, just an inch above his black blazer, also gave her a clue as to his neatness. Her eyes drifted to his hands on the steering wheel and it was then that she first noticed the absence of a thumb on his right hand.

Maybe it was an accident, perhaps the result of military conflict? She looked again at his hand but there were no clues there to help her reach a positive conclusion about the missing thumb.

Suddenly, she saw his eyes in the rear view mirror. Deep brown. Serious. Calculating. *Was he watching her or routinely checking the traffic behind the car?* Quickly, she turned her head away with no answers.

In time Hubert finished his business call, closed his briefcase and fondly patted Brandy's hand. The call to his secretary was of the utmost importance, he casually explained.

"You will meet Miss Borden next week at my office. There are papers for you to sign."

"I look forward to meeting her," Brandy said, all the while wondering what type relationship existed between her husband and this Miss Borden. With their return to Boston, she had a sense that the honeymoon was over.

Hubert, she suspected, would soon be absorbed by his business.

As they turned onto Beacon Street, within a few block of Hubert's Boston residence, he told her all about Queen's Garden, the gated high priced development in which he had investments. With noticeable pride he described how Queen's Garden was a three-year-old complex that consisted of five high-rise residential buildings. The investors had taken an area of decaying real estate and transformed it into a planned community.

Federal money was made available to the project because they had demolished older structures of lesser value, replacing them with high quality condos. The neighbors approved the fashionable appearance of Queen's Garden and the politicians loved the new tax rolls.

"I personally own one building, living on the tenth floor and renting out the other nine."

"After seeing your apartment in New York, I'm really anxious to see where you live here in Boston," Brandy said excitedly. "I think I will know more about you when I see where and how you live away from the glamour of New York."

When they approached the divided drive, Brandy marveled at the beautiful red, yellow, and purple blooms trailing in front of and down the sides of the stone fencing. *The Garden of Eden* thought Brandy, in this her virgin view of her new home.

Shields passed through the opening gate, waved to the guard and drove up to the first building known as The Boxwood. At the front door, Hubert introduced his Brandy to the doorman. "Nathan, this is Mrs. Berman. Shields will be taking charge of her driving needs."

"Welcome to The Boxwood, Mrs. Berman. You are in very good hands with Shields," Nathan responded.

"Oh my gosh, our luggage!" Brandy exclaimed as she saw Shields pull away from the curb.

"Not to worry, my dear. Shields will drive around to the chauffeur's garage and use the service elevator up to our floor."

In Hubert's private elevator, they were politely silent as the express button sent them directly to the tenth floor. Brandy's knees were knocking so hard that she feared he would hear them. But he had already zeroed in on being home.

Returning to the reality of everyday life came quickly for when the elevator doors opened into the marbled and mirrored foyer of the penthouse, Helga VonSmitten, his private housekeeper, was standing there waiting.

"Helga, it is so nice to be back. And this is my surprise for you. Meet Mrs. Berman, my new wife."

"Yes, I've already heard about the wedding," replied Helga with the rudest of an icy posture completely ignoring Brandy. "Mr. Berman, your daughters and son-in-law will be here this evening to visit with you."

As Shields arrived with all the suitcases, Helga, fuming under her collar and making no gesture to unpack for the new Mrs. Berman, turned sharply on her heels and retreated into the kitchen.

"It will take her a while to adapt; this was probably a shock to her. She was Catherine's, that's my first wife's name. Well, she was Catherine's personal maid. I'll soothe things with her before the girls arrive tonight."

Brandy, weary from the flight and outwardly struggling with the newness of the place and the tenseness of the greeting, just wanted to stop and restart slowly.

Hubert sensed her stiffness and sweetly guided her through a mini tour of the master bedroom and dressing rooms. He pointed out the centralize controls by the bedside that operated all the lights, the TV and sound system. He wrote out the codes for the in-house phone system. Finally, he showed her the large Jacuzzi that was located in an alcove off the master bath.

"Perhaps a nice soak with the scented oils will help you relax. It has been a long day."

"Yes, thank you. I'll do that soon. Right now, I'll just kick off my shoes and unwind a little."

He left her there to go downstairs for his talk with Helga. Brandy wandered freely about the bedroom, observing all the small items that revealed something more about her new husband.

From a round draped table she picked up a variety of silver framed photographs, each with the happy faces of young girls. She had no names for the girls in the photographs but she correctly assumed that they were of his two daughters at different stages of their growing years.

By the table stood a masculine, leather chair in rich, dark color of chocolate-brown. Close by, on an antique table, was a humidor of Zino cigars. She casually sat down on the edge of his bed, a sturdy four poster that was to become her nightly place. She wondered what side was his and how strange it was to be away from her own bed.

Gosh! Her apartment! With all this newness, she had finally remembered her own things. There would be bills and magazines crammed into her mail slot. The rent, telephone, and utility bills had to be paid. The milk would have soured by now and she still had clothes at the laundry.

These things sorely required her attention and soon. But for tonight, she had to adjust to Hubert's home and then lay a plan as to when and how she would get back to her own apartment.

"Brandy," he said, coming back into the bedroom. "We'll reorganize the closets to accommodate your things. I'm afraid this penthouse was designed more for a man. Catherine died over ten years ago and my daughters pressured me to keep her house. After seven years alone in that old house, this penthouse became my haven from the past and well, it has suited me. That is, until now."

"Oh Hubert, I've been selfish thinking of myself, not understanding how many adjustments you are making. Together we will work things out."

"Sit down, my dear. Let me tell you a few things about my daughters before you meet them tonight," he insisted. "Caroline is 40 and married to David D Trump. Cynthia, I believe, is already 36. She is a stockbroker and vows to never marry. They were spoiled girls and now they are spoiled women. Catherine performed her role in society and I was rarely home. So it was natural that my daughters were more dependent on her."

Brandy could relate to the father part about never being home. The big difference was that her drinking father never worked and came home only to take hard-earned money from her mother. These things she had not told Hubert and, now with all this wealth around her, it would be extremely difficult and down-right embarrassing for her to bring them up.

She dismissed it all and focused on what Hubert was saying. He tried to be brief, yet each halting sentence revealed more and more about his own past and the events that had held him captive.

"Catherine was Catherine Abigail Adams of the original Adams family of Massachusetts. Her heritage could be traced to John Adams and John Quincy Adams, the second and sixth Presidents of the United States. Most of her relatives were all loyal red, white, and blue citizens."

"How proud of your wife you must have been," Brandy remarked, voicing more confidence in her understanding of him.

"No, don't let me off that easily," Hubert responded; his brow tensed into deep furrows. "I married into her family to add to my own wealth. We were married for thirty-two years, but it was a terrible marriage of lies and pressured commitments. During those years, we lived in an historical home that Catherine had inherited. The girls never let me forget that."

"Hubert, we have many things to learn about each other." Brandy replied, trying to halt more of the heavy facts that she was trying to digest. "Let's just take it slowly and calmly. Tonight, I'll meet your daughters and son-in-law and then tomorrow we will work on the next stage. Okay?"

"All right, Brandy. But I am sorry that I didn't prepare you or, at least, warn you before we married. Maybe you would have backed out."

"No, don't even go there!" Brandy said it solidly. "I married you because I wanted to. There was no pressure and I have no regrets."

Their guests had already arrived, when they came down the sweeping staircase. Brandy drew in a deep breath, exhaled and walked into the drawing room, holding onto the strong arm of Hubert.

His two daughters were seated on a fancy, green sofa and his son-in-law stood by an unlit fireplace, the carved mantel of sturdy English oak, offering a perfect backdrop for his snobbish presence.

The three of them made no comments and the rigidity of everyone in the room halted any attempts at polite greetings. Finally, Hubert stepped forward and addressed his daughters straight on.

"Caroline. Cynthia. This is my wife Brandy."

"Father, we had hoped to speak to you alone," his waspish daughter Caroline remarked, glaring at him. "There are family matters that must be discussed and frankly, an outsider need not be present."

The younger Cynthia, in a saucy admonishing voice, jumped right in. "Mrs. Capalo couldn't wait to call us. I should have been there. I would have stopped you. Really, father, she's a piano player. Oh, how **could** you?"

"Enough! Say no more. Brandy is now a part of this family," he sternly snapped back at his two, fussy daughters. The steel blade of a knife could not have cut their icy-cold glares.

Hubert, with stronger resolve, turned Brandy to face the man at the fireplace. "My dear, this is David D Trump, Caroline's husband."

"Hello David."

"David **D**, I prefer to be addressed as David **D**," he spoke abruptly with no gesture of a handshake or a gentlemanly nod, not even a simple how-do-you-do as Brandy's relatives would have said.

"Yes, of course. Nice to meet you, David **D**," she quickly added, correcting her mistake, the first mistake of the many that would follow.

How they made it through the rest of the taxing evening would never be fully remembered by Brandy as she plowed her way through it all. As it went, they, meaning Hubert's family, argued and argued.

Nosey Helga, smugly content that things where in chaos, came into the room on two occasions to announce dinner, but there was no dinner. Caroline and Cynthia, with David D trailing behind, left in a puffy huff over the marriage which Hubert flatly refused to discuss.

With their steamy departure, Hubert was beyond consoling and went directly to his office for a cigar.

Brandy went upstairs and lay quietly in the darken room, worrying about her blunders that she feared had added more fuel to the family's hostile arguments.

The masculine four-posted bed was too wide, too cold and too empty. It was not the way her first night at The Boxwood should have gone. Not close to the way Brandy had dreamed that it would have smoothly gone, lying with Hubert in his bed in her new home.

Rejected for the present, she could not close her eyes as she listened for him.

But what she heard were the padded swish of footsteps, like those made by house shoes. The sound stopped at the bedroom door. Brandy then heard a light rustle of movement.

No one knocked. No one touched the doorknob.

Silence, just empty, questioning silence stilled the room.

Her ears perked up, straining harder to hear. She got up from the bed, moving across the carpeted distance towards the door.

Immediately the footsteps started again, faintly fading off into the distance.

8

Mildred Brown was in a rebellious mood; the devil could have had her that morning! She was sullen and hostile as she slammed the door to the three-story walkup.

For two long days, she had unwillingly participated in her father's long-winded revival, an attendance that was required; yes, literally demanded by the self righteous and overbearing preacher.

Out in the Monday sun, Mildred stopped mid-way on the sidewalk, closed her eyes and deeply inhaled the morning air. It was uplifting, now, to be on her way to the beauty shop where she would find refuge in her morning clients, the people who meant more to her than those who were bending their knees in fake piety.

Two customers were waiting for her when she walked into the shop and, without the slightest hint of toil, her ritual with friends began. But, when Daisy told her the good news that Brandy was coming in for hair and nail appointments, Mildred's spirits soared beyond the height of mere satisfaction. A big smile raised her jawbones and lifted her brow.

At about the same time, Shields pulled the limo up to the front of the Millennium Bostonian Hotel on North Street. As usual, he opened the car door for Brandy. She thanked him and asked that he return for her around 3:30; that would allow ample time for her appointments and the shopping she wanted to do at Faneuil Hall Marketplace and, perhaps if time allowed, at Quincy Market.

"Very well, Mrs. Berman, I will be here. Have a nice day."

He drove away wondering why she would choose this location when there were so many exclusive salons nearer the penthouse. But he was not the one to question his boss's wife and such an intrusion into her personal life would be against his own code of honorable conduct.

Brandy entered the hotel through the main door and then cleverly made a quick exit. In an alleyway, she hurried over to a taxi-stand, located nearby for the convenience of the hotel's guests. Instructing the driver to a West Broadway address, Brandy sat back and nervously endured the ride across the channel into an Irish neighborhood, the route that would take her directly to Daisy's Beauty Shop.

Guilt rode with her. She had openly lied to Shields and had deceived Hubert, withholding the true facts about her day.

After the deplorable evening with his daughters and the weekend abuses from Helga, she needed to be with good friends, regardless of Hubert's understanding.

"It's you. I can't believe it," exclaimed Mildred when Brandy entered the shop. "Oh, how we have missed you and we can't wait to hear all about your wedding! Oh hurry, please tell us everything!"

"It was a fairy tale with flowers, gifts, a harp, and the sunshine. His name is Hubert and he is a wonderful man."

"What's he like? Do you have pictures? Tell us everything, don't leave out a single thing," Mildred wildly chattered as Daisy mixed the bouncy-blond color for Brandy's hair.

"All right, just give me a chance. Hubert is very nice, well educated, very polite, and just a little older than I am. We enjoy things together and he loves my music."

Brandy was radiant when she spoke of their shipboard romance and, as she continued with a collage of fanciful details, every lady with curlers, conditioner, or styling gel, turned to listen.

"Do you have pictures for us to see?" Mildred giggled like a child stealing glances at the personal diary of a school friend.

"Oh, I don't have our wedding picture with me today. I was in a rush this morning and my mind was so full of other things."

"New brides do get nervous," laughed Daisy. "They got other, more important business to attend to. Right, girls?" And the shop filled with female laughter.

"Was New York awesome and crowded with lots of people?"

"Yes, Mildred, it **was** truly impressive! Of course, it was so big and noisy. But we had our quiet lunches and did a little shopping and a good deal of sightseeing."

Not quite telling the full and truthful story, Brandy found herself withholding more and more information from her friends. The extensive shopping she had enjoyed in New York would sound so pretentious to these dear ladies and the places where they had their quiet lunches were the kinds of restaurants written up in travel magazines.

But it was the ring, the 5-carat diamond ring, which drew most of the attention. She smoothly sidestepped their comments on its size and, surely, its staggering cost. With the hair dryers humming heavily, the disclosure of immense wealth never had a chance to completely surface, nor the full details of Hubert Franz Berman.

Once her hair was dried and styled and her nails freshly polished a tomato-red, a beautiful Brandy caught a cab back to the Millennium Bostonian Hotel. She dashed inside and went immediately into the hotel's gift shop, where she selected four rather large and thick books on Boston architecture, several bookmarks, and some boxes of note cards and Boston logo pens. She quickly thought to pick up two big, white gift bags.

"I bought all these things as presents," Brandy told the clerk, handing her a credit card. "Just put everything into these two bags. I don't want others to know that I made these purchases here in the hotel."

"No problem. We do this often," responded the cashier.

Outside, Shields waited patiently as he watched for Brandy to return to the limo. Just five minutes late for the 3:30 pick-up, Brandy came out the main entrance and slowly strolled over to Shields.

He took the two shopping bags and, as usual, opened the rear door for her. But when she slid across the leather seat, her skirt caught on the seat belt and it accidentally hiked upward, revealing a generous view of her curvaceous legs.

"Any other shopping for today, Mrs. Berman?" he asked, not taking his eyes from the sudden, but pleasurable, look at her shapely figure.

"No, that's all today. Take me home, please," Brandy responded, straightening her skirt in a more lady-like fashion.

In a way, it was a small blessing that this unexpected embarrassment was overriding her nagging fear that he might be aware of her lies about where she had been and what she had been doing.

At The Boxwood, Nathan the doorman, in a jovial mood, welcomed her back and told her that Mr. Berman had not yet returned from the office. That meant that when she went up in the elevator to the tenth floor, Helga VonSmitten would be the only person there to meet her.

But, it was not to be a friendly welcome. The ornery woman, a sour look plastered on her face, stood firmly in Brandy's path, blocking her passage. The bomb for a full declaration of warfare had been lit.

Hissing sharply with the deadly force of a venomous snake, Helga struck with a wicked, verbal attack, catching Brandy unprepared to retaliate. A shock of terror appeared on her face and an erratic shaking quivered about her shoulders.

The lengthy strap of her black purse slid down her arm and tangled itself into a twisted mess onto the plastic handles of the two, shopping bags. The weight of the books inside, anchored Brandy to the terrifying spot.

"Woman, you hear me well! I will **NOT** call you Mrs. Berman; you do not have that right! Catherine Adams Berman held that title and no one else deserves that respect!" Helga's eyes blazed and her hands knotted tightly into locked fists.

Jumping to the side of the crazed woman, Brandy ran up the stairs, her purchases heavily dragging and bouncing on each step. Just inside the master bedroom, she threw her purse and the two bags to the floor, reached back and slammed the door, clicking tightly the brass lock.

In a panic, she pressed her back hard against the closed door, slowly sliding wide-eyed to the floor. Body limp and blood pressure soaring, it took all her efforts to keep from passing out.

Two hours later, when Hubert returned from his office, Helga, showing no signs of her earlier malice, happily greeted him, took his briefcase and offered to prepare his favorite martini.

"Thank you, Helga. Where is Mrs. Berman, perhaps she would wish to join me?"

"I doubt it, sir," Helga reported. "She has been in your bedroom all afternoon and has not asked for anything."

Fearing that Brandy might be ill, Hubert immediately went upstairs to check. He knocked loudly on the locked barrier; a worrisome expression solidified on his face.

"What's wrong, Brandy? You had the lock on. Why, my dear?"

"Oh, I'm sorry about locking the door. You know, it is a routine practice in my apartment building," Brandy quickly explained, offering a feeble half-truth.

"You'll soon adjust to our built-in security. Were you reading all afternoon?" Hubert inquired as he picked up the architectural books, strewn across the end of the bed.

"Yes. Never too late to learn, you know, especially now that I am on the other side of town."

"Let's go out for dinner tonight. You choose the place," he suggested as he went into the dressing room to change from his business suit.

"No. I prefer that you choose," she called out to him from her refuge at the foot of his big bed. "Surprise me, I like that."

He made reservations and they soon said good-night to Helga, leaving her alone in the penthouse. Their dinner-date gave Brandy a stay of execution. Other attacks might be in her future, but, for this one evening, Brandy had strong protection in the company of her Hubert.

The bed felt empty the next morning when Brandy reached out for her husband and discovered that he was not there. She was terrified at the thought that he had left her alone again with Helga. Instantly, she grabbed her robe and raced downstairs, hoping and praying that he was still at home.

She found him in the breakfast room, drinking coffee and reading the Boston Globe.

"Did you sleep well, my dear?" He smiled, giving her a morning kiss.

"Yes, until things went downhill when you were missing from the bed. But, I'm better now."

Helga came from the kitchen and poured Brandy some coffee. It was so blistering hot that she could barely take a brief sip before gingerly replacing the china cup back on its matching saucer. Their fiery eyes locked in a mutual glare, but, with Hubert in hearing range, no words were exchanged.

Helga politely set a plate of bagels, cream cheese, and sliced fruit in front of him and then she turned to Brandy, dropping, with sheer tint of malice, a plate of the same items onto the table.

The loud crash caught his attention.

"You seem a little jumpy this morning, Helga. Perhaps you need a day off. After all, since Mrs. Berman and I have arrived, you have been quite busy taking care of us."

"Oh, that's not necessary, Mr. Berman. It has always been my pleasure to take care of your needs. I'll be in the kitchen if you want anything else." Helga flipped around, shot another arrow of disdain at Brandy and then smugly retreated into the kitchen.

"Helga," Hubert called out to her.

She came back through the swinging door, taking a position by his chair and deliberately turning her back to Brandy. "Yes, Mr. Berman, more coffee for you?"

"No, we are fine. Mrs. Berman and I will not be here for lunch today. And, I will call you later about dinner. We may or may not be home this evening." As always, Hubert gave his instructions with a steady air of authority.

Without hesitation, Helga withdrew from the room with much less arrogance than she had previously displayed. Brandy, sweetly and silently, enjoyed her turn to smirk.

She blew her coffee to an acceptable temperature, drank it and finished off most of the food on the china plate. She purposely wiped her lips with the white napkin, leaving a lipstick smudge for Helga to handle.

Hubert put down the Globe, and, still innocent of the friction between the two women, affectionately touched Brandy's hand. "My dear, we'll go to my office this morning. There are important papers for you to sign. Wear one of your new outfits. And I'm hoping you will choose the green St. John. I especially like that one."

Brandy's temporary victory over Helga had come at a price. Her nerves were being stretched way beyond the usual, jittery tension of a new bride. This ever-growing animosity about her entrance into Hubert's life was like hitting a stone wall that she had never anticipated, weeks ago, aboard The Lily Pad.

But she was determined to conquer the position as his wife.

Later, when they entered the reception area of Berman and Rothchild, Hubert had his arm comfortably around Brandy's waist. He was glowing over her stunning appearance in the fashionable St. John, the green knit he had asked her to wear.

The smile on his secretary's face quickly faded when she saw that the current Mrs. Berman was with him. It was to be their first meeting, though she had already received numerous telephone calls. Calls announcing the same messages: That woman was a piano player on the cruise. That woman, with dyed-blond hair, had turned his head. That woman only wants his money and is making a fool out of him.

"Miss Borden, this is my wife Brandy," Hubert proudly announced.

"Hello," the secretary responded with a polar tone.

"My dear, this is the best employee in the firm," Hubert said. "Miss Borden keeps everything on a smooth schedule and everybody loves working with her."

"Congratulations, Miss Borden," Brandy remarked. "That is a very high praise for a secretary."

The attractive Miss Borden, with hostile resentment, shot back a blast of cold air, plainly indicating that the visit was not to her liking.

"Secretary is not my only title," she grunted in a rather evasive reply. "Mr. Berman, I have an important business agenda that requires your immediate attention."

"Yes, of course, you are so right. I should get to that. But first, bring in the new insurance papers," Hubert called back as he and Brandy went into his private office.

It was large and resembled a library with numerous shelves of accounting books and tax codes, and more shelves of architecture, art, and a collage of fiction and nonfiction books too many to absorb in one scan.

Solid, tinted windows filled the wall immediately behind a sturdy, walnut desk, the very type that Brandy would have expected. Two leather club chairs sat at the front of this desk and, on its left, stood a mirrored, custom bar where crystal decanters were displayed. A durable leather couch, side tables and several, silk-shaded lamps filled out the rest.

Brandy sat down in one of the club chairs as Hubert took his place at his desk. Miss Borden brought in the requested insurance folder, but said nothing and curtly walked out.

"These papers are rather simple. This is an insurance policy just to prepare for financial needs after death. Sign here on this form and we are done."

"Hubert, we didn't spend much time talking about personal money before the wedding. But frankly, I just did not realize the legal complications about mixing your money and mine. I know I would be absolutely phony if I told you I had," Brandy reacted, rather perplexed.

"Oh, I don't want your money. This is just a policy on my death. I wish to provide for you," Hubert said, smiling at his wife's honesty. "Signing this form only indicates that you are aware of the policy. My lawyer feels that, perhaps later, this document might be required."

"What about your daughters? Have you thought of them? I'm a little frightened that they might be more upset, especially when they learn of this insurance policy." Brandy took a tissue from her purse, sniffed and dabbed at a few, misty tears.

"Let's get this straight right now and no further discussion is necessary. And, I don't want to see tears. You are my legal wife and as your husband I intend to take care of all your needs. Leave the other family matters to me; those things will not interfere with us. We will enjoy the years we will have together."

He went to her side of the desk, lightly stroking her blond hair. He smiled and winked, handing her the pen. She signed and dated the form. And, just as he leaned over to kiss her, Miss Borden returned.

"Excuse me, Mr. Berman. New York is on your private line."

"Of course, I must take that call. Put it on the private extension in the conference room." He managed a quick peck on Brandy's cheek and left through an adjoining door, leaving the two ladies in his office.

"So, you and Hubert married on the cruise?" quizzed the agitated secretary.

"Yes. It was a beautiful ceremony, but a small one on Deck B. The captain, Captain Dover, did a marvelous job." Brandy said, trying to be friendly.

"I don't care about the ceremony. I only care about Hubert. If you are some little tramp trying to get his money, be warned! First, you will have to get through me. I'll be closely watching Hubert's accounts and I have ways to sabotage your greedy efforts."

The heavy-handed secretary stormed out the door, leaving Brandy wide-eyed in the leather chair. For twenty long minutes, Brandy waited alone and still Hubert had not returned from the conference room. Finally, Miss Borden, with renewed joy, came bounding into the private office.

"You'll have to leave now," she said pointedly. "Hubert has an important meeting to attend. I have arranged separate transportation for him. Downstairs, you will find Shields waiting for you. Let's face it, dearie, you are definitely in our way. I strongly suggest that you collect your tacky, little purse and go."

"I don't understand? Leave without talking to Hubert? He will want to know that I'm alright. I should, at least, leave him a written note."

"No, there isn't time for such foolishness. Hubert will hear what he needs to know. Go now," Miss Borden ordered, holding the door open to exile the boss's wife.

Shields was waiting at the side entrance, exactly as instructed by the feisty secretary. He was enjoying the view of Brandy as she walked towards him in the flattering green suit that so alluringly accentuated her good looks.

Like most seasoned males, he had an appreciative eye for female beauty. He suspected that this one was about his age, but her looks and youthful gait made her appear much younger. That emotionally-stimulated idea sent a steady stream of warm pulsations, exactly the kind that most seasoned males hoped that they could feel.

"Where to, Mrs. Berman, I didn't get my instructions on where I am to take you?" he asked, slowly driving away from the imposing building of Berman and Rothchild.

"I can't think right now," she quivered, twisting soiled tissues in her nervous hands.

"Perhaps a quiet, calm ride out of the city," Shields suggested.

Before she had time to respond, his cell phone rang loudly in the front seat. "Yes, Mr. Berman. Yes sir, I understand and I will do that. Yes sir, she is already in the car. Hold please."

He handed the phone to Brandy.

"Hello," she stammered. "Yes. Me too. Oh I do; I do know that you hated to leave. I understand that you are busy, but still I was surprised that you left so unexpectedly without telling me good-bye."

On the other end of the line, Hubert was explaining the importance of the meeting. He was making promises that this was just a brief interruption for them, and explaining his other directives that Miss Borden was there to help and that Helga would gladly prepare lunch and dinner.

"New York? No, I didn't know that. Miss Borden didn't tell me you were going to be gone overnight for the meeting," Brandy hurtfully added.

Shields, looking up at the rear view mirror, watched the painful expressions on her face. He wasn't allowed to tell her that her husband often made unexpected trips and that he had never learned anything from Miss Borden about those trips. Certainly, he couldn't tell her that the secretary had ridden with Mr. Borden in this same limo. No, for now, he had to be silent and watch her suffer through this wide, rough bump in the road.

"Okay, until tomorrow." Brandy sadly sighed and clicked off the phone. She lightly sighed once more before handing it back to Shields.

"He's a busy man, our Mr. Berman," Shields appropriately said, still watching her sad face through the rear view mirror.

The phone call had drained Brandy. She was ashy white and sick to her stomach, far more devastated than when she had first left the office. In the attempt to escape her hurt feelings, she temporarily blocked out everything and everyone around her.

"Shields, take me anywhere," she finally said; her weepy voice breaking the stillness of the sullen air trapped in the car between them.

He drove north out of the city, connecting to highway 107, using a route leading to the community of Salem. It was a sunny day, with the traffic thinning as they traveled further and further from downtown Boston, onward towards the clean, open air, flowing freely without motor fumes.

Brandy looked out the windows at the passing trees; thickly leafed as they were, they held no real interest for her. Yet, when she caught her own image in the glass window, it shamed her to see such an unhappy reflection. And, whenever she turned her focus back to the car, she would see Shields' brown eyes in the rear view mirror.

However, this time, she was sure that those searching eyes were not checking the traffic behind the car; no, this time he was studying her face, a drawn and unhappy face.

Brandy never looked at her watch, nor did she have any concept of how long they had been riding or exactly how far they had traveled.

For her, the minutes drug by like heavy plows, forging through the hard, rough thoughts in her mind.

Finally, the car reached a small hamlet before the roadway would eventually reach Gloucester, a coastal town on Cape Ann.

Shields slowed to the posted speed in the quite, traffic-free community. A convenient service station was to his right and he eased the big limo to the gas pump. Next door was a coffee shop, where they settled into a booth and ordered hamburgers and black coffee, just the strong caffeine pick-up required by the sluggish pair.

Nothing special occupied their stay; yet, they were joined together with trivial conversations of the weather, the coffee shop, or the bright, red cardinal on a tree branch just outside the window. Not once did they mention any personal items, including the sensitive subject of Hubert.

Brandy could not bring herself to expose the ache in her heart and Shields was her employee, not licensed to talk on such a personal level.

There were virtually no other patrons in the quaint shop, save an attentive waitress who kept them supplied with refills; routinely she stopped by their table during the next hour, trying to tempt them with her friendly down-home suggestions of apple pie or blackberry cobbler.

When the hour to leave finally ticked by, it was obvious to both of them that their little, chit-chat period was over. It was appropriate that they leave, though neither one actually announced it.

Shields opened the car door for Brandy and then took his position behind the steering wheel. He drove slowly through the small town and made a final turn back onto the highway, bound for Boston. Settled into their proper rolls as limo driver and boss's wife, they safely distanced themselves. One stayed busy at the controls and the other sat quietly, alone on the back seat.

Silence ruled again and, for all practical purposes, it seemed acceptably normal.

He watched the road and she watched the back of his head. Occasionally, their eyes met in the rear view mirror, the reflective link between them. Finally, it was Brandy who first spoke.

"Shields, I don't want to disturb your driving, but may I ask you something?"

"Yes, of course, Mrs. Berman," he answered, pleased that he would have another opportunity to hear her voice.

"Were you in the military? I mean..., I'm guessing, maybe you were? Because of your haircut and the way you walk, well, it looks fairly obvious that there may have been some military influence in your life. Did you serve?"

"Yes, I did, then on the police force, later as a private investigator. Now, I work exclusively for Mr. Berman," he stated without hesitation.

"The thumb, was that from your military duties?"

"You mean the no thumb," he laughed, lifting up his right hand with only four fingers. "No, I can't blame the military. I lost that thumb chasing a suspect in a blackmailing case. I caught him. But he ripped me with a sharp knife. I might have died if a store clerk had not spotted me in the alley."

"Oh, that was terrible! Was he ever arrested for attacking you?"

"No. But after my brief recovery, I did target where he was staying and I called Mr. Berman. Someone, I don't know who, shot the suspect and he died before reaching the hospital. That ended my case."

"You mean my husband was involved?"

"The guy was blackmailing the boss, demanding millions of dollars. But, of course, with the shooting, the thug wasn't around any more," Shields told her, not adding any gruesome details.

"Did you stay around in that kind of business before you started to work for my husband?"

"Well, it is hard to be a sharp-shooter with missing fingers. So, Mr. Berman's offer was a generous one. Now, I'm quite happy to say that I work as a driver for him. Oh, and now, of course, I am also in your service."

"Thank you, Shields. I am very comfortable knowing that you are around, especially today."

It was getting late and the sun was rapidly disappearing behind city buildings. The afternoon traffic was thickly brutal, slowing their progress. Brandy suddenly felt a longing for her own things. She wasn't ready to return to The Boxwood and to Helga.

Following street directions, Shields soon stopped the limo in front of the Boston Arms on Flaherty Way. He offered to help her, but she insisted to go it alone, claiming that she had many personal things to do and would just stay overnight.

"As you wish, Mrs. Berman," Shields responded, sensing that there were deep, hidden reasons for her uneasiness. Yet, she had not willingly shared any such emotional secrets to him.

In his travels, he had experienced enough women to recognize those tell-tale signs when women are lonely and most vulnerable. He saw those very indicators in Brandy.

But, that particular, golden opportunity was definitely not presented to him. Though he had his own private visions of how delightful the night might have passed.

9

Mildred Brown had been in her kitchen some thirty minutes or so when she received a telephone call.

"Hello," she said, answering with flour on her hands. "Brandy, oh what a nice surprise! How are you?"

"I'm alright. No, I'm not alright Mildred. Could you meet me for dinner tonight? I know that this sounds strange, but it is so important to me. Can you, tonight?"

"I don't know, Brandy. I'm cooking Wilford's dinner right now," she whispered. "I don't think that I should do that. I...... let me think. Yes. Yes, Brandy, I will. If I could come about 8:30, he will be asleep by then. But where will I meet you?"

"Oh, thank you, Mildred. Let's meet at Luigi's; it's about three blocks from you. Do you know that restaurant?"

"Yes, I do. I've never been there but I know exactly where it is. I'll hurry and meet you," Mildred responded in her usual sensitive way.

Her heart was racing as she placed the dinner of mashed potatoes and pot roast on the table. Wilford paid no attention to her as his knife and fork went into action. Robustly he devoured his food, asking for his mandated second portion. Halfheartedly she nibbled at her food, not diverting her look from the plate. So afraid that he would notice her nervousness, she kept her shaking left hand in her lap.

What if he doesn't go to sleep? What if he wakes up before I'm back? Unsettling questions tumbled about in her brain. But it was her wild thoughts of getting caught that sent rare, emotional charges, fueling her desires to go. Never before had she known such exhilaration. It felt like she was on fire!

Fortunately, there was no change to Wilford's dull routine. He left the table, clicked on a favorite TV program, and promptly fell asleep on their old naugahyde couch. Mildred cleared the table and washed the dishes, stopping only briefly to peep around the corner to check on the sleeping man. As usual, his big bulk was slumped over. Even his loud, aggravating snores were as predictable as his lifeless presence on their couch.

At 8:20, she picked up her purse and tipped-toed to the apartment door with the big worry that the creaking sound might awaken him.

I can do this. I can do this. Over and over she reassured herself as she silently prayed for the courage to get it done.

Her fingers were crossed for extra measure.

She forced her feet onto the three flights of steps that led straight to the front door. Each landing had its own unique creak, squeak, or clunk. She knew them and sidestepped her way to the bottom. Having made it that far, the odds were getting better and better.

Out on the street, she was extremely careful not to be seen by the neighbors. If someone saw her, especially at such an hour of the night, that subject would surely be the damming theme of her father's sermon at Sunday's services.

Yet she continued on, with a braver determination.

As she drew nearer to the restaurant, she stopped for the third time and looked back; once again, her eyes were wide, searching and checking!

Her hands were sweaty!

Her heartbeats were loud thumps!

Briefly, she huddled in the shadows of Luigi's doorway, catching a last, deep breath before entering.

Brandy had asked for a table for two in the far, back corner. The lighting was dimmer there and she had noted that no other diners were close by. She sipped on a hot cup of coffee.

"Oh, thank you. Thank you for coming," Brandy said as Mildred sat down, clutching her purse in her lap. "I ordered two salads with Italian bread sticks and some decaf coffee. Do you want something else?"

"No, that's really too much. Wilford was eating his dinner and I attempted to eat a little so that he wouldn't suspect anything."

A 300-pound bearded waiter named Little Leno rolled up. His fat hand held the coffee pot that refilled Brandy's cup and splashed into Mildred's. He brought back the two salads and placed the garlic bread sticks in the center of the table. With no other orders from the two ladies he left them to gossip, the usual type of conversations that he overheard in the restaurant.

But these two friends were not gossiping at all, far from it. They huddled closer together, leaning in and whispering. Their own troubles took priority on this night.

It was Brandy who dropped a few tears before she could say a full sentence. Mildred, dear sweet Mildred, patted her friend's trembling shoulder with warmth and concern.

Finally, Brandy began the sad drama about all the verbal abuses concerning her marriage and the unexpected resentments that had so surprised her. And, she couldn't rationally explain to Mildred why Hubert had left so suddenly for his trip to New York.

"I had to get back to my apartment so that I could think more clearly. I'm at a total loss of what to do about his daughters and especially the housekeeper Helga," Brandy continued, controlling her tears now.

"Maybe if you just give it time, they will come to love you like we all do. Why at Daisy's you are our favorite customer," Mildred remarked with tender compassion.

"Yes, I had hoped that time would be the answer. But when his secretary was so snappy to me, I realized that they are all supporting each other. I am an outsider. Hubert just doesn't see it happening and now, with this trip, I'm afraid that he may be having his own doubts about us."

As if Mildred did not have enough dissatisfaction with her own marriage, she was now deeply sharing her dear friend's agony. A painful agony involving love, a subject of which Mildred had no real experience.

"I shouldn't throw all my problems at you. I'm so sorry to involve you like this," Brandy apologized. "You must think me crazy that I acted so foolishly, like a love-struck school girl, jumping into this relationship.

But I want to save it. I have to make Hubert talk about our marriage and his family. Don't you think it best that I do?"

"Oh, Brandy, you can do it, I just know you can. Wilford won't talk about marriage, especially anything related to emotions. And, I've certainly never been comfortable to say how I feel. One day, please, oh please, teach me to be assertive. You always know what to do."

The two had merged into a sisterhood. They took from each other the support and understanding they needed, and they provided each other with a friendship based on trust.

Though words were not necessary to express this trust, it was silently noted that whatever needs had passed between them, those emotional secrets would stay within them, never to be shared with others.

"Thanks for the compliment and thanks for the encouragement. I'm better now. You have helped me find conviction. I know what to do."

"I'm proud that I could help, but I really have to leave," Mildred said, checking her watch.

It was already 9:30 and if she didn't hurry home things might get dangerous. As she stood for her good-bye, she clutched her small purse tightly against her breasts. Then, like a frightened little child, she lowered her head and rushed through the restaurant.

As she frantically retraced her steps back towards her dreary house, she realized that, for one night in her life, she was needed by someone. That very warm feeling planted seeds of desire deep inside her heart!

10

New York City is a large cavernous place. Hubert Franz Berman had been drawn back to this city every six months for so many years he had lost count. He was thinking about his brief phone call to Brandy, how he had casually told her he had to be in New York on business. But he did not and could not tell her the true nature of that business.

Out on the city's jam-packed sidewalks he was headed to the offices of Steinberg and Leftwich, an impressive, upscale law firm specializing in corporate law. Some of the firm's best and most profitable cases had occurred in the courtrooms, defending CEO's of high caliber companies.

Samuel Steinberg, near eighty years of age and a long-time friend of Hubert's, had an outstanding reputation among his peers. Many of his closing arguments were used as study guides in the regional law schools and numerous honorary degrees covered the walls of his office.

"Welcome Hubert. Lewis is waiting for us," Steinberg said, greeting him in the reception area.

Lewis Capalo, another boyhood friend, was a successful plastic surgeon, enjoying an expensive and adventurous lifestyle. He spent his clinical days in Washington, but always joined the other two men in New York at their regular business meetings.

"Lewis, glad to see you," Hubert said as he extended his hand to a warm and friendly handshake.

"Good to see you too, Hubert. So, how's the bride?"

"She's wonderful. But it's difficult to leave a new wife and not tell her exactly where you are going."

"Don't worry, old boy. Soon it will be a routine thing," Lewis reminded him. "Just as Samuel and I do with our wives, you simply tell them that you are busy making more money. Women like hearing that."

"I think Brandy is a little different from that type of woman. In fact, I've never known a woman like her before. She has asked me for so little that it has been a joy giving her gifts. Never once has she openly sought out the material things so many other women constantly ask for, and I'm including my own two daughters."

"Gentlemen, settle down. Our business first and then the women," Steinberg spoke up, redirecting the conversations.

The three men stopped talking and stood in silence by the round conference table in Steinberg's private office; the door was locked and all cell phones were off. They joined hands, bowed their heads, and, in unison, repeated their secret oath; the powerful oath that had endured the lengthy span of time from their boyhood days.

> **"We, the three members of the Honor Guard Secret Society, promise to keep our secret from all other friends and from all our family members. We are bound together for life in this secret, like blood brothers, one to the other. Each member is dependent on the other two. We are therefore one."**

"Gentlemen, please be seated," Steinberg said as he opened his briefcase and removed some legal documents. "With Hubert's permission, we start our meeting today with the first drafts of his Last Will and Testament. I have redone parts of this Will to include his new wife. I felt that it was important that we all know his intentions and that we should discuss how they might possibly affect us as a Society. These are copies of the drafts for us to go over."

"Samuel, I think you are wise to discuss these new changes. And, I want to thank you again for preparing the prenuptial right before my wedding. At the time, I don't think Brandy fully understood what we were doing. I have, however, assured her that it is always best to be prepared."

"No problem. I was there and happy to do it. Legal matters must be handled correctly when there is a great deal at stake."

Capalo, looking directly at Hubert, quickly asked. "The Honor Guard is not in jeopardy by your Will? Do we dare reveal anything now, regardless of the reasons? I think that it is too dangerous to introduce new things."

"Let's face facts," Hubert responded. "One of us will die first. And I am a few months older than Samuel and over six months older than you. We have been foolish in not addressing this issue before."

"It's time, really past the time." Steinberg nodded, strongly agreeing with Hubert. "I have been worried about how to settle-up on the Society's accounts. When we were young, we never thought we would die."

"I hate to discuss death. It makes me feel old. I want to think young and feel young," Capalo responded with a big grin on his face.

"Death will come as surely as those big taxes you pay every year. And, we all know that you cannot avoid those taxes. You might as well start realizing that you are not exempt from death," remarked Steinberg.

"Let's vote on this matter," Hubert said. "I propose that each man prepares a Will, as I have done, with special instructions as to his income from our secret accounts. Certainly, I did not name the Society. I plan to set up some type of trust fund in Brandy's name. At my death, I am hoping that one of you will channel my share into that fund. Then, regardless of who dies first, the other two are bound to the wishes of the deceased."

"Wait. No, I don't see it that way," Capalo strongly objected. "The three of us started together so I think that we should have three members in continuum. We should have secret and separate instructions, pertaining only to the Society, creating a successor for the deceased. I want to prolong my membership and continue my participation even in death."

"Well said, Lewis," Steinberg responded. "You are right. The funds should stay concealed as they are now. Like you have proposed, we would still be beating the system and, at the same time, our Society of three would continue to exist. By a secret Will, if that is what we choose to call it, we are simply indicating our hand-picked successors."

Hubert nodded in agreement. "I got over zealous about Brandy. But I understand what Lewis is saying and I do agree with him that we should not expose any of the funds. It will take a little time to rework the distribution of my personal estate, but, know now, that my Will for the Society will name Brandy as my replacement."

"We are all together on this issue," Steinberg said. "I will redraft your changes. This also puts the difficult pressure on me to decide on my own successor. Lewis, get into the ballgame; you better start thinking about your own Wills."

"Yes, I guess I better. But it will be hard. I've made a few commitments here and there to some lady friends and my wife will explode if she ever finds out," Capalo confessed, though the other two were not the least bit surprised.

"Lewis, you should be more careful and not get into those bad situations. It could end up being life threatening and, we all know, that you don't always have the best of luck," Steinberg teased.

"Yea. Like that night when we hid some tuition money behind old Mr. Judd's brick steps. He was in the hospital or something. We forgot about his dog and that ugly mutt came charging towards us. It sure scared the crap out of me and Lady Luck was no where around."

"I remember that dog. He was more than a mutt, he was a big furry chow with fangs down to his knees. Was his name Jackson?" Steinberg asked.

"No, it was Geronimo," Capalo said. "Regrettably, I remember running and hollering 'whoa Geronimo'! But, he kept on charging. I painfully recall, ending up on the brick wall, trapped like a possum, with that vicious dog, yapping at my heels."

"Yes, I do remember you sitting up there. Hubert and I were outside the gate, unable to lure him away from you. That was a rough night; thank goodness things have definitely gotten better for all of us. And, that's why we are here." Steinberg said. "So, we better get to work and follow our regular agenda. Go ahead Hubert, start things off."

"Right, time is too valuable to waste. Please take note, that since we eliminated that troublesome transaction, our system is, once again, running like a well-oiled engine. I assure you that all the kinks are out and, as you will see, this quarter, we have heavy profits in our accounts."

"Great! I love it when you say profits to me, especially when you say **heavy profits**," Capalo laughed.

Though he had said it like a joke, he was really very serious when it came to gaining more money. He didn't have the skills of Hubert Berman who, like a shepherd, could always herd his money into profitable places. And, he bore no resemblance to Samuel Steinberg, who could maneuver legal documents in ways that never smelled of corruption, though some may have boarded on the brink of such discovery.

Dr. Lewis Capalo, cleaver or not, was their childhood friend who just happened to be along on the night that they buried the box of money.

"I know you two prefer the Caymans as the safe harbor for your accounts; but I'm very satisfied with my Swiss bank accounts and I certainly plan to continue with them," Steinberg announced.

"As long as the money keeps flowing, I know that I don't plan any changes," perked in Capalo. "After we finish with all this business I would like to address the issue of our next party. Stanley Fizer called and he is ready to begin the preparations for the next charity function. Save some time for that, Hubert."

"Lewis, if it had not been for the money we found there would be no parties. We need to keep our minds on business and move this meeting along." Hubert reacted, pointing his finger in an emphatic gesture.

"Whoa, Geronimo," Capalo laughed again! "Okay. I confess that I remember how you and Samuel had to force me into that cemetery that damn, scary night. Maybe I not putting enough emphasis on all the right details, but I have never forgotten how much I owe you guys."

"Sorry, Lewis, but you know that I am edgy tonight. Brandy and I are still new at marriage and it was tough leaving her. Especially tough, since I feel so bad about the lies of why I am in New York."

"Fellows what do we have here, racing hormones? You two are acting like pimpled-faced boys; one wants his girl and the other wants a party."

The trio had come so far in a friendship that had spanned many, many years, and now was not the time to destroy what they had shared. In grade school they were just ordinary boys, playing stickball on neighborhood streets until things changed when they found the money. In their twenties they had carefully used small amounts of this hidden treasure; money well spent on colleges, graduate schools, law schools, medical schools and all the fringe benefits.

By their mid-thirties, they were secretly investing and reinvesting all the money for greater gains. And it had all worked to their financial benefit. Later, as they reached their fifties and sixties, each man had become a pillar in the community, soundly recognized for his success in a chosen field.

Through all those years, with unwavering loyalties, they had met in New York, professing their secret oath and rejoicing in their lucrative rewards. As this meeting ended, as with previous meetings, all Society papers were shredded, leaving no trail that the meeting had occurred at all.

It was late when a tired Hubert finally returned to his fourteenth floor apartment. He wanted to call Brandy, wanted more desperately to be with her in Boston. But calling at such an hour might frighten her that something was wrong.

Waiting for the morning, however, was lonely. The emptiness of the bed made him realize how much he missed his wife. He tossed and turned, fluffing the pillows and kicking off the sheets. Finally, his aging and achy body surrendered.

Dreams of Brandy came easily and their soothing images caressed his soul. But it didn't bring forgiveness for the white lies he had made to her.

11

Throughout the middle of the night Brandy paced the floor, her frazzled body finding no restful spot. Being with Mildred earlier in the evening had been helpful, but now that she was alone in her apartment, away from the support of a friend, it all seemed much harder. It was one thing to tell Mildred; it would be a more difficult thing to actually have it out with Hubert.

Clusters and clusters of wild thoughts bumped about in her mind, offering her no practical reasoning to formulate any solid solutions. The more she walked the floor, the more confusing everything seemed to become. With clinched jaws and tense shoulders, she was constantly vacillating between the 'I **will** do it' and 'they **can't** do that to me'.

She fought these mental goblins until the warmth of dawn replaced the coldness in the apartment. Having given it her all and being just completely bone-tired, she crawled across the end of her bed and fell into the softness of her pillow. Sleep was a necessary reprieve.

Some time later, and somewhere in the distance, a telephone rang. One, two, three rings broke the silence around her bed. Four, five, six piercing sounds. By the eighth ring, Brandy stretched her arm over towards the nightstand and pulled the telephone receiver to her ear.

"Hello," she mumbled in a low, raspy voice.

"Brandy? Brandy, is that you?" Hubert's voice echoed through her head. "Brandy, can you hear me?"

"Yes," she muttered, her arm resting across the bridge of her nose, shielding her sleepy eyes from the imposing glare of the sunlight.

"Thank God you are safe! When I flew in from New York early this morning, Helga was frantic. You didn't call her last night. And Miss Borden was so sure she had made proper arrangements for you. What happened?" he asked, completely misinformed about what had occurred while he was gone.

"I am tired and sleepy, but I guess I'm okay. I just had to come home, just to be with my things, to remember who I am."

"But you don't live at Boston Arms on Flaherty Way and Shields told me that's where he dropped you off. He didn't even know your full name. This morning when I called him to find you, he had to trace you through Mac's Bar. Why did you lie to Shields?" Hubert's voice was sterner now, laden with an annoyance at her confusing behavior.

"I didn't feel it appropriate to have Shields come to my apartment, especially with you out of town. At the time, it seemed best not to tell him my real address. I guess I messed up on that."

"Brandy, this is rather confusing to say the least. I'm not used to all this bantering back and forth. Shields has a job to do and driving you places is part of that job. He is paid for his services and his has been a very faithful employee. Surely that is simple enough to understand."

"Hubert, I know that you are put out with me, but try to understand before you get really angry. There is a great deal of pressure connected to our relationship and I needed familiar territory where I could do some heavy thinking. I didn't want to involve Shields with any of my private troubles. Only you and I need to talk about these matters."

"Oh, I understand now what you are saying. You missed me and you were fretful about sleeping alone at The Boxwood. I felt the same way. It hurt to be away from you and all alone in New York. Be patient and I will send Shields to pick you up. He can help with whatever personal attachments you need to bring for you own comfort. When you are back here at the condo, Helga will prepare a late lunch for us."

"No, I don't want Shields and especially not Helga. You come. You come to my apartment and spend the rest of this day and tonight with me. You come **here** where I live and see who I am," Brandy said, strongly wording her plea. "If things work out and if you really understand the problems of our relationship, then I will go with you. And I won't need any of these worthless items from this place."

For a few seconds there was no response on the end of the line. In that instant Brandy lingered in a limbo, fearful that he would not accept her ultimatum. Yet, she knew of no other way to approach him. If he couldn't defend who she really was, then he was in love with an impostor from his own imagination. Nervously she held onto the black receiver, her breathing strained and her hands sweaty and cold.

"Brandy," he spoke with warm affection. "You are my wife and a few interferences are not going to change that, nor change the way I feel about you. I believe that by saying that I missed you, I'm expressing how I have grown to know more and more wonderful things about you each day."

"I did miss you too, really I did. But the way you left so abruptly was an insult to me and I was annoyed and embarrassed in front of Miss Borden. It really hit me hard and totally knocked the support out from under me. I'm new at this way of living and the adjustments have been difficult for me. In honesty, from the very beginning I have been dependent on your guidance."

"Miss Borden assured me that she had explained everything to your satisfaction and I knew that Shields would handle his responsibilities. So I thought everything had been taken care of without me here. I even had flowers sent to the condo for you."

"Hubert, all I require is you. No gifts or flowers are necessary, and no family members or employees involved in the privacy of our personal life. Our relationship is shaky because these things have come between us. How much of this can you change in order to keep us together? That is the most important question we have to answer."

"From the moment I first saw you, I knew that I had never known anyone like you in my life. I needed your wit and your laughter, your sensitive affection and your unselfish requests," Hubert said, loaded with the compliments he could so lavishly bestow.

"Listen to me, Hubert. I'm a plain person. Admittedly, you swept me off my feet with the Cinderella courtship and the romantic backdrop of the cruise. But now, I'm faced with the reality of a daily life together and that is an entirely different matter. Take me off the pedestal and see me as I am. Take your blinders off and see the others as they are. I desperately want to be accepted."

"My daughters are the blame for soiling your entry into my household. But I thought I had explained that to you," he replied.

"It's more than your daughters' attitudes."

"Okay, Brandy. I may not fully understand how all this confusion came about. I'm a businessman and I am accustomed to having others handle the small details. But I assure you, I'm coming there to talk so that we can correct whatever went wrong. Don't be hasty; give me a chance. I promise you that you can depend on me."

"I'll wait for you," Brandy responded, placing the receiver back onto its cradle.

12

At that same hour, across town, Daisy's was the hub of electricity as Mildred told every customer about dining with Brandy at Luigi's. Most of Daisy's clientele could never afford to eat out; they were dining vicariously through the romantic scenario that Mildred was describing.

The women walked with her through the flawless interior of the Italian restaurant; they smiled at the heavy-set waiter named Little Leno. They inhaled the aroma of the garlic and felt the white cloths that covered every table.

"Imagine, just imagine," Mildred said with enthusiasm, "opera music in a bathroom! Never have I known such a thing."

Maybe she did stretch the truth, but who would know? Certainly her spellbound group of customers would never doubt her. They hung onto every word, laughing at the funny tidbits that Mildred added with such animation to her part-true, part-fictional saga.

No mention was ever made of the tears and the pain, of the uneaten salads or the jittery nerves. Mildred had pushed aside those things and her memories of that night would forever be sealed with happiness.

At her coffee break in the backroom, her spirits were still soaring and she could not calm herself to an ordinary day. To keep the happy feelings in tact she decided to call Brandy.

"Hi, it's Mildred," she chirped. "It may be too early, but I was already at work. I was hoping that you were still at your apartment."

"No it's not too early and I am glad that you called. Are you okay this morning? Was there any trouble with Wilford?"

"No, everything worked out. He never woke up, so I made it just fine. I'm surely glad that I went last night. And today is a marvelous day here at the shop! But I should really be asking about what is happening there?"

"Hubert is coming in a little while. I was firm, Mildred, and I think now I can tell him everything. Say those prayers of yours for me. Listen, I won't ever tell anyone that you met me last night. I would never get you into any trouble."

"Don't worry about that. I told a few people here at Daisy's. But I don't think Wilford will ever find out. But, today, I just don't care," she chirped again. "Today, I feel free. I finally did something, thanks to you. Can we do it again sometime?"

"Yes, let's do it again. And hopefully it will be soon. Maybe the next time there won't be any need of secrecy or lies. We'll meet just to have fun. When I get through all this mess, I'll call you. Thanks again for being such a good friend. You really helped me so much."

Mildred's call had reinforced Brandy's commitment to face Hubert and since he had agreed to talk things out, she had no regrets about the pressure she had applied. She sat at the window watching for him, hoping that it would all go the way she had planned.

The limo pulled up to the curb in front of O'Ryan House, an apartment building five doors down from the Boston Arms. Shields popped the trunk, got out and removed a suit bag. Hubert stood on the curb, scanning the array of windows in the tall building. From her own window she looked down at this proper man in a pin stripe suit; he appeared lost, not knowing exactly what to do or where to go.

"Mr. Berman, shall I carry this bag up for you?" Shields asked, being more accustomed to performing that role.

"No, Shields. I need to do this myself. I'll call for you when we are ready to leave."

As the limo pulled away, Hubert pushed an entry button under the name – Irma Lou Delaney. His firm touch released a long, steady buzz. Then, the solid, wooden door opened. He was on his way to Brandy. Yet, as he began to climb the four flights of steps, a masculine mind-set crept in. How could a person of his proclaimed prominence and immense wealth been reduced to an errand boy, carrying a bag and following the orders issued by a woman?

Never in his adult life had anyone put him in such a position.

Under other circumstances and with someone else, he would have said 'the hell with it' and walked away. But this was Brandy; this was too important to dismiss so easily without discussion.

She was waiting at her door and motioned for him to come inside. At first, he stood coldly away from her, causing their casual greetings to be awkward and strained.

Though she was full of confidence only a few moments earlier, now she struggled to get things started. "Hubert, this is very hard for me," she stammered.

"Let's sit here by each other and together we can work on this," he replied. His years of breeding as a gentleman came to the forefront and overrode his negativity at submitting to a woman. He cared too much not to offer his wife the opportunity to explain herself.

"I can't sit that close to you just yet. I need to sit across from you," she sputtered, at first going too fast then regaining her composure. "Hubert, look around. This is how I live. Throughout the years I have had several lousy lovers live with me in this cramped place, but I never married any of them. You were the first man I ever wanted to marry."

"Is this really necessary? What happened before is over," he immediately said, not wanting to hear these events about her life. He knew all that he required to know about Brandy.

"Yes, it is very necessary for me. Recently, I lied to you and I am not proud of myself. You deserve better and I don't want to lie to you again. No, I need to clean the slate. I want you to know the real me. I am an honest person."

"You must have had your reasons to hide things from me. Sometimes situations require less than honest approaches. Things can be destroyed if people are too honest," he remarked. "There has been no serious harm here and all this worry and pain can be over."

"No, it cannot be covered over so easily. It will never be settled if it is not explained. The reasons for my lies had to do with the people around you. Everyone wants me out of your life. But I don't think you know what they are doing. Do you?" Brandy put her issues out in full view.

"Brandy, I know that my daughters were rude and that your first meeting with them went badly," he frankly responded.

"They were very rude. I tried to overlook their behavior hoping they would eventually see how much I love you," she replied.

"Caroline and Cynthia are not going to change any time soon. Don't expect that. I felt that you would have understood their attitudes given the early death of their mother." Hubert sank back into the chair as he watched Brandy's eyes for some sign of acceptance.

"I'm not trying to take her place in their lives, surely they understand that," Brandy sighed. "Help me figure a way to gain their support for our relationship."

"Wait, it is much deeper. Catherine and I were going home from a party at the club, we had the top down on my sports car and there was an unexpected blow-out on the front tire. I walked away with a few bruises. But Catherine, poor Catherine, she was thrown from the car and received serious facial injuries and a shattered shoulder." Hubert folded his hands together, tightened his lips as if to fight back tears.

"And your daughters blame you for the accident? How many years have they tortured you like this?" She exploded in a heated rush at the idea of their insensitivity to their own father.

"Catherine was only forty-seven when we crashed. Then she lived about ten years in total misery before her death. My daughters were about twenty and sixteen at the time of the accident."

"My heavens, they should have understood that it wasn't your fault."

"Catherine was an attractive woman and they literally screamed and hit me when I had to tell them about the horror to her face. There were numerous operations, requiring extensive plastic surgery; unfortunately, without enough success. Beauty was Catherine's very essence. She could not survive without it. The girls have never forgiven me for that."

Brandy waited quietly. She had already said too much. Having heard all these additional details about the tragic conditions that had led to Catherine's death, it was obvious that her hasty overreactions were not justified. In her own repugnance on how badly she had been acting towards Hubert, all she could do was to reach across and pat his arm with an enormous amount of sympathy.

"You are getting more than you ever expected, Brandy, but if it's honesty you need, I'll cooperate," he mustered up the effort to continue. "Helga came into my employ and cared for Catherine. At the hospitals and at home, day and night for years, Helga was there for Catherine and the girls. They had stopped talking to me and Helga became my only source of information about my wife and my children. I was literally expelled from their lives."

"Now I understand better why Helga has such animosity towards me. It was her fear that I would replace her. That I would start taking care of you and she would be lost without someone to hover over. After the funeral, why didn't your daughters just move away from you?" Brandy asked, remembering her own bitter resentments of her parents, moving as far away from them as her money would allow.

"I'm sure that they made a pact to stand together against me and to stay around and make my life miserable. At that time Caroline was dating David D, and, as you probably guessed, she married him to spite me."

"That certainly was not hard to figure out. She could do much better."

"I agree. I arranged to have him checked out. He was penniless. But regardless of how much I had warned Caroline about him, they dashed off to Mexico for a quickie marriage. He claims to be closely related to Donald Trump, hence that David **D** business. It is a fake kinship, just as fake as the diamond that he gave to Caroline."

"But she made that decision herself. What more could you have done to stop her?" asked a concerned Brandy, correctly guessing the answer before Hubert could speak.

"Nothing," he said emphatically. "In her state of anger, she absolutely was not listening to me about anything. To this day, I give him a hefty paycheck just to keep him from Caroline's money. She knows what a loser he is, but just too darn stubborn to get rid of him."

Hubert added more with the sordid details about his youngest daughter Cynthia. Through her free-spirited sexual behaviors, she had destroyed her reputable reputation as a Berman, causing a great deal of embarrassment to the family, which of course, was exactly what Cynthia wanted.

"Oh, Hubert, I am so sorry. How stupid I feel complaining about a few insults thrown at me, when you have endured so much."

"Sometimes I believe that I deserved all their hatred. The truth is I really didn't love Catherine; our marriage was a society thing, really just a serviceable arrangement. We both had affairs and tried to be discreet," he confessed.

"You are not the first man to say that about marriage."

"Well, regardless of the way we behaved, Catherine did not deserve such pain. She had intended to ride home that night with one of her lovers, but I insisted that she go with me, just to keep up appearances because the girls with there with dates. I literally caused her death by my insistence of her being in my sports car. The damn, stupid blow-out ruined all our lives."

"Was the blackmailing scheme connected to the accident?"

"Shields told you? I'm quite surprise at his disloyalty about such a private matter."

"Yes," she voiced a note of uneasiness. "Shields mentioned it only because I pressed him about his thumb."

"The thumb, oh yes. Well, it is true. After Catherine died I did receive various photographs of the accident. The anonymous sender claimed that I was drunk and that he would prove it to the police. At first I thought maybe my daughters were behind it, so I hired Shields to investigate."

"Shields said the man was killed," she remarked with inquisitive prying.

"The police report indicated that he died as the result of a provoked gambling-fight in some dump of a bar. The other man was later released on a plea of self-defense," Hubert declared. "There was never any evidence that the girls had anything to do with the blackmailer. So, with his death, that ended all blackmailing threats to me."

"I can relate to bar room fights. I have avoided many in my career." Brandy stated as she moved from listening to his explanations to asking one important question. "Hubert, about your affairs, was Miss Borden one of them?"

"Brandy, we are treading on troubled waters here. All that business is far in the past. I really prefer not to say any more. I honestly fail to see that we have an issue and it just might create uncomfortable feelings when you are around Miss Borden."

"It is an issue for me, because she is a part of our problem."

"I'm hesitant to do this. But please remember that you are the one pushing for honesty. Yes, we did have an affair. It was an insignificant situation during my struggles about Catherine. I will admit to my weaknesses, but there was nothing romantic on my part."

"I think there is a great deal to **IT** on Miss Beverly Borden's part! She was over protective of you and flat-dabbed sent me packing," Brandy snapped back, releasing the green-eyed monster lurking within her emotions.

"Hold still for a moment, Brandy. Affairs of that nature don't really have merit to them. It didn't mean anything then, nor does it mean anything now. Especially now," he responded. "Brandy, I love you. And that is plain and simple. Hopefully, you can forgive and forget all these things of the past. Let's just move beyond all this nonsense."

"I do want you," she admitted, "and right now I really feel stupid about the way I have been going around pouting and puffing, blaming everybody as I did. On the front end, I just didn't have enough wisdom on how to be a second wife. I really started off on the wrong foot, didn't I? Now I wish I knew an approach that would appease all of them so that you and I could restart our honeymoon."

"That, my dear, is the invitation I am glad to hear. Let me do what I do best and I will fix everything just for you," Hubert said in a firm voice. "My daughters can be appeased with more money. Helga will go to work at Catherine's house. I will speed up my retirement. And, I'm sure Miss Borden will gladly stay to work with my replacement. As of this moment, she is also out of my Will. All that should do. Anything else you need?"

"Hubert, you are an amazing man!" Brandy said, swelling in pride over a husband who so willingly would correct all their problems.

"In your forgiving eyes I guess I am amazing. But it is **you** who has given me the desire to really live again. What a beauty you are to love an old man like me."

"Aren't we two lucky people, I see a knight in shining armor, my dream man come to life. And you see a young, thin girl."

"That's a truth in what we see and not in what we really are. When you have lived as long as I have, you will recognize that, sometimes, we fight truth until we mold it into our liking. Yet, perhaps, I have long ignored the part about youthful enthusiasm and you are teaching me something."

"Right on the button, we will be as young as we feel!"

Brandy's cherry-red lips brushed his check, a rosy glow surfaced on her face. Softly, and with tenderness, she lowered her searching lips.

With confidence she lured him into her embrace. She kissed him.

Sweetly, they kissed again, deliciously savoring the tantalizing feel.

His arms went around her waist. His hands moved under her blouse; his fingers, gliding slowly across the moist heat on her back.

In that precious moment, age had no importance.

13

Helga VanSmitten handed two fully packed suitcases to the cab driver waiting at the delivery exit on the south side of The Boxwood. It was degrading to her, having to go out the rear door of the building and leave the private compound in a public taxi. Spoiled by her generous boss, she was more suited to using the owners' elevator directly to the garage where she was quite free to come and go in the Toyota Avalon that Hubert Berman provided for her. Those pampered days were over now that her household services were no longer required.

How curt he had been on the phone when he called her. That Brandy! It was that Brandy who caused her to be fired, she thought as she slammed the door of the taxi.

"Dreary morning," mumbled the cabby, watching the rain pelting hard against his windshield as they left the protection of the canopy-covered exit.

"What? Oh, yes. Dreary for sure and more than the rain," she snapped back. Having no desire to chat with the stranger, she lifted her newspaper high in front of her face, putting up a conversation barrier that the driver would not try to penetrate.

The taxi ride to Caroline Trump's house would not be long but it would be slow on the rain soaked roads. There was no rush though, since Helga was still fuming over her dismissal, she was in no hurry to leave the contented position she had in her service to Hubert Berman.

The driver pulled around to the back of the Georgian styled, red brick house. Helga put on her rain bonnet and made a mad dash for the rear door where a uniformed maid of Mexican heritage was standing. The driver, loudly cursing the wind swept rain, hurriedly dispatched the suitcases from his trunk to the rain soaked steps of the back porch.

"It's raining the cat and the dog," remarked the maid as she and Helga hurried to gather up the two suitcases. The short, stocky woman then led Helga a short distance down the hall to a small bedroom.

"Senora Trump, she will be pronto," the maid said, leaving Helga alone in the crowded room with its twin bed, chair, dresser, and a small TV on a metal stand.

Helga hung her dripping raincoat on the shower rod in the tiny, adjoining bathroom. Still feeling damp and chilly, she was just unpacking drier clothes when Caroline popped open the door.

"Helga, we are so delighted to have you work here," Caroline began in a most proper but patronizing manner. "You'll soon discover that things are different here than at my father's. I entertain quite often. You will help in the kitchen, and also serving and tidying up after our little parties."

"You know that I have always been a good cook. Remember all the special things that I prepared for you and Cynthia."

"That was long ago. I have already retained an excellent cook. I meant that in my kitchen you will help by doing dishes and polishing silver," Caroline smirked as she turned to leave. "Oh, one thing more, yesterday just as soon as father called about your employment, I had Ramona secure several uniforms for you. She has put them in your closet. Please change into one and then assist her in the kitchen. Of course, you understand, Ramona is in charge of our staff."

A strong taste of bile crusted in Helga's throat and she tensed trying to fight off the nausea that was about to spew. Leaning against a well-worn chair, she swallowed and forced control.

Caroline made her uppity exit and Helga was left alone in the tiny room, far removed from the status she had fully enjoyed over the past years. When she changed clothes, the ugly uniform hung disgustingly limp on her small frame and her desire to perform well completely died at the very moment she saw her reflection in the bathroom mirror.

The coldness of Caroline's greeting and the coldness in the small bedroom were but the introduction to the cold family life that daily went on in the Trump household.

Outside the historical home, the severe weather continued with the blowing rain saturating the soil and flooding gutters and curb-side drains. Nothing good could be said about the day or about the future that was in store for Helga.

Across town, an annoying drip, oozing through the sheetrock ceiling, pitter-pattered into a plastic bucket that Daisy had placed squarely under the steady leak. She was quite busy with her morning customers who had kept their appointments regardless of the miserable storm.

When the phone rang, she routinely balanced the receiver between her chin and shoulder so as not to stop working on Mrs. Kilpatrick's silvery hair.

"Daisy's Nail and Beauty Shop, where it is dry inside," she laughed at her comment, looking at the red mop bucket catching the rain.

"Daisy, this is Brandy. Good morning," rang out the familiar voice of her favorite customer.

"Brandy, it's great to hear from you. What can I do for you on this miserable day?"

"I know that it's short notice, but I desperately need hair and nail appointments today," Brandy inquired with a sweet, begging tone; the gray in her hair growing faster than the clock was ticking.

"Honey, for you, Mildred and I are always available. Let me check for an opening." Still holding the receiver with her chin, she looked at the appointment book and marked out their lunch breaks. "Noon is good, if you can make it then."

"Thank you. I'll be there," Brandy responded. "Tell Mildred that Hubert will be with me."

"What? Are you kidding? She will be so excited that I won't get any work out of her! See you two at noon." Daisy hung up the phone and told all her patrons to stay around, Brandy's new husband was coming.

The rain would not alter Hubert's and Brandy's enthusiasm on this special day as they prepared to start, again, their public life. The prior two days secluded in her apartment, talking and planning, had settled all their differences.

True to his word, Hubert had made the phone calls that would take care of all his promises to Brandy. With trust, they had compiled a lengthy list of where they would travel and the many fun things that they would do as a couple.

"Ready, dear? Shields is downstairs waiting for us. With this rain, we need to leave now to make your appointments," Hubert called out, waiting patiently by the door.

After checking the stove and turning off lights, Brandy took her last look around.

A dull, unflattering light filtered in through the dingy window-shades, and she wondered, now, why she had spent an entire Saturday morning, picking out the green paint that was on all the walls. It was cheap paint when she had bought it and it was cheap looking as she was leaving it.

The meager furnishings were chipped and scratched and the cream bedspread looked more like taupe. It was threadbare and old, as was the couch in front of an out-dated TV.

She had called the apartment HOME. Had invited friends, like Patrick O'Reilly, to stop by for coffee. Had even insisted that Hubert come to see how she really lived.

She should have felt embarrassment that she had exposed Hubert to such a pathetic place. Yet, he had not said one unpleasant word about the apartment. He had come only to be with her.

"I'm ready," she called out to him, "when the landlady sells my stuff, I'm sure she will be lucky to get pennies for it."

"It's all behind you now. Somebody else will come along and be quite content to be in this nice building."

"Hubert, you are right. For years I could only afford this type of living and I should never forget my roots."

"I'm proud of you and all that you did to support yourself. Now, my dear, you absolutely deserve to enjoy everything that I have. You have earned it."

She left her only key in the lock.

Hand in hand they walked down the four flights of steps and she never looked back.

14

Mac's Bar reeked of thick, heavy smoke like the kind that permeates into walls and continually yellows upholstery and draperies. It was if no fresh air had visited the premises in years, even sunlight was barred from entry. But Ox Moran had seen these kinds of places before, many times before, as he silently roamed around the city following wayward husbands or cheating wives.

Being a private eye was a lonely and often times dangerous job, but it was his profession ever since he was booted out of a football career, short-lived because of bad knees that never mended properly. Forward years ahead and damned the stiff knees; his detective snooping was a good career and he liked it. His size and muscles – big – coupled with a fantastic memory for faces were great assets that served him well.

Sly as a fox, his style of spying didn't often require chasing his subject, but rather simply watching their little rendezvous from a safe distance. After each episode, he reported his sordid findings to the interested party and then gladly squirreled away his fee.

Mac's Bar was a neighborhood joint. It was crowded and disagreeably loud when Moran climbed onto the nearest bar stool. At least he was out of the pouring rain and maybe, just maybe, the beer might be cold and the glass reasonably clean.

He lit a cigarette and set it on the edge of a dirty ashtray, letting it smolder more as a prop, giving the impression that he belonged in the place like any other hard working stiff, stopping off for a brew and a smoke.

Never having worked this particular Boston neighborhood before, he was a little leery not being familiar with the side alleys and back doors. He checked around for exit signs and sized up the guys sitting along the bar.

Nothing seemed too threatening at the moment.

"A draft beer," he yelled out to the bartender, a burly grimy looking character the others were calling Mac.

"Two bucks," Mac bellowed picking up a glass, wiping it with his apron and filling it from the tap with a little beer and a lot of foam.

When Mac slid the glass across the bar, Moran laid down the two dollar bills and asked, "Where's the john?"

"Back in the rear, on the left," Mac answered, pointing his hairy arm in the direction past a stage and down a shabby hallway. "It's a one door deal. Lock it or some broad might stop in and jump your bone."

The roly-poly drinkers all along the bar let out disgusting yells and cat-call whistles at Mac's bad attempt at humor. Their obese beer-bellies rolled in unison and Mac slapped his fat fingers on the bar as he whooped it up with the rest of them.

Moran left the half-empty glass on the scratched-up bar and the cigarette wasting away in the broken ashtray. He weaved by cluttered tables of rowdy patrons who were cheering on a brunette at the piano, her raunchy music wilder than their behavior.

In the rear, he located the poorly locked exit next to the restroom into which he momentarily entered for a passing shot at the urinal, though the call wasn't for real.

Heading back to the bar stool, he mentally recorded that the place was just a local dive and, should things go soar, he was more than pleased with the simple, escape route. The case, so far, was moving along routinely; no one was questioning his presence and there appeared to be little danger of exposing his real identity.

"Shove me another cold one," he yelled to Mac when he got back to his hot, flat beer. "The guys really like that piano player you got in here. Later, maybe I better send over a tip."

"Nay, don't waste your dime. That's my niece and she's a dud on the piano. Not as good as my other girl Brandy who went off and got herself married. She's high-stepping these days; or so she says, if you can ever believe a dame."

"That's right," Moran replied. "They all lie and cry."

"Buddy, you sure know dames. My niece over there has been strutting around here milking these guys, getting into their paychecks. Just ain't no telling what big lies she's been feeding her mama. I'm working overtime trying to keep her straight."

"So, the girl Brandy moved on. Think her old place might be available to rent? That is, if it's an apartment around here."

"Don't know. Never went there. See O'Reilly back in the dressing room, he might know because he was always hanging around her."

Moran wandered into a small hallway just back of the bar; there he found a cluttered storeroom that had more empty boxes than those containing beer and wine.

He pushed open a small, weathered door to a broom size closet where he came face-to-face with Patrick O'Reilly, sitting before a mirror that was streaked with heavy layers of dust.

"Excuse me," Moran said from the doorway, the space being so tight that he could get no closer to the other man.

"The restroom is down the back hall," O'Reilly replied without stopping his applications of stage makeup.

"No, I don't need that. Mac sent me. He said you might know where the former piano player used to live. I need a place to rent, just can't stand living over at my friend's anymore. I like to bring home a lady or two and old Frank is always there. Know what I mean?"

"Sure," O'Reilly answered with a grin. "You would be talking about Brandy's apartment; she lived at O'Ryan House on Flaherty Way, just a good walking distance from here. You can check with her landlady Ruthie O'Connor, she'll know if it's available."

"Thanks, I'll go there tomorrow after work. Is that Brandy in the photo there on the mirror? Looks like you, and I'm guessing that's Brandy at the piano."

"Yea, last New Year's Eve. She's a great girl and fabulous with music! New in the neighborhood, are you?"

"Yea. Just doing some day work now, but soon I hope to get on regular. Frank has some good leads on a job for me."

"Come around after you get all settled. Marsha plays six nights a week and I do my comic gig before and after her spot. Too bad Brandy's no longer here; she added a sweet dignity to our little place."

"Too bad I missed out. But I'll start stopping by anyway," Moran said with absolutely no intent of ever returning to the lousy joint.

He hung around the bar for another thirty minutes, nursing the warming beer and acting out the role of a bored, wage earner. Mac bounced back and forth, telling him jokes and fussing about Brandy and all the dough he had paid her. Moran casually asked more pertinent questions in between the rough comments about how good Brandy had been, how bad Marsha was doing, and how the damn, rotten weather was ruining his business.

Mac, not smart enough to see beyond his own selfish speeches, never once realized that Moran was actually interrogating him on the main subject at hand – Brandy. But Moran knew how to work weaknesses when he was pumping for information. He was way too skillful for most people and Mac pretty much fit the bill as the weakest of the lot.

Satisfied with all the answers he had weaseled out of the dumb and dirty bartender, he retreated back to his car. Drenched from the rain that was still pouring heavily, he decided not to go by the office. Later, in some dry underwear and the comfort of his own bedroom, he would simply dash off a hand-written memo about the findings in Mac's Bar.

Moran was a man of the streets and like a bloodhound he could catch a scent and follow it. By early morning he was back on the trail, this time in the bright sunshine, a fact that pleased him a great deal.

Over on Flaherty Way at the O'Ryan House apartments, he found Ruthie O'Connor to be a very talkative landlady. She took him to the fourth floor, to apartment 4-C. The conditions in Brandy's old apartment looked good even though it was vacant and the green paint on the walls was peeling.

"Brandy was a neat housekeeper," the landlady said. "She plays the piano for opera stars and she just married a famous man with a limo. They wanted to live here but I don't allow no two people in my smaller units."

The shabby dressed woman may have stretched the truth about Brandy but, in the end, Moran had enough factual information that filled a half-page for his report.

The local butcher, across the street, remembered Brandy as a woman who always paid cash for her meat and, also, as a good neighbor who once sent him a get-well card.

Father Murphy at St. Matthew's Catholic Church had not seen Brandy at church in years, but he confided in Moran that a good Catholic girl like Irma Lou Delaney would find her way, confess, and rejoin the flock.

Back at his office, Moran hit the computer keys for the final report. In a quick-read format, he provided the name and address of the apartment on Flaherty Way and the amount of salary Mac had paid Brandy as his star attraction.

Also, from his notes, he compiled a list of adjectives in alphabetical order: Attractive blond, bouncy and witty, fabulous with music, friendly person, good neighbor, great entertainer, neat tenant, and new bride.

In his final paragraph he keyed in the name Irma Lou Delaney, her current age, and her fallen faith from an Irish Catholic background.

Moran didn't know why his client Beverly Borden wanted the data but he absolutely didn't care; she had not blinked an eye when she had hired him at an hourly rate, including his driving time. And, when he called her about the Confidential Investigative Report, she arrived at his office within the hour.

He presented her with a rather thin envelope that he worried might just cause her to complain about its size.

But she didn't.

She quickly wrote out his check, made no comments or asked any questions. She simply scooped up the envelope and was gone from his premises.

Sitting in her locked office, Beverly Borden tore open the envelope and read with delight how Brandy was a lowly-paid piano player, working in a cheap bar, in a disgusting ethnic neighborhood. Those words not being exactly the way Moran had written his report.

Immensely fixated with the lumps of defiling tidbits, now spread out across her desk, she read and reread them with delight. Her consuming appetite continually soared over the description of an Irish Catholic girl, named Irma Lou Delaney whose mother did laundry for money and whose father was a worthless drunk.

As far as she was concerned, her little scheme had worked beautifully to support her suspicions. Now, with the convicting evidence documented, Hubert would certainly congratulate her on her resourcefulness in hiring the private detective.

There would be no doubts, that when she showed him all this incriminating data, he would promptly decide that he had made a big mistake with his marriage to Brandy.

Beverly Borden was content, once again, in the intimate surroundings of her office, the office adjoining Hubert's. The office she rushed to every morning, where she had been at his side over the many years of their compatible, working relationship.

Confident in her role of knowing what was best for Hubert, she advanced her scheme to more detailed and professional arrangements.

Preparing appropriate folders, she attached tabs to each one: first the detective's report, then Hubert's financial statement before Brandy's appearance, and then one, for his future statements, following any activity where Brandy might be digging into his money.

Finally, she labeled a folder - BRANDY, where she would keep her own personal comments about the other woman. Such a term was now official in her vocabulary.

First entry: The other woman is no match for me. Being of a ridiculous and ill-prepared background, she will not meet the high standards that Hubert requires.

Second entry: Re: The Subject of LOVE. She could never measure up to the sensitive and sophisticated style that I have provided for his specialized desires.

15

The Cessna Citation was reserved for a 10:00 a.m. flight.
Passengers: Mr. and Mrs. Hubert Franz Berman
Departure: Boston.
Destination: Lexington, Kentucky
Return flight: Not yet requested.

Fifteen minutes out from the Lexington runway, Brandy, excited about her first view of the land below them, peered out the small window of the aircraft. Thousands of feet below, she saw a vibrant palette of blending greens. In various hues, these patches of color intermingled from the lush evergreen of tall trees to the blue-green of rich grasses.

As the Citation proceeded into its final descent, she could more clearly define a wonderful geometric design of fields, streams, barns, and buildings.

The day was perfect, blue skies and soft breezes, with no strong gusts to disrupt the private plane's landing. Then, just as smoothly, it taxied to a secured spot a few yards away from a waiting automobile, its driver already proceeding towards the plane.

"Jefferson, this is Mrs. Berman," Hubert said to the elderly black gentleman who was gathering their four suitcases from the tarmac and placing them into the trunk of a Lincoln Town Car.

"Yea'sa! I's glad to meet you, Mrs. Berman," replied Jefferson. "We's all excited you dun come here."

"Thank you, Jefferson. I look forward to seeing a lot of Kentucky." Brandy politely responded as she shook the driver's hand.

From the airport the party of three traveled out Highway 60, eventually passing through various sections of Lexington. Finally, after connecting to Paris Pike, they made an exit onto a paved, county road near Elkhorn Creek. Neat split-rail fencing flanked both sides of the roadway.

This rural area was but a sampling of the sprawling land of horse country that made up the diversity of Lexington. Going further along this narrow lane, Brandy had a ringside seat, up close to the numerous barns and wide-open land she had observed from the air.

"Just down the road a few more miles and you will be at the farm, our home for the next month," Hubert happily announced.

"Oh, Hubert, the fields are so beautiful and wonderfully green! I just can't describe what I am seeing."

"Pastures, my dear. These expensive acres are for the expensive horses." He laughed, but not at her. His joyous laughter was from the blissful zest that surrounded her.

The car's tires made crackling sounds on a gravel drive and then a stronger crunch as Jefferson stopped at the front door of a stone and cedar house.

A large heavy-set woman of color, her shiny chocolate complexion glistening in the high humidity of the day, was standing on the porch with her hands resting on full, rounded hips. She wore a clean, white apron and her coarse, graying hair was neatly pulled up into a round bun.

"Mr. Berman, we's ready for you. And, we's mighty glad to see you back. Yea'sa, the Lord has dun blessed us today." She sang out, "Yea'sa, indeed the Lord has!"

"Thank you, Mama Eve. I want you to meet Mrs. Berman," he said. "I know you will take good care of her."

"Lord, you knows that be so. It's gonna be my pleasure. Now, you two be a coming on in here and gets your lunch," she blurted out with enthusiasm. Then, without fanfare or apologies, she abruptly turned and pointed her finger at Jefferson. He seemed to shrink, waiting for her orders.

She obliged with a direct command.

"You gets this luggage up to Mr. Berman's room. And don't be a lagging about!"

Jefferson immediately responded to her dictate and it amused Brandy that Mama Eve could smile so gaily and fuss so sternly, all at the same time but in two different rhythms.

The Bermans followed her into the coolness of the house, which was rustic casual with a real down-home look of cozy chic. Old beams supported a high ceiling in the main room, where an odd assortment of eclectic antiques had been staged into an inviting conversational area.

At the far end of the room, a massive stone fireplace rose from floor to ceiling, with a heavy iron grate centered in the large, blackened opening. Highly polished plank flooring ran throughout the rest of the ground floor.

In the dining room, a sturdy farmer's table had been attractively set with green place mats and folded napkins of a burgundy and green plaid. The drifting aromas of home cooking announced, 'come and get it'!

"Thank you, Mama Eve. I have missed this country ham," Hubert remarked to the housekeeper as they sat down while she served ham and garden peas, a basket of hot cornbread, and a side platter of ruby red tomatoes.

"Oh my, this is so tasty," Brandy joined in. "Even the smell is delicious!"

"Good! You two eats up everything while I's go and unpacks them suitcases," Mama Eve said as she showered them with yet another big, happy smile.

"Is Scottie out at the barn?" Hubert asked.

"Yea'sa. Mr. McInbrew, he wants to sees you when you dun finished that lunch or either later."

"I'll see to that. Thanks," Hubert said, slowly sipping, without much hesitation, on a large, frosted glass of iced tea.

Lunch took a slow mouth-watering hour. Certainly they had no need to rush, for each bite was more delectable than the one before and they had no citified appointments to keep.

Hubert led Brandy down a winding path that rambled from the back of the house to a big, white barn with a green metal roof and bright red doors.

"You'll meet Scottie, he is my superintendent," Hubert explained. "He knows everything about horses and I completely rely on his good judgment. He literally runs the farm twelve months a year and I am only here maybe twice a year, usually for about three weeks at a time."

"Maybe I can convince you to change that limited schedule since it is so peaceful here," Brandy cooed, linking her arm in his and resting her head on his shoulder.

When they entered the massive, air-conditioned barn, Scottie McInbrew was in his enclosed office but he could see them through a large glass panel that faced the barn doors.

"Hubert," he shouted out, leaving the office and quickly moving towards them. "Glad to see you back. We had some rain last week and, fortunately for your visit, we have this great sunshine today with more in the forecast for the rest of the week."

"Glad to hear that," Hubert replied, taking Brandy by the hand and gently leading her towards the foreman. "Scottie, this is Brandy. Didn't I tell you she was beautiful?"

"My, my, Brandy, it **is** a delight to meet you. Hubert gave me the wonderful news about your marriage. But, I see now that he failed miserably in telling me how beautiful you are! Hubert, get some new glasses, you didn't say enough."

"I think I am blushing," replied Brandy. "But it's a nice feeling. Thank you for your compliments."

"No false statements, Brandy. I sincerely meant it. And, by the way, welcome to Kentucky," he said. He then turned and playfully gave Hubert a light jab on the arm that was his way of saying – 'you did well, old man'.

Scottie McInbrew was an intriguing prototype of an equestrian manager, attributable to his mixed resume of rugged outdoorsman, knowledgeable horseman, and astute businessman. He wore dusty boots and a blue work shirt, but his delicate wire-framed glasses, balding hairline, and intense eyes more appropriately suggested a man of learning.

And indeed he was. As a graduate from Louisiana State University he had early plans to pursue Veterinary Medicine. Later, he diverted to the University of Kentucky where he completed a Master's in Business.

But his real love, his self-proclaimed only love, always remained with horses. Scottie's immigrant grandfather had fostered this love by exposing his young grandson to the world of thoroughbreds. Though, for years, he had fought this natural inclination; at fifty-two, he officially returned to his roots in the barns of Lexington.

Five years had passed since Hubert purchased Unbridled Farm and during those short years, Scottie, as the site manager, had turned the declining property into a very prosperous venture.

Brandy did not know all the details about Scottie, but it would not take her long to observe him in action and to come to realize, as others had, that Scottie McInbrew was a man to be respected and to be trusted.

"Brandy, I hope you will excuse me for mentioning business at our first meeting and I promise not to completely occupy your husband's time," he said to her. "But I do need to go over this month's figures with him."

"Oh, I understand that business must come **second**," she smiled and winked. "But I do expect you and Hubert to save some time to show me more of this beautiful area."

"She's a dandy lady," Hubert quickly laughed. "Scottie, tonight and tomorrow morning belong to her. But you and I can meet later tomorrow afternoon. Whatever time suits your schedule."

"That's perfect. Brandy, may I show you our layout? A nice tour of Unbridled Farm will explain why we love doing business here."

Using a golf cart he drove her around the privileged acreage, pointing out various facilities and explaining in simple language how modern technology had taken control of an old industry.

"What great-looking animals," she exclaimed!

"Thoroughbreds. High strung and frisky thoroughbreds, they love to run. Though we are not exactly in the racing business, here at Unbridle Farm we are in the breeding business."

"I think I have the idea," Brandy nodded. "What a wonderful business you are in, bringing such gorgeous thoroughbreds into this world!"

When they reached a third barn, the home of the stallions, they walked inside along a sanitized hallway, lined with sturdy, iron gates. He stopped at the first three stalls, calling each splendid animal by name and gently stroking their groomed manes.

"This one is the famous Our Bad Boy and this one is Jetstream," he said as he continued with descriptions of weights, heights, previous racing records, and the number of foals that each had sired.

"My goodness, what ancestors they must have had! I never knew the real quality of thoroughbreds. Now I am totally captivated by them," remarked Brandy, following Scottie from stall to stall.

"Here is G Two. He was sired by Gyration and out of Gemini. He may look small for a stallion, yet he was a big man on the track. He is devilish and a handful for the groomsmen. Regardless of his attitude, he deserves our respect because of the bloodlines surging in him."

To Brandy's delight the stallions, confined in their separate stalls, put on a splendid show, prancing about and pawing at the soft surface. They swished their coarse tails and snorted their authority, dipping their heads up and down.

She showed no fear and, when she climbed back into the golf cart, her comfortable posture beside him, let Scottie know just how much she had enjoyed her tour.

"Thank you," she said.

"Believe me, it has be a great pleasure. I'm not usually this relaxed with female visitors. Some ask how much money we make, breeding the stallions. Many of them simply complain of the smell when visiting the barns. No, not you. You actually appreciated their pure-breeding. So, I thank you, Brandy."

She sat beside him, full of confidence that she had found a new friend in Scottie McInbrew. And, with the warmth of the sun brushing across her shoulders, she had great faith that Kentucky was proving to be the best beginning for what she and Hubert had planned.

They rode back past the fenced pastures and the three barns, headed to the terrace where Hubert was waiting.

He waved to them.

"Did you enjoy the tour?" he asked when Brandy walked onto the terrace and gave him a quick kiss on the cheek.

"Oh, very much! Scottie explained everything," she replied. "He said to tell you that he will be in his office if you need him."

"Good. Oh, while you were at the barns Mindy Morningstar called. She is hosting a little party on Saturday night at her place," Hubert said, conveying the news of their first invitation to a social gathering.

"I remember Mindy from the cruise. She was with that group of nine ladies. Does she live near here?"

"About ten miles down the road. She owns Twin Oaks Farm, a successful stable of winning thoroughbreds. Right now her trainer is working with Indy Go, a beautiful black yearling that was sired by Our Bad Boy and out of Black Roses."

"So you and Mindy are like partners. She had the mare and you had the stallion and then Indy Go enters the world." Brandy laughed at her amateurish explanation of the important work done at the farm.

"Well, my dear, you almost have it right, except for the part that Twin Oaks will be the winning stable when Indy Go takes the big races that everyone expects from her. However, the more she wins the more publicity this farm gets for Our Bad Boy."

"That's a cute name! I think that I shall call you my Bad Boy because you can be so wickedly romantic. Thank you for opening up this world to me," Brandy said with a broad smile.

"As always, dear wife, it has been my pleasure."

Together they quietly shared the rest of the day in the slow pace of short walks and good books.

Early the next morning, the sounds of a working horse farm roused Brandy from her sleep. Hubert was not in the room but the smells from the kitchen offered the best clue for his absence. She dressed and rushed towards the tantalizing aromas of bacon, eggs, and homemade biscuits.

Mama Eve greeted her with a stemming mug of black coffee.

"Thanks," Brandy said. "I followed the delicious smells straight to your kitchen. And, may I say, all this makes for a glorious morning!"

"Yes'um, it is a fine day and rightly so! The Lord's work dun give us this glorious morning," Mama Eve agreed as she turned six slices of thickly, honey-cured bacon.

She handed Brandy a large platter of the breakfast treats, then motioned for her to take it out to the terrace.

Hubert was waiting there. "Good morning! We have such lovely weather this morning. And, today will get even better when a special surprise arrives for you."

"Oh, Hubert. You are always full of surprises. What have you done this time? Is it big or small?" she gleefully asked like an excited child, too wiggly to sit still.

"Now patience, my dear. Just enjoy your breakfast for now and then, by 10:30, you will have your little surprise."

Mama Eve had been told about the arrangements and she was almost giggling when she brought out more coffee. "I's got everything in the right place," she snickered, as she hurried back into the house.

"Hubert, am I the only one who doesn't know what is going to happen? Gosh, I'm really getting nervous over this."

"Have control, my dear. I know that you are in the dark. But I bet that a few of the horses haven't been told either," Hubert laughed.

His habit of giving her gifts was in itself a gift to him. With Brandy it was so easy and so appreciated that he found no reason to ever stop.

Time moved slowly after breakfast. Brandy checked and rechecked her watch. Hubert even lured her upstairs with some simple pretense of looking for his glasses. Though she knew it was a trick, she played along not wanting to upset his plans.

When he finally heard a truck coming onto the gravel drive, he asked her to wait by the bedroom door.

"You will know when to go down. I'm sure of it," he said.

She waited as he had asked.

In no time, the wonderful sounds of a piano drifted up the staircase! Excitedly, she turned and raced down, following the music. In the corner of the large front room, she spotted the most beautiful Steinway that she had ever seen.

Bobby Joe Bradley, the local salesman, was playing a tune until he saw her. He stepped away from the piano stool and let her take over the keys.

Notes struck in tune. Her style of music flooded the air. An ordinary room was transformed into a concert hall.

Hubert had followed her down the stairs, but at a much slower pace. He came towards her now, eager and excited! With admiration and a twinkle in his eyes, he leaned against the new piano.

If smiles were the only language of lovers, then Hubert was publicly broadcasting the greatest love of his life.

Mama Eve stood off to the side, by the hall door. Her large, round figure swayed back and forth in a steady tide with every beat. Near the end, when Brandy began to play - *When the Saints Go Marching In* - Mama Eve, with choir quality of Sunday services, jumped right in.

"ALLELUIA! ALLELUIA," she shouted out!

Brandy was more inspired and the music grew louder and faster. Bobby Joe Bradley, with his eyes closed, moved his head up and down. Selling that piano had made a good profit for him, but hearing that music flowing from it at Brandy's touch, was a powerful treat not to be forgotten.

Jefferson popped into the room. Wide-eyed and grinning from ear to ear, he strutted about, kicking his legs side-to-side. With arms a flapping and his head a bobbing, his feet clicked like the tap dance of a New Orleans street man.

Never had the household at Unbridled Farm ever shared such a celebrated day! And, never had Brandy's fingers marched up and down on such an expensive keyboard!

16

A royal sunset cast long shadows at Twin Oaks Farm. Rustic weather vanes atop the barns beckoned like large spotlights, luring people to the festivities.

Cars were parked along the country lane, many more were off to the sides of the large circular drive, and even more were in neat rows out in the front pasture.

There were, however, no twin oaks to greet the guests, only the grassy, wide-open countryside and the miles upon miles of white fencing. If the farm had originally been named after oak trees, they had long been cut down and, now, not even abandoned stumps remained to suggest that two, tall trees had ever been there.

Twin Oaks Farm was very similar to the dozen or so other horse farms in the neighborhood, only it was the largest and most prestigious. Mindy Morningstar was the mistress of the house. By trade she was a radio super star, famous for her outrageous talk show.

How she had acquired the property or why, no one was quite sure.

Many in Kentucky simply assumed that, seven years ago, she had bought the farm for personal investment. However, the local busybodies spread tall tales of her mysterious dealings and the strange comings and goings at all hours of the night.

Mindy was called a witch by some, a fortune-teller by others. There were those who even labeled her a rogue gambler, adding more pizzazz to their stories.

But when she threw a party, no one in the area of Lexington and points beyond would dare miss the event. Tonight's guest list included Washington politicians, high-paid athletes, movie stars, pencil-thin models, powerful business tycoons, and the elite from the thoroughbred racing society.

Brandy was breathless when she walked through the threshold of the 15,000 square-foot house. Like an erupting volcano, words shot through her mind – pretentious, showy, overwhelming, chic, expensive, and flashy.

Ultimately, she settled on one of her own words - **Highfalutin**!

If only she had a camera to capture it all. Why Mildred and the ladies at the beauty shop, would go crazy over such an incredible place.

"Stay close to me," she whispered to Hubert. "Let my shaking knees settle before you leave my side."

"Take it all in, my dear. And then dismiss it. Everyone here is too busy, boasting their own credentials to take note of each other."

"Easy for you to say, you are used to all this. But I am star struck. I think that woman by the fireplace was in a movie that I saw and the man beside her, I'm sure, he was on a television show."

"See there, you already know celebrities. But watch them closely. All evening, they will check their own images in the mirrors. Stand tall, my dear," he said, putting his arm around her. "You have more genuine quality than any other person in this room."

"Well, this one person needs some liquid reinforcement. How about getting me a reinforcing glass of chardonnay?"

"Good idea. I could use one too. I'm hot in here and a wine might just cool me off."

With a determined effort, they wedged a path and claimed a tiny spot by the built-in bar just outside the French doors. With a panoramic view Brandy could see several sheltered cabanas, bordering the pool on three sides. These small, canvassed retreats, though closely clustered, did not open directly into each other.

Additionally, and this was with amazement, Brandy noted that a truly intimate privacy would be guaranteed by the thick backdrop of large, tropical plants. Straight out of paradise, they were not natural to the gardens of Kentucky.

"With all that privacy something must happen here. My goodness, what really happens?" she whispered to Hubert.

"I've heard about some nudity. Not my cup of tea, but let's ask one of her closest friends," Hubert suggested when he spotted Greta Donna Cupani on the other side of the pool.

They did a quick zigzag through the crowd and cornered Greta Donna where she was perched on a cushioned chaise in front of one of the cabanas.

Her third glass of Merlot was empty for which she sent Hubert back inside for a refill of the very expensive wine that Mindy kept hidden in the kitchen.

"So how's the new bride doing? The girls and I have been wondering just how you two have managed," Greta Donna wedged her nosey questions as Hubert walked away.

"We are very happy," Brandy responded.

"Honey, you and I put on our panties the same way every morning. And even though I may take mine off more often than you, I do believe that you understand what I mean?"

"We are a loving couple and quite content with our marriage. And that's all that I care to say," Brandy replied.

It really didn't matter to Greta Donna for she had many other sources to seek the answer and she would surely try in her best, snoopy way.

"Look at all these free-loaders," she said, redirecting the conversation. "I could rattle off a truck-load of dirt on most of them. But then, that's Mindy, she loves to stir the pot at her parties!"

"Since you know about these things, what about the cabanas? Hubert said that there are wild parties."

"Are you suggesting **wild** like with nudity and who knows what? Sorry to disappoint you, but Mindy started those sexy rumors just for the publicity."

"Oh, I see. Hubert did warn me not to believe everything I might hear or see tonight. I guess he was right."

"Honey, he was so right! And, just as I told you to expect **dirt,** take this as a warning - watch out for the wolves. They love to howl over new blood and it doesn't look like you have been soiled, yet. But believe me sweetie, with your looks, it won't take them long."

Maneuvering his way back through the blocked doorways, Hubert returned, carefully balancing three glasses of wine. "It's noisy in there and too darn crowded! Stay out here where you can get some air."

"I was worried about you. It took so long," Brandy said, taking the glass and lovingly patting Hubert on the arm, more as a display for Greta Donna's benefit than as a necessary act.

"I ran into Lewis Capalo; we stopped to discuss a little business. Sorry to worry you, my dear."

The other cackling hens from the close-knit flock, sauntered by two by two. They clucked their girly exchanges with Brandy and their teasing congratulations to the groom.

After two hours of standing on the hard concrete, Hubert had smiled enough and drank enough. He and Brandy worked their way through the growing crowd, back to the main foyer. It was solidly crunched with the loud late-arrivals, bunched together in elbow-rubbing huddles.

"Shouldn't we say good-bye or at least a thank you to Mindy before we leave? It seems the proper thing to do."

"We are not likely to see her this evening. At most of these parties, she usually stays upstairs, predicting financial windfalls to the gullible guests who believe her. That's a big part of her mystique that I never let myself get involved in," Hubert said with some distaste.

While they waited for Jefferson to bring up the car, Hubert asked Brandy to find him a glass of water. She had only been away two or three minutes when she returned to find him on the floor, surrounded by a circle of onlookers.

Doctor Lewis Capalo was giving loud orders for everyone to step back and, with his cell phone, was calling for an ambulance

"Hubert," she screamed! "Let me through, he's my husband!"

"I feel sure that he had a fainting episode. The medics are on the way and I will go along to the hospital. He'll be fine."

"I'm riding with him," she nervously replied to Capalo.

"No. Just stay calm and don't upset him. Right now his vital signs look good and I'll continue to monitor him in the ambulance. Your driver can bring you along and I'll see you in ER. I know one or two of the doctors on staff; they are good physicians. Don't worry."

Someone standing behind her at the edge of the pressing circle, tried to coax her into a chair. But she would not leave the spot where she was, kneeling beside Hubert.

She squeezed his hand. But the limp response to her touch and the weak look in his eyes frightened her that this was far more serious than a mere fainting spell.

In seconds, his eyes rolled shut.

Brandy walked beside the gurney and watched helplessly while they loaded her sweet Hubert for the rush to the hospital.

Jefferson, his old eyes wide and the diameter of his pupils straining for more light, tried to chase the ambulance; its sirens wailing and its red lights brightly flashing in the blackness of the country lane. But the faster the speeding vehicle went, the further and further the big town car lagged behind.

When he finally got Brandy to the entrance of the hospital, Hubert was already in one of the treatment rooms, well beyond the security passage that stopped her from finding him.

Brandy was trapped in the confusing confines of the waiting area! Babies were crying and children were restless. The injured and sick moaned and anxiously waited for their names to be called.

Frustrated and exhausted, she could do no more than pace the floor.

A befuddled Jefferson slumped off to the side. Totally out of his element and scared stiff about being around sick folks, he waited nervously for any excuse to get out of the place.

Finally, Brandy asked him to use the car phone and to call Mama Eve and explain what had happened.

When a nurse came through the swinging doors, Brandy rushed towards her. "Is there any news on my husband, Hubert Berman?"

"Doctor Capalo and Doctor Kruger, our Chief of Staff, instructed me to tell you that your husband is stabilized. They are doing the paper work to admit him for the night."

"Oh no! I must be with him," Brandy responded in a shaky voice.

"He is fine, I assure you. It is wiser to let patients get plenty of rest. Too much commotion back there can unsettle them and totally disrupt our necessary observations."

"I don't know what to do out here. I am his wife, he needs me by his side," Brandy said, loudly pleading.

"Quieter, please, Mrs. Berman. You will disrupt this entire waiting area. You are not a special person here, these other people are important too. If you persist in these hysterics, I'll be forced to have you removed."

"Yes. Yes, I understand. But surely you realize how unnerving something like this can be."

"Certainly, I do. I work twelve-hour shifts at this hospital and we see cases far more serious than your husband's present condition."

"Okay. Okay. I'll wait here, until you can give me updates on what is happening."

"No, it is much better for you to go home and wait there. Dr. Capalo said that he intends to call you in the morning."

This devastating night had crumbled all the joy that Brandy had stock piled since the days in her apartment when she and Hubert had so amicably settled all their past problems and set forth their new plans.

Now with his hospitalization, those plans lay in chaos. Once again she had been abandoned, totally alone in the hostile world of the people who surrounded Hubert.

Leaning against a wall near the hospital's exit doors, Brandy was trapped in a daze. She was numb.

She could not feel, nor think, nor reason.

Jefferson reappeared and gently guided her out to the parked car. He slowly drove towards Unbridled Farm. There, he knew for sure, Mama Eve would have ways to ease the pain of this troubled woman.

17

Stanley Fizer was in the Cessna Citation headed for Lexington before Brandy had time to reach Unbridled Farm. Without her knowledge he had been urgently summoned to manage the current situation.

Before 6:00 a.m., with a command post actively set up in the downstairs office, he had already conducted the necessary business of contacting Hubert's daughters. And, he was well into other affairs that had to be discreetly handled.

He had arrived by dawn and Brandy and Mama Eve were totally unaware of his presence in the house. They had been shut up in the master bedroom ever since Jefferson had delivered his shivering boss-lady. When the two women finally came downstairs to perk the morning coffee, they were totally surprised to see him.

"Why are **you** here? Hubert is in the hospital," Brandy thundered at him as Mama Eve took flight into the kitchen.

"Brandy, regardless of the hour and how far I have to travel, when I am told that there is a need for my services, I immediately respond and take charge," he replied, seeking no input from her.

"Need? What need? Has something else happened at the hospital? I've been waiting all night and all this morning for Doctor Capalo to call me. I don't understand why **you** are involved; this is a medical matter."

"I have already talked to the doctor. They have moved Mr. Berman to a private room. In the mean time, I will be making arrangements for the flight back to Boston and for his personal doctor to meet him at the airport."

"Boston? When was all this planned? No one has told me anything about this move. I want to see Hubert. I need to be with him." She screamed louder, in a high-pitched, angry voice, "I **am** his wife!"

"Yes, you are his wife. That's true. But, that's it. I am his personal administrator and I take the full responsibility of handling all details. I suggest that you get a better understanding of your position. Plainly put, stay out of my way and out of the business at hand."

"Jefferson will take me to the hospital and I will see for myself what Hubert needs and if he really wants to leave for Boston," she forcefully rebutted.

"I don't think so, Mrs. Berman."

She turned to leave the room, but he grabbed her arm.

"Dr. Capalo and I have left strict instructions that only medical personnel are to be allowed in that private room. So for now, I will tell you what you can and cannot do. And when and how you will travel from this house to Boston."

His words could not have been more riveting and his powerful, stern attitude jolted Brandy from her immediate concerns over Hubert's condition to the more stressful concerns for her immediate future.

She mulled the situation as she bolted away from him and rushed to the safety zone of Mama Eve's kitchen.

All morning long, the foyer of the manor house was alive with a steady stream of people arriving from the airport. Samuel Steinberg, the first to report in, brought his briefcase and locked himself in the front office with Fizer. Muffled voices could be heard from behind the closed door but no others in the household were ever informed of the nature of their clandestine business.

Caroline and Cynthia, traveling together, were very explicit about not staying in the same house with Brandy. And they were rudely firm with Jefferson that he was to put their luggage in the furnished rooms of the poolside cottage.

Unexpectedly, Caroline's husband David D appeared on the doorstep and, without asking anyone's permission, carried his luggage upstairs and unpacked in the guestroom nearest to the master bedroom.

With all this meandering about, the household routines were totally disrupted. Mama Eve frantically fluttered about, keeping a steady pot of hot coffee in the kitchen and a full tray of food on the dining room table.

Jefferson was busy driving from one end of town to the other; most specifically, driving Caroline and Cynthia on shopping trips. But Mama Eve saw to it that he got his household chores done regardless of what the two women demanded of him.

With no quiet place to avoid all this turbulence, Brandy found much needed solace in the barn with Scottie McInbrew.

"I am sorry that Hubert is not well and so soon after your marriage," he said, welcoming her into his office.

"Scottie, it is awful! I am kept in the dark about what is going on and it is rattling my senses. I should be concentrating on him. I should be there."

She wept loudly.

Supportively, he pulled her close, her head resting on his shoulder. His blue shirt spotted with the wet droppings of her flowing tears.

"Easy now. Give it time. They are running about in a greedy stupor like they always do. Unfortunately, you have been pushed to the sideline. Just as soon as Hubert's strength is back, he will stop all this interference and get those people out of your house."

"They are openly brutal to me because they think that I cornered Hubert and made him marry me. That's not true," Brandy sighed. "It just didn't take us long to know that we wanted to be together. I hope you saw it when we arrived here."

"He has never been happier. I know that sure scares the hell out of that crew up at the house. Listen, they still treat me like I am a stable boy."

"I guess then, you already know what I am just learning. Being an outsider is a tough thing to overcome."

"Brandy, for a lifetime we have to live with what we can handle. Deep inside, we are what we are. That's the way I look at things."

"You are right. Yet, I don't know how Stanley Fizer stands to live with himself. He's a power freak and I hate him for that."

"Yea, he's a yellow-bellied sapsucker."

"A what?"

"A yellow-bellied sapsucker is a perfect description of how I see him. Like a woodpecker, he drills holes into people and drains out the sap of their nourishment."

"May I borrow that from you? Because whenever I am near him, he literally drains me dry."

"Yes, I gladly give you the term. And I hope that when you call him that, it acts like a voodoo pin. He won't know what hit him."

"Yellow-bellied sapsucker sure gives me a lift. I'll say it again, yellow-bellied sapsucker." She laughed aloud in spite of her misery.

"Come to the barn as often as you need to. I'm here and the horses are too," he softly spoke, hoping their conversations would make things a little easier for the long days ahead.

"Thank you, dear sweet Scottie. I'll try to keep going. I must. I must keep going for Hubert's sake!"

The emotional pain in her heart was a stabbing ache that would not stop and without Scottie she would have had no refuge.

Stars twinkled overhead as she made her way up the path from the barn to the rear of the house. Through the dining room window she could see that dinner was being served. She had no interest in food and certainly no interest in sitting at a table with the enemy.

Without their notice, she crept up the back flight of stairs and went directly down the hall to the master bedroom.

Her body was tired and achy; she needed rest.

Around midnight, she heard a knocking noise. Thinking Mama Eve was coming to check on her, she left the tussled bed and unlocked the door.

Opening it, she came face to face with David D Trump!

Without a word, he forcefully pressed his hand against the bedroom door and promptly wedged his foot so securely in the opening that she was unable to slam it shut.

"What do you want?" she screeched in a frosty tone.

"I'm here to fill in for old Hubert. You must be very lonely in that big bed," he said with a smirk that turned Brandy's stomach.

"Get away from me, you miserable piece of shit," she snapped back, her eyes flashing a fighting red.

"Take it easy, dear step-mother-in-law. We don't want to wake everybody up. No one needs to know about my little charity visit."

"There is nothing for anyone to know. Get away from this door," she screamed, her shrill cries echoing throughout the hallway!

Like thunder, feet hit the stairs! And when he heard the close sound of those fast footsteps, he recoiled from the doorway and fled back to the guestroom.

Brandy, still tightly gripping the wooden door, was shaking so hard that she could hardly stand as Mama Eve's big arms caught her and helped her back into bed.

"A slimy snake, that Mr. Trump," she said, stroking Brandy's hair. "Tomorrow Jefferson is gonna move his thangs out yonder to the cottage where that man should have dun been. And, properly so! A man rightly ought to be with his own wife."

"Thank you," Brandy weakly muttered. "He tried to get in here. What gave him the idea I could possibly be interested in him? I've never led him on. Never, did I do that."

Mama Eve bent down closer to Brandy. "That white man, he dun been a wrapping-up himself in trouble every time he comes here. He's one of them wicked womanizers, a plain low-life. He ain't got no right being in here. A fine, proper woman likes you don't be a smutting out them sinful callings for such thangs. Why, I knows, if Mr. Berman gets a wind of this, he be a skinning that man alive!"

"We can't tell Mr. Berman, especially not now. No, Mama Eve this must be kept quiet. The others would surely blame me."

Stone-faced and with resolve, the big woman reached into the pocket of her robe and withdrew a small caliber pistol. She wiped it clean with the sash of her robe and passed it towards Brandy.

"Here baby, you puts this here gun under that pillow. If'un that Mr. Trump comes a knocking again, you points and you shoots."

"Oh my goodness, a gun," Brandy gasped and shook her head. "Oh no, I couldn't shoot a gun."

"Hush then and you sleeps now. I's plan to sit over yonder in that rocker tonight. And, when I's sees them snaky eyes of that slimy man in this here room again, I's ain't be too scared to shoot that sinner. Yes'um, the good Lord knows it's a gonna be righteous for me to shoots this here gun. Ain't no way that wicked, white man a gonna be seeing them pearly gates. No sir, he's be bound for hell. Praise the Lord!"

18

Miles away, by land and by sea, Shields Mason knew nothing of Hubert Berman's hospital confinement. On the very day that the private jet had flown from Boston to Lexington, Shields had also flown from the Boston area bound for much warmer weather, particularly the tropical temperatures of the Caribbean.

Quite vividly, Shields remembered the last direct orders from his boss. *'Use my boat. Get out there and catch some fish while Mrs. Berman and I are in Kentucky. Enjoy it. You deserve some time off.'*

The boat in question was the 48-ft Queenie B purchased by Berman on a business trip some three years earlier. Signed, sealed, and delivered to a harbor in Antigua, the boat became another Berman possession; though never used by the man himself, it was always on loan to others.

Shields, as a faithful employee, had enjoyed the good fortune of using the boat whenever he had time off from his Boston duties. It had been a relaxing payback since Shields was on call 24 hours a day, 7 days a week, diligently attending to the needs of his generous employer and now Mrs. Berman, the new lady of the house.

The way Shields saw it, there was no one waiting for him at his home so why not enjoy these free getaways.

This trip, however, was already quite different from all the rest. Tropical storm warnings had repeatedly been received over the boat's radio and the radar screen was displaying large areas of bright green for the approaching rain from the south, south-east. But Shields observed no signs of any threatening weather in the isolated spot where he was fishing.

Not to be flippant about it, he wisely trusted the weather reports and watched the sky with a serious stance as he prepared for the worst. Piloting the boat into a well-protected inlet, one having a heavily vegetated gooseneck entrance, he sailed onward into a larger embayment that was shielded on three sides by high cliffs.

Clearly defined as a dogleg right, the waterway cut sharply to starboard; rocky cliffs, on both banks, jutted in staggering layers out into the water's edges. As he traveled inward, the channel drew to a stop against massive bluffs of solid stone, rising from sea level to some 200-feet in the air.

Trees peppered the terrain on all sides; the earth's surfaces of sand, soil, and hard rock tightly gripped and forcefully held their meandering roots. Somehow, in spite of this poor nourishment, the determined trees thrived to soaring heights.

Shields brought the Queenie B about and cut her speed to idle. He then clicked the proper switch to activate the release of the anchor from its locked position on the bow of the boat.

A heavy, well-built chain was securely fused to the shank of the anchor; attached was a line linkage, growing longer and longer as the pointed anchor disappeared into the water. The procedure created a pronounced, rugged dragging; an ugly noise that can rattle nerves much like fingernails on a blackboard.

The forceful sounds of the screeching and scrapping bounced against the stone bluffs and then echoed, at full volume, back across the bay. Birds, innocently slumbering in their nests high in the trees, suddenly took flight, scattering wildly into the bright, blue sky, turning it into a muddle of blackened masses.

Shields had only temporarily set the anchor until he could determine a more secure position, one that would allow a safe ride should a storm thunder in during the night. When he finally shut off the twin engines and the anchor motor, the Queenie B floated at ease, bobbing on the ripples of the water.

The frantic birds reformed their scattered ranks and flew back to their nests. The sheltered cove, once again, returned to a peaceful state.

Inside the galley, Shields sat at the table with his nautical charts and a seaman's manual. Using the seven to one rule, he quickly multiplied the water depth of 12 feet by the number 7, giving him a scope of 84 feet. With this calculation, he was sure that the Queenie B would have a safety zone with more than a 360-degree clearance to the shorelines.

He was confident that if there were to be high winds, the boat would swing freely on the measured line with no apparent danger of shifting too wide in any direction, thus avoiding dangerous contact with the jagged shorelines that flanked his chosen port.

Restarting the engines, he drew up the anchor and edged the boat forward a few feet to the exact spot that he had calculated as the proper measurement.

Again the birds took their chaotic flight, until Shields finished his task and, finally, silenced the engines.

Following a mental checklist, he prepared the Queenie B as best he knew how. The hatches were properly shut. All loose objects were tightly secured or stowed below. Life jackets were on hooks at the exit ladder by his cabin and on the upper deck by the helm. His personal fishing gear was returned to storage boxes. With total confidence he was ready to ride out a storm if it blew in his direction.

The weather reports came in clusters now and, with every passing minute, he intently charted each one. So far, the storm seemed to be headed towards the Island of Dominica, a pin-point on the map that was south of his location.

He x-marked the spot and drew lines along the coordinates of the latest reports of the storm. Accurately adjusting his communication system to channel 16, he radioed his own coordinates to a Coast Guard Station located miles away.

Having completed all his jobs, Shields could only wait and see what would happen. He sat back with a hot brew of coffee and his favorite camera.

All about him there was an ample supply of photographic subjects like the aloof heron wading in the shallow pools near the shore or the large snake silently slicing through the still waters surrounding the boat. He captured those and then zoomed in and snapped a shot of a colossal tree on the distant shore. Its leaves, brilliant and a striking pepper red, had an exotic shape that he had not observed before.

Brandy would enjoy this, he happily thought. This wasn't just a simple, passing notion. Rather, it was an emotional longing, a real sense of wanting to share this view with her, to be beside her, just the two of them, alone in this beautiful Garden of Eden.

How strange it was, it seemed to him, that all these emotions would rise up now when he was so far removed from where she was in Kentucky. On the day he had driven her to Weston, had coffee and a hamburger with her, their time together had all been so innocent and friendly.

And when, on the night that he left Brandy at her apartment, his strong urge to stay with her was real but it was, at the time, a sympathetic opportunity, more like a Sir Galahad helping a damsel in distress.

Seeing this beautiful paradise all about him had escalated his deepest emotions and made him realize that he was in love with the woman, the wife of his boss.

No guilt surfaced to make him realize that it was the sin of lust to want another man's spouse. That truth didn't stop him; it didn't distract him the least bit.

He carefully aimed his Canon at the objects that he knew she would enjoy. Every subject, patiently centered in his lens, was a deliberate and careful selection, just for her. With his heart racing, his excitement grew wilder! His fantasized that she loved looking at these special photographs. And, in the joy of it all, she would say how much she loved him for being so thoughtful and caring.

Later that night, while the Queenie B gently rocked, his illusions about Brandy turned into sensuous dreams of being beside her in his bunk. He dreamed of the soft feel of her skin and the intoxicating aroma of her cologne. They were wrapped lovingly in each other's arms, without a care about others; with no regard for space or time.

But his peaceful slumber was shattered, when, in the early pre-dawn hours, a vociferous blast of thunder discharged a resounding boom; like a bombshell it shook the boat, vibrating his bunk. He bolted upright, grabbed a life jacket, and virtually shot up the ladder to the open deck.

All was dark and ominous until lightening bolts streaked across the distant sky!

Heavy rain began to pelt down like pea gravel, their sting biting into his exposed skin. Angry, turbulent waves rose up and slammed against the sides of the boat, thrusting it into a repetitive pitching.

Shields alertly clipped a metal hook, latching his swaying body to a lifeline so as not to be propelled into the sea.

Frantically leaning into the barreling wind, he pushed forward to the bow, to the location of the anchor's line. It was holding!

Thank God, it was holding!

At the bow, the unmerciful wind was a powerful foe; with a deafening roar it was proclaiming victory. Without letup, the driving rain followed suit with its own drenching fury. Yet, Shields stayed at the bow, daringly checking and rechecking the anchor line.

His very life depended on the accuracy of his earlier calculations for the safe swing of the boat and on the soundness of the anchorage. If she broke loose the Queenie B would surely crash against the boulders along the shore or capsize into the murky, swirling water.

For what seemed like a fruitless battle, Shields fought the raging forces of nature's worst elements. Regrettably, though it would do no good now to whine and wail about it, he realized that he had miscalculated the variances of the wind in the bay and he was totally unprepared for such erratic wind shifts at sea level.

The eerie pitching of the commanding currents stirred nausea within him. His attachment to the secured lifeline was all that prevented him from falling overboard whenever he bent over to vomit the green slime of the awful seasickness that spun his bowels out of control.

The repetitive whirr of the strong air flow was enough to scare the hell out of the best. And the dense screens of blackness literally blocked all presence of position for man or boat. It was if the world was stranded in an abnormal, black hole.

When there were a few, brief breaks in the storm, though those moments could be counted on one hand, he could hear the crisp snap of tree limbs, faintly though it was, off in the distance. These were just the usual sounds expected in a storm.

Erratically anticipating more extreme dangers, he would desperately lean towards the bank, straining to hear the distinct splash of big rocks dropping into the sea. Rockslides off the high cliffs would be brutal if they created a water vacuum, trapping his boat in their funnel spirals.

It was then that Shields would have unsettling visions of the boat's bow, pivoting downward, bringing him to the pits of a drowning death.

"Concentrate, damn you! Concentrate! Keep a clear mind on what must be done," he screamed aloud to no one but the Queenie B.

Had it not been for the weeks of survival training, he would have been too feeble of mind to concentrate. Even though he had earlier radioed his position, no Coast Guard boat was likely to suddenly appear in the cove to rescue him. It was his own skills that would guide him through this mess. And concentrating was the only way to execute such skills.

Yet, at other times and without control, he shivered; his body soaked and drained. His mind lost in a daze and concentration not retainable, it was then that he would withdraw to the dryness of the cabin only to crazily climb back to the deck, defiantly and courageously hanging on while the storm's terrifying movements ransacked the area.

Not an overly religious man, the stress and uncertainty of these treacherous conditions prompted Shields to pray. And, with each shaking breath, he begged for divine intervention to save him from certain death.

"God....God, please help me," he prayed in sincerity as the back and forth gush of emotions were testing his very being.

At some point in the madness of the day, though no clock stopped to mark the hour, the heavens decided to call back these ugly doers of disaster and to send forth the tranquil beauties of nature.

The deafening roar of the wind gradually began to subside and just the whisper of a breeze could be heard. And slowly, very slowly, the uneven spurts of rain relaxed, followed by a light mist that seemed to gaily dance on still waters.

The Queenie B had ridden at anchor. Shields had beaten the monster. He was safe! He was alive!

Though storm weary as he was with purple bruises and callused hands, he forgot those aches and pains and immediately radioed the Coast Guard to report his position and to provide information about the storm.

"United States Coast Guard, Virgin Islands unit," he shouted into the mike three times. "This is the Queenie B."

"Queenie B, switch and answer on 22 Alpha. Over."

"Affirmative. Over and out." Shields responded, moving the channel dial up. "United States Coast Guard on 22 Alpha. This is the Queenie B. I have ridden the storm of a lifetime. Over."

"Affirmative, Queenie B," replied the voice over the radio. "We receive you clearly. From you coordinates you have been in the outer bands of a Category 3 that pounded islands south of St. Lucia. It has veered more to the south-west. New tracking has it headed towards the Venezuelan coast."

"Affirmative, Coast Guard. I'm glad to hear that update. Over."

"Queenie B, we have received numerous reports of surges and heavy debris in many harbor areas. We will advise later for your safest port of return. Remain at your location for another day. Over."

"Affirmative, Coast Guard, I understand the situation. My supplies are adequate and my fuel is ample and intact. The boat appears to be solid. I anticipate no problems anchored here. Over."

"Affirmative, Queenie B. We need secured information about other passengers on you boat and if you are transporting any dangerous materials? Clarify. Over."

"Negative on both items. I don't even have fish aboard. I am definitely alone. But this cove is so beautiful that I would gladly share it with someone while I wait. Over," Shields responded into the mike, knowing exactly who that someone should be, though it would be ungentlemanly to reveal her name over the airwaves.

"Roger, Queenie B. This is Officer Graham; we have recorded your location. Stay safe, enjoy the view. Over and out."

Well before nightfall, Shields was absolutely dead tired. He had no appetite for food but forced himself to drink bottled water. After discarding his soiled clothing, he showered and fell nude across the bunk.

A strong carnal hunger for Brandy invaded all other thoughts. Though she had never asked him to hold her, to caress her; he could literally smell her scent and feel her warmth. He wanted her there, physically beside him.

Dream. Start dreaming and put Brandy here in this bunk, he groaned.

Maybe forced or maybe spontaneous, the sweet dreams of his beloved came to him. They provided what he wanted. What he needed.

With Brandy curled up beside him in the best of dreams, he could sleep contented.

The clarity of a new morning intensified the awesome display of nature as the rays of the rising sun parted the sheer veil of dewy fog. The cove came abundantly active as Shields climbed up to the deck. He stretched his arms high; spread his fingers wide. Rolling his shoulders to relax the slightly knotted muscles, he felt renewed and alert.

Being alive was a wonderful experience that he promised not to take for granted!

Clothed only in jeans, he leaned against the railing and quietly stared out across the bay. Thoughts of his past life drifted freely and for his own pleasure he allowed them to entertain his morning.

Navy buddies and the antics they pulled on each other brought a smile to his face. And the remembrance of his favorite partner on the police force made him sadly realize how many years had slipped away.

He recalled, with some amusement, the high school championship when he fumbled the football, losing the team's last effort for victory. His coach had stood by him, slapping him on the back and encouraging him not to quit the team.

'*Boy, there are going to be tougher times in life,*' the coach had said on that embarrassing night. And, of course, the coach had been right. Life went on and he grew to be stronger.

There had been many other tougher events in his life, where strength and daring had dictated the results. He did not smile when he remembered the men he had killed, all honorable acts in the line of duty to his country or to the law.

What startled him the most was the sheer fact that all his best memories seemed to center on relationships with other men; not that those memories shocked him or sent up red signals of alarm about his sexuality. No, after all, he was a normal, stud of a guy who had dated a lot of women.

But the more that he pondered his past behaviors, the more he realized there had been few relationships with women. Most of his episodes had been fleeting one-night-stands or a girl-in-every-port, as some sailors often tagged their conquests.

Of all the women that had passed through his arms, he couldn't even recall their names or their faces.

He didn't like the unsettling way his mind was wandering. He gave it up, finished his coffee and set about doing his boating duties. As the morning past, he cleaned away wind-blown leaves on the deck and reclaimed his fishing gear from the storage boxes. He ate a can of tuna and some fruit for lunch and then took an afternoon swim in the cool water.

Just after sunset, when things were quiet, the callous memories of his affairs began to resurface.

He played a game with his mind, trying again to remember the names of the women who have pranced through his life. He could not recall one name.

Meeting Brandy had changed his behavior. When he was with her, he actually delighted in having purpose, sharing with another being, worrying about their problems, and feeling love, a captivating emotion that warmed his body.

Shields smiled. He raised his mug of coffee to the sky and saluted the horror of a storm that had shown him how quickly life could fade away. The victory of his battle with nature had offered him a second chance to be a better man.

"God, I jumped on religion last night when I thought I was going under. And today, this review of my life has been strange. Perhaps it is a message from you. Brandy is a good woman, so don't be confusing her with the rest of them. I hope for a chance to win her over and tonight sure would be nice! But that's not likely. I could promise you that I'll be in church everyday, but that's not likely. Just think about it. Okay?"

19

Nervous tension ruled as uneasy days passed in Kentucky. Since that Sunday morning when Stanley Fizer took full control of everything in the Berman household, he had continually dictated the daily agenda that everyone was to follow, while providing little information to any of them about Hubert's hospitalization.

Caroline and Cynthia, grown women with little affection for their aging father, had come into the house with their cocky attitudes and had uncaringly left Tuesday morning when they realized that he was still breathing and that his Last Will and Testament was not going to be read.

Samuel Steinberg had flown in from New York, conducted business with Fizer for three straight days, and then abruptly left town on the private jet.

The tease and brazen David D wanted to stay put but, after his little episode at Brandy's bedroom door, he was no longer a welcomed guest. Mama Eve cleverly suggested that he high-tail-it for safer ground when she deliberately displayed two inches of her midnight-special from the front pocket of her apron.

It didn't take a rocket scientist to get her message that she knew how to make the little pistol do some big-time harm. David D sped out the gravel drive in his rental sports car and headed for Twin Oaks to sponge off the hospitality of Mindy Morningstar.

The big house was quiet again with Mama Eve singing in the kitchen, Jefferson outside tending to the Town-Car, and Fizer strangely disappearing for long hours. Even if he returned, he withdrew into Hubert's office.

Brandy was the only one who refused to adjust to the changes at Unbridle Farm. Remaining steadfast in her efforts to learn more about her husband's medical condition, she had tried endless ways to sidestep Fizer's unyielding authority.

But her telephone calls to the nurse's station were put on hold and then promptly cancelled with a buzzing disconnect on the line. Even her Monday night attempt to sneak into Hubert's hospital room was forcefully obstructed by a uniformed guard stationed just outside the door.

"What harm would there be with a wife staying beside her ill husband? I don't understand," she had yelled at Fizer more than once.

Mama Eve was the only one who could tempt Brandy to eat. She prepared chicken soup and green tea, bringing them up late in the evenings and literally begging Brandy to take a few bites.

This emotional roller coaster had taken its toll on Brandy. Gone was the happy smile on her face and the pleasant laughter that had pleased so many of her friends. What one saw these days was the drawn and gray appearance of a woman looking ten-years older. So totally camouflaged behind drab housecoats, there was simply no beauty left to behold of the once, bouncy bombshell.

On Friday morning, the sun was shinning but Brandy lay in a state of exhaustion and depression. Curled up in the bed with a blanket drawn up tightly around her neck, her eyes were blurred sockets with no expression of visual interest for this beautiful morning or for the fresh flowers by her bed, placed there daily by Mama Eve.

After having spent the whirlwind months in the company of Hubert, she found no comfort without his presence. Energy had fleeted from her and she had no resolve left to change the confinement placed upon her.

Mama Eve tapped on the door and slowly opened it, allowing the sweet, alluring aroma of freshly baked cookies to precede her into the room. The large woman then moved forward with a glass of warm milk and a saucer of chocolate chip cookies.

"Sweetie, I's got a little treat jest for you," she said with concern for Brandy's well being.

"Please put them down, Mama Eve. I'll eat them later," responded Brandy, her voice faint; not to be believed.

"Yes'um. Here's they be on the table. But, I's reckon to jest sit a spell and share one or two of them cookies before I's be a bending my knees down them long stairs back to the kitchen."

The faithful housekeeper dutifully handed her the glass of milk and a cookie before sitting down in the rocker. Brandy made feeble attempts to nibble on the baked morsel and to sip the milk; its warm fluid easing the constricted muscles of her throat worn sore and scratchy from the hours of crying that had besieged her these last few days.

"Mama Eve, I truly appreciate the way you have pampered me, but I have given up. I tried to fight back, but I failed."

"Sweetie, we's all has to struggle, day in and day out. Life jest ain't always easy, even for rich folks. But the good Lord knows that, lately, you dun seen plenty of problems. They sure dun been enough to pile up a heap of sorrow. But, now, the time dun come for you to think another way."

A long silence followed. Brandy rolled to her back, her eyes starring upward to the ceiling as she pondered the older woman's words. But she stayed quiet, not agreeing or disagreeing.

In time they ate a cookie or two, while Mama Eve told her about the house chores that Jefferson was slow to finish and what Scottie McInbrew was doing out in the barn with the horses. Though Brandy cherished Mama Eve's company, in no way did she truly believe that such a caring woman could understand the anguish of rejection.

"Sweetie, I's reckon that these here cookies was jest one of them white lies, likes them there wooden ducks that Mr. Berman dun be a having in that office with his shotguns. I's really dun comes up here to announce that Mr. Fizer telephoned the house. And he dun told me that Mr. Berman is gonna be a moving on Sataday, over yonder to Boston. He dun said that you is to stay right here untils next week when that airplane comes back."

"Did he tell you how Mr. Berman was feeling? Did he give you any other information about the hospital or any tests, or just anything that would tell me if my husband is better?"

"That's be the message, jest what he be a saying over the kitchen telephone. That Mr. Fizer dun said that there ain't no need for any more dinners. Ain't nobody coming. And, right then, he dun told me to forget you, if you ain't eating. I's was to go on about my house work, he tried to tell me. But I sure ain't a going to forget you."

"Oh, my God, what is he up to?" Brandy screamed!

"Lord! Lord, Mrs. Berman, all this mess was more than you be a needing. I's knowed it! You soon be a working yourself up into one of them crying spells."

"No Mama Eve, I **am not** going to cry anymore! But, if I had the strength, I would cuss him out for the way he keeps knocking me down!"

"Now, Mrs. Berman, that there jest ain't be doing no good. Only you and me be a hearing them bad words. It be's the time to get up and go on. Ain't nobody but you, can fix yourself."

Mama Eve left the rocker and sat on the side of the bed. Taking Brandy by the shoulders, she straightened her up, higher onto the pillows.

"Now, listen to me, baby," the older woman began. "I's had myself a husband once, but he dun been dead some twenty years. Back yonder in our days together, some woman strutted by and tried to get him away from me. She being one of them reddish-black kind with smooth, bright skin; a right pretty woman, she was. Most men jest admires them pretty ones. Like Mr. Berman dun admired your beauty. You is a beautiful woman!"

"Thank you, Mama Eve. But how I look is not what I am worried about. What's happening to Hubert is far more important than all that. And, really, I fail to see what you are trying to tell me."

"Well, I's be explaining how you gotta find something to be a doing about your troubles; my troubles, at the time, was that woman. She lived in a rooming house down yonder on Third Street and she didn't have herself no kitchen, jest herself that one, little room."

"Mama Eve, I'm angry right now and not really up to your story."

"Ain't be no story. It be's the truth the way my Rufus dun loved to eat. I's cooked up a buncha food every night. And when my Rufus got in from his job that food be's a sitting on the table. Lord, that man and eating was jest like a hand a fitting into a glove. Ain't no worry crossed my mind that he ever be a bothering to go out looking again."

"I don't think that food actually matches the severity of what is happening to me."

"Well, sweetie, we's all be a needing to busy our minds. It don't need to be cooking. For a well-bred lady likes you, it jest be a social calling on some friends, maybe them proper Boston ladies. They be joining up with you and giving you back your strength. Likes when I's talk to my Lord, I's feel uplifted, like I's be sure that I's got me somebody!"

"I see what you are saying and you are right. Having someone, even if it is just a good friend, can offer a lot of support. Mama Eve, besides being a wonderful nurse, you surely understand human nature."

"That's it. I's dun spoke my mind, Mrs. Berman. I's got my work to do and you best to get out of that bed."

Mama Eve picked up the empty glass and the half-eaten cookies. At the door, she turned and smiled her golden-tooth smile.

Somehow the room didn't seem as dreary and Brandy didn't feel as alone. Words of wisdom had come her way from the dearest and sweetest lady she had ever met.

Though it was tough at first and the weakness of her condition made it even harder, she finally sat up in the bed and crossed her legs into a simple yoga position that she had once learned in a YWCA class.

One breath at a time, she thought hopefully. *Show them what you are made of.*

Deeply inhaling a lung-filling breath, she promptly exhaled, pushing out the steady flow of air until her shoulders eased downward and relaxed. She repeated this same procedure over and over. It was a healthy cleansing of the recessed impurities that had been holding her down.

It didn't take long for the tension to ease and for an energetic sensation to completely engulf her body. With closed eyes and with rhapsody of musical notes, she began a slow hum.

Gentle air flowed in and out. It flowed, in and out.

Up and more alive, Brandy reached for the phone and called the airport for time schedules to Boston. Without hesitation, she booked a first class ticket on the earliest flight available.

Then she dialed the long distance number to her old neighborhood, to Daisy's Beauty Salon where she made Saturday appointments for her hair and nails.

On the other end of the line she heard the soothing voices of friends who had missed her and really cared about her. She knew that Daisy and Mildred would always been there, ready and waiting for her.

20

When Brandy unlocked the condo door at The Boxwood, a musty smell of stagnation fouled her nostrils. Going further into the sitting room, the uninviting sight that greeted her was like a ghostly mausoleum, for no one had been there since a cleaning service had covered all the furniture with large, drop cloths.

To dispel the cheerless darkness, she went about pulling back the drapes, letting in the late, afternoon sun; its brightness already pouring life back into the rooms. The French terrace doors she fully opened and a clean breeze brushed past her. It lightly circulated fresh, cool air, pushing out the stuffiness that felt so dusty and heavy.

Protective sleeves had also been hung over the museum quality paintings that Hubert prized so highly. Their brilliant colors that once had set the theme of the styled décor now were hidden from view. At once she set about removing all these drab, ecru cloths. She neatly folded them and put them out of sight.

Color abounded! A lively exuberance transfixed the room.

Hubert would be so pleased, she thought, for this was his haven and she treated it with due respect. If only he was there now, with her; everything might be close to perfection. But soon, he would be there and she would have things ready for his arrival after his long confinement in the hospital.

She busied herself with many other mundane tasks of preparing the condo; but, in the end, there was little else to do but to pour a glass of wine, kick off her shoes, and curl up in a big, inviting chair.

Mama Eve had been so right about changing one's attitude, about getting up and seeing things in a different way. Brandy was convinced of this now and she was definitely prepared to charge forward.

Her icy conviction to outsmart Stanley Fizer was working, at least on this day. *He'll blow a casket when he finds out I booked my own flight and got myself back here to Boston. Let him. I am Mrs. Hubert Franz Berman with a credit card and a wallet full of money,* she said to herself.

The more red wine she consumed, the looser her tongue as she spoke aloud of her devious plotting against the regime that was trying to destroy her. Though no one heard these boastful expressions, she had, and she believed them. And when she finally had her fill of the wine, she tired of her own bragging. Her eyes closed and she nodded off.

The sun had set while Brandy slept, drawn up like a little ball in the big, comfortable chair. An undisturbed quietness surrounded her with the room being refreshingly peaceful without the glow of lighted lamps.

Suddenly, something stirred in the distance; a noise or a movement that was apart from the stillness of the room. At first it was a faint sound that deepened louder as the private elevator reached the tenth floor.

Wedged between the protective arms of the chair, Brandy listened, pulse pounding and wide-eyed! "Yes?" she haltered, recognizing the sound of the elevator door opening directly into the foyer.

It was quite upsetting when she realized that she had not closed and locked the interior door.

"Who is there?" she called out with a frightened voice, the creepy blackness of the room intensifying the mystery of what she could not see.

"Mrs. Berman, is that you?" A voice responded, definitely male and not quite recognizable to her at that unsettling moment.

"I warn you, I am armed. Do not come any further until I know who you are," Brandy forcefully yelled.

"Mrs. Berman, wait, don't shoot, it's Shields Mason. I didn't mean to scare you. The place was dark and I had no idea that anyone would be in here. I came to check the condo as Mr. Berman had asked me before he left. May I come in?"

"Yes, of course. But you scared the crap out of me! Yes, yes. Do come in," she said, with sleep still in her eyes and a big yawn erupting from her mouth.

She clicked the lamp on by her chair just as Shields turned on the overhead fixture in the entry foyer. The brightness from the light bulbs caused both of them to put their hands above their eyes as a protection to the instant glare. They laughed aloud at the absurdity of the situation.

"Please come in, Shields. I'm sorry that I sounded so harsh but I was asleep here in the chair and I think that I was so tired that I just didn't realize what was happening. And, I don't have a gun," she said to him as he walked into the sitting room.

"I'm glad to hear that. I am sorry about barging in on you. But I thought that you and the boss were in Kentucky."

"You don't know? Stanley Fizer didn't call and tell you that Hubert was taken to a Lexington hospital last Saturday night?"

"Oh no! No, no one called. I just got back into Boston about an hour ago from my fishing trip. Even if he had tried to reach me, I never got wind of it. Tell me what has happened."

"I know very little because Stanley Fizer flew into Lexington and immediately took charge of everything. He kept me from seeing Hubert, telling me that the doctors had ordered complete rest. I'm hoping that the doctors found it to be just stress or overexertion. Hubert will be back in Boston tomorrow and I plan to ask him what exactly the doctors found and how they are treating it."

"Are you alright?"

"I'm trying, Shields. But it was very rough over these last few days. I am so glad that you are here now. I'll need your help," she softly said. She did not know nor could she tell from his appearance that the very sound of her voice sent a flush of fever through his body.

"Of course I am here to help," he tenderly replied.

They stood a short distance apart, he just inside the doorway and she by the lamp table. Awkwardly lost for words at their unexpected meeting, it was Shields who finally stepped forward and stood closer to her, perhaps too close to his boss's wife.

"Do you need me tonight? I mean, do you have any need for me to help out tonight, with your luggage or something like that?" He felt foolish and tongue-tied like he had just said something really stupid or perhaps something that could be conceived as too suggestive.

"Coffee?" she blurted out, not knowing his hidden feelings. "Do you want a cup, Shields? I need one myself."

"Right. A cup of coffee and a snack would help," he added, quickly retreating towards the kitchen. "Let me do that for you. I know how to prepare simple little meals; we bachelors have to fend for ourselves."

"Shields, you always seem to appear at just the right moments. It must be your special radar that detects when I need you the most," she grinned, following him into the kitchen.

He filled water to the 8-cup level and added measured scoops of regular coffee to the black Mr. Coffee sitting on the counter. He clicked the brew switch and headed towards the pantry. From its neatly organized shelves, he selected a sealed box of crackers and a can of soup.

"Not exactly a chef's delight, but I think we can get some culinary satisfaction from this chicken noodle soup," he laughed as the can spun around on the electric can opener. "A quick fix, anyway."

"Thanks. I hadn't thought of eating before you mentioned it. Now, I feel like I am starving. Chicken noodle soup is considered the remedy to mend the body and the mind. And the soup that comes out of cans is what I am use to. You have planned the perfect meal."

"Maybe I do know just what you need!"

"You do remember that Helga left our service when we flew to Kentucky, so there hasn't been anyone here for awhile. With Hubert coming home, I guess I better get to a grocery store tomorrow morning," she said, spooning in another taste of the hot soup.

"Not your job, boss lady. I'll take care of that for you. And, I'll locate a housekeeper to start work right away. With Helga gone you will need someone to cook and clean."

"It was difficult for Hubert to send her over to Caroline's house since she had worked for him all those years. She and I just didn't hit it off and it was going downhill from that. Actually, I doubt she will ever be back; so we will need a housekeeper. I certainly want to be free to take care of Hubert."

"Helga was definitely a headstrong woman. The other drivers and I called her Hardheaded Helga, the terror of Berlin. She pretty much controlled things with this family, sometimes including me. With Mr. Berman working all the time, he just left the household to her."

"It's weird to be back at The Boxwood. Kentucky was so enjoyable until Hubert was rushed to the hospital. Without a second thought, I have tossed away all ideas of traveling. Right now, I'm not sure what will happen next. But, thank goodness, I have you to talk to. It's good you came tonight."

"Probably, it was just fate. I'm back earlier than I had expected. And you certainly didn't expect to be here."

They sat at the kitchen table and, in between Brandy's sips of hot coffee and spoonfuls of soup, they talked. She did most of the talking, telling Shields all about the beauty of Kentucky and how excited she had been to see the thoroughbreds.

She went on and on about how relaxed Hubert seemed, that was, until he passed out at Mindy Morningstar's party. From that night, there had been uncertainty and confusion. She told him about her alliance with Mama Eve and Scottie McInbrew, and how Hubert's daughters had refused to talk to her. Most importantly, she explained how secretive Stanley Fizer had acted and how they had battled through a few, shouting matches.

Ignoring his own soup and coffee, quickly cooling at his finger tips, Shields listened attentively; his eyes fixed on her, absorbing everything she said. Without comment, he showered his agreement with a mere nod.

Inwardly, he sensed the pain that he knew was holding her captive. He, too, was a prisoner, but of his own making. He had let love into his heart and, now, the very one that he loved was there beside him.

Finished with her pent-up venting, she slowed to give Shields a chance to speak. "Enough is enough, I'll stop," she said, half-laughing. "Did you catch any fish?"

"Caught some, cooked some, and threw the little ones back. The weather turned pretty sour, but I found a convenient cove that offered good protection. The Queenie B and I survived the outer bands of a hurricane."

"Oh my heavens, a hurricane, you say! I haven't paid any attention to the weather or to the news. I should be asking you, are **you** alright?"

"Yes, of course. I'm a tough guy," he laughed, not daring to tell her the truth of how scared he had been. So very scared in fact, he feared that his life was about to end and that he would never see her again.

"I know you are tough and you have faced danger before. But I can't conceive how very frightening it was for you, alone out there in a raging storm! Oh, Shields, I just couldn't bear losing you, especially not now. It would be dreadfully empty here without you. You are such a big part of my life here in Boston."

In that brief moment, that tiny interlude between the sound of her voice and the aftermath of silence, something sparked! Something that bordered on a profound sharing with an unexpressed nervousness that quivered in their bodies.

They felt a joy of closeness, a private closeness of mind and spirit. Nothing around them seemed to be real; their bodies were transposed into another existence.

Their eyes reflected the truth that something was pulling at their emotions, something beyond their control. The buds, of which, were beginning to blossom in the short, open space between them.

And then it happened!

Shields leaned closer to Brandy, her fragrant cologne intoxicating his repressed desires. He willingly inhaled the stimulating aroma. He put his right hand behind her neck and very gently drew her to him.

He kissed her, warmly kissed her, holding back the intense passion that was hotly waiting to be released.

She willingly encouraged his advances; her sweet lips transmitting an immediate acceptance of what he had done. His tongue traced the edges of her ruby-red lips and she opened her mouth in response to his soothing persuasion.

His left hand moved slowly up her arm. Then, ever so lightly, it slid across her breast. He had no thoughts of her double-Ds as physical objects of fascination. He only wanted to caress her and to feel her tremble beneath his sincere touch.

Their bodies brushed against each other with a contagious heat, permeating from the throbbing blood, hotly flowing through their veins. She sighed, knowing that he should stop; but, in candor, hoped that the special moment would never end.

She brought her arms up and lovingly draped them about his neck. They kissed again, a longer, more emotional kiss; one that was exceedingly expressive.

Their arousal heightened!

Shields wanted desperately to win her there – on the table, on the floor. He passionately longed to go way beyond a kiss.

Instead, he reluctantly drew back from their embrace, intently holding his focus on her blue eyes as if to analyze her deepest thoughts.

Did she truly want more as he did? Hope swelled in him.

His profound love came with the sensible respect he held for her, a proper respect due to her as a woman and as his potential lover. He waited for her to say that she desired him and that this kiss was to be the beginning of an active and committed relationship.

She made no sounds.

Her facial expressions were strained and no words came forth, providing him with the answer he so desperately wanted. *Yes, yes, please let it be YES.*

Over and over his mind rushed for that one, simple yes. But, if Brandy understood his hopefulness, she did not acknowledge it.

Rather, she lowered her eyes from his steady, almost pleading gaze. And without words, she slowly inched away from her cozy position, that warm, sensitive position, pressing against his willing body.

"I'm sorry," he reluctantly said, releasing his embrace. "Maybe kissing you was wrong, but I wanted it. I have wanted to kiss you since the first day that I met you."

"Shields," she softly said his name, not looking up at him nor adding another word.

A silence, a threatening silence, lingered, frozen just above his heart. He was tempted to speak out. But, instead, he said nothing. His jaws tense in refusal.

For a long time, she quietly studied her folded hands that lay clinched in her lap. The five-carat wedding ring was still on her left hand.

"Please, don't say anything more. Give me a moment," she said.

Unable to sit still at the table, Shields retrieved the coffeepot and topped off their mugs, painfully delaying what he suspected would soon become a proclaimed dictate for him to leave.

He lingered near the kitchen counter, sipping the hot coffee, allowing amble time for her to regain her control.

"I'm married," she calmly and quietly said. "And, of all days, this is absolutely the worst situation for something like this to happen. I am lonely, especially tonight of all nights. And, I feel very sure that you sensed that. But quite frankly, I was starving for more than just a hug and a kiss. I have been longing for passion."

"Me too," he said, gaining confidence that she was ready to allow the passion he planned to provide.

"Let me explain before you misunderstand. Hubert and I have had sex many times. But, unfortunately, it was rather awkward and never with the total intensity of that kiss. His age was a problem, though we tried our best. But... But...damn it, how cruel of me to have said that. I have already told you too much!"

Then she looked at Shields, strangely, as if she were inwardly fighting the opposing demons of her natural, sexual desires and those of her legal vow to a husband. He felt compassion for her confusion and for her need to confess these uncertainties. Yet, none of that stopped him from pushing forward to claim her as his own.

"Brandy, maybe I should feel guilty; but I don't. Mr. Berman is an outstanding man and I owe him for a lot of things. But I can't stop thinking about you, wanting you, and literally needing you. And those strong desires override my contract with any boss."

"And, without a doubt, I find you desirable, perhaps too desirable. But it is wrong, absolutely **wrong!** I agreed to marry Hubert and he has done nothing to warrant this disrespect from me, actually, from both of us."

She got up and walked to the other side of the kitchen, expanding the tiled footage between them.

"I love you," Shields professed with tenderness.

"No, you cannot say that. It's not right!"

"But it is true. It is the absolute truth. I do love you."

"Oh, Shields, what a mess we have created. What if we satisfy our sexual yearnings? After tonight, what then? Would you and I ever know if we shared real love or simply indulged in a one-night affair, rushed and sneaky?"

"I'm sure of my feelings and it would not be just for tonight. My God, Brandy, I am a man deeply in love with you," he sincerely replied, lacing his words with an urgency of expectation.

"Stop," she shouted, her voice breaking!

He rushed to her side, taking her in his arms.

Again, she fell into the sensitive allure of his touch. His arms were familiar and inviting and, for an instant, she almost gave in to his persuasion.

"No, I'm so sorry Shields. I just can't. And, I'm not trying to tease you," she said, pulling away from his caress.

"Brandy, relax. I'm not going to force you. Let love take you were you want to go."

"I'm so confused and way too upset to think clearly. Right now, I really don't want to push you away. Right now, I want you more than anything. But, tomorrow, I must faithfully perform my responsibilities as a wife. So please, please be patient with me. Give me time."

"I'll try to be patient and stay in the background until you decide where your happiness can be found, with me or with Mr. Berman. Have no doubts that I really want you with me, forever. But one day, and God I hope it is soon, you will have to determine what you truly want."

"For now, that's all I can promise you. Once Hubert is healthy and we are alone together without his menacing family and friends, then I will learn what kind of feelings I truly have for him. In the beginning, I was so sure it was love; maybe I was wrong. If our marriage doesn't work out, I'll have to assume the blame. Hubert has been nothing but an honest man."

"Brandy, it won't be blame. It will be the truth and he will know it. I will wait for you to know it, too."

Shields picked up the coffee mugs and the soup bowls and went to the dishwasher. He emptied the small amount of coffee still in the pot and clicked the off button.

There was no more to be said about love and physical desires.

21

Mildred bounced out of bed before 5:00 a.m., a peppy routine that she had recently cultivated thanks in large part to comments from Brandy, though she herself had no idea of these contributions to Mildred's new persona.

This flame of change grew out of past conversations with Brandy, when she had casually mentioned an informative, new book - **<u>A Firm & Glowing You</u>** - a best-seller that could be purchased at a 35% discount in Wally's Book Store, next to the beauty shop.

Mildred, gushing with the admiration of a student for one's beloved teacher, had intently listened to Brandy, taken in this self-help information and then, with robust energy, was eagerly acting upon it.

The 35% discounted hardback had detailed illustrations on how to touch toes, tuck in the tummy, pull up, stretch tall and hold the pose; which of course, Mildred enthusiastically and whole-heartedly followed along.

And, she loved it!

Leaving her rumpled husband asleep, she would bounce up every morning from their double bed and go into the living room. From under the couch, she would pull out the hard-bound book and the two-lb hand weights. Then with mighty gusto, she rigorously jumped into these reshaping exercises.

Strong-minded about the project, she was determined that one day she would look just like the firmly packed models in the book's illustrations. She equally expected to become a gorgeous, thin-as-a-rail, long-legged beauty with clear complexion, perfectly arched eyebrows, and high cheek bones as glamorized in the spiffy tabloids on the magazine racks.

Most readers of these advertising exploits believed what they read or saw on their tempting, fully-colored pages.

Mildred was no exception, having spent money from her shoe box to purchase the book and a stack of magazines.

Daisy and the clients at the beauty shop had noticed her livelier gait and happier disposition. Their compliments encouraged her all the more.

The very one who had not taken note of the disappearing plump and plain Millie, was her husband Wilford. Of all the concerned parties, he should have been the first to enjoy the new sight.

Yet, he didn't. And Mildred took to working longer hours at the beauty shop.

On this particular morning, she was already at work, ready for Brandy's 8:00 a.m. appointment. Normally, on Saturday mornings, the shop didn't open until 10:00 a.m., which is why Mildred happened to be alone when the phone rang.

"Daisy's Beauty Shop."

"Mildred?" A man's voice was direct and quick.

"Yes, this is me."

"I'm Shields Mason. I am calling for Mrs. Hubert Berman."

"Wait, hold a second," she remarked as she lowered the volume of the shop's radio. "Did you say Shields Mason, the friend of Brandy's?"

"Yes, I am calling because she won't be at her appointment."

"Is something wrong? Can I give her another time later or next week?"

"Well, I'm afraid it is serious. Mr. Berman passed away and Mrs. Berman is in a state of shock. I'm really not sure when she will be able to come. I think it best to leave that up to her."

"Oh," exclaimed Mildred! "This is terrible! What can I do to help?"

"We just got the call about thirty minutes ago, right before I was to drive her to your shop. I don't think we know what to do just yet. As you can imagine, she hasn't had time to recover. I'm here at The Boxwood now and she is in quite a state."

"I'm coming there," Mildred shouted! "That's what I can do for her. Tell her that I am on my way."

Without a good-bye, Mildred slammed the receiver down. She grabbed her purse, left a scribbled note for Daisy, and dashed out.

At the street corner, she hailed a taxi and gave no thought to the cost for the ride over to the other side of town. Brandy needed her and that was too important to worry about money.

Though Mildred had no details, the telephone call that Shields was describing had come from Kentucky. Mama Eve had tried to ease the blow of the bad news, but her own muffled tears could not prolong the dreadful message that she had been required to deliver.

Upon hearing the words that Hubert was dead, Brandy had dropped the phone and Shields had barely caught her as she sank to the floor, her wobbly knees unable to support her upright.

He had put his strong arms around her and carried her to the couch. She was pasty and lifeless with a blank stare that registered no recognition of where she was.

Removing her shoes, he had then covered her with a cashmere throw, trying to warm her and calm the shaking that had begun to take charge of her body. Not knowing exactly what else to do, he had poured her a shot of whiskey and helped her sip the strong drink.

With her somewhat stabilized on the couch, Shields had picked up the receiver from the floor and had heard the loud sobs of the distraught housekeeper.

"Mama Eve, stop crying! What happened? Tell me what happened?" He literally had to scream into the phone because of Mama Eve's loud wailing.

"Oh, Mr. Mason, it's awful," she had cried out in a voice loaded with heavy sobs of dismay! "I's so heartbroken for that poor child. Lord, she dun waited so long to have Mr. Berman home; she be a wanting him to be healthy. And now, the Lord dun let him pass."

"Stop your crying and tell me **exactly** what has happened," he had impatiently shouted into the receiver!

"Mr. Fizer, he dun called me. He says to me that Mr. Berman was dead. He directly said for me to goes and tells Mrs. Berman. He had himself a hissy fit when he learned that she's already dun gotten herself back to Boston. After he dun fussed and fussed about that, he said something about being on his way back there to Boston with the casket."

"You mean that son-of-a-bitch didn't even have the decency to call here," Shields had said forcefully, with full revulsion over the way things had been handled. "What time is that damn plane expected to arrive?"

"Mr. Mason, that's alls I'm a knowing."

"Go slower and think, woman! This is too important."

"Well, Mr. Fizer dun went on to order that I was to gets Jefferson ready and that he was a gonna send a private plane to picks us up with Mr. McInbrew. He dun laid down the law. The three of us best be at Mr. Berman's funeral. Oh, Mr. Mason, it be's hard to be a saying that."

"Funeral! You mean Fizer already knows the plans for a funeral?"

"I's reckon so. The airplane it suppose to gets us Monday at noon and we's to bring a small suitcase for staying over. Lord, that's all I knows. Oh, my goodness, the Lord's gotta help us!"

"It's okay, Mama Eve. It's okay. Do what you were told to do there at the house and I will handle things here for Mrs. Berman," Shields had said, trying to comfort the nervous woman.

"Lord. Oh, Lord! What's a gonna become of me and Jefferson? We's old; ain't never been off this home place."

Waiting for Mildred to arrive, Shields couldn't erase the memory of the whistling sound of Mama Eve's hearing aids. Her shaking hand, pressing the receiver too tightly against her ear, had set off an irritating and piercing shriek.

That damn, annoying noise and her uncontrollable sobbing had created such a strain that he couldn't reasonably make any sense of the whole, ghastly incident.

Only with repeated persuasion, on his part, was he able to calm Mama Eve, and then, that was only with the guarantee that he would personally meet the plane in Boston and immediately drive her to The Boxwood to be with Brandy.

Shields couldn't dwell too long over the long distance call and over any concerns he might have about the pressures that Stanley Fizer had put onto Mama Eve. The poor woman was certainly distraught, and that was putting it mildly. But her condition was a problem far removed from his immediate concerns.

When Nathan the doorman buzzed the penthouse that Mildred Brown had arrived, Shields put aside his fury over the asinine handling of this sad and serious occurrence.

Mildred flew into the room like a fired-up, relief worker. It was the first time in her life that she was to be in full control of another person and, with respect for Brandy, there would be no mistakes.

Without asking about the sordid details, Mildred went to work, gently guiding the ghostly lady from the couch to the bedroom where she removed her clothing, including the suffocating and restrictive double-D bra. She dressed the grieving widow in a comfortable and loose-fitting gown and helped her into the king-size bed.

"I'm here for you, my special friend," she softly said, pulling the covers up and tucking Brandy in.

"Mildred? Oh, Mildred, you're here! It's bad, really bad! I never got to see Hubert; never got to explain things to him. I didn't get to apologize, and now it is too late, Hubert is dead."

"Let the guilt go. Let it go," Mildred replied with gentleness.

Shields walked back and forth, just outside the closed, bedroom door. He could hear the muffled sounds of female voices. But, the two women were in a chamber where he did not belong. His work lay ahead in the world of male commitment, where real men defined their masculinity in the pursuit of defending a woman's honor.

22

Stanley Fizer had worked day and night over the past week in Kentucky. Few would ever know all the details he had shuffled around, corrected, redid and, quite expertly, put back in place.

His secretive duties were drawing to a close as he stood stone-faced by a charted aircraft. He was alone in a semi-darken area, guarding the last remains of Hubert Franz Berman.

Slowly from the entrance gate, a white van came towards the plane. It made a half-turn, then backed up to a full stop near Fizer. Two husky men got out and proceeded to load the unmarked crate, containing the casket with Berman's body.

Later in the week, a black hearse and a parade of limousines would transport this same body to its final resting-place. But here at this sinister and darken spot, the van carted away the deceased without formalities.

Nasty clouds hung heavy over the small, Boston airport and unsettled winds robustly blew across the concrete tarmac, causing traveling whirlpools of sandy particles and crunchy leaves. Fizer pulled up the collar of his lightweight raincoat and walked into a nearby hanger where he made a series of telephone calls on his cell phone.

He had already made the announcement call to Mama Eve and, even now, he was still quite disturbed to have learned that Brandy had left Lexington on Friday. She was forever causing wrinkles in his plans.

"I won't let that woman create havoc this time around. She's been a real problem," he said to Dr. Lewis Capalo when he called to tell of the body's arrival in Boston.

The Washington doctor agreed to alert Samuel Steinberg in New York that the transfer had gone smoothly and that the death particulars would soon be public.

Fizer made a call to his secretary Gigi, giving her the go-ahead to release the news to the press. He had composed the information himself and cautioned her not to answer any questions without consulting with him.

"Make sure that you hit all the newspapers especially in Boston, Washington, and New York. I want Berman's obituary to have every detail that I dictated to you. Got that? Now get on it," Fizer sharply told her.

The tiring trip was beginning to affect his attitude and he knew it. He decided to take an hour or so in the local snack bar; sitting down to a hardy breakfast certainly couldn't hurt. Time, after all, was on his side since the embalmed body was now in the hands of the funeral home.

Besides the attending doctor at Presbyterian Hospital in Kentucky, there were only three other persons who knew that Hubert Berman had died on Tuesday evening. Those three being Fizer, Capalo, and Steinberg.

The data on the death certificate would long be guaranteed because Fizer had threatened the not-so-honest doctor with the sordid dirt about his extra marital activities with a blond nurse. By adding the red-head and the brunette from the year before, the doctor's lips were definitely zipped.

Still sipping on the hot coffee, he made a final call, this one to Shields Mason's cell phone.

"This is Stanley Fizer," he hawked out. "I am at the private airport just beyond Logan. Pick me up in the next hour!"

"I didn't know that I was at your beck and call," Shields shot back, his anger still raging over Fizer's announcement to Mama Eve and the calamity of the situation that the bad news had stirred up.

"Shields, you have been around long enough to know that when I am representing the old man's business, you are on call."

"Was it **just** business to so coldly announce that Mr. Berman was dead? And, exactly what authority do you still have that lets you make demands of me?"

"Listen, meat-head. I have not been dismissed by anyone. I still belong to the Berman dynasty. Is that perfectly clear? In fact," he roughly continued, "as long as I choose, **you** will drive me when **I** request it!"

Smoldering, with his teeth grinding, Shields silently considered the fact that being with Fizer might help to uncover some of the details of just what was going on. And, if he was to be of any help to Brandy about who to trust, this could be a good-link.

"Okay, I'll be there," he said.

"It's good that you agree. There is no need for your ruffled feathers, it's best to show respect for the good man that has passed away. I certainly have made sure that his body has been treated with care."

"Mrs. Berman is very shaken by her husband's death. Perhaps you should show a little respect for her loss. At least in her presence, try a pretense at feeling sorry," Shields coldly remarked.

"Maybe your interest in the little widow is a bit too strong and you are strutting your manhood. Am I right?" Fizer laughingly quizzed.

"You bastard! Be ready, I'll be there in twenty minutes," Shields snapped back as he clicked off his cell.

His blood was boiling and he threw the phone across to the passenger side. Regardless of whether he would ever have Brandy as his own, he was going to make damn sure that he settled the score with Fizer.

Throughout their ride to Fizer's office, there was no further discussion between the two. Shields kept both hands tightly on the wheel in a determined effort to keep from turning around and punching his passenger in the nose.

Fizer, in his own arrogant world, ignored him, going about the task of paperwork. Never once, even out of a gentleman's courtesy to another, did he try explaining about Hubert's hospitalization or why he had kept Brandy from seeing her husband.

When they reached the curb in front of Gala Enterprises, Fizer had just closed the rear door when Shields shot away, leaving a breezy wake of squealing tires. His heavy foot put the limo's speed well past the limit.

Still hotly upset, he drove two or three blocks before he pulled into an alley, turned off the engine, and tried to realign his volatile nerves.

"Stop it! The military and the police academy double-trained you on situations of anger," he shouted aloud!

He drew on those past experiences and calmed down before picking up his cell phone and calling The Boxwood.

"Mildred, is Brandy better now? Do you think we need to call in a doctor for a sedative or something more powerful to help her? The more things keep piling up, the more my worries have pumped up. I'm determined to get a grip on things so that she will have some answers."

"She has been sleeping off and on. Let's wait about the doctor."

"Okay. I got tied up driving Stanley Fizer to his office; but I couldn't get anything out of him. The jerk is involved in something that's smells sour, but he's not about to spill the beans. I would really enjoy beating it out of him, but I don't want to do jail time over a scum-bag like him."

"I understand. Brandy has been mumbling about him. I think that the less we say about him right now, the better for her."

"Yes, I know you are right. Still, there are things that a man must do. I'm going now to check on Monday's arrival time for the Kentucky plane. Then, I'll be busy doing a little detective work."

"Shall I call you when Brandy wakes up?"

"Do that, Mildred, I would feel much better knowing that she is alright. By the way, when do you need to leave?"

"Leave?" She blurted out the word as if it was not in her vocabulary. "Leave? I hadn't thought about that. Brandy is in no condition to be left alone, so I definitely will stay longer."

"Great, that makes it easier for me. I'm too charged up to come back to The Boxwood. I don't think I would know what to do there."

"This is woman's territory. God designed us to be better equipped for these things. It's the basic nature of women to confide in each other and, somehow, we seem to thrive on it. I am very sure that when this sad news gets out, all her other friends will come to help."

"I hope you are right. Because from the beginning, she has been fighting too many enemies."

"Yes, hasn't she. We have shared many of our problems like the ones I have with my husband. Oh, how stupid can I be? In all this rushing around, I forgot to call my house. I'm rarely gone from there except, of course, to work at Daisy's."

"I'm finished; I was just checking on Brandy. Go ahead and call."

"No hurry, Wilford works on Saturdays. I'll call mama about cooking his meals; if he eats, he won't care where I am. We never talk much because he is such a bore and cooking for him is a thankless job."

"I'm sorry to hear all that. I've been rambling about Brandy's problems and I really didn't know about your own."

"Well, it's nothing new. I've been the cook and the slave, forever."

"Oh, about food, there's not much there in the pantry or the freezer. Nathan, the doorman, can give you the telephone number of a grocery store that delivers to the complex. Brandy probably won't have any desire to eat, but the group coming in from Kentucky will need food. Would you mind preparing something for them, just in case?"

"Sure, that's no big deal. I really do enjoy cooking, except when it is on demand for Wilford. Maybe Brandy would eat some soup?"

"That's a good suggestion," he said with the fond memory of watching Brandy eat the canned soup he had prepared only the night before.

The vision he held of Brandy was the fuel that would drive him. As long as he knew she was safe and sound under the protective watch of Mildred, he could direct all his attention to uncovering the truth about the mystery of his boss's death and why that bastard Fizer wouldn't let Brandy know any of the details.

"Mildred," he said, before hanging up, "things are going to get better. I'm determined to see to it. And, I want you to know that I think you are a special lady to help out like this."

"Gosh, thanks. It's wonderful that someone believes I'm special. Thank you, Shields, you've made my day," she replied, not expecting such a compliment to come her way.

Immediately, she felt the heat of a blush that prickled onto her face. It fully bloomed into a blazing red! He was not there to see it, nor could he have known that such a simple compliment would have the impact to light this roaring flame.

Her fingers traced the blush across her check bones; she felt the steaming warmth. She smiled.

Neglected though she had been over the years, never having received a compliment from a man, Mildred was not likely to forget that her first exposure had come from Shields.

23

With the Sunday edition of the Globe clutched in his hand, Shields was sweating as he raced from his parking spot at The Boxwood over to the elevator; he had to get to Brandy before she read the obituary and the lead article.

He had reacted to them with such fury that he could barely catch his breath now. He wanted to scream, to slam his fists against the concrete walls; to do anything, just anything, in retaliation against what Fizer and the Berman family were doing to her.

Damn them for not acknowledging her as Mrs. Berman. She's alive and legally a member of their family.

His mind was wildly racing as fast as his heart was pounding while he paced the width of the elevator as it slowly ascended ten floors to the penthouse.

Mildred greeted him in the foyer. "Brandy is in the shower. I think she's better. At least, she seemed better when she got up."

"Has she seen the morning newspaper?" he asked with such fury that he was literally shaking the paper in Mildred's face.

"No. And, she hasn't asked about it. Do they deliver it up here or should I have gone down to the lobby?"

"Nathan usually brings it up. Maybe he was hesitant about coming up today. What those reporters wrote is not good. The rats did not acknowledge Brandy's marriage. She will be very upset."

"Who will be upset?" Brandy asked as she came from the bedroom wearing a robe and hearing only the last sentence of the conversation.

"It's the Globe. Mr. Berman's obituary and this accompanying article are totally lop-sided against you," Shields responded, her very presence injecting sympathy into his heart.

"Let me read it for myself," she said, taking the newspaper from him.

Mildred sensed the stress of the same old rhetoric. "We'll probably need some strong coffee for this. I'll get that started," she said, heading off to the kitchen.

With a deep frown embedded above his eyebrows, Shields walked back and forth while Brandy silently read the full details of what he had only briefly described to her.

His hands were clenched into knuckle-white fists and his heavy breathing was still audible. His broad shoulders had tightly drawn up, almost touching the base of his ear lobes. He was, in fact, posed and ready for a boxing match.

Looking up from the folded pages, Brandy calmly said, "I'm not at all surprised. No, I'm not surprised. Hubert was a Boston leader. They had to write about his importance and mentioning a blond from the south side wouldn't add anything of value. With the family having their private, burial service at the Adams Estate, that pretty much says that Caroline and Cynthia have gotten what they wanted. All of them, the whole blasted bunch, have held the upper hand. It's all over, the power people have won."

Shields stopped his pacing but kept his fists locked in place lest he would walk over to her and wrap his consoling arms around her, speaking again of his love.

Yet, he could not let himself be that weak; not now, in this mournful period of her husband's death. He had to wait as he had promised, wait for her to be totally free in her own mind and eagerly choosing to accept his professed love.

"I was awake most of the night, following up on some leads," he spoke up, explaining his rumpled appearance. "I learned that Fizer had Mr. Berman secretly admitted to that Presbyterian Hospital. For some reason, he was trying to keep it hush-hush. The big question is **WHY**? Something more was in the works than just keeping you away. I've got friendly sources still checking on it for me."

"Shields, you are persistent about looking for an answer. But, I believe that this newspaper glorifies Hubert's life in business and purposely compliments his family. The very way everyone in Boston would expect. It is obvious that Caroline and Cynthia are still banded together. They had no intentions are letting me know about the funeral."

"Don't give up you lawful rights. The public should be made aware of your existence. You are entitled to something as Mrs. Berman, even if it is just decent respect for you as a human being."

"You are right! I do deserve more. The obituary says that the funeral service will be at noon on Tuesday at Faith Presbyterian Church. By damn, I'm going there just to spite all of them. I'll make my public statement, whether they like it or not!"

"That's good! I'm proud of your spunk. Yet, I want to make very sure that you are safe. You won't be alone. I'll be in that church and I know that Mildred and the Kentucky group will be there too."

"I realize that they all care what happens to me. And, I know that you have made yourself perfectly clear on how much you care."

"You've got that right!"

"Shields, I'm talking big right now, but getting through that funeral will take all the fire that I have. I don't need the additional worry about you disappearing in some mysterious way. You must be very cautious about what you do. You have no evidence and you don't really know who is involved."

"The funeral will be the very gathering of all the major players and Fizer will be among them."

"Perhaps Caroline and Cynthia were paying him to keep me at bay and uninformed about their father. If I'm right, I would guess that they will send Stanley Fizer packing. His work for them will be finished."

"Okay, Brandy, that's one way to look at it. Remember though, as a professional, I am trained to keep a sharp lookout. Yet, at all times, I'll have my nose to the ground. And, if any of them try to harm you, I'll be very eager to let them know, in no uncertain terms, exactly what I think about them and their plot against you."

"What a good protector and a good detective you are, even with a dirt smudge on your nose," she added.

"Thanks," he smiled. "I'm glad you've noticed my best trait. And, you can add that I am a darn, good driver. Mama Eve, Jefferson, and

Scottie McInbrew are due in on Monday. I'll do my job and get them here. You just concentrate on yourself and leave the worries to me."

She loved the way he always stood guard. His self-assured stance was enough to reassure her that he knew what to do. As in the past, he managed to replace the worst with a confident plan of action.

Brandy moved from the chair and walked towards him.

He took a step or two forward, but he had no realization that he had moved. His mind was totally fixed on her. His eyes closed when he felt her gentle stroke across his lips. He kissed her suggestive fingers tips.

They stood quietly there in a waiting zone, decently apart from the passion they may have been seeking.

One step more and they would have been close enough to find what they really wanted.

Instead, Brandy was the first to back away. She retreated to the chair where she had been sitting. The front of her robe parted at her knees and she tucked it into place before he had time to comment on the exposure of her bare legs.

"Let's go to the kitchen and have that coffee Mildred is preparing. We need a break," she quickly said.

"No coffee for me," he replied with a manly assertion to ward off further temptation. "I really need to get out of here. If Mildred wants some of her clothes, I'll go now and pick them up for her."

"We have planned for her to stay longer and I have loaned her some things. I gave her a few more ruffles than she is used to wearing. And, I must admit, she looks quite different in them."

"I guess that's a woman's thing, ruffles and lacy outfits."

"Yes it is. But for sure, most guys seem to enjoy it," she remarked with a wink and a smile.

"I like to see you light up like that! It builds hope for me. And, I definitely have an image of you in ruffles and lace."

"Smiles do lift my spirits, and you seem to inspire them."

"Yea, I understand," he said, his own emotions hitting a high over the presence of her half-clad body in the silky robe.

24

Quietness ruled the morning. Only the faintest hint of whispers was the exchange of conversation at Faith Presbyterian Church, as a large contingent of mourners gathered to pay their last respects to the deceased.

In this quietness of proper etiquette, echoes of foot steps bounced off the interior stone-walls while the masses selected the cherry-wood pews that best positioned them as close to the funeral service as the crammed sitting spaces would allow.

The black draped coffin stood center stage, royally positioned at the very end of a long, wide center-aisle. Numerous candles flanked it, their wicks hot with flame and their smoky aroma a mixture of vanilla and melting wax.

Yet, in this crowded gathering, it was a difficult task to distinguish one aroma from another with such a fragrant assortment of floral arrangements stretching the width of the large sanctuary and the various personal colognes, mingling so heavily in the crowded pews.

When Brandy entered the massive church, Reverend Wayne League was in the back talking to Caroline and Cynthia. They made no effort to speak and quite rudely shunned her arrival. The good Reverend knew that his loyalty remained with the Berman daughters, who were more likely to pad his donation box than was this lowly, exiled woman.

But Brandy was there with the full intent to be seen.

She wore a black suit, a noted haute couture creation; its lines splashed with sophisticated flair. The reporters, crammed into nook and cranny, took notes and flashed cameras to record such style!

She, with the grace of a ballerina, head held high and shoulders erect, ignored all stares and walked the long aisle to the first pew, the very seat of honor for the family members.

Muted murmurs lowly rumbled across the back of the church. From the reserved pews rose the audible gasps of the prim and proper blue bloods; their noses pointed skyward in their snooty posture of contempt for the gall of this dressed-up misfit.

Regardless of their horrified gawking, Brandy remained steadfast.

Daisy and a few of her patrons had managed to sneak upstairs to an unused corner of the choir loft. They were there for Brandy as much as for the opportunity to see the fancy folks. What they experienced at this funeral would be the talk in the beauty shop for months to come!

Shields, Mildred, and the Kentucky clan, watching from the rear pew, would have gladly sat up front next to Brandy, but that was something that she had professed to do on her own.

It was obvious that Caroline and Cynthia were not pleased about their own seating arrangement as they roughly slid into the second pew. The heat from their anger penetrated the back of Brandy's blond head. Yet, with so many eyes directed towards them, there was little else they could do but to silently fume over their displacement.

Music settled the issue.

The organist and her accompanying violinist began their musical introduction, soon joined by the robed choir dressed in impressive robes of vivid purple. Finally, a soprano from the Opera Company sang two of Hubert Berman's favorite arias.

At the conclusion of the musical presentations, bells rang out from high in the steeple, heralding the entrance of twenty ceremonial pallbearers. In procession too, were uniformed policemen and local politicians. This large assembly marched in and took their assigned positions in folding chairs along the front and off to the sides.

Reverend League rose from his velvet chair and began his sermon with the promising words of Heaven; a must belief, he preached, for those of Christian faiths. In his rambling oratory, those keeping time would have said an hour or so, he spoke about charitable contributions and encouraged all present to be charitable in their own daily lives, donating time and money to their communities and to their churches whether Presbyterian or not.

Several men came forward to eulogize the business success of Hubert Berman and how he had achieved it in such a Christian fashion. A young, talented surgeon spoke of how various Berman scholarships had rescued her from the inner city and had provided her with the unbelievable opportunity for medical school.

In the end, the congregation prayed for his soul. "Amen," they prayed in unison and the funeral was over.

A line of limousines waited curbside as the select group of family and friends prepared to leave for the private gravesite. Led by a police escort, the caravan slowly moved from the church, heading towards the Adams Burial Garden on the Adams Estate in nearby suburbia.

Shields had not been detected when he had positioned the limo into formation at the rear of the convoy. With Brandy, Mildred, Mama Eve, Jefferson, and Scottie McInbrew all aboard, they were underway and unnoticed by the family entourage containing Caroline and Cynthia.

The long, black parade finally snaked to a stop at the burial spot. As the mourners departed from their expensive cars, the Berman sisters caught a glimpse of Brandy and her little troupe, departing from their limo parked at the rear.

If the hateful glares of these two adversaries could kill, most certainly, Brandy would have been a dead stepmother.

But Stanley Fizer, directing the motorcade, alertly collected the two women and guided them to the side of the coffin where the Reverend Jason Abbott and the twenty pallbearers were waiting.

Dr. Lewis Capalo and Samuel Steinberg and their two families, along with David D Trump and Beverly Borden, quietly formed a circle with the other invitees.

Brandy and her friends gathered on the far fringe of the tightly-knit enclosure.

"Peace unto all," Reverend Abbott said in his opening remarks. Everyone bowed their heads and he continued with a previously selected menu of inspirational prayers. Reaching down to the turned soil, he picked up a handful of dirt and cast its loose particles over the expensive, mahogany casket.

"Unto dust we shall all return," he said, ending his portion of the sterile service.

Caroline and Cynthia, with little emotion, threw white carnations into the open grave. The Reverend signaled to the pallbearers and they, on his nodding cue, removed the boutonnieres from their lapels and laid them one at a time onto the brass cross that was an attached ornament on the top of the highly-priced casket.

No one shed a tear, except for Mama Eve who sobbed so loudly that Scottie McInbrew and Jefferson had to lead her back to the limo. Mildred, steady and calm, held onto Brandy's arm while Shields, adamantly determined that she would have her moment of closure, stood protectively near by.

When the mourners began to leave, Caroline walked right up to Brandy and loudly confronted her. "How dare you! You are not welcomed here! This is my mother's place of honor."

"Yes," hotly chimed in Cynthia. "You are so crude to exhibit such poor manners about social protocol! You **were not invited** to this private service, especially here at our mother's family estate! No, you will never be welcomed here!"

"**We hate you**," Caroline whirled around and sputtered! "And, don't you dare plan on spending father's money. Our lawyers will stop any of your efforts to claim an inheritance."

Wild-eyed and red faced with her black cape loosely flapping in the breeze, she grabbed Cynthia's hand and they made a speedy beeline to their limousine. David D, lagging a short distance behind them, casually strolled up to express his own petty, little comments to Brandy.

"Well, lady in black," he grinned with a snotty air. "I guess they will see you in court. While you spend nights preparing, I'll be available to give advice or whatever you might require."

Shields stepped in front of Brandy and roughly shot out a threat to the younger, but wimpy-sized man. "Beat it or you'll go home in pieces. This lady doesn't need any of your vulgar remarks."

"Sure, sure. I am a lover not a fighter," he responded and, with his usual greasy voice, he then leaned over and whispered to Brandy. "Think about it when this big-mouthed bodyguard is not around."

She shuttered at his arrogance. But he smugly sauntered off and joined Caroline who was impatiently waiting for him.

"Damn! That creep is a total ass; he shits where he steps!" Shields, fuming at the collar, roughly shouted out the remarks before he turned to face Brandy.

"Excuse my language. I'm really sorry I lost my cool here of all places," he said. "Probably, right now, you would prefer a quiet moment by yourself. Take all the time that you need. I'll be with the others, but you know that I'll be standing close by."

"Yes, thank you Shields. It would be better if you waited in the limo. Right now, I'm struggling with something that I need to say and I want to do it by myself."

"Yes, I thought so. There's no rush, it will give that group time to get out of here."

While all the other limousines were slowly moving up to the main house, the settled mood of the gravesite provided Brandy with the crucial opportunity to face facts.

She was officially a widow now. The casket of her deceased husband stood directly in front of her and no wishing or praying could change that.

Though there had been rough days during their marriage, this abrupt ending to their relationship was not what she would have expected. In all their talks of age and time left for life, it never occurred to her that Hubert would leave her so soon and without any last words.

She had time to talk now and though it was a strain she managed to speak up. "My dear husband, funerals services and burial rituals are for the living. We tend to hang on as long as we can before we say good-bye. All that I did wrong is here in my mind. I regret that I never got the chance to explain. I deeply apologize for the emotions I have for Shields. Yet, there are no doubts that I would have told you about them."

If tears could have come, that moment would have been her finest moment to cry. It would have been a normal reaction as a new widow. But there were no tears left to shed, too many had already fallen in too short a span.

The forgiveness she was searching for would probably give her nightmares. Though she knew that Hubert would have understood and forgiven her, she would have to find ways to forgive herself.

Good memories of her days with him overrode the bad. She knew that they would forever remain with her, untouched or distorted by anyone else.

No dark clouds or unsettling winds marred the beauty of the place. The sun was shinning and it was a calm day with blooming flowers all about the burial grounds. For Brandy it would be another good memory.

From her purse she removed an expensive Zino. She reached over and touched the casket with a steady hand. With the hand that still held the five carat diamond ring, she let the unlit cigar drop into the abyss below.

"One for the trip," she said.

25

Editorial   THE BOSTON GLOBE

It is a sad statement that this week's largest event was the well attended funeral of Hubert Franz Berman, one of this city's outstanding leaders. Yesterday, at Faith Presbyterian Church, the pews were filled to capacity with prominent people. But we, the ordinary citizens of Boston, the uninvited and lacking in prominence, we were also there. We gathered in somber groups outside the church or in our homes or our offices, watching the funeral on televisions screens.

As proud Bostonians we were joined together for this one funeral, expressing how much we knew of this man and how much we respected him for his endless contributions to our special and beloved city.

This illustrious philanthropist was, for many years, actively successful in many facets. And we have prospered under his seal in the social, financial, and artistic sides of our community.

Mr. Berman's wife, the former Catherine Abigail Adams, has been deceased for some ten years. Yet, how can we Bostonians ever forget her charitable

donations and her colorful horticultural campaigns that provided annual plantings to otherwise neglected areas of the city.
Generous neighbors are not easily forgotten.

Helga VonSmitten placed the Boston Globe on a silver tray and brought it into Caroline's bedroom. "I knew that you would want to read the wonderful editorial about your mother and father," she happily announced.

"Where is my coffee and breakfast?" Caroline snapped back at her. "How many times do I have to tell you to follow the routine that I outlined? You just work here!"

"Yes, Miss Caroline. But... but this is a tribute to your family and I just assumed that you would want to see it right away."

"You don't assume anything in my home. You simply do as I say. Now, get that newspaper out of here and bring me my breakfast. I will read what I choose and when I choose to do so!" Caroline bellowed loudly, broadcasting her heated insults all the way down to the kitchen.

Helga, glowing red with embarrassment and devastated over the callous shouting, rushed back to the kitchen for the breakfast tray.

The others of the household staff knew well the selfish injustice that Mrs. Caroline Berman Trump could distribute; but they did not know, nor had they been around years ago, when Helga cared for the two Berman daughters and consoled them through the trouble years of their mother's illness.

With boundless loyalty, even to this date, she did as she was told and brought the breakfast tray up to the bitchy woman who had not moved from the bed.

Helga went about the prescribed routine of laying out towels and colognes and running warm bath water. She picked up the discarded, soiled clothing that Caroline so repeatedly threw on the floor. Finally, she laid out the day's outfit and then meekly returned to the woman's bedside.

"Helga, Mr. Steinberg will be here this afternoon around 2:00. Have coffee and cake set out. I'm sure that my darling husband will be about the house all day, since we are to have the reading of my father's Will."

"Yes, Miss Caroline, I'll see to that. And Mr. Trump is still asleep this morning. He was rather late coming in last night."

"Helga, I'm quite aware of my husband's hours. Stop fluttering about and get this tray out of here. I can't tolerate the odor of stale food," Caroline said, shooting her rapid fire of orders as she dropped her dressing gown to the floor. Then with the theatrical flare of a B-grade movie queen, she made her nude exit, stage left into the bathroom.

Disgusted with Caroline's behavior, Helga was tempted to slam the door on her departure from the bedroom. But she knew better. Such an act would give Caroline a flimsy excuse to dismiss her from this job, and she could not visualize another placement after all her years with the Berman family.

Across town, Mildred was handing the Boston Globe to Brandy. "Shields called right before Nathan brought up the paper. He told me to prepare you for this morning's editorial about Hubert and his wife."

"Shields worries too much about me. I'm strong enough now to read about those things," Brandy replied. "Why this is a wonderful recognition of his generosity. We all should be very proud of him, though I must confess that I never really knew the full extent of his importance in Boston."

"I guess citizens like us from the south side are the last to know about the powerful ones. If it wasn't in a hymnal or the bible, I never knew about significant things going on in Boston," Mildred said.

"We have both failed in that area. I spent long hours in those smoky bars. But, none of that is Hubert's fault or that of his first wife. From what I see here, she must have been well respected."

"That's all over and done with."

"But we are the living and we have to move on. I intend to grow from all the things that Hubert has shown me. He opened so many doors of a new world that I never knew existed."

"Brandy, I feel the same way about you. Thanks to your friendship, I am becoming a new person and I am not going back to the old, mousy me."

Mildred stood up, collected their coffee cups and was headed towards the kitchen when the phone rang.

"Berman residence," she said.

"May I please speak to Mrs. Berman?"

"Let me check on that," Mildred responded, cupping her hand over the receiver as she whispered to Brandy. "It's a man. He sounds nice. Do you want to talk?"

Brandy took the receiver with no hint as to who was calling. "Hello," she said cautiously.

"Mrs. Berman, this is Samuel Steinberg. I'm calling to request your presence at Caroline's home, around 2:00 this afternoon. We will have the reading of the Will."

"Today? I thought that it would take weeks to get everything in order," she responded, completely puzzled that the legal activities could be addressed so soon.

"Caroline and Cynthia are quite anxious to resolve all the matters associated with their father's death," Steinberg stated. "You see, Mrs. Berman, we had everything properly prepared some time ago, so there really is no need for a delay. Hubert was always quite emphatic about the details associated with all his business dealings and, of course, this was also true about matters concerning his estate."

"I understand."

"Shields will pick you up. I just left word for him to retrieve Mama Eve, Jefferson, and Scottie from their motel. You might not have expected that the four of them are named in the Will."

"To the contrary, Mr. Steinberg, I'm not surprised about that. Hubert was a generous man. Why would I expect anything less of him?"

"Oh yes, of course. Well then, I shall see you at Caroline's. Good day, Mrs. Berman."

"Was that bad news?" Mildred promptly asked, seeing the frown on Brandy's face.

"Maybe? Yes, I feel sure that it will probably end up being bad news. They are reading the Will today at Caroline's," Brandy said. "I'm afraid that the two of us might be on the streets by nightfall."

"Oh surely your husband left you this penthouse or something. At least he would leave you a place to live. He had given you so many gifts in the past, surely he would have provided for you now. Wouldn't he?"

Brandy could not answer that question with any certainty. She walked around the kitchen, trying to collect her thoughts, trying to recall anything that Hubert might have told her.

She remembered the prenuptial she had signed and the fact that Hubert had so willingly introduced her as his legal wife. She had the photos from the wedding, the notarized papers for the insurance policy and even the one, credit card. But beyond those things, she knew very little of what could be considered as legal evidence for her cause.

Troubled by the urgency of reading the Will, she finally stopped her useless walking and sat down at the kitchen bar to test her thoughts on Mildred.

"Think about it this way. Hubert may have privately promised me many things, but I have very little to produce in the way of signed documents. I'm rather empty-handed."

"Don't you worry about those things, Shields will tell you what to do," Mildred quickly suggested.

"He's coming to pick me up, but I can't keep dumping my problems on him. His own position will be at stake. When Caroline and Cynthia get through with all this, you know that they will surely yank his job."

"Should I pack up our things while you are at Caroline's?"

"No, by heavens, I'm not leaving here so willingly! I will insist that they give me time to find another place. I'll flat out demand it if I have to!"

"Do you know a good lawyer, one that you could afford?"

"Now that's a sensible question. And, unfortunately, I only know bail bondsmen. Those Berman daughters have pin-stripped lawyers. So, if the very worst scenario happens, I guess I may have to get my job back at Mac's Bar. Though I know that would feel like going to hell after the way I have been living."

"You're too smart not to figure out something."

"I didn't marry Hubert for his money. But now that I am faced with supporting myself again, I'm terrified. I'll be starting over, but not fitting in. You know, just knowing too much to go back and still not polished enough to go forward."

"Do what you have been telling me to do," Mildred suggested. "Keep your chin up and believe in yourself. It sure is working for me."

"Thanks for your encouragement. You are right. There is no other way. My mama always told me to face the truth and just keep going. She would say if you quit, then you have nothing. I'll be at Caroline's, but I'll be there with just a hope and a prayer."

"Good. Then instead of packing while you are gone, I'll just do some heavy praying and you know that I've got tons of experience in that field," Mildred said with a reassuring smile.

26

Greeting those summoned to Caroline's two-story brick home was the task assigned to Helga VonSmitten. Clad in a prissy uniform with a white, dainty apron, she was stationed outside on the concrete porch.

Her skirt fluttered out like an accordion; its indecent length stopping at an embarrassing six inches above her aging knees. And, it was obvious that her small breasts were a total mismatch for the blouse. Scantily of material, it had been designed for a much younger woman with perky boobs.

This idea to display Helga at the entrance was, in many ways, Caroline's sick and bitter mentality to belittle her and to demonstrate that the upper-crust rich possessed superiority over lowly people, a disgusting term that she spewed about when speaking of the hired help.

It was precisely these hard working people who kept her possessions spotless and organized, never receiving a kind word or a dollar bonus from the high and mighty princess. It was also a fact that employment at the household was most often of short tenure.

But Helga was of the longevity type. Her faithful commitment to Caroline went back too many years for her to be labeled as a 'lowly'. Yet, despite the meanness of her boss, she showed no hint of the degradation over the uniform. With reserve, she deeply suppressed this excruciating emotion, concentrating more intently on the obedience for her own survival.

Graciously, she received the guests and directed them into the library where chairs had been suitably arranged, in descending prominence, towards an antique desk of historical registry. Like other antiques in the household, this expensive possession had been in the Adam's family for generations.

Everyone in the crowded room soon grew quite impatient that Samuel Steinberg had not yet arrived, he being already some thirty minutes late.

Restless feet shuffled and a light coughing began circulating about the room. Silent thoughts of 'I have had enough or just get on with it' were being telegraphed about, but with little to no results.

David D, having endured his fill of the confinement and always the first to go against all rules, got up, grunted loudly, and left the others to their own discomforts.

Within five minutes of his departure from the room, Jefferson asked permission to go out back and smoke a cigarette or two. But Mama Eve, lightly rocking back and forth in her usual posture, gave him one of her threatening glares and he quickly sat back down, quickly suppressing his desire for a Camel.

The chair arrangements, conceived and controlled by Caroline, coldly stated her constant affinity for hierarchy. She and Cynthia occupied the first two on the far left, those being classified as chair #1 and chair #2, while Brandy had been relegated to a chair awkwardly arranged by the door; Caroline's snippy little way of letting her know that the chair with no number was in the position of the least importance.

Brandy did not let the sisters' arrogant attitudes get the better of her. Without seeking their permission, she quietly got up and left the room. As she passed through the wide opening of the dining room, David D caught sight of her and, without hesitation, pounced with one of his sharp jabs.

"Join me for a cup of coffee. It's much cozier in here than in that room with the serpents, namely my dear wife."

"Look David D, I've told you before that we have nothing to say to each other."

"It's just a cup of coffee, no need to freeze up. A nice looking woman like you should know how to handle a gentleman's compliments," he told her and, with that not being enough of his flippant approach, he added more. "I plan to go where the money goes and Caroline thinks that you are about to upset her apple cart. Of course, she despises you. But you know that."

"Yes, I caught on real fast! Yet, I have tried to be nice to Caroline and Cynthia. I never meant them any harm. But it is your behavior that really baffles me. To what gain do you continually badger me?"

"Come, come you must have discovered by now how this family has operated all these years. Big Daddy controlled the money; little daughters expected to get it all. And, naturally, I would take half of what Caroline received. But, alas, you bounced in here as the big unexpected. BAM, they had acquired a step-mother. And **you** are, indeed, a fine looking one!"

"Stop it! You are a worthless gigolo. Your wife is in the next room. Have you no decency at all?"

"Honey, I'm not a decent guy and never professed to be one. I intend to follow the money any way I can."

Brandy forcefully turned on her heels, holding back the temptation to scratch his eyes out; a fate he would have justly deserved. With the word **shit... shit... shit**... ramming against her gritted teeth, she flew from the room, leaving the despicable cad shrugging his shoulders as if he had done nothing to warrant her scorn.

Blindly rushing through the entry foyer, she almost knocked down Samuel Steinberg and Stanley Fizer as they were coming in the front door. They had no idea of what had just transpired, nor any idea, what-so-ever, that all the others were still squirming in their seats, waiting on their arrival.

"Surely, Mrs. Berman, you are not leaving?" Steinberg asked.

"No, I'm just annoyed at the long delay. Everyone has been waiting for you. You're late," she puffed, taking his arm, leading him to the others.

Fizer dutifully followed behind, carrying a large briefcase that he promptly placed on the antique desk.

"Sorry ladies and gentlemen," Steinberg apologized just as David D reentered the room and sat back down. "Well, it looks like we are all ready now. I have here copies of the entirety of Hubert's Last Will and Testament. But in order to save time at this meeting, I will read a synopsis of those related passages dealing with each of you. Are there any objections to this procedure?"

A boisterous '**hold-it**' shot full force from Caroline's mouth, catching the others by surprise that she would so quickly intrude with her expected objections.

"I do protest if you are about to use your own words rather than the exact words of my father. I have doubts that you might be using your own interpretation of what my dearly, departed father may have indicated in the full text of his Will?"

"Come now, Caroline. Surely you know me better than that. First, I am a lawyer and my own credibility in the legal profession would not allow such an act. And secondly, your father dictated to me exactly what I am about to read to each of you. And, I do have his signature for your inspection. Satisfied?"

"Well, perhaps. But I do retain the right to have my lawyers review those papers," she demanded.

"That's your right, Caroline. And you will receive legal copies of the full text," Steinberg convincingly replied.

"Ignore her belly-aching and get on with it," David D shouted out!

"Did I speak to you?" Caroline roared back.

A stunned silence gripped the room as the others waited to see if these domestic outbursts would somehow completely stop the proceedings. But the reasonable voice of Scottie McInbrew intervened.

"Perhaps if we would all just listen, we certainly could move along much quicker."

"That's true," Steinberg replied as he picked up the legal papers and started to read. "To the very faithful and innocent Jefferson Washington, I leave the Lincoln Town Car and five hundred thousand dollars in a trust fund. This amount is to be allocated on a monthly basis for his living expenses and any medical and/or other appropriate needs."

"Oh, I dun hits the jackpot," Jefferson jumped up and shouted towards Mama Eve!

"Hush up! Ain't no jackpots in life; it's only the blessings of the Lord. And you best be thanking the good Lord for a worthy man likes Mr. Berman," Mama Eve preached, grabbing Jefferson by the shoulders and pushing him back into his chair. "Go ahead, Mr. Steinberg, I'll sees to it that he's a gonna be quiet."

"Thank you. Now, to the very talented horseman and astute businessman Scottie McInbrew, I leave Unbridled Farm, all the acreage, barns, thoroughbreds, the house, cottages, and all assets associated with the workings of the farm. The sole item of the Steinway piano, one of my gifts to Brandy, is to be removed and relocated for her."

"My goodness, I never expected anything like this," Scottie said with sincerity. "We were so successful these last five years and now this. Unbelievable! Unbelievable!"

Caroline and Cynthia both jerked around and watched Brandy's reaction when the mere mention of the piano was announced. But Brandy wouldn't yield an inch. She withheld all facial expressions and sat somberly posed, waiting for Steinberg to continue.

"To my housekeeper Mama Eve Horton, I express my deep appreciation for the humble and Christian manner that she was of service to me. I request of Scottie McInbrew that he retain her living quarters at Unbridled Farm and allow her to continue her service there until such time that she wishes to retire. It is a joy to leave to Mama Eve, the sum of one million dollars in a trust fund.

"Oh my Lord, oh my Lord," Mama Eve shouted, jumping up and dancing! "Y'all gots to excuse me folks, my old heart is jest a'fluttering!"

"Though this behavior is quite irregular, I'll allow you a moment," Steinberg responded to the jubilant woman.

"Get on with it. Get to the real part of my father's wishes," Caroline loudly screeched!

Brandy could not restrain herself any longer. "That was a real part," she said. "The real part of how deeply your father felt about other people. He constantly demonstrated his compassion. What a darn shame that you never appreciated him like they did."

"You people were all just simple employees, mere trinkets in the old man's world," David D butted in. "And Brandy, face the fact, regardless of how worthy you may feel, just like me, you were a taker on his payroll."

Shields left his place and crossed over to stand behind Brandy's chair. He waited, arms folded, just daring anyone else to speak against her.

Mama Eve had never returned to her seat; she stood in the middle of the semi-circle, right smack in the middle.

"Oh, Lord," she shouted again and again! "Oh Lord, this bunch of money dun made us all crazy! It's like the devil dun run through here and sturred up his fire. We's doomed! We's doomed! All this here money will be a changing our lives!"

Steinberg stood upright from his chair and leaned hard against the desk. "Alright, ladies and gentlemen, everyone needs to calm down. We cannot continue in this fashion. Unless you remain seated and quiet, I simply can not proceed."

"Helga, open the bar. We all need a drink," David D yelled!

"Order," shouted Stanley Fizer! "Mr. Berman's business is too serious for this commotion and as his Administrative Assistant I am taking charge to end this right here and now."

Was it the firmness with which he spoke or the sheer fact that everyone wanted to know what else was in that Will?

Who was to get something? How much was it to be?

Regardless of their motives, whether selfish or curious, they calmed their ruckus and refocused their attention to the business that lay unfinished on the antique desk.

"Now that's better." Fizer said, relishing in his own, glorious control.

"Yes, thank you Stanley," Steinberg said as he picked up the papers and began to read again. "To my longtime housekeeper Helga VonSmitten, I leave three million dollars in a trust fund to be administered for her well being and safe keeping."

"**NO!!**" Caroline exploded in total disgust. "That's absolutely preposterous that an employee in my household would be included in a Will with me! It is absurd. It…it is totally absurd!"

"**Caroline**," Steinberg shouted! "This Will is precisely what your father wanted and **his** wishes are what this agenda is about. Your personal opinions will not affect how his money is to be distributed. **Sit down!**"

Caught by surprise at the directness of his words, she sulked into her chair and a childish mask of indifference immediately covered her face.

Picking up speed, he began again. "As I was about to explain before these rude interruptions, Hubert also indicated that because Helga's salary was being paid from his accounts, that arrangement will continue."

"What? I never knew that," Helga blared, her words taking flight towards Caroline. "I can't believe that I blamed Mr. Berman for everything. You ungrateful brat, I quit! Yes, I quit before I'll give you the satisfaction of releasing me!"

Seeing the furor of Helga's outburst, Brandy could not remain silent. "Hubert thought that you would be happier here. He wanted you to be settled in a place where you would be comfortable. I'm sorry that we started off the way we did. Hubert and I should have worked it out with you before he sent you away."

"Yes, from the very beginning, we should have talked more openly. I definitely over-reacted to your arrival. My own stubbornness put me in this pit hole," replied the penitent woman.

"Perhaps you two might settle your reconciliation later; as for now, let me continue," Steinberg said. "To my loyal driver and bodyguard Shields Mason, I leave the limousine that he may keep or sell. And I bequeath the Queenie B, the boat he loved and the one I never sailed on. His diligent service warranted my faithful and lasting friendship. So, with due respect, he is also to receive five million dollars in stock and cash."

Shields made no response, but quickly glanced at Brandy with an expression that conveyed troubled thoughts of his failures and of their secret dishonesties.

Unaware of the eye contact between the clandestine lovers, Steinberg never stopped reading.

"To my son-in-law David D Trump, my estate will provide ten million dollars in a monitored trust fund, based on the binding conditions that he obtains a divorce from Caroline, never pursues her again, and that he seeks permanent residence outside the city of Boston. Any failure to abide by these terms equates to forfeiture. This legal arrangement will be supervised by an Executor."

"Well now, ten million dollars is peanuts compared to what this estate is worth. I refuse the offer," David D snarled. "I won't be bought off so cheaply. Right, Caroline? You'll pay more to keep me around. You have always enjoyed showing me off. I was your great catch, a real stud of a handsome he-man. And, now, you will keep me just to smear the old man's legacy. Isn't that right, my darling wife? What mind games could you play with people if I wasn't your toy-boy?"

Brandy, passionate against such repulsive remarks, suddenly felt a deep sympathy for Caroline. Here was a husband so money hungry that he would blatantly defile his wife in front of all these witnesses.

They, too, may have felt the same compassion, but Steinberg paused only long enough to remind David D that he could express his refusal at the office of the Executor and that now was not the time to respond without proper representation.

"For the present, Mr. Trump, you have had your turn," Steinberg remarked before proceeding to the next issue. "To my wonderful and loving wife Irma Lou Delaney, known affectionately to me as Brandy, I leave all the gifts that I so enjoyed giving to her. I further grant to her a residence at Seahaven, a beach house in the Cayman Islands. To provide for her a comfortable and proper life-style, I leave the sum of five million dollars in stock and cash."

Caroline jumped from her chair, shouting, "We did it Cynthia! We two will share the bulk of the money! Read it, hurry up and read it."

"Yes, read it," Cynthia joined in.

The two sisters stood together, comrades in victory, awaiting the final pronouncement.

"At this point there is an important tape left by your father that I am to play for the two of you. Please, be seated," Steinberg said, clicking on a pocket-size recorder.

My darling daughters, this message is being prepared for you the very morning that I am to marry Irma Lou Delaney. Samuel Steinberg will hold in trust this tape, should the occasion not arise for me to explain things to you in person. An exciting relationship has suddenly captured me and it is affords me a marvelous, new beginning. Please join me in my excitement for I do love you both.

Hopefully you will feel this love when we next meet and this tape will never be necessary.

A lightening bolt could not have caused more charge as emotional rushes surged in different degrees. Hubert's voice on that tape had brought his presence to the forefront. It was as if he was there in that room, the paramount, imposing figure as he had always been.

"Go on with the Will, don't stop now. I heard what he recorded," Caroline smugly snapped, forgoing any acceptance of her father's request.

"Very well, if that's how you want it," Steinberg said with a slight shake of his head, demonstrating his disbelief at the rigidity of the obstinate woman.

"To my youngest daughter Cynthia, I leave my penthouse at the Boxwood and The Boxwood building. She is to receive one-half of the remaining estate after all bequests and debts are satisfied." Steinberg clearly read. "And to my daughter Caroline, I leave the other half of the remaining estate, provided that she agrees to the following terms."

"**What?** Stop right there. **Terms?** What do you mean by **terms**?"

As she posed her heated questions, she was literally shaking despite the tight grip onto her sister's arm.

"Yes, it is true that there are terms. Your father was quite determined to add this existing clause. Shall I continue?"

Nervously, she nodded.

"The following terms, not in my words, but as your father dictated, are these," Steinberg reported. "Caroline will receive her share of my estate only by agreeing to a divorce from David D Trump, thus allowing him to receive his ten million dollars. Furthermore, she shall never see him again and never offer him any monetary assistance and/or payments of any type. And finally, I request of her that she legally return to the usage of her given name Caroline Catherine Adams Berman, a name that I hope she honors more than the name Trump. She may accept the terms of this agreement that will rid her of her bondage. If not, she will forever forfeit her legal entitlement."

"Accept it? I would be a fool not to. I happily accept my father's offer and even happier to be rid of that contemptible man," she screamed, pointing a shaking finger directly at David D.

"He really loved us and didn't forget us in the end," Cynthia said, leaning over to be closer to Caroline. "He loved us in spite of all our malicious ways."

"Yes, yes he did," Caroline uttered, wiping at the rush of tears that erupted to a full, heavy flow.

Brandy wanted so deeply to reach out and hug Hubert's daughters, to tell them that they would be okay now. Their father always understood their pain over the loss of their mother. He understood it because he had also suffered with the loss and with his guilt. But this moment offered no proper way for her to approach them. She was still the outsider.

"Well now, everything for today is done," Steinberg said with detached emotion.

Picking up his briefcase, he and Stanley Fizer left together through the front door where they had entered some two hours earlier. David D, frantic over the change of events, jumped up and promptly raced after them.

"Wait, listen. Please listen," he shouted to the two men. "I'll sign the papers. Give them to me now. I'll gladly sign and do whatever you want about Caroline. I don't care about her. I want the ten million dollars."

"Call me tomorrow," Steinberg shouted back, getting into the car and slamming the door.

"He's a real jerk," Fizer commented, putting the car in reverse and backing out, leaving David D standing on the drive in monetary distress.

"Yes, you are absolutely right," Steinberg replied.

"I have business with you myself and I don't particularly want to wait," Fizer said. "I'm positive that Mr. Berman must have included me in his Will. After all, I have been very successful as his right-hand man. Why didn't that come up today?"

"Well, Stanley, I didn't think it appropriate to include you with this group. They were closer. Let's say, they were family in one form or another. And without any intent of criticism, I considered you in the classification as office staff. Understand?"

"No, I don't clearly understand it; definitely not in dollars and cents. Just how much does office staff add up to?"

"You were remembered by Hubert as you so accurately expressed. Right now I can give you an estimated figure or you can see me tomorrow and we can go over that portion together."

"I think that right now will do just fine. How much is that portion?"

"Hubert always felt that you had the great ability to go beyond your current employment level. He recognized that you are talented and clever. And, he definitely put value on your service. So I would estimate that the figure might be in the neighborhood somewhere near five-hundred-thousand. Give or take a few."

"That's it? I'm rewarded with the same amount left to that old, simple-minded servant from Kentucky?"

"Yes, but you have such potential, Stanley. That poor fellow is near his end. Clearly among the ranks, you have outstanding status. That's what counts."

"At the moment it counts to about five-hundred-thousand. Not nearly what I had expected."

"Expectations are not a barometer of reality. Your personal drive will be your gateway, Stanley."

27

Mildred, aimlessly wandering from room to room in the spacious Boxwood penthouse, was intensely worrying about Brandy and the outcome of the Will. Would the two of them not have a roof over their heads by nightfall or would Brandy return as the rich widow, fully endowed with Hubert Franz Berman's estate.

Mildred, hoping for the latter, had no clue which would be true.

Hectic days had passed since that Saturday morning when Shields had called the beauty shop to cancel Brandy's nail appointment. So much had happened during those few days and Mildred prided herself on all the resourceful ways she had participated. After Brandy's collapse over the devastating news of Hubert's death, she had, without hesitation, come immediately to take care of her best friend.

And when the three Kentuckians had arrived for the funeral, she had prepared meals for all of them. She had calmly consoled Brandy when the Berman daughters had boldly attacked her; like stinging scorpions they had pierced their step-mother with their noxious sting and she was the one to apply the ointment of love and compassion.

Through all of this mayhem, Mildred had put aside her own personal life. Now, out of some sense of duty to her husband Wilfred, she called their apartment to offer an apology about being away for so long.

Yet, when the answering machine kicked on, she was glad that Wilford was still at work and not there to ask questions or to demand that she come home immediately. It was much easier for her to leave the brief message than trying to explain her acts of friendship.

"Hope that you have had plenty to eat," she quickly added as an empty good-bye.

One hour and one glass of wine later, the penthouse phone rang.

Mildred jumped!

Afraid that her mother may have intercepted the message left for Wilford, she hesitated, staring at the phone, dreading the prospect of hearing another religious lecture from her suspicious mother.

Oh, but then, could the call be from Brandy?

It was not. Instead, it was the voice of a husky-throated woman.

"This is Greta Donna Cupani. Is Brandy Berman there?"

"No, she's not right now and I am not sure when she will return. But this is her best friend Mildred Brown. May I give her a message?"

"Why Mildred, I remember seeing you at the funeral and that's exactly what this call is about. We are back in Kentucky and our little group wanted to extend our condolences about poor Hubert's demise. We just didn't have the opportunity to visit with Brandy at the funeral."

"I know that she will appreciate your call. Is there a phone number I could give to her? Maybe she could contact you later today or at least by tomorrow."

"No. We are like a band of gypsies, you see. We roam around too much, mostly going from parties to parties and I am not sure just what tomorrow will bring. I think she will understand how we are since she saw us in action on the cruise. Just tell her that we called and that we are sorry about Hubert."

"I want to write your name correctly. It is Greta Donna Cupani. Is that 'C u p a n i'?"

"That's right. Oh wait Mildred, don't hang up yet; a few of the others want to speak with you. Just a sec, here's BJ."

"Hi, this is BJ Turner. Please tell Brandy that our group has made a sizeable donation to the Boston Pops Orchestra. There will be acknowledgements sent to Caroline and Cynthia, but we wanted to make sure that Brandy is made aware of this contribution in Hubert's name. We all noticed that there was no communication between the three of them."

"I think everyone noticed that," Mildred responded.

"You will remember to tell her about this contribution. It is sizeable and the Pops might contact her, perhaps for a statement or to extend an invitation for the gala that we are planning in Hubert's memory."

"Oh, my! That does sound very important. I'm writing all that down for Brandy. She put a note pad by the phone so that I wouldn't forget any of the telephone calls.

"That was a good idea. Hey, do you mind giving us a few more minutes of your time. This may all seem a bit pragmatic; but it's just the way we operate in our little group. Hold on, Mindy Morningstar has something to say."

"Mildred, I've been listening on the speaker box and you do sound like a sweet person; one that can be trusted. It's my profession to observe and connect to the nature of people since I am a soothsayer and a child of the spirits."

"Oh my goodness, a soothsayer," Mildred cringed! "I've never met nor ever heard of a real soothsayer. Is that the same as a fortune teller?"

"No. I don't use a crystal ball," Mindy answered with a laugh. "I simply rely on the transmitting waves that I receive from the natural aura that surrounds all of us."

"Is that really true? Do we all have a natural aura? I can't imagine something like that," said a confused Mildred.

"I would be happy to explain the essence of our natural aura to you on another occasion. But for now, will you do something special for me?"

"Sure. What do you need?"

"Please hold the receiver over your heart for the count of ten and then return to the line. Do not be afraid, just hold the receiver. Please, do it for me."

A little leery about what was about to occur, Mildred, shaking like a leaf, held the receiver over her heart to a speedy count of ten. "Was that right? Did I hold it long enough?" she asked, her voice quivering and a lump rising in her throat.

"Oh yes, you did it right. Your aura tells me that your heart and not your head will guide you sooner than you think. I foresee a whirlwind of changes just beyond this minute and perhaps even extending into your distant future. Do you believe me, Mildred?"

"Oh my goodness, this is weird! I don't know what I believe. This is too fast. Gosh, I'm so nervous right now that I might forget to tell Brandy everything. Can you tell that I am nervous?"

"Why yes, that was easy to do just from the sound of your voice. But I know for sure that you won't forget. Your confidence in yourself rises with each heartbeat. Trust what I am telling you."

"I don't think I will forget. No, I am sure that I will **not** forget."

"Good girl, Mildred. Now please follow these instructions for me. First settle yourself. That's good, Mildred. I can sense you are trying. Now, write down what I am going to say."

"Wait," Mildred struggled, "Let me hold this pen steady; it is literally wiggling in my hand. Alright, go ahead I'm ready."

"Mildred, I sense that you will do fine. Now, write these exact words and give them to Brandy," she said, waiting a few seconds until she was sure of the right moment. Then she softly continued, "Okay, write this: **The end is not the end until everything is over. Then, and only then, is it ended.**"

"That's it?" Mildred asked, frowning and still full of questions about such a silly combination of words.

"There is no more to the message. Now look at it, are you satisfied with how you wrote it?"

"Yes, I did it right. Shall I read it back to you?"

"No need to, Mildred, I have full confidence in you. Just as I predicted, **your** confidence level is already rising. But unfortunately, I cannot continue in this space, I've lost the sensory perception and I cannot now predict just how or even if you and Brandy will experience the intent of that message. However, the day will come when a clearer view will emerge. Thank you, Mildred. Good-bye."

Locked in place, a foggy Mildred held onto the empty line. Whether it was a witch's hex or a magic spell that had been cast on her, something certainly had caused a real transformation. From somewhere deep within, a new posture emerged and she walked away from the phone, head held high with shoulders relaxed and straight.

By the time that Brandy returned to the penthouse, Mildred had celebrated with a canister of her favorite cookies and a full bottle of Cabernet. Yet, she had not consumed enough to forget to tell Brandy that there had been an important phone call.

In her inebriated way, she was, however, much too light-headed to fully understand Brandy's explanations of the serious consequences of Hubert's Will.

"We have to leave this penthouse," Brandy kept saying over and over. "I have a limited amount of time to redirect my life. Pay attention to me. This is serious business. Do you understand that Boston is over for me?"

"Yes, I hear you. But these messages, they wanted you to read them right away." Mildred's garbled words were not exactly hitting the target.

"What are you trying to say?"

"Mindy Morningstar forecasted that changes were coming. I believed her; good things......good for you and me. Read it. In the end it won't be over; or was it that the end ends it all? I'm a little cloudy right now about remembering parts of it, but I know that good is coming. Look, I wrote it all down."

"You have had too much to drink to clearly remember anything! And, you don't seem to grasp that I have to move to the Cayman Islands? If something good is going to happen about that, it better happen very soon."

"But Mindy said that more vibes or something, maybe something spooky will come to her. I don't think that she was quite sure just when it would arrive."

"You wait for it to come. I've got to seriously think about the here and now. You've been such a wonderful friend and I know that you are sincere about what you have been told. But Mildred, that's all just a wild prediction. Don't let it launch any kind of false hope."

"I truly believe what Mindy told me. I actually felt something different even before she could say good-bye. Some kind of odd vision came into my mind, like maybe the two of us are there at the end and we are happy like in a fairy tale...and they lived happily ever after," Mildred giggled, the consumed wine altering all normal brain cells.

"I'm too practical to accept fairy tales. I focus on the reality of what comes each day," Brandy said, watching her friend sink down onto the couch. "Let me see those darn messages that you keep blabbering about."

"There. They are there by the phone."

"What's this, a gala? Those women have parties all the time. Well at least this one will be a tribute in Hubert's memory. Mildred, you can say that is a good thing. …Mildred? Mildred?"

There was no response. The bottle of wine was warmly flowing in Mildred's blood stream, her checks red and her eyes blurry. She was the epitome of a content woman, totally relaxed and smiling about it.

Back on the night when she had been with Brandy at the Italian restaurant, the seeds of her transformation had first been planted. Mindy Morningstar felt the aura of that hidden breath of change. She had taken it to another notch within her prediction.

Now peacefully, with that crooked smile plastered on her lips, Mildred's head softly dropped onto the wide arm of the couch. In two seconds she was gone, drifting off, far, far beyond Brandy's words.

28

A large, brass award for Secretary of the Year hung prominently over Beverly Borden's desk in her immaculate Boston apartment; an award that was a well-deserved recognition of her professional talent.

Having worked for twenty, committed years as an executive secretary at Berman and Rothchild, she was a high caliber and proficient career woman admired by colleagues and friends. And, if there was a flaw in her porcelain character, few would have been able to detect it.

With the utmost care, she had successfully shielded her private life from the rest of the world. Through all those years there had been no fear that her deepest secret would ever be exposed to anyone. Yet, that carefully guarded secret, her profound love for her boss Hubert Franz Berman, was totally shattered on the very day of the announcement of his death.

Surviving his funeral had to be the hardest accomplishment she would ever encountered. It had sickened her beyond belief and its torment tugged heavily. Her emotions were totally drained and her nerves knotted to the point of an eruption. Had it not been for pills and her Bostonian pride, she would have perished at the funeral.

Two days had passed since that fateful day and still she could not bring herself to be seen in public. Her eyes were too puffy from the tears and her functioning mind a log jam of memories, so many memories that they came in torrents. There was simply no way she could avoid thinking about the massive loss of the love of her life.

"Shirley, this is Miss Borden. Is Mr. Rothchild in?" she barely managed when the cute, blond receptionist answered at the office.

"Yes he is, but Mrs. Cahill just put him on a big conference call. Shall I buzz her?"

"That's alright, Shirley, things sound very busy there. Tell Mrs. Cahill that I'm sick with flu-like symptoms. I think it best that I stay in bed for a few, more days."

"I'll tell her Miss Borden. Hope you feel better. Gosh, we are all sorry about Mr. Berman's funeral. It's really sad to walk by his empty office. Did you see the flowers that the staff sent?"

"Yes, Shirley, they were very nice. Tell Mrs. Cahill to handle things until I'm back at work."

"Sure thing, Miss Borden," the young receptionist responded, smacking on a piece of chewing gum. "I'll do that. Bye."

Beverly Borden's knees went weak and the receiver weighed heavily in her hand. Then, without control, the painful crying began again; for a steady five minutes she wept bitterly.

Wadded tissues were everywhere, cluttered in messy piles across her desk and overflowing the capacity of the wastebasket. Though her hands were shaky, she returned to her task with the scissors, cutting out the editorial from the Boston Globe, the well-written one about Hubert's many business accomplishments and his hefty contributions to the city of Boston. She knew all too well the man being honored by the press, but she also knew what was not in print, those items of his personal requests and his masculine desires.

Vivid memories of their days together flashed before her – how she bought his favorite Zino cigars and how she knew his preference for one drop of cream in his morning coffee. She remembered sadly the little personal things she had done when he needed a haircut or the private memos reminding him of physicals or dental appointments. Oh how wonderful it was to read his thoughts before he actually asked for things like clients' folders or the morning mail. They had been a fabulous duo in his private office, moving in tandem.

Again she reread the editorial and then slid the cutting into a plastic sleeve and clicked it into a thick, three-ring binder that was both an album and a scrapbook full of photographs, press releases, and magazine and newspaper articles all about Hubert. This was her private collection of his life that she had been faithfully updating for years; even he was never aware of its existence.

No one had ever accused her of flirtations with Hubert. Even at the funeral, she held her secret intact with a calm, false composure in front of all the others. Caroline and Cynthia had hugged her and Samuel Steinberg extended his condolences over the death of her boss.

"Fine man," he had said. "I expect that you'll miss him in the office?"

MISS HIM? It was like missing the very air she inhaled. No man had ever shared her bed except for Hubert when he came to her after his wife's accident. He desperately needed her then and she had lovingly ushered him back from his despair.

"*You are a wonderful woman,*" she kept remembering those very words that he had spoken so many times after their lovemaking. Though he had never made promises to her or actually said that he loved her; she had dearly loved him.

Her woman's intuition knew how to handle these things and if Hubert wasn't ready to return her love back in those days, she had been, through the following years, slowly leading him in that direction.

But curse the very entrance of Irma Lou Delaney who had spoiled a romantic future that would have changed her Borden name to Berman. If only that woman, a socially unacceptable piano player, had not been on the cruise in the first place. If only, after his New York trip, there had been more time in their private world, boss and secretary, alone and comfortably away from his family life. If only he had not traveled to Kentucky and died in that wretched hospital.

If only...if only....

Sullen and consumed in her world of misery, Beverly cursed the shattering ring of the telephone.

"Hello," she grudgingly said, her voice echoing her soiled feelings.

"Beverly, are you alright? This is Margie Cahill; I hope I haven't disturbed your rest. Shirley told me that you were not feeling well and I called to see if you need anything."

"No, I'm taking it easy, trying to get rid of a cold or maybe the flu."

"Well honey, you are missing the **big** gossip here in the office today! I overheard Mr. Rothchild say that Mr. Berman's daughters got the bulk of his estate and that new, blond wife just got five million dollars. Of course, five million to me is a big, big inheritance."

"They have read his Will? Did anyone call looking for me? Wasn't there a need to get into Hubert's…Mr. Berman's office? I'll quickly dress and try to get there right away."

"Stay put, Beverly. According to Shirley there have been no calls for you, business or otherwise. And there is no need for you to be worried about the office. It's all over," Margie Cahill replied in a jovial, careless voice that rubbed Beverly's emotional sore-spots.

"All over, what do you mean, ALL OVER?"

"Mr. Berman's office has been completely shut down today. A crew came in early and carted off his things. It looks bare in there."

"What's happening? We just buried the dear man."

"Well, Beverly, it seems he had made arrangements with Mr. Rothchild to move you over to the new partner, a Mr. Robinson. We are in for some renovations and the company is going to be Rothchild and Robinson by the end of the month. The deal had been in the works since Mr. Berman came back from New York and no one around here, except Mr. Rothchild, knew a thing about it. I suspect you weren't savvy to these big changes."

"I can't do this now. No, I can't. Oh God, I'm sick!" Beverly cried out through parched lips. Tossing the telephone aside, she reeled as a bloodless, white-stoned coloring washed across her face.

She flew to the bathroom and threw up! Again and again, the sour fluids erupted from her throat, splashing murky brown into the water of the commode.

Hanging onto the rim of that toilet, the white, hard receptacle of those sick of stomach, her head was spinning and her guts churning to the most putrid ejection that she had ever endured.

She crawled to the tub and pulled a damp wash cloth from its edge and dabbed her lips and chin. She yanked the soiled robe away from her body and left it by the tub as she crawled back to the bedroom and slumped onto the beige carpeting.

Pathetic with a broken heart, she lay partially nude, shivering and unable to rise to her bed.

The raw truth of being alone hits hardest when there is no one there to witness your despair. No, in her bleak, black episode she withered alone; ever to be alone without her Hubert.

If one's bidding could bring instant death, Beverly Borden, Secretary of the Year, would have cast herself forth from this wasteland.

29

A new day brought some tempting fresh air that lured Brandy outside for a slow stroll around the landscaped, private grounds at Queen's Gate. She needed the stimulating air to clear the cobwebs of the past few weeks and to erase the more disturbing thoughts of her dishonest behavior had she pursued the secret relationship with Shields.

Twice she had asked him to wait for the proper timing and twice he had agreed to come to her when she was settled.

Still it was all very strange to be leaving Boston for a beach house in the Cayman Islands, a place far removed from the busy, crowded city that had served her well for many years. Stranger still that Hubert would have left her such a place.

Seahaven was an unknown word to her. Hubert had never mentioned that he had property in the Caymans nor had he ever suggested a Caribbean trip for the two of them.

As Brandy strolled along the manicured walkway she thought of what the house would be like. With no descriptions given to her, she could only imagine a quaint cottage, surrounded by palm trees, perhaps near the beach.

In this next phase of her life she expected no more bitterness from Hubert's daughters nor did she have need of the green-eyed jealousy over his secretary. Why bother? Hubert himself had given no value to it, nor had he broken his promise to leave Beverly Borden out of his Will.

One of the hardest changes that Brandy faced was her separation from Mildred, who had packed and left for her apartment on West 5th Street. Their friendship had been so reassuring at a time when everything else was lopsidedly wrong. Yet, now, they were headed down different paths and soon they would be miles and miles apart.

Brandy did not hear a white sedan as it pulled near the curb. Samuel Steinberg rolled down the window. "Good morning," he called out. "I was on my way to see you and the doorman said you were out walking. Do you mind getting in? We need to talk privately and here in the car might be one of the better places."

"If you have come here to evict me, I am planning to leave in a reasonable time," Brandy coldly responded, positioning herself at a safe distance from him on the front seat of his car.

"No, it's not concerning that. There's no rush for a week or more. Even before Cynthia can begin to redecorate, Hubert's art pieces are to be removed from the penthouse on family loan to the museum. Caroline is furious about that, but it was one of his instructions and quite legal."

"They won't let him rest in peace. How sad that the bickering still goes on. Hubert certainly must have anticipated that this would happen; that's why he provided protection for me and also wisely protected his favorite art collection. Are there other bequests that I should know about?"

"Yes. There are many, many others; mostly, however, those items are to be handled by trust funds or the accountants and the lawyers. And when it is all settled, Caroline and Cynthia will still be very wealthy women. I have with me, your complete copy of the Will," he announced, reaching into his briefcase and removing a thick, manila folder with the name Steinberg and Leftwich embossed across the front.

"How strange that a man's life can be reduced to a folder," Brandy responded.

"I guess that is true. Yet, for Hubert's life, it required a rather large folder," Steinberg said, smiling.

"I will cherish this; not because others may think of it as money, but because it will always remind me of an intelligent man and a wonderfully, kind person."

"You are a very intuitive woman, Mrs. Berman."

"Thank you," she meekly replied, utterly surprised to hear such a compliment from this elite lawyer.

"There is more that I need to tell you about. But, this part cannot be discussed with accountants and lawyers. It is quite serious and must not even be shared with your family or closest friends. However, before I explain these things, I must request that you swear an oath of secrecy not to reveal any of what I am about to say. Are you willing to subject yourself to this oath as Hubert wanted you to do?"

"I'm not sure. It is difficult to commit to an oath without knowing more of what might be required. But, I respected Hubert and if this is what he asked of me, then I cannot refuse," she softly replied.

"Very well. Repeat this oath. **We, the three members of the Honor Guard Secret Society, promise to keep our secret from all other friends and from all our family members. We are bound together for life in this secret, like blood brothers, one to the other. Each member is dependent on the other two. We are therefore one.**"

Not realizing the severity of these vows, nor the commitment she would soon assume, Brandy, true to her professed respect for Hubert, followed along, repeating each of the special words.

"You are brave to have such blind faith in all this, Brandy. Excuse me, may I call you Brandy?" he asked.

"Yes, of course. Actually I would be more comfortable if you would."

"There is much more to tell," Steinberg continued, looking around to be sure no one was watching them. "Are you ready to share the greatest secret that Hubert ever held?"

"Yes, I am," Brandy replied with heighten curiosity.

"When Hubert, Lewis, and I were teenagers, we found a great deal of money. We hide it and never once spoke of the money to anyone. Through the years, we parlayed the money into successful fortunes, eventually mixing it into research departments, charitable foundations, and art acquisitions for public museums or parks. The Society's money has continued to feed on itself, producing more than we could have ever imagined."

"It's almost impossible for me to understand all this, but I know that Hubert was a very intelligent man and obviously you and Dr. Capalo are too," Brandy responded.

"Thank you. But now this whole issue centers on you," Steinberg spoke, closely observing her reaction. "Before Hubert's death he named you as his successor and he cleverly had certain arrangements made to prepare for your entry. Can you now comprehend the importance of why I asked you to declare our oath of silence?"

"It's quite obvious that your secret can never be uncovered or there could be serious complications. But you must realize that I know nothing about finances. What could I possibly contribute to the Society?"

"Don't labor over that, in time it will all be easier for you. Our system works smoothly and the profits automatically go into separate accounts. Hubert's accounts are in the Cayman Islands that's why he wanted you to have the beach house. All clear now?"

"As clear as mud is what we would say in my old neighborhood. But, here at the Queen's Court, it seems to make sense. With your guidance, I will try to do my best."

"Good. We start with your move to Seahaven. By the time you arrive there, everything you will need for the Society's business will be in a small safe, concealed under a floor tile. Memorize this rotary-lock number and then properly destroy this paper. I'll fly down tomorrow and personally deal with the preparation of the safe."

"This makes me think of a cloak and dagger movie and I'm not sure just what part I would be playing. Probably, I would be the one with the big wide eyes, telling my feet to get going. I'm not making light of this serious business, it's just my way to try and calm my nerves."

"Eventually you'll adjust and it will become second nature. It is **imperative**, Brandy, I repeat, **imperative** that **no one** is ever given a clue to our activities! Stanley will see to organizing your move. He'll do his petty job exactly as I tell him to, but he has absolutely no knowledge about the Society and its members."

"It amazes me how things are always so carefully constructed way before I ever know what is about to happen. And, it seems, that out of the blue, Stanley Fizer suddenly appears. He's certainly not too pleasant to me when he does."

"I know that Stanley can be a boorish annoyance, but he does follow instructions. He'll arrange the shipment of your possessions; just prepare you personal items and leave him to me. In no time you will be relaxing on a tropical island. That doesn't seem like a bad way to live, now does it?"

"No, not at all. It does sound good."

"Brandy, I must tell you that Hubert made a very wise decision when he selected you as his wife."

"Oh, that's very kind of you."

"Not kind, my dear lady, but a positive statement of proven data," Steinberg remarked in a lighter tone, his head nodding agreeably.

He drove her back to the front door of The Boxwood, got out and gave her a gentle hug in front of Nathan the doorman. No suspicion could be unleashed that his visit was more than a friendly, social call.

"We will miss Hubert," Steinberg said aloud, performing the perfect act of a friend consoling a new widow.

She waved good-bye as he drove away. Nathan, holding the door for her, extended his own condolences, "Yes Mrs. Berman, everyone here will miss your husband. I will especially remember his happy greetings whenever he went in and out. Always a kind word, that man always had a kind word."

"Thank you, Nathan. My husband always spoke fondly of you."

Brandy casually carried the folder that Steinberg had given her, while she tightly clutched the small piece of paper with the numbers for the safe. Once inside the privacy of the condo, she read the numbers several times, repeating them over and over until she knew that they were securely tucked away into her long-term memory.

She closed her eyes, visualized the numbers and recited them one last time. Without further hesitation, she burned the paper in a small ashtray, cooled the ashes and mixed them into the soil of a potted plant on the terrace.

The feel of the loosened soil released images of Hubert, puttering around with his gardening hobby as she had seen him do in the cool of the evenings. Breathing in that lone, endearing memory, she felt as if he was there, beside her, encouraging her with his own strength.

"I'll do it for you," she said aloud. "But stay close until I get it right."

Later, in the laundry room, she found a cardboard box and went about collecting all the framed photos of him; these tokens of his life would be the first boxed items to travel with her to the Caymans.

Stanley Fizer could come to finish the packing. But there would be little on her list for him to move. The potted plant, Hubert's opera tapes and his favorite humidor, her own clothes, and a few trinkets of emotional value would be all that she would need for her transition to the beach house called Seahaven.

30

No enthusiasm accompanied Mildred when she returned home. The aroma of the dingy apartment had a strange, uninviting scent that she attributed to her own disdain for returning at all.

At first, things about her seemed shabbily familiar. Yet, it was a gapping emptiness in the living room that shocked her to the realization that this slight ting of strangeness was more than just her gloomy mood.

For right smack in front of her was a vacant area where Wilford's prized 27-inch TV once stood. Without a TV, there could be no Wilford!

Gone, too, from a hook on the back of the door, were his work uniforms that always hung there after each washing. His black-soled house shoes, the ugly ones that made those hard-to-remove streaks on her clean linoleum floors, were not to be seen in front of the tattered couch.

Finally, in the kitchen, she found an empty refrigerator, completely void of the cold beers that Wilford so selfishly harbored.

He has left me, Mildred accurately reasoned, a situation that was not totally repulsive to her.

Perhaps it was even such an event of magnitude that it invited a celebration. Pondering a yes or a no, it took no time for her to happily react with a yes.

With her fist stretched skyward, she shouted, **"YES! YES!"**

That brief moment of jubilation was shattered to bits when her mother exploded through the door, "Well, the she-devil has returned! Did you think you could just sneak back in here without offering your repentance?"

"Mother, I told you and Wilford that I would be gone for a very short time. I was needed there to help a good friend with her problems. Didn't you brainwash me about charity?"

"Charity begins at home where your first duty belongs exclusively to your faithful husband," preached the harsh woman. "You have totally failed to be submissive and obedient as the bible plainly requires of a married woman. Leaving your husband alone is disgustingly unacceptable for a Christian wife. **You....you** are a **she-devil**, a wicked and sinful woman!"

"That may be the shallow way that you and father live your lives. But I believe in a charity with faith, hope, and love – especially love! I have done nothing wrong and I am not ashamed of myself," proclaimed Mildred, a ram-rod going up her back, allowing her not to give in.

Though her jaws were tense and locked, she composed herself so that she could release what she had been harboring for so many years.

"Wilford failed to acknowledge my presence," she spoke forth with determination. "He never talked and rarely touched me and then, only if he felt some type of carnal desire."

"Sins have stained you and led you from the righteous path! You have let the wicked world corrupt your very soul. A demon such as you will face the Lord's wrath. You will be damned for speaking so explicitly of a woman's marital duties!"

Her mother cringed and stiffened, turning her face away, unable to squarely face her own daughter over a subject that had never once been openly discussed in their household.

"**SEX!** Yes, mother, **SEX!** Look at me and believe what I am telling you. There was so little of it that I assure you that Wilford long ago abandoned his marital duties to me as his wife."

"Oh, you are indeed **corrupt**! Your words are of filth. Your words are the burning words of the devil. Wilford is a faithful provider and a faithful bible-reading man. The Lord has sent His blessings to this household, allowing that decent man to live with us now. Like a loving son, he has come into my arms."

"A son is born, full-grown! Is that what you have been praying for? Your Christian principles seem to work only in your selective ways. Finally, you have gotten exactly what you have always wanted. You prayed, and prayed hard, while you totally ignored me as your biological daughter. Now, it comes easy for you to pamper a new-found son."

"I have no daughter! And the quicker you gather up your junk and leave here, the better for our family and our Church. Two worshiping members from our congregation will soon live here," shouted the stringy haired woman.

With cold and callous eyes, she turned and abruptly abandoned her daughter, slamming the apartment door as her final gesture.

Mildred released a sweet sigh of relief. It was finally over. She was finally able to leave the bonds of this house. And there would be no twinge of guilt associated with her leaving, for hadn't her own mother made it abundantly clear that no one at West 5th Street wanted her there.

Without remorse, Mildred went into the closet and took down the box that once housed her wedding shoes. Removing her treasury of tip money hidden there, she threw the shoebox on the floor, looked over at the sagging double-bed and made no pretense at saying good-bye.

Some months later, a letter from Mildred arrived at Seahaven, the small, celery-green beach house nestled among tropical foliage. The neatly written, two-page letter brought the announcement of her new job in the beauty salon aboard the Mermaid, a luxury liner registered in the Caribbean.

Enclosed, too, was a photograph. It literally took Brandy a few seconds to recognize that it was Mildred. What a change she had made; a real beauty she was. Very tanned and slim, she was wearing a blue and white bathing suit with a victory sash ---MS CABERNET.

On the back of the photo, she had written - **I won! Can you believe it? I am Ms Cabernet! Remember me this way. Your friend, Mildred.**

Her letter contained other personal information about the exciting job, her new friend Johnny, the lively music at the Cabernet Festival, and her plans to see Brandy if the ship ever sailed to the Cayman Islands.

But the 4 x 6 photo told Brandy more than the written words had described. The honest lens of the camera had captured a vibrant woman, full of life, with eyes that sparkled and a lovely smile that wooed the viewer. Brandy looked at the picture again and again, finally hanging it on a bulletin board above her computer.

It prompted her to dash off this good news to Shields. Though they had agreed not to see each other for a socially-proper separation, they had continued to communicate, using e-mails.

Shields answered immediately: Glad to hear about Mildred's rebirth. So who is Johnny? Let me know. Been busy today planning another fishing trip. Tomorrow I take the boat out. Reregistered her yesterday and now she is the Brandywine. Guess why? Hope you like that name. Miss you dearly. Love, Shields.

Click, click she sent her response: Hello Captain. Couldn't wait, had to reply right away. Thanks for renaming the boat; a lovely compliment! Hope Mildred writes again. Don't know enough about her Johnny. Take care and stay clear of storms. Make sure you return safely to port. Until next time, Brandy.

So far the agreement with Shields had gone exceptionally well. She was always content after hearing from him and it always added to her day. She went to her piano, just as she had been doing every afternoon since her first day in the islands, and played one of his favorite songs.

Outside, a man stopped at her front gate to listen to her music. He was, for that moment, her audience, a simple stranger who had passed her way on his trek to the beach. He stood there for a short time before continuing down the sandy lane.

As the warm rays of the descending sun dropped lower and lower onto the windowsill, Brandy caught their cue, picked up her glass of Chardonnay and went outside, curling up on the stripped cushion of the swing, her favorite spot to toast another super sunset.

The horizon glowed with vibrant red and powdered purple. And, as if a master artist had painted the scene, radiant dashes of orange and yellow swirled about the sky, creating a mixture of tantalizing colors, lively broadcasting day's end.

The air was cool and clean, refreshingly clean.

There was no question that Brandy had grown to love every inch of her beautiful surroundings and it required no effort to celebrate the occasion. She remained curled there on her porch, until darkness settled in.

But, later that evening, her mood changed when she had to attend to serious business on her computer, the very one that had been in Hubert's office at Berman and Rothchild.

Stanley Fizer had personally packed it when he orchestrated her move from Boston. Though he had not actually accompanied the movers to Seahaven, he had sent along sheets of computer instructions, along with his own advice to chuck the whole system and go to a laptop.

Beyond the simple e-mails that she had begun to send as soon as she had arrived, Brandy was not a friendly user for detailed business entries and on her first few solos she had given up in desperation.

Fortunately, she happened upon a small computer store in George Town where a knowledgeable technician clearly explained the basic programs, giving her enough advice to get her started on some practice drills.

All that was behind her now and this particular night belonged to the Society's secret accounts. She rolled back a small, area rug and removed the large, floor tile that rested over a hidden safe. The very safe that Samuel Steinberg had described to her and had so strongly cautioned about keeping it concealed and always securely locked.

Within its darken recesses there was a back-up CD and various items of identification namely a birth certificate, driver's license, passport, check book, ATM card, and a AAA motor card. The fictitious name Jane Banks appeared on all these counterfeit documents.

Brandy clicked on-line and brought to the screen three separate accounts that held her share of the money from the Honor Guard Secret Society. Listed under fake charity names, these interest-earning accounts received generous deposits that steadily increased their balances. It was her job to transfer funds and to safely back-up the work by saving it to the disc.

How easy it was to mentally plan her movements with this task, yet her fingers resisted the keyboard. They were unable to touch the correct keys that would transfer money out of these three accounts into one account defined as the major disbursement fund, the safety net of a secured checking account at a local bank.

The voice of Steinberg repeatedly pushed her on. *'You must do it often; you must keep the money circulating. The future of the Society depends on the transfer of funds. Lewis and I do it, you must for your own protection and the security of our society of three.'*

His words had been firm and almost threatening, as if she would not be permitted a single mistake. He had years of practice at this and yet he expected, no demanded, that she be of equal ability.

Her mind was focused.

Her will was strong.

Her fingers would not move.

They froze like ice, cold and hard, as she tried to place them on the keyboard. Instantly, she withdrew them and they responded with a fearful tremble. She tried again, then again. Maybe the other two members had performed the routine of shifting money, but she had not been able to execute the simple task.

Not once!

The splashing sounds of the sea drifted in through the windows and the overhead fan gently hummed as Brandy sat and stared at the computer. What should have been peaceful was not. It was, in fact, sheer misery for Brandy to sit there, struggling with the moral issue of her involvement in this mysterious society.

She questioned the level of guilt that could be charged to her if she participated in the illicit act and actually used the money. Going to jail for doing something someone else had instructed her to do was not exactly an innocent plea and she knew that.

Still, according to Steinberg, the money had been around for over sixty years and not one of the original three members had ever once been found guilty of anything.

"Okay, you promised," she said aloud. "Do what you must do."

Commitment or not, her hands and her mind would not jell in rhythm. For when she reached towards the keyboard, her rebellious fingers froze again.

31

Some two weeks later Brandy rode a rental Vespa, a red two-seater scooter, out of bustling George Town into the north where, near the end of the island, she kept a mailbox at a rural post office in the town of Hell.

This small town had a steady flow of tourists who seemingly traveled there seeking out the postmark of Hell, not exactly the sort of thing that was accurately descriptive of a beautiful paradise surrounded by the sea.

Brandy's postal box in that small community was used exclusively to receive all communications from Samuel Steinberg, he preferring to use novelty postcards and always writing his messages in code.

From her postal box, she withdrew a single card, displaying a colorful photograph of the Statue of Liberty. Taking no time to read the message, she hastily returned to the Vespa and headed down the road, where, at a secluded spot, one safely nestled among several shade trees, she stopped the scooter just long enough to read what Steinberg had carefully worded:

Hi, friend. NY is big! Ten a.m. and already I'm lost again. Friday, a drop-dead meter maid helped me with directions. October is her last name; think MISS OCTOBER of the centerfold type. 28, she said, but she looked like a shapely 22! Meeting her tonight at a bar - the stud works again - ha! Money spent on drinks always does the

trick for guys and I am sure glad you are not here to spoil things. Where will I woo her in NY? Later I might tell if you are lucky. Sammy

Early on, when he had prepared the hidden safe for Brandy, Steinberg had left instructions in it as to the code for his messages. By extracting the first word of every sentence, she could easily reveal the information for her activity concerning the Society.

As a caution while on her postal runs, he had advised her to use different routes, wear a wig and sunglasses, and, at all costs, try to blend in with the throngs of tourists. Additionally, he strongly insisted that she never reveal her true identity and that she should avoid traveling at the same hour - on the same day of the week - or with another person.

At that time Brandy had committed to memory these detailed directives and had then destroyed Steinberg's memo, as she had done with the tumbler numbers for the safe's lock.

Riding out of Hell, she followed a mapped course and did a zigzag through neighborhoods, ultimately making a turn near the airport that allowed her to return into George Town from the east. The rental agency was in a decent location there and she returned it without delay.

She headed home to reconfirm the coded message and to shred the postcard, destroying all evidence of its existence.

It would be two, long weeks before Brandy would travel to the post office again. During that wait, she spent her days with ordinary routines of long walks in the morning, playing the piano in the late afternoons, and watching glorious sunsets from her porch - her favorite past time.

It was on an afternoon of playing the piano, or the lack there of, that she came face to face with a Garrett Grayson.

Seasonal weather, unpredictable and uncontrollable, had a lot to do with their first meeting. Early morning rains on that particular day had been cool and delightfully soothing but, by afternoon, the winds had shifted, blowing powerfully hard and pushing the rain back towards the sea. What followed was a hot, heavy depression that settled in and refused to let up.

Brandy, miserable with the suffocating warmth of the house, forgot about the piano and sat on the front porch all afternoon trying to find relief from the heat that radiated like a blast furnace. Tiny sweat beads rested at the crevasse of her 40 double-Ds and damp ringlets of blond hair curled about her forehead and cheekbones.

"Excuse me," a man in a red bathing suit called out to her from just beyond her front gate.

"Yes? May I help you?"

"Maybe you can. I've used this lane several times and have often heard music. Who plays the piano?"

"That would be me," she laughed.

"Your music is delightful and it has added extra entertainment to my afternoon walks. I'm Garrett Grayson, obviously a fan of yours."

"Why I am flattered Mr. Grayson, but I'm afraid no concert today. It is too ghastly hot to stay indoors."

"Yes, the temperatures could well set a record today. Perhaps tomorrow you might be playing again?"

"Yes, maybe tomorrow," she replied just as he turned to leave. "Oh Mr. Grayson, before you go perhaps you would care for a glass of tea with this dreadful heat and all. I have a cold pitcher here on the porch."

"Thank you. That is certainly too tempting to refuse," he said, rearranging a colorful beach towel across his broad shoulders in a more modest attempt to cover his bare chest.

It took only a second for her eyes to scan his firm build with its glistening smooth tan; but she made no verbal acknowledgement of these things as she handed him a glass of the cold, sweet tea. Still her female mind enjoyed what she saw and he was left to guess that the smile on her face was no more than a polite gesture.

They sat on her porch discussing the weather; she lightly pushed herself in the swing and he seemed comfortable in the large, wooden rocker. In time the sun began to set and from their positions they could watch it drop behind the low shrubbery at the end of the lane.

When he stood to leave, cooler air was circulating about the porch and the cold pitcher of tea had long been consumed. Garrett thanked her for her hospitality and promised to stop by the next afternoon for music and more of her tasty refreshments.

She shook his hand, smiled into his bright blue eyes and said a pleasant good-bye. As he stepped from the porch, the scent of his cologne lingered in the air and she inhaled a deep breath, savoring the pleasing aroma. *Was it Armani or Calvin Klein?* She wasn't sure, but she knew that she liked it.

He walked down the lane, turned and waved to her. Waving back, she watched him disappear beyond the bend. It seemed too comfortable to leave the porch so she remained there, silent in thought, thankful for the afternoon, and immensely happy about meeting such a handsome man.

Suddenly, amorous sensations swirled about in her very being!

Her mind filled with the lingering visions of his sexy blue eyes and of his repeated smiles; mischievous ones like that of a little boy and others like alluring invitations – I'm open to your advances. She hadn't thought of them that way, until now, when these sizzling flashes heated up her emotions.

Brandy's arms folded across her breasts and her slender fingers moved back and forth over her shoulders and up and down the base of her throat. A warm flow of blood seeped through her veins. She did not try to stop her own caressing, but simply closed her eyes and allowed these emotional feelings to swell and captivate her desires.

Not once since Brandy had arrived on the island had she paid any attention to a man. She had committed herself to avoiding sexual activities in her state of widowhood. Yet this man, this handsome stranger, was enormously bewitching to her; his close presence had pressed her buttons and she was not quite sure at what moment her innocence ended and her female interest began.

Whatever had occurred earlier on the porch between the two of them, it had caused this stirring that was now racing through her body. This whole stimulating encounter was not planned, certainly not expected. Nature or fate or lady luck seemed to be dealing the cards and Brandy was holding a winning hand.

Though the twilight of early evening was taking over the day, she could not draw herself from the porch. This ordinary, wooden structure had become her den of elation; it was possessively cradling her with profound contentment.

She sat there for the longest, looking down the path to the spot where she had enjoyed the last glimpse of him. And, when darkness and fire flies finally took charge, the euphoria of the mood was still about her within her cozy home.

Cherry flavors of the red wine she drank were like an angel's potion of sugary lightness that lifted her still higher and higher into a rose-colored bubble. Easily, so wonderfully easily, a mental review of Garrett Grayson's stunning good looks stayed with her. His manly voice echoed in her thoughts.

Oh how she wanted to talk about this perfect day! If only Mildred or some friend from the south side were there to hear about this heavenly joy. It would provide her the opportunity to describe all that she had seen, felt, sensed, and savored!

Brandy clicked on the computer for her e-mails, the fastest way to shorten the distance to old friends.

Daisy had sent one with gossip about the beauty shop and the announcement about Mildred's position on the cruise ship. Brandy dashed off a reply:

I was thinking about you and Mildred this very night – friends are dearly missed. I heard about her job, I think it will do wonders for her. I'm so proud that she moved away from that family. Yet, there are times when I am sad that I've moved on, away from you guys. Wish all of you were here to enjoy these islands with me. We would have our fun in the sun and all become streaky blonds. Now wouldn't that be great for your business! Brandy.

Scottie McInbrew had great hopes for the next breeding season. He also relayed the latest details of Jefferson's death which had prompted Mama Eve to give all her inheritance to her church. The devil was at work is what that sweet soul kept telling him. Brandy delayed her reply for another time; no sad news would spoil this evening.

A lengthy message had come from Patrick O'Reilly, who e-mailed her often. This time he was ecstatic that he had finally proposed to the widow Kathleen O'Connor. His mother had approved, he had written, but only on two conditions: Father Murphy would officiate at the wedding mass and the marriage would not take place for another two years.

Poor dear Patrick, Brandy sighed as she recalled the sour look of his controlling mother.

With a true fondness for her sensitive friend, she replied with encouraging words that she suspected he sorely needed. Court your lady with flowers and cards, she tutored him, and the romance should certainly keep the fires burning. Two years is not as long as you have waited for the right one to come along, Brandy typed, closing her lesson on love.

But finally it was the e-mail from Shields that she was most eager to read.

Sheer luck today that I ran into Mildred on the docks. She sends you a big hello. Said her Johnny is just a good friend. Wow, she looks great! Why in Boston did she camouflage a figure like that? We had a beer or two. She's coming aboard with her Johnny. I'm grilling steaks. Wish you could join us. Fondly, Shields

Captain: Wish I could join you at the party. Being near you would be the greatest thing, especially tonight of all nights. I got a compliment this afternoon; a wonderful man named Garrett Grayson said he enjoyed my music. I hate that there is no one here to share that with. Hug Mildred and take some pictures for me. Miss everybody, especially you. No, more than that, I miss you dearly! Kisses to you, Brandy

Boston and all her memories of Shields were still held dearly, and, after reading his e-mail, she cursed their agreement to stay apart during this interlude following Hubert's funeral.

It had been her own persuasion that had forced Shields to go. But, tonight, she could not deny the intensity of womanly desires that burned to the core. She regretted that she had been so firm about needing time.

Tonight, that agreement seemed foolish for she wanted Shields the way she had wanted him before. Physically she longed for his touch, especially now that a stranger had awakened her suppressed passion.

To the brim with wine and overflowing with thoughts of torrid romance, Brandy went back out onto the porch and sat down in the wooden rocker.

She drew her bare feet up under her and gazed upward at the vast array of stars, their points of light brightly twinkling. The smell of the Armani or Calvin Klein cologne still lingered on the rocker's cushion.

She breathed in the special aroma.

Midnight came before she finally went to bed and, even at that, she tossed and turned before settling down. It was in the wee dawn, the time between darkness and light when the rising sun first reveals its glow, that she was drawn to the window by the hooting sounds of a nocturnal owl.

The large-eyed bird, partially hidden from her view, was perched in safe seclusion, high amid branches whose woody forms were slightly visible in the haziness of the hour.

Brandy listened to the soft, feathered creature; his distinctive call a signal for a closure to the night.

In response, nature opened its full symphony with sounds of playful crickets, chirping, and deep-throated frogs, croaking their boisterous song. Beyond this assembly of critters, she could hear the splashing sounds of the sea, cresting onto the shores close to her house.

In the bathroom, she raised the small, frosted panes, allowing the outside sounds to join her there in a soaking tub of creamy bubbles and silky oil beads.

Reclining in the warm bath-water, Brandy allowed herself to feel her own femininity, a private reach for self-fulfillment. It was with emotional movements of physical touching that released in her the moist sensation of a heightened state, a womanly state of profound arousal. Quickly it manifested itself, bringing a blissful conclusion to her private affair.

She hadn't planned these actions. No part of it had been based on any set formula like lessons one, two, and three found in a how-to manual. No, this performance was but a spontaneous exploration. Like a free-spirited joy ride, it had taken her down a secluded road of pleasure.

No one else needed to know.

Without guilt or self-reproach, Brandy went directly to her piano, letting the notes whirl about and dance with the chorus of the morn. If her music brought her continuing satisfaction, it also brought the reward of Garrett Grayson at her front door.

"Hello," he called out through the latched screen. "Hello. I was passing by."

Before rushing to greet him at the door, Brandy, trying to protect the exposure of her nude body beneath the cover of a flimsy cotton robe, hastily looped the pink sash tighter about her waist.

"Good morning! My goodness, you have already been to the beach," she gaily chirped, noticing the sand trapped on the edges of his sandals.

"Yes, I have. And it was absolutely beautiful this morning. The sunrise was outstanding! Did you see it?"

"No, not at the beach, but I took it all in from my window. I could hear the crickets and frogs having a great time."

"I guess I am being utterly rude by stopping by so early. I didn't even give you time to dress," he remarked, taking a closer look at her natural beauty, needing neither lipstick nor makeup.

With the way her 40 double-Ds pressed against the pink robe, he also took stock of her shapely, nude body beneath its delicate covering.

Brandy could literally read his mind by the way he was staring at her with his gorgeous blue eyes. She clutched the top of the robe and bashfully tried to avoid those penetrating eyes.

"Please forgive me, but I was thrilled to hear you playing this morning. Remember, you promised me a concert."

"Oh yes, I do remember," she responded. "It's still early so let's have a cup of coffee. I was just about to put on a fresh pot and we could sit out on the porch. Perhaps those darling creatures will start to sing again."

"I could use some coffee. I didn't take time before I left."

"Good. Pick your spot and I'll get the pot started. I'll take a minute more while I grab some clothes," she slightly cooed as a blush of embarrassment appeared perky pink on her cheeks, a color that matched her fluffy robe.

She smiled as she walked back into the house. He was there, again, and so soon after their first meeting. Her body was still tingling from her bath and, now, his appearance at her door excited her all the more.

When she returned to the porch with two mugs of coffee, she was wearing blue shorts and a white sleeveless blouse; her hair had been quickly pulled back into a ponytail, tied with a blue ribbon.

As she bent down to hand him the coffee, two long, loose strands of blond hair fell across her forehead. Without a word he gently tucked the strands behind her ear.

"Thanks," she uttered, stepping aside and taking her place on the swing.

He took a few sips of the hot coffee. She held her mug between her hands. They sat there in silence just enjoying the comfortable delight of being together.

"This is good - the beautiful sunrise, this relaxing porch. And you," he finally said.

The words floated in the air, soft and gentle, with no rush or pretense, spoken by him with true sincerity.

"Yes, it is nice sitting here," she replied. "You said it right about this being a relaxing porch for the two of us. Darn, that came out a little too strong."

"Let's make this easier for both of us. I think you already know that I am a safe character and a fan of your music. And, I've already said I am Garrett Grayson. Now I'll add that I am a guy about ten pounds overweight and somewhere close to being fifty-six. I divorced a good friend about twenty years ago because we were better at being friends than being married. No children and no pets. I can't stop watching sunsets and sunrises. So you probably guessed that I prefer the simple things in life. Just consider me an average Joe with only a few oddities."

She giggled. Then she quickly brought her hand up to her mouth to cover the girlish giggle that had so instinctively followed his friendly directness.

"Oh no, you are no average Joe and I don't believe there is anything odd about you. Name one and let me decide."

"Alright, here's one. I can't brush my teeth unless the cap is back on the toothpaste."

"No," she laughed in full force without the girlish giggles. "You are making that up!"

"I swear it's true. Call my ex-wife; it literally drove her crazy. Now it's your turn. Go ahead, think deep and try to surprise me."

"Well, oh this is silly. Let's see. My oddity is some dumb ritual that I inherited from my mother. Don't laugh. Whenever there is a terrible storm with loud thunder and flashing lightening, I have to arrange a knife and fork like a cross and put them in a window."

He tried to withhold his amusement but it leaped out into a hardy laugh. His eyes sparkled and the ensuing smile stayed on his face.

"See, I told you so. It is silly and ridiculous."

He curbed his rolling laughter, but a few snickers managed to sneak out before he settled down.

"Have you ever been struck by lightening?" he asked in a more serious tone.

"No. Oh, heaven's no!"

"Then, that ritual works and during the next storm I'll be in your house by that window."

They both burst into hysterics.

More coffee brewed in the kitchen and more pleasantries, peppered with chummy laughter, flowed effortlessly back and forth on that porch.

By mid-morning Brandy had told him about her early days in Boston and how she developed a career at Mac's bar. And then, because Garrett made it so painless, she told him about the shipboard marriage to Hubert and his recent funeral.

Somewhere in the conversation she candidly dropped the name of Shields, though she called him just a good friend who had helped her through some very rough days.

Through all of what she said, he listened with intensity, conveying his understanding of what she must have felt. At no time did he rush his own words when he gave her bits and pieces of his childhood, how it was lonely being an only child, but how great it was getting all the toys at Christmas.

He shared his family stories with a wit that was cute and cheerful. All the while, his moderately flirtatious manner was alluring to her.

The amorous mood of that morning, at least on Brandy's part, was like the perfect setting for a scene right out of a romantic paperback. The jungle air was lustful, the sky tantalizingly blue, the exotic birds singing songs of passion, and the dreamy sounds of the sea so close that the lovers stripped bare and dashed for its swirling waters.

No doubt Garrett Grayson possibly saw no more than a lovely lady sitting on a porch with a clear sky overhead and the balmy breeze of the island brushing past the two of them.

But had he moved from the rocker to be beside Brandy on the swing, she would have jumped into his arms and kissed him like any heroine would have done in such a fictional book with three-hundred and sixty-nine heated pages of sizzling love!

But he failed to follow any written script.

Garrett stayed at a gentleman's distance. He remained on the rocker with his sandaled feet casually propped up on the railing of the porch and she, quite adorable, sat on the swing, her legs bent and her bare feet gracefully tucked beneath her tanned body.

32

Back in Boston on a Friday night, limousine after limousine brought the one thousand dollar, per-plate-elite to the threshold of the fund-raiser that was honoring the legacy of Hubert Franz Berman.

All dolled up, the throngs of paying guests were greeted with a red carpet treatment from crowded curbside to the fully opened, ballroom doors where they passed under rose covered archways, reminiscent of an English countryside.

Inside the noisy and body-filled ballroom, twenty-foot ice carvings, securely anchored in oval ponds of Asian koi, were being admired and photographed from every angle.

Arrangements of petunias, hydrangeas, verbenas, and wispy ferns had been professionally placed in decorative boxes all about the massive room, giving the whole area the fragrant aroma of a greenhouse in full bloom.

Mindy Morningstar, buzzing about like the queen bee, was the Chairperson of the Gala. Her black hair was plastered in place by an expensive spray. A jeweled tiara, perched upon that velvety mane, sparkled brightly, as if on public display upon a royal cushion.

Exercising her full authority, she had commandeered three VIP tables, center aisle and stage-front. Joining her, and just as eager to be seen up front, was her favorite group of eight friends, notably the bubbly socialites who would scratch, claw, and back-stab to be included with the cream of this festive crop.

Seated in the reserved chair next to Mindy's, was David D Trump, her escort for the evening. Since his divorce from Caroline Berman, he had claimed residency at Twin Oaks, Mindy's estate in Kentucky.

At every private party or society bash that she attended, he tagged along, like her shadow. She let him hang about in this useless manner more out of sympathy for his predicament than as a true fondness for his companionship.

Her more serious guests, seated at the two other VIP tables, were the families of Lewis Capalo and Samuel Steinberg, the medical attendant for Mrs. Steinberg, the mayor of Boston and other political dignitaries.

Always creative and eternally mischievous, she had concocted an idea to hire waiters of various nationalities to serve the seven-course dinner of international foods. For the Italian service at her own reserved tables, she had handpicked a young waiter named Salvatore Fiorelli.

He was, without a doubt, a gorgeous stud with penetrating brown eyes and a cocky, egotistical smile that advertised, without meekness --- 'Of course, beautiful one, I am here for you!'

The eight cackling socialites, immediately addicted to his captivating charm, adored every solid ounce of what they saw. Each one called out his name, clamoring for the attention of the dark-haired Roman god. They summoned him back and forth to their plates, far more than was necessary.

Mindy, too, did her own share of flirtatious maneuvers. She stalked about and pounced upon him, brushing her slender legs against his hindquarters as he bent to serve. Without words, she flashed predatory eyes, readily broadcasting her wild intents.

When she slid her telephone number into the pocket of his white jacket, he nodded. Without breaking his stride with a silver tray securely held in his right hand, his left hand moved down and rubbed her rear.

Then with a strut, he was gone, back into the kitchen.

The party roared on! And, with the ruckus, there came a detachment from table to table as the guests leaned in closer, into a touching distance with their nearest reveler.

Suddenly and without warning, Mindy's playful activities came to an abrupt ending. Her psychic vibes invaded her fun and, almost on a trot, she bolted from the laden table and sought refuge in a deserted hallway that led to the backstage area.

There, alone and undisturbed, she zeroed in on the very source that was scrambling into her receptor.

Using her cell phone, Mindy pressed the contact buttons for Seahaven. "Brandy, you are missing one hell of a party," she said. "Our little group thinks that you need a touch of glamour and some R and R."

"You are right about the glamour. I spend my days in flip-flops. But I'm really too involved right now to get back into Boston."

"Brandy, this is more than a friendly call. I had this engaging impulse to speak with you. Right now, there is a powerful, magnetic attraction that is elevating my supernatural powers. Remember that I get mental connections to another person and, most often, I know when that person is speaking the truth or is speaking with denial."

"Well, right you are then; what I just told you was not the truth. I was sure that Caroline and Cynthia would represent the Berman family and I would be an unwanted distraction. Besides, I never received an official invitation and I bet that they were responsible. Honestly, Mindy, I really had no desire, what-so-ever, to be at the Gala."

"I sensed as much when you answered the phone. Your wellbeing is still in jeopardy, in part because of that family. Those two, selfish daughters are here and will walk across the stage, accepting the plaque honoring their father. They are such DRAMA QUEENS!"

"They may need that public fanfare to exhibit their own status. But, as you well know, my breeding would have soiled that fanfare. Having me near them is like having mud on the tires of their squeaky, clean limos."

"At some point in the future, they will suffer the consequences of such prejudice behavior. The paths they have forged will close in on them."

"I seek no revenge with them. Hubert was generous to me and now I have this new life that is comfortable. Actually, I'm content."

"Are you sure of that? Your vibrational substance is erratic and I am not getting a reading of contentment. I fear that you are deeply suppressing something. Open up and share your feelings with me?"

"No, Mindy, no, there is nothing to share with you or to add to any of your revelations."

"Well then, how about making some arrangements for a vacation? Join us later in Kentucky. The cutest waiter at the party tonight, an import named Salvatore Fiorelli, will be at my farm in two weeks to teach the girls his romantic, Italian language."

"Mindy, you certainly have a talent for redirecting conversations. But again, I am telling you the truth; I'm not ready to be around a group of people or to sample new experiences in any language."

"It is not good to spend so much time alone."

"At this point in time, I am leading an idyllic life and I am not alone. I have a few acquaintances here that I regularly see, one on one. And, I also have my music and my adorable house."

"Acquaintances, you say. That word just sparked an image, a rather cloudy image of a man."

"Okay, yes I do have a new friend. He's a decent sort of guy, outgoing and fun to be with. I'm not trying to be rude about this, but some things are very personal and just not open to public review."

"Well, my dear, it is also the truth that you would find Salvatore quite interesting, both to look at and to listen to, whether in privacy or outdoors. He is dashing, strikingly tall, with an extremely sexy smile and the most enchanting eyes. Oh, those gorgeous eyes! Believe me, if there ever was a diversion from troubles, an intriguing man like Salvatore would fit the bill."

"You do put it bluntly. But right now I have no desire for a handsome waiter," Brandy responded, knowing that she already had her mind on Shields and often, as of late, too much on Garrett Grayson.

"Sure, sweetie," the soothsayer responded, "I must offer you this: **Pose the question correctly and you will receive the answer for whatever secret is now being shielded.** So, my friend, prepare for that forthcoming truth. Heed what I say and stay in touch."

The phone call was over and Brandy was left guessing. Had Mindy, with all her telepathic abilities, uncovered the existence of the Society? Did her powers really receive vibrations, exposing future plans and wishful dreams, especially those of Shields and Garrett?

Not sure if any of these unexplained powers really did exist, she made a firm resolution to avoid further exposure to the magic. Remaining out of circulation and tight-lipped would be her best defenses against the oddities of Mindy's world.

Ox Moran was positioned in a strategic location on a low elevated ramp near the hallway where Mindy had made the phone call. Innocently, he overheard most of her comments. Because they made no sense to him, he dismissed it as useless jabbering, bordering on the premise of a nutty lady full of mumbo-jumbo.

He did not know that she was the chairperson in charge, the high priestess, the main nutcracker, and the supernatural, clairvoyant female deeply feared by many.

He had been hired for the evening by the law firm of Steinberg and Leftwich with the simple assignment to report any contact between David D Trump and the former Mrs. Trump, who was seated at a table for six on the far side of the room. Neither of the parties under observation had made any moves thus far, polite or otherwise, to be nearer to each other. Or, for that matter, neither had even acknowledged the existence of the other, by frown or by grin.

His repeated yawning proved how boring the whole stake-out had become and the evening was not even half over.

Inside the ill-fitting black, rental shoes, his corn-crusted feet felt like concrete. And, he was near the point of strangulation from the starched shirt collar and bow tie of his rented tuxedo. Any reasonable flow of blood to his brain had been tightly constricted and to say that he was in misery, was describing it lightly.

Moran wondered at painful lengths how these black-clad men of money could possibly sit around all night, in such torture, and live through it. But they did; and he watched them talk, eat, and drink.

And drink! And drink!

But pain-relieving drinking was not on his agenda, nor could it be; his very attendance at this society bash was for official business only. And, in all the years of being a detective, he had proven over and over how important a clear head meant when his job had him tailing unsavory and guilty human beings.

Among the festive merrymakers, he recognized a few former targets he had trailed and photographed. On those occasions, quick snaps with his trusty zoom had captured some of them in compromising positions and the others, greedily taking kickbacks or bribes. Their prominent families probably had tons in a slush fund to silence the publicity of their misdeeds.

Yet, Moran never lost any sleep over how those guilty targets ended up. He always remained completely detached from his professional snooping. He comforted himself with the reward of the fee, the feel-good padding in his wallet.

Bored with the current stakeout, he changed locations and circulated more freely about the room. Drawing closer to the VIP tables, he overheard the name Brandy Berman battered about. That name he recognized from the case he had investigated for a Miss Borden, a jealous secretary.

But the more interesting bits of fumbling words came when the arrogant David D described his ex-wife – quote: **'a rich bitch that wasn't as heart-warming as the ten million he had inherited just to leave the Artic iceberg.'**

Alert! Alert!

Moran saw green, bright, crispy GREEN, in the shape of neon dollar signs. "Ten million bucks! Hot damn! My palms are itching and I'm going to track this strutting roaster to the coop."

The clerk at Steinberg and Leftwich had not told him that the two parties were up to their necks with a big bundle of inheritance money. In fact, he was led to believe that it was only a love triangle that had resulted in a quickie divorce.

What a stroke of luck that he had picked up this new data. Feeding it into his calculating mind, his mental gears hit GO and he began arranging the pieces of what had become a more, fascinating puzzle.

The trail of the dough might lead him to a jackpot, just the extra spice for this otherwise hum-drum case. A jackpot was a hell of a lot more interesting than trying to catch two people out on a dance floor, lustfully fondling private places.

He circled the table, moved away towards the bar, and then crossed over to the other side of the room.

He hoped that anyone who had been watching his movements would probably surmise that he was a stag invitee, seeking out a loose lady for the night. If they only knew that on this night of truths, his detective wheels were speedily turning, in spite of his cramped toes and stinging blisters.

"Detective work can be dog-eared drudgery," Moran whispered to himself on the way to the restroom. "But it is damn rewarding when you sniff out things that no one ever expects you to be smart enough to uncover!"

He whistled lowly. He whistled the fairy-tale tune of the seven dwarfs: High-Ho, High-Ho, it's off to work I go.

33

The Brandywine, docked in the port of Martinique, checked out to the mechanic's highest approval rating as he completed the full maintenance schedule for the 48-footer. He had attentively run the boat hard and fast on a final shake-down, as his boss required on all service contracts. Then, very precise with the Maintenance Summary Report, he wrote that the ride was solid with absolutely no indications of mechanical malfunctions.

However, if she had been his own boat, a boat he certainly could never afford, he would have handled her with kid gloves. Sapphire Diamond would be her name; a real jewel, she was!

Shields, reclaiming his sturdy boat, performed his own tests by taking the Brandywine out past the harbor where he did practice maneuvers, using the recently installed Raymarine Navigation Network. After his near-fatal adventure with the turbulent hurricane, he wanted more current technology on the panel and this particular integrated system had been repeatedly advertised as top-notch and state-of-the-art.

Completely satisfied with the day's drills and feeling especially competent with the new hardware on board, he took her back in. The next day would be equally as busy, stockpiling the galley and filling the diesel tanks in preparations for the first leg of a planned journey.

The idea for the boat trip had actually come from Mildred who had expressed an interest in such a voyage. Even on her first visit to the Brandywine, she had been quite taken with the boat and, in the days that followed, she had rambled on and on about quitting her job and doing the islands with Shields as her guide.

He was flattered by her compliments and overly enthralled with her love of his boat and, when their plans began to take life, he cheerfully agreed to set sail for a fun-filled excursion.

Charting a course out of Martinique, he drew a northerly line for a scenic run through the various islands that Mildred asked to see. However, such a trek would be extremely long and time consuming, given the nautical distance from the Lesser Antilles to St. Croix, hugging the coast lines of Hispaniola and Jamaica, ultimately reaching the Caymans.

Though the layers of flattery from Mildred pumped his enthusiasm, her sweetness completely clouded his better judgment. Indeed, the whole experience would be more of a dangerous odyssey.

Mildred knew absolutely nothing of nautical miles and detailed charts, all that being quite boring to her. She much preferred the fantasy of shell collecting and sunbathing. And, how exciting it would be when they surprised Brandy and showed up on her sandy doorstep, unannounced!

But Shields, the bigger worrier of the two, was uncomfortable with that plan; so, on his own, he e-mailed Brandy that he was leaving port and would eventually anchor in the Caymans, not providing a time frame or the fact that Mildred was aboard, leaving that item as the big surprise.

Prepped to go, he eased the boat out through the pass while Mildred leisurely reclined on the sun pad, working on her tan. They traveled in their respected positions for most of the day; until, just safely before the intruding darkness, Shields maneuvered the Brandywine to harbor in the first of the smaller ports he had originally charted.

In a quaint, hut-styled restaurant within walking distance of the docks, they shared a native treat of crabs and fresh fish, along with their best remembrances of Brandy. It wasn't hard to pass the time since they both had such pleasant Brandy-stories to share. But too much of the local rum, mixed with the late hour and their day-long exposure on the water, soon prompted a sleepy weariness.

Being the gentleman that he was, Shields yielded the main cabin to Mildred, which of course she fully expected. He would sleep just outside her door on a bunk that miraculously appeared when the table was removed from its latched position in the galley. He didn't require the comforts of pampering; in the past, he had slept all over the Brandywine and one spot was just as good as the next, be it padded bunk or hard deck.

As a seasoned sailor, he was easily lulled with the slow, gentle pitch of the moored Brandywine and, if Mildred was having difficulties adjusting to this marine movement, that would be their first problem to discuss the next morning.

But he heard no restless sounds drifting from her cabin. Things remained relatively quiet aboard his boat, except, of course, for the ZZZ's of his own snoring.

After their first week of island hopping and shell collecting, Shields went ashore to a small, port store where he purchased galley supplies, the likes of leafy vegetables and fruits, nuts, bottled water, coffee and an assortment of other items for refrigeration, namely fresh fish for a special mid-day meal.

Mildred stayed on board to shower and dress for the day. Oiled and glistening, she stepped into her skimpy, leopard-print bikini and returned topside to her favorite spot on the sun pad.

While in the open-air store Shields, still not comfortable about surprising Brandy with Mildred's visit, faced the hard decision of what to do about it. Happening upon the readiness of the harbormaster's computer soon solved his dilemma and made it quite easy for a solution.

He promptly sent an e-mail to the beach house, announcing the truth about the excursion.

Dear Brandy - the Brandywine is underway to the Caymans. She moves through the water so easily that I have little to do. Oh, did I mention in my earlier e-mail that Mildred is traveling with me? Well, anyway, she was very insistent that we take this trip together because she really wanted to surprise you. However, I thought it best to tell you ahead of time. Not sure about the arrival. The weather might slow us down and we are making a lot of port stops. Mildred wants to explore every island along the way. She is taking photographs of everything, including the galley sink. That girl can really get bouncy! Are you thrilled about our visit? I am excited, even though I know it will take days and days.   Shields

When he returned to the boat he never told Mildred about the e-mail, all the while reassuring himself that it had been the best thing to do. He reasoned that Brandy would be worried if he was alone at sea. He quite rightly remembered that she had said the same when he had told her about the hurricane.

This clean slate of conscience easily opened up Shields' acceptance about being with his younger, traveling companion. She was, in his opinion, just a carefree spirit with no desires for commitments.

From the very beginning, he had accepted her adventurous style as a part of her new personality. Yet this boundless, energy drive had not yet spread towards Shields, changing his reserved behavior.

Once they left harbor and were back on the vast emptiness of the open waters, Mildred gave up her tanning and stood directly behind Shields on the bridge, watching him at the navigation table, complimenting him over and over about his nautical skills.

He, flattered to the hilt, explained every gadget and every dial; his manly ego absorbing each and every puff of her praises.

The oily sheen of her sunscreen and the very nearness of her half-clad body provided more temptations than one man should have to fight off.

Though he tried!

Trying first in Brandy's memory and, later, he tried again as a reasonable man, respectful that he was her senior.

She was a gorgeous, deep-tanned Barbie doll and her female scent encased him, driving his resistance beyond its limits. His mind dangerously wandered from the operating controls. The thick hair on his arms and groin were like electric jolts, charging him with desire.

When her first kiss gently brushed the back of his neck, he lost the last bit of bodily control. All other commitments were tossed aside, expelled from thought, definitely not needed at the moment.

Passions soared!

Breasts perked up!

Muscles flexed!

Shields instinctively shifted into idle gear. He turned and, with a lustful appetite, kissed her wet, receptive lips. With his searching, roaming fingers, he easily released the bit-of nothing bikini top. One move more and the tiny bottom of her leopard-print lay in a wee puddle at their bare feet.

Their torrid sex affair began right on the open, exposed deck of the Brandywine. It continued again and again in the master cabin and in the galley. Shields, like a man driven from deprivation, could not get enough of the wild tiger he held in his arms.

The sounds coming from her throat were low and murmuring with each elevation of her own passions; completely uninhibited, she repeatedly opened her consent and deliciously, deliciously drew him in!

All their travel plans lay dormant now, as the Brandywine held anchor in a tiny, tranquil cove. It was if they had found their own private paradise. They shed their clothing of civilized living and were like the unembarrassed patrons of a nudist colony.

With probing hands, they groped their way through the newness of their fantastic, exploratory sex.

Mildred was a sly, alluring, and saucy woman leading Shields into all directions, letting him think that this physical escapade was of his own doing. She was cagey enough not to mention Brandy's name, keeping Shields' attention directed towards their current, pleasurable frolicking.

Whether she had planned to seduce him before they left on their journey was a question never asked and one he never even considered. He had become a changed man, completely possessed under her feminine, sexy spell.

"I love you," she sighed as they lay in a balmy embrace; the sun just breaking through a morning mist.

"You are something else," he replied, stroking her smooth, tanned shoulders.

He meant what he had said. Yet, he fumbled for a better combination of nouns and adjectives to describe how he felt; unadulterated love not being the exact description he was ready to select.

"I'm something else, like what?" She lured him on, prodding all his attention towards her. "Tell me, excite me!"

"A woman-child is what you are. Full of energy and playful games, you literally melt my concentration. It's like I am on a stimulating drug, wanting more and more of you."

"WHEW! Oh, my captain, those are definitely **stimulating** words and I like how they make me feel! Say more; melt away my resistance."

"What resistance?" He smiled at her with a wink. "You are too free to have resistance. I see you like a playful kitten, pouncing on a ball of yarn or snuggling up close to stay warm."

"A kitten; no, that's not powerful enough. I'm more inclined to claw like a jungle tiger," she sensuously added, dragging her Passion Plum coated nails along the center of his bare back.

His body shivered and he stirred as if to leave the bed. She pulled at his arm.

"Five minutes, give me five more minutes," she teasingly pleaded, "I need to sharpen these painted claws. G R O W L!!"

The rush of her breath crossed his ear in sugary, floating waves. Her manicured toes slid up and down his leg; from his ankle to the top of his calf, the rhythm of her strokes was steady, inviting. Her slender fingers traced the wiry hair above the elastic band of his white, cotton briefs.

Expertly, without disturbing her purpose, she lifted the Fruit-of-the-Loom band and slid her hand to her point of interest, his cornucopia of abundant pleasure.

The tiger in her had captured her morning prey.

She growled again and again!

Their five minutes extended into an hour-long romp. Breakfast was forgotten, including the first mug of coffee or sugar-free tea.

As the many days passed, Shields gave up shaving and grew a manly beard. This rugged bush of facial hair was neatly shaped and Mildred could not pass him without reaching out and touching his sun-streaked face, reaffirming her approval of his new look.

To change his appearance all the more, she trimmed his pepper-gray mane into a wind-swept style that replaced his outdated, barber cut.

For convenience, she sometimes kept her own hair pulled up in a tight ponytail; but when she released the rubber band, letting the silky strands fall loosely on youthful shoulders, she was ravishingly gorgeous!

Shields would often stand adoringly to the side, entranced in awe over her natural and native-toned beauty! With such a distraction, work was not on his calendar anymore; each day brought an exciting newness and he voluntarily went along with whatever came their way.

On an uncharted island, with few inhabitants, Mildred befriended a shy, stray cat that she rescued from a cluster of broken sticks and cracked sea shells.

"It will be our mascot," she coaxed Shields when she went aboard with the shivering, half-starved, and tightly-clinging feline.

The helpless, little thing was somewhat of a dingy brown to a dusty, shade of ugly mushroom. But somehow, be it the intervention of a miracle or a good bar of soap, the cat emerged from the pail with a healthy coat, slick and black.

To honor the occasion of their new found friend and to officially proclaim her as the new inspiration to continue their voyage, Mildred insisted that the boat required a name change. THE VENUS.

Yes, THE VENUS – the mythological, Roman goddess of love – yes, that was the very name she wanted.

And what Mildred wanted, beautiful Mildred got!

When they were at sea again, Shields became uneasy about a persistent noise, coming from one of the engines. Though he had some mechanical skills, he realized that the noise was beyond his best efforts and that a maintenance marina would be better equipped for the situation.

To their disadvantage, their previous routes had been a zigzag pattern through small Caribbean islands. He explained this to Mildred, telling her that by backtracking directly to a qualified port they would save time and be able to correct the mechanical problem in its earliest stages.

She pouted about turning back, not fully understanding the potential danger of a malfunctioning engine. Though he tried to be firm with her, she stubbornly refused to accept any scenario of being stranded at sea.

"There's more to life than deserted islands. We have to tend to business once in awhile," he insisted.

"Don't be so serious and old," she puffed!

Yet, despite her bitchy complaining, Shields wisely headed back to the working harbor of Pointe-a-Pitre on the island of Guadelopue, in the French West Indies. They had previously purchased fuel at the marina and he felt confident that it was the place to be.

Without romantic fanfare, they set up daily housekeeping on the boat, assuming a more normal existence while waiting on the arrival of a replacement part for a faulty, engine valve.

Shields stayed busy with wash up and paint up chores; spending a great deal of his time preparing the stern for the boat's new name THE VENUS, which of course Mildred repeatedly insisted that it must be painted in bold, red letters.

Every day, without acknowledging his meticulous efforts at the precise spacing of the letters, she sat apart on the deck, tanning to deeper tones, in the over-head heat of the morning sun.

In the afternoons, she strolled among the crowded boutiques, only to return empty-handed and dissatisfied. Sulking at the prospect of little else to do, she would go to the stateroom for what she dictated to be an undisturbed nap until dinner was served.

There was no pleasure or excitement for her in this crowded, touristy town. And, night after night, she would continuously grumble that her cravings were left unfulfilled. They should move on, she kept insisting.

The final straw came when Mildred had tolerated all the boredom that she could absorb. With little compassion for Shields' feelings, she spent her last few minutes writing a Dear John note.

Though her actual departure from THE VENUS was indeed abrupt, she had purposely picked the timing of it to coincide with one of his trips to the paint store.

In his absence that day, she tacked her note just above the cabin door. It was not sympathetic or apologetic, merely two brief sentences, on target and hand-written on the back of a diesel ticket from the marina.

I'M GONE, WON'T BE BACK.
FEED THAT DARN CAT.

The once-adored mascot, deliberately left behind, prowled the empty deck, searching endlessly for her mistress. But to no avail. Even the cat food that Shields patiently put in her personalized bowl, offered no reprieve; the brooding cat would not eat.

Shields, too, never suspecting such a ghastly departure, was totally shattered and listless, with no wind left in his sails. He stopped the painting and stopped caring about the boat.

In his lustful pursuit of Mildred, he had always given in to her demanding whims. But this dreadful rejection was not just another of her foolish impulses.

It was for real.

She hadn't climbed back on board with her pouting smile and her purring voice, the way that he hoped she might. And, with the many passing days, it appeared that such a longing wish was not to be granted.

When he finally accepted the hard, cold certainty that she had dumped him, the manly self-assuredness that he had once possessed, vanished into thin air.

What was left of him was but a hollow shell of a man with no recognizable traits of his old self. At first, he was trapped in a zone of nothingness; numb to the core and defeated.

Mood swings soon started, with hate and pity fighting at odds, and the ugly side of revenge trampling harshly across understanding. Dreadful doubt bombarded him with questions, so many questions; the answers always elusive or down-right weak.

How stupid can one man profess to be? Stupid enough to begin a long sea voyage from Martinique to the Caymans, a dangerous undertaking in a boat of 48-feet and, certainly, even more dangerous with a female temptress aboard.

In fury and in sickening disgust, he ripped apart the charted maps and threw their remains into the trash. He splashed the paint against the stern of the boat and the words, THE VENUS, disappeared beneath the running red.

He shouldn't blame the boat and he knew that. Yet, he couldn't separate Mildred's presence from the boat. And, why couldn't he sleep in her absence? Sleeping was nothing more than a functional activity and the boat had always been an adequate place of rest.

"She is gone from this stateroom. Man, be done with it," he would loudly preach and the cat would meow from her place at the cabin door.

There was more beneath the surface of his anguish than these things. There was a big knot, a tormenting ache, down deep in his masculine gut. And, when it finally erupted, it lay before him, nakedly exposed as a hideous truth he agonized over.

An oath to Brandy had been shattered!

With deceit, he had piled up a heavy heap of unfaithfulness and, with that, the prospects of their future together were doomed.

Painfully, he called to mind his promising words to wait for her, allowing her ample time to respond to his faithful pledge of deep love. He would wait, he remembered saying, without pressure or hesitation.

Maybe he could learn to live with his disgust over Mildred, dumping him like she did. And, maybe, he could lightly brush off the sex, boasting that he was only normal, doing what comes natural to a guy.

But breaking his personal vow to Brandy was no simple matter. This breach of trust, acknowledged as a broken trait of honor, was too important and too sensitive to leave it unattended.

Without honor, just how worthy was a man to his lady?

Shields spent many hours, brooding over his past actions, replaying them, not for the memories, but for some clarity of why he had been so weak, so incapable of avoiding the pit falls that separated him from Brandy.

At other restless times, he dropped all thoughts of her and filled his glass to the brim with local rum. But even those bottomless drinks never totally coated the sting.

As to his appearance, it boarded on that of a vinegary vagrant, reeking with the lack of daily bathing. Gone, too, was the once flattering hair, the wind-swept and youthful style that Mildred had created. That fashionable flair was distorted now with greasy and matted ends.

A bumpy rash had pranced across his throat just above his Adam's apple, the area where his wiry growth of beard was left unattended. Added to that disarray was his noticeable weight loss and blood-shot eyes.

He was, by all measures, a repulsive mess!

Absolutely nothing about him reflected the spit-polished shoes and starched shirts that had once been his secure world.

Ultimately, it was the cat's litter box that ended up being his salvation. For as time dragged by, the cat's needs could no longer be denied.

She had stopped her forlorn meowing, curling up by him during his brooding spells. She offered him warmth and comfort and in return, he provided food and, most importantly, fresh boxes of kitty-litter.

Forced to the store for the purchase of these boxes, he began to stay out for a beer or two, which then led him to the final soul-searching moment. In a local, internet bar, his right hand tightly gripped a long neck beer and, the other, idly rested on the black keys of a rent-by-the-minute computer.

With a long, purposeful sip of the cold brew, he was fortified to face whatever consequences lay ahead with Brandy.

Words flowed towards her as he keyed his e-mail plea for her acceptance of his failures. Within the first few sentences, he described, in sincere frankness, every painful emotion of the total disgust that he felt about himself.

He confessed that he had lied. That he had failed to honorably respect her feelings. And, most importantly, that he had violated the sincerity of their promises to each other.

Yet, with all that he had typed, he could not find a kindhearted way to describe for her what had passionately transpired with Mildred. That dilemma of what to say and how to say it wore heavily on him; it required three more beers and another hour.

Finally, he revealed that there had been some flirtations with Mildred, perhaps too many. Yet, in this weak confession, he carefully avoided all the sexual details of their reckless episode, there being no further need to hurt Brandy with lurid details.

Enough said on the matter!

He clicked and sent his three paragraphs.

34

It should have been fun, riding a Vespa down an open, tropical roadway; but Brandy was in no mood for fun, her heart broken over Shields' long e-mail. Without regard for the safe operation of the motor scooter or any acknowledgment of the speed limit, she was driving way too reckless and entirely too fast, her mind wildly trying to erase the unforgivable news that she had received.

The wind whipped harshly across her bare arms; the grating repetition of the small engine whirled in her ears, droning on and on like a drill in the hands of a dentist. The headache that developed pumped angry blood to her temples, making her blurry eyed and crazy!

It was her obligation to the Society's mailbox that had put her on the road this day, of all days. Provoked, outraged, steam shooting from her ears – damn, was she to be chained forever to the deep secrets?

What a scene she made as she drove bolder and faster!

Small insects pelted against the plastic visor on her helmet; the bloody smudges hardly fazed her. Her knuckles were icy white and polar cold, latched, as they were, to the handlebars in a death-grip.

Rows upon rows of trees narrowed into her space and, unless the trees had ears, the sounds of her frustrating screams went unnoticed.

"How could he? How could he?" She repeatedly shouted into the airy emptiness of the wind!

For the longest time, she dwelled on the idea of leaving the Caymans and returning to her old job at Mac's bar. A basement lifestyle would have to do, if it would replace the loss of Shields and put everything back to the way it had been between the two of them.

Double-damn! She had lost him and even Mac's Bar couldn't cement the broken pieces.

She didn't care about anything. She just didn't care!

In the background she heard the wail of a siren and then shockingly realized that the officer in the patrol car was pulling in behind her, signaling for her to pull over. Obediently she cut off the engine at the side of the road; removing the hard helmet, she quickly straightened the black wig.

"I clocked you going over the speed limit. I need your identification, please."

The officer didn't smile and with a sternly serious frown, he walked to the rear of the burgundy Vespa and jotted down the tag number.

With heated palms she handed him the counterfeit driver's license and passport. **JANE BANKS**. Would that name pass his professional inspection?

"I'm sorry officer; I guess I was having too much fun with this cute, little scooter. I really didn't realize that it could go fast," she said with a feminine flutter of her eyelashes.

"Jane Banks. Is that correct? Off the cruise ship, are you?"

"My, officer, aren't you clever!" Again, her eyelashes fluttered.

"Let's see the receipt for this rental," he snapped and she dutifully reacted, reaching back into her tote bag, pulling out the legitimate, yellow copy.

She waited sheepishly, watching him compare the information on the properly dated and stamped receipt to that of her fraudulent license and passport. His dark sunglasses rested squarely over his eyes, shielding the movement of his dissecting eyeballs as he read over the documents.

She was stumped as to what this immense frame of a man might decide to do.

With the papers in his total control, Brandy tried to calm her rapid breathing, hoping he would not ask for a reason why she was on this particular road, alone without other tourists.

"Jane Banks, hmm." he slowed, pushing the suspense deeper into Brandy's nerves. Then with the three documents still clutched in his official hands, he asked the very question she had feared.

"And just where were you headed?"

"I was just enjoying the scenery and seeing more of the island."

"I hope you have a map, Ms. Banks," the officer stated. "The clerk in George Town should have told you that this type rental is a legalized form of transportation. It can be very dangerous if you don't know how to properly operate it. I'm tempted to write a citation and get you before a judge, but I'm going to warn you this time. Keep your speed down to the posted levels. If I have to stop you again, there will be trouble."

"Yes sir."

"And, Ms Banks, I was glad to see you wearing that helmet. At least it showed that you have some regard for safety. We want every one of our tourists to leave in one piece."

He did a quick, military salute, handing back the yellow receipt, along with the fake driver's license and passport. She slowly took them into her clammy hands and smiled one last time. The uniformed officer, with his holstered gun and shiny badge, had definitely scared the bitter wits out of her.

She watched him pull away before she heaved a fretful sigh, the very type so often expelled when all words falter in a woman's attempt to regain composure. Cautiously looking up and down the empty roadway, she eased onward; the speedometer becoming her focal point as she resumed her trip to the post office.

Once inside the rural building, staying vigilant was a must, so afraid was she that the officer might have followed her. Deliberately avoiding any contact with other customers, Brandy reached into the private box, took one last look around, and then grabbed a single post card, resting in the back of the otherwise empty container.

Get the hell out of Dodge, she thought as she stuffed the card into her tote bag, delaying until later the dreaded reading of Steinberg's newest message.

On her return into George Town, she aborted what would have been her first attempt to withdraw money from the Society's disbursement fund, by using the ATM at the local tobacco store. With the officer so freshly in her mind, any kind of secret business was out of the question.

She also chose not to mail money she had previously wrapped in a securely, tapped box. Father Murphy, at St. Matthew's Catholic Church in south Boston, would not have the excitement over an anonymous donation that his church sorely needed. Even though it was a meager amount of cash from her own money, Brandy was afraid to drop the small, brown box into an out-going slot.

All acts of charity would have to take a sabbatical until another, braver day when luck was visiting more in her favor.

After returning the Vespa, Brandy eased out the side door of the rental office, using a back alley that led to a public restroom. There she removed the black wig and changed into different clothing, handily available in her tote bag. She fluffed her blond hair, quickly changed her lip color to red, and straightened her 40-double D straps before heading out.

The sidewalks along the main road were teeming with a ship-load of busy tourists. Brandy wasted no time, weaving her way through their turtle speed. She was in a hurry to get home, back to the safety of Seahaven.

Though the beach house was peacefully waiting for her, Brandy was far from being peaceful herself. The daylong episodes had been frustrating, irritating, and scary.

The black wig had been hot and uncomfortable. And, dressed up in clothes she would not normally wear and playing the part of some fictitious Jane Banks, was an acting role that Brandy did not like, did not want, nor did she look forward to replaying the performance again.

She fixed herself a stiff drink, trying with little result to throw-off the bad experiences of the day, first the news from Shields and then the officer. And, as terrible as all that made her feel, she still had Steinberg's postcard in her bag. It took another sip before she could drag it out.

> **Hi, friend. Dead wrong about the beautiful meter maid, she was an iceberg. Doctor No Pills convinced me not to see her again. Wait, don't laugh, she had a left hook and I have a busted nose that hurts like hell. Accident, a bad accident is my story and I'm**

**sticking to it. YOU, however, would have guessed the truth anyway. Me, I was wrong to pick up that girl. Only the two of us can understand or even stand each other. Problems, as you always preach, seem to follow me around. Stay put, see you soon.
Sammy**

If there had been any way she could have smiled at the humor in Steinberg's fictitious story, that smile might have helped her. But his message was no joke; it was serious, very serious, with deadly overtones that she hadn't expected.

She used a pencil to circle the first words of every sentence and, regardless of how many times she reread the words there was still no mistake about them. A very grim message was there.

Problems, the noun that Steinberg had chosen to write, never came close to describing what Brandy perceived to be a major **catastrophe**. It was, indeed, what Steinberg had not said in his message that scared the holy crap out of her!

Sitting there, turning the postcard over and over in her hands, she imaged all kinds of potential implications. But one was magnified as the most important. Her obligations to the money, she perceived, would surely increase with only two members left in the Society.

An uncontrollable laughter surprisingly erupted, a nervous, lengthy laughter, followed by a wet infusion of crying that saturated her eyes. The drink shook in her trembling hands until she poured the remaining ounces of the stiff brew down the drain.

She blew her nose, dried the tears and went outside to her beloved porch. But sadness didn't belong there. It was out of place with the tranquility that always surrounded her spot.

Her sadness, however, eventually disappeared as the fragrance of the night, like a cleansing bath, washed it away. And that was a good start.

By the next morning, Brandy had convinced herself to get out of the house and to do things that would keep her mind occupied. She headed down to the local community center where, on three previous occasions, she had played the piano for the senior citizens who came each day for morning bingo, a free lunch, and an afternoon of activities.

That evening, she went to an art opening in George Town. The advertisement had been tempting with the offer of chamber music, a wine tasting, and the attendance of the famous oriental artist Aoe Missu, whose work she had seen in local galleries.

While admiring his famous Showering Mist, Brandy caught a glimpse of Garrett Grayson, standing by the doorway on the opposite side of the room. She sidestepped more to her left in hopes that he might see her; but he made no indication by hand or eye that he was aware of her presence.

As the steady flow of people moved from canvas to canvas, often corralling her in, she persisted as she worked her way to an open spot near a center beam. Yet, Garrett still did not look her way.

Suddenly, a young woman walked up and casually slipped her arm about his shoulder. From Brandy's spying vantage, such behavior surely meant that this woman knew Garrett and knew him well.

He leaned in as if the woman was whispering something to him. On the very heels of his actions, a blazing spurt of deep-green jealousy flared in Brandy. Full-blast, it hit her hard!

She conjured up all kinds of intimate conversations that the two of them could be sharing. Her jealousy drove her to hide behind the round beam while she plotted her next move.

Unfortunately, when she peeked for a second look, the elusive couple was gone. She twisted and turned, but even with the clearest of views they were not to be seen.

Suspicions ran rampant through Brandy's mind! He had not been around for a few days, nor had he called her. Now, she had caught him with another woman. It was too much! Garrett would have some explaining to do and she was hoping that it would be soon.

For the next few afternoons, an hour or so before sunsets, Brandy played her music in case he would happen by. She even rearranged a wall mirror so that she could watch the front gate from her piano stool. But, her wayward Garrett never came along the lane.

One very chilly morning, when the temperatures dropped to a record low for the islands, Brandy put on her only warm-up and walked to the beach for what the late news had promised to be a spectacular sunrise.

She hadn't expected to find such a large gathering already milling about at the beach. But others, like her, had come to see the show. Wanting to be alone, she stood off to the side, preferring to watch the sunrise in a silent, reflective mood.

The sand felt unusually crunchy under Brandy's bare feet on this strangely, dark morning. Yet, as the sun peeked out, just above the eastern horizon, the lively, intense sight was so glorious that everything around and under foot was left unnoticed.

Luminous and full of a dazzling display of swirling colors, the predicted spectacle burst forth, God-sent and people-admired!

Those along the shore stood spell-bound; then, as if rehearsed for the proper timing, they whistled, shouted, and applauded this solar reward, rising from afar.

With all eyes to the sky, no one was watching the actions of the sea as a solitary figure, clad in a black, synthetic wetsuit, swam in through the rolling waves. He stood upright in shallow waters, gradually wadding further inward, onto the sugary shore.

The salty sea water dripped from his skintight wetsuit and, as he began to remove the hood covering his head, Brandy immediately stopped her clapping. Even before she could clearly see his face, she knew, instinctively, that it was her handsome Garrett Grayson.

She wanted to run towards him, apologize for her jealousy and admit that she had no hold on him. Yet, she did not move.

No, it was his place to do some explaining. There was an accounting to be given about why he had been avoiding their sunsets together and why he had ignored her at the art show. And, more importantly, she wanted an explanation about the woman he was with.

"Hi," he said in a friendly voice as he walked up beside her. "I'm really glad to see you again. It's been awhile."

"That's true."

"I just had to get out here and swim with the sea life in these unusual conditions. The weatherman was right on target with his prediction."

"Being at home alone, I had plenty of time to watch TV."

"Regrettably, I haven't been able to call you because I've been extremely busy. I was planning on calling you later. I needed to tell you that this is my last day here. I leave on a flight tonight."

"Oh?" She managed to get out, absolutely dumbfounded that he had just made a big announcement about his departure. "I'm really sorry to hear that. I had thought that I might get to watch more sunsets with you."

"I knew you expected that. And, about the other night, I did notice you at the gallery. The thing is, I was on assignment and I had to move on. I just couldn't stop to talk," he confessed.

"She was a beautiful woman. Do you label all your dates as had-to-do assignments?"

"The woman was no date; she's my partner. I have literally been working almost 24 hours a day. It's difficult to explain my situation."

"Yet, you said earlier that you are leaving the Caymans?"

"That's true. It all happened so quickly. Late last night, I was pulled from the job. I'm a field agent with the FBI and the Bureau placed me on an urgent assignment in Tennessee," he explained and continued with more information than perhaps his superiors in Washington would have preferred.

"I had no idea that the FBI would be in the Caymans? What would they do here? Is it about illegal immigrants or drug smugglers? Can the FBI tap into telephones or into personal computers?"

Her voice quivered as she rapidly asked her scattered questions, not giving him a moment to respond or herself a breaking breath.

"Whoa! Slow down, Brandy. Yes, we do have agents here who work with the local Immigrations Department and we do help to monitor drug traffic. I'm not involved with any of that. I'm a specialist, dealing mainly with acts of embezzlement, racketeering or money laundering."

"Embezzlement… racketeering… money laundering," Brandy stuttered.

"Jennifer, my partner, had set up a contact with an informant. She met the woman in the ladies' room at the art show and with the information she got, we now have enough evidence on an embezzler hiding in the Caymans. It's been a long case and there are many details that I cannot disclose."

"Yes, I understand. But it is all seems so dangerous, especially for a woman like your partner. Will Jennifer be traveling with you?"

"No, she won't. She's the lead agent and has been assigned another partner. Their team will still work with local law enforcement. But don't be fooled by Jennifer's looks. She is a damn good agent, well-trained and highly disciplined."

"The two of you must be locked into very controlled lives?"

"We are not handcuffed to the Bureau. There are free times, like those that I shared with you. Remember? I sure do."

"I remember."

"Brandy, I'm not at liberty to tell you everything. But, after a few weeks, the Memphis case will surely ease. Come there for a visit and help me spend my time," he said with a wink.

"Yes. That does sound nice," she answered, a smile returning to her rosy-red lips.

"No, don't just nod your head and say yes. And don't just flash that gorgeous smile at me. I'm really sincere. I would very much enjoy having a relationship with you. The failure of my marriage has made me move slower than perhaps most other guys might choose to do. But with you, I feel like trying a bit faster than I ever have."

"That's an interesting proposition. Get settled up there in your Tennessee and then call or e-mail. If things are going smoothly, maybe I will come to see you."

"Good. Very good! I hope that's a promise," he said, giving her a warm hug.

They stood together, his arm about her shoulder, watching the sun climb higher into a cloudless sky.

Soft opal foam came gently onto the shore, circling their bare feet then retreating back into the shimmering spearmint waters of the sea.

35

Brandy sorely missed Garrett's soothing presence, which had offered her a reprieve from the ugliness of the other side of her life. Left alone to wait for his phone call or an e-mail, the waiting was hard.

She found odd ways to keep her spirits up and her mind busy. Still there were those times when she was fearful about the FBI agents and their undercover work in the islands.

When this fear would manifest itself, she let paranoia overpower her.

Once she thought she saw a man, lurking across the street. And, on a windy night, when she was startled by strange noises at her back door, she had hidden beneath the covers for one full hour, suspecting that it was footsteps.

She had taken to the habit of not leaving the house as often as she had before. But she never lost her fondness for the comfort of her front porch. She was sitting on her swing the very afternoon that a FedEx courier made a delivery to Seahaven.

"What the devil?" Brandy sparked in surprise when she saw that the return address was GALA ENTERPRISES, Boston, Mass.

The contents of the over-sized envelope consisted of a two-page letter from Stanley Fizer, along with a clipped newspaper headline, a map, and a confirmation slip for a chartered flight to Florida.

Her breath halted and then rushed into spurts of total shock over what she read.

SAMUEL STEINBERG, NEW YORK LAWYER, FOUND DEAD IN HIS HOME.

"Oh my God," she said, her hands clutching the neatly-cut headline. "No, I can't believe this. Not now!"

The dollars in her accounts had piled up like an unyielding log-jam. Their bulging balances were altering the historical flow of the Society's money and Steinberg had sternly warned her of that danger.

At their next meeting she had planned to beg for his help. His death had drastically ended that plan. His death and that of Dr. Lewis Capalo had left her as the only member of the Honor Guard Secret Society.

Going to that funeral was a must, for she had to find out who would replace them.

The next day, when a taxi pulled up in front of Seahaven, Ox Moran was crouched in the bushes across the street. He watched the driver put Brandy's suitcase in the trunk, a lucky sign that she might be gone for awhile.

He let the taxi clear the area before he left his hiding spot and headed to the rear of the empty house.

Brandy's backyard was nothing more than a full collection of scrambled vegetation, all indigenous to the area and thickly thriving. To the left, the neighboring beach house was unoccupied and, on the right, there was nothing but an empty lot where a maze of wild, tangled foliage blocked any view to the yard from that direction.

As a precautionary measure, Moran put on leather gloves before approaching the backdoor. It was tightly bolted, just as it had been once before in his attempt to turn the handle.

He slowly did a visual sweep of the rear exterior, alertly searching for another entry point. Bingo! He smiled a big 'thank you'.

A small, bathroom window had been left ajar, perhaps no more than one inch. He wondered if Brandy had raised it earlier for one of her soaking baths; a female ritual of preening he had been fortunate enough to observe while on another surveillance of her house.

Regardless of why she had failed to close and lock the window, Moran didn't bother to analyze; he quickly put her tiny mistake to his best advantage by raising the window to a full opening.

The exterior ledge was no more than shoulder high for a man of his height. Yet, the brute effort of lifting his entire being up onto that ledge and through that window, might have proven to be an impossible task for a lesser man. But Moran was no ordinary man; he prided his abilities on tackling difficulties and taming their drawbacks.

What could be correctly termed as an unlawful entry, and Moran knew that it was, began, when headfirst, he wedged into the now fully-opened space.

Teetering on his belt buckle, his left hand reached down inside to steady his approach for a smooth landing. Unluckily, that gloved hand grabbed hold of a loose towel, resulting in a comical but loud slide of his big hulk right into the middle of Brandy's white tub.

He might have chuckled had it not been for the newly-acquired bump starting to protrude through his thick hair. He rubbed the sore spot and, with an audible groan, checked his face and arms for scratches or blood, especially blood, not wanting to leave behind any personal evidence of his illegal visit.

Wasting no more time, he got down to the serious business of finding a paper trail of credit card receipts, bank statements, travel brochures or anything else that would lead him to the BIG money that he intended to find.

His twitchy snout, angled from breaks in rough football games, had never failed him before and even here, in this out-of-the-way cottage, it was pungently inhaling the scent.

Rifling through the top, dresser drawer, Moran hit gold when he found the envelope from Stanley Fizer. Brandy had, haphazardly and without much afterthought, thrown the envelope into the clutter of the catch-all drawer never suspecting that it was of any value to anyone else.

But in Moran's detective clutches, it was the forge-ahead clue.

Inside, he found a visitor's map of northern Florida and the first page of Fizer's letter, providing an excellent briefing of what was going on: (1) A chartered jet to Florida, departing the Caymans and arriving in Destin at a private airport on Airport Road. (2) A funeral service on the beach by the Hilton Hotel, the deceased being Samuel Steinberg.

"Alright, female suspect, I know exactly where to find you," Moran chuckled, putting the map into his pocket.

He dug through other bedroom drawers, finding nothing out of the ordinary, only an odd assortment of shorts, t-shirts, bathing suits, and other feminine apparel plus a flashlight, paperback books, and reading glasses.

Moran continued to prowl about, quickly checking the obvious and the not-so-obvious places where clues might be found. The piano stool and the end tables were big negatives. As were the top shelves of closets, the pantry, and under the cushions of the couch and chairs.

He slid his hand behind mirrors and pictures, finding nothing but traces of household dust. And, when he opened the freezer, he was blasted with a spurt of frosty air. As refreshing as the dewy coldness was, it proved to be a total waste of snooping time.

By Brandy's desk, he rummaged through a self-standing shredder where he found an assortment of colorful paper strips, apparently the remains of a postcard. Thankful that she possessed the vertical cut and not the more precise, crisscross model, Moran placed the slender strips on the table and easily aligned the severed pieces.

From his back pocket, he removed a small plastic bag, a handy container for the strips, until he had time to tape the pieces together and scrutinize the written note.

Finally, from a bulletin board above the computer, he retrieved a photograph of a woman in a bathing suit. A 'wow' grin spread across his face!

"Hmmm, MS Cabernet," he said with a wolf whistle!

To better enjoy the almost center-fold pose, he slowly traced his finger along the curves of the woman's figure. Flipping the photo, he read the brief message on the back, signed with the personal message 'your friend, Mildred'.

Whistling again, with more lust, he returned it to its position on the bulletin board, directly above a to-do list and below an advertising leaflet about local art galleries.

Powering on Brandy's computer, he easily brought up Microsoft Outlook and clicked for her e-mails. Slowly scrolling down the unsecured list, the names of Daisy, Patrick, and Shields appeared on the screen.

"Oops," Moran remarked, backing up to the long e-mail containing the recent apology from Shields.

"Mrs. Berman, what's this?" he quizzed. "It appears that you had troubles with a boyfriend and all because of another woman. And it was Ms Cabernet, a.k.a. Mildred. ZAAP!" His hand grabbed his chest, mockingly removing an imaginary arrow.

Another click and the printer came on; he had a copy of the e-mail for later review. Shifting over to the sent messages, he searched for Brandy's reply to the boyfriend, but there didn't seem to be one.

With a slight frown he muttered to himself about the missing piece. But he moved on and put the copy of the apology into his pocket containing the map. Those items, along with the shredded postcard, would soon be catalogued in his briefcase back at the motel.

The details in Fizer's letter and a few notes about Daisy and Patrick, he had duplicated in his keen memory and that was almost as good as paper copies.

He frowned again.

The big scoop he wanted had not been found.

Monitoring Brandy's computer files was what he really needed to do. And, though he was a good bloodhound on the trail of tangible clues, he was never classified as a qualified hacker. Throughout his formative education, his tenure as a scholar dealt strictly with football plays and that had brought only the painful reward of a gimpy knee.

Not one of his brain cells had ever traveled to the playing field of technical application.

But he had talented allies who were true technicians and, on his return to Boston, he could hire an unsavory fellow who was an ace with spying devices and surveillance software.

His nick-name was Caffeine and, like his moniker, he was highly stimulated by the hyped-up and fast-paced mechanics of the internet. He readily knew the vocabulary of this specialized world better than Moran knew his ABC's.

In Caffeine's arsenal of hardware and software, he had ways to drain data from one computer to another. Moran, in his limited mentality, jokingly described the process as jumper-cables. How it really worked was not the issue to him. The fact that Caffeine made it work was all that really mattered.

For the added measure, Moran jotted down Brandy's e-mail address, the brand names of all of her equipment and the on-screen icons, these things the clever Caffeine would stir, like a sweet sugar, into his mug of computer tampering.

Next, on the snooping agenda, was the safety recap of his final walkthrough of the entire house. With white-glove accuracy, Moran would make doubly sure that everything appeared normal to Brandy whenever she returned.

He was a master at this stage of the prowl! Given that he had walked about in stocking feet and had not removed his gloves, no lingering concerns would surface about noticeable footprints or traceable fingerprints.

He made sure that closet doors and furniture drawers were closed and that he had not left his hand imprint on the bedspread when he had leaned down to look under the bed.

Additionally, he had been careful not to sit down, drink water, use the toilet or dial the telephone.

All seemed to be okay by his standards, leaving his mind freer to focus on retrieving his luggage from the motel and purchasing an airline ticket for that important flight to Florida.

How quickly an hour had passed since the search of the house had begun; the fast, second hand movements on his Timex wristwatch made that point, perfectly clear. It was his habit to check the time every ten minutes.

Moran knew that staying too long in an empty house was not a good idea for an uninvited prowler. He had been practicing that theory since the day when an irate homeowner had tried to kill him with a hand gun.

But those unpleasant memories eased off as he reached the exit point in the bathroom. There, he picked up his shoes from their resting place by the tub; and, with an easy pitch towards the window, they were out, dropping in a final, soft thump onto the thick grass.

As an extra precaution, he ripped off ten or twelve inches of Brandy's toilet paper; leaning into the tub, he pressed the streamer into circular passes around the porcelain to remove tiny particles or smudges he may have caused.

The cleaning job instantly reminded him that his own tub back in Boston had never seen such stroking motions by his hands. And, it also reiterated his old belief that males could tolerate living in soiled areas of unidentifiable spots and smelly clutter.

He smiled about it but, just as quickly, reverted back to his professional side, wisely tucking the wadded streamer into his shirt pocket.

Little effort was then needed to slither out the window and slide easily to the ground, which he executed with quiet precision. Standing tall once again, Moran handily repositioned the bathroom window back to the slight, one-inch opening, just as he had found it.

With the confidence of a self-proclaimed he-man, he removed the gloves, put on his brown loafers and silently walked away.

36

The jet banked left and Brandy had a parting look at the island. It was her temporary good-bye to the rainbow colors so vivid of land and sea, and to the British sophisticated essence of life retained for generations in the Caymans. Those proper residents, mixed with the casual new inhabitants, had been quite a contrast to how Brandy had lived in Boston.

Her recent plight with topsy-turvy events had painfully disrupted her attempts at living the comfortable island way. Even the stiffer, upper-lip Brits might have tottered under the emotional pressures so rapidly crushing in on her.

For the time being, however, all the problems of Shields, Garrett, the secret accounts, and her own instability had been put aside and her thoughts seriously concentrated on the unknown that lay ahead in Florida.

After all, this was no joy ride; she was on her way to a funeral and, quite possibly, to the total collapse of the Honor Guard Secret Society.

As the vanity jet climbed higher into cruising, colder altitudes, Brandy lost track of time and distance, never noticing the plane's advances past Cuba and across the vast expanse of the Gulf of Mexico.

"Mrs. Berman," the pilot announced, breaking the silence of her private cabin. "The millionaires' airport is just ahead. Tray table up and belt securely tightened, we are in our approach for Destin."

The custom-built, six-passenger, high-quality aircraft landed with a smooth touch; effortlessly, it glided along the short runway. Brandy collected her personal items in preparation for her next stop – The Hilton Sandestin Beach Golf Resort and Spa.

Perhaps not the usual spot for a New Yorker's funeral; it was, without her understanding of the matter, the announced location for Steinberg's final send-off.

Her hotel room in the main building was nothing out of the ordinary, though she was the first guest to occupy the freshly renovated junior-suite. With the pleated drapes pulled wide, the sliding, glass door afforded her an unobstructed view of the rolling surf and the straight line of beach chairs and umbrellas along the pearly-white beach.

Unpacked and freshly showered, Brandy stretched out on one of the double-sized beds. With her wet, shampooed hair against the headboard and her squeaky-clean feet up on a pillow, she was enjoying this quiet distraction from her troubles.

Tossed across the bed were her reading materials. They were scattered there in no particular order; a cheap-read paperback, a local magazine, courtesy of the hotel, and the second page of the long letter from Fizer.

The specifics of his agenda outlined her free time after check-in and for the rest of the evening. Three lines down, his commands specified the next day's attendance at both the brunch/eulogy, 10:00 a.m., and at the spiritual service on the beach at or near sunset.

There were, additionally, other directives for proper attire at both functions: business suit, skirt or slacks for her morning appearance and a black sundress or black Capri pants at the beach service. He preferred the pants over the sundress as a more respectable choice.

Perfectly aligned, as everything was, under the business letterhead of Gala Enterprises, Brandy surmised that the total presentation of page two had been dictated with strict orders to his secretary Gigi.

"Everything about this is just so Fizer! He is callus, obstinate, and demanding," she muttered aloud as the phone on the nightstand rang before she could finish charactering Stanley Fizer to no one but the bed post.

"Come down and join us," Mindy Morningstar said.

"Thanks, but no thanks. I just shampooed my hair."

"That's a flimsy excuse for now. So I'll change the invitation for dinner. The girls and I are going to a recommended restaurant at Crystal Beach. It's Chef Creehan's Beach Walk; I insist that you come with us. Besides, you have to eat something."

"Okay. That makes sense. What time?"

"About 7:00, the limo is picking us up. Be downstairs."

At the local restaurant, at a table by the window, the hens all wailed about starvation and, without any regard for the final tab, ordered endless dishes of tomato and shrimp soup, eggplant and crabmeat, Caesar salads, grouper, red snapper, tuna, and a rack of lamb.

Yet, throughout their food orgy, with winks and giggles, they kept complaining that their favorite Bostonian waiter Salvatore should have come along to serve them.

"He is a dream, Brandy. I'm telling you, he is the very best of all Italian men. You just **must** meet him," Greta Donna Cupani drooled.

"OH, can that man ride horses! The sheer sight of him up on a big stallion; well, honey, it's just too much to describe," Arnette Lincoln edged in, with the contented smile of a person telling the truth.

Brandy smiled back, but with little interest in their man.

Mindy leaned-in to face Brandy. "The girls do get carried away. You should come to Twin Oaks and judge for yourself. Salvatore is there right now. You will be happy to know that I got rid David D; without Caroline, he is a social has-been."

"Maybe one day I'll go back to Kentucky."

The group continued their chattering until the platters were empty. They then perched upon ten of the bar stools. The cute bartender gave them his spill about being the best Cosmopolitan mixer in all of Destin; and maybe, he went on to boast, maybe in all of Florida.

It was only a matter of time before the pinky brew of his talented skills flushed their faces and they were dizzily plastered.

When they finally emerged into the cool, night air their limo driver obeyed their requests and took them to his favorite spot – The Boathouse Oyster Bar down at the harbor.

It looked like a boathouse and it had been one in years past. But in modern day terms it was THE place for THE party, as the driver enthusiastically described it to them. The rustic building had screened windows that might have been put in place to keep bugs out; but, in no way, did they impede the rollicking music from drifting out and flooding the parking lot.

Once inside the small restaurant/bar/watering hole, the ladies got down to being as casual as the rest of the partying patrons. Off went their expensive high-heels and, in no time, BJ Turner was shouting out her musical requests. With the support of her closest friends, they jumped up and formed a conga line that bumped up one short aisle, then down the other.

Brandy threw away her troubles and joined in the high-stepping procession. Without a doubt, it was the most festive time she had enjoyed in a long time.

All this wonderful jubilation was expressed in this noisy gathering, with a group of ladies she was now describing, in a slurring way, as 'my goodest and bestest friends'!

Later, she had no recall at what hour during that long night that she had been delivered back to the Hilton and assisted upstairs via the elevator to the fifth floor.

Brandy, suffering in a comatose state, rested heavily on the far side of the hotel room, in a double-bed nearest the window. She was sure that there was a window because of the traces of light that filtered in. And, she was sure that in her prone position she was on a bed, propped up on two pillows and covered by cotton sheets.

But little else registered on any cognitive level. And in her condition she had neither the energy nor the balance to do anything else.

It wasn't long before spastic dreams, definitely alcohol induced, began to rumble through her cluttered and woozy mind. Those dreams came and went without her control.

Uneasily, at one point, she could see a woman standing on a tabletop, stapling her bra to overhead rafters already loaded with similar unmentionables.

In another dream, and just as bizarre, that same woman, slightly out of focus, still not identifiable, could be seen kicking her bare feet high into the air, while singing a Bostonian rendition of Dixie, the spirited, national anthem of the South.

These wild displays of behavior would filter in and out with few interruptions, except, of course, when Brandy became painfully aware that the bed seemed to be going in circles.

It was during those spinning and swaying moments that she, one sick little puppy, would hold tightly to the edges of the mattress, praying for help from the goddess of booze and, with every intention of full commitment, promising never to touch one, single drop of a Cosmopolitan, ever – ever again!

The tighter Brandy held on, the more she became embarrassingly aware that she had no clear recollection of **why**, or **how**, or **exactly who** had removed her clothing and had put her into that bed by the window of this strange hotel room.

Each uncontrollable spin brought her swirling view near, on, or around the only chair in the semi-darken room. There, through bloodshot eyes, she caught glimpses of her black skirt and sleeveless blouse, loosely hanging across the chair's wooden arms.

Her Victoria Secret bikini-cuts, the beige French ones, she could feel were appropriately located on her body. Yet, noticeably missing, was a beige bra, size 40 double-D!

37

Large, dark sunglasses helped to shield the elevator's bright lights as Brandy struggled to press the down button. She held onto the side railing as the elevator began its descent to the ground floor. It felt like a rapid, speedy plunge; much too fast for the hang-over that she was nursing.

When the metal doors slid open, the sounds of the lobby echoed brutally in Brandy's sensitive head. Stepping from the carpeted elevator, her three-inch heels clicked across the polished tiles of the lobby.

CLICKETYYCLICK! CLICKETYCLACK!

An excruciating pain thundered in her temples!

The time was 10:20 a.m. and she was unfashionably late for the Steinberg brunch/eulogy in the Coral Room.

"Hey, this way," shouted Mindy Morningstar, motioning for Brandy to join them at the breakfast table for ten. Brandy saw her, but the idea of breakfast food or any food was certainly unappealing, considering the unrest bubbling in her stomach.

"You look rather unsteady," BJ Turner said, laughing as if nothing had happened to the rest of them.

"How can all of you look so fresh? I feel like road kill," Brandy mumbled.

"Practice makes perfect. We are seasoned party girls," Arnet Lincoln snickered. And the eight others knew that as the truth as they laughed while Brandy eased down, propping her hand under her chin and shrugging off such gaiety as being entirely too penetrating for her shaky condition.

Samuel Steinberg's two daughters sorrowfully began the eulogy followed by his partner, Isaac Leftwich, who fondly reviewed the many successful years of their law firm under Samuel's brilliant leadership. Next, capturing the spotlight as she loved to do, Caroline Berman used the mike to drone on and on about her late father's relationship with Uncle Samuel, the touching name she accentuated repeatedly.

Brandy pushed the dark sunglasses closer to her hypersensitive eyes, shielding them as best she could from the high wattage of the overhead lights. She heard little of what was being said and was totally detached from the other living beings in the room.

Her hand never stopped supporting her heavy chin and the black coffee in front of her, never left the cup.

As the final expressions of sympathy gushed through the sound system, Brandy hastily retreated back to her fifth-floor room. It was to be a quiet, solo time to sleep off the dire consequences of overdosing on pretty, pink Cosmos.

Near sunset, the assembly of mourners began to gather on a large, wooden deck where toddy-time was in progress at the hotel's outdoor bar, appropriately named The Barefoots Beachside Bar and Grill. It was the last opportunity for some of them to seek the alcoholic support they required before facing the spiritual send-off of the man-of-the-day.

They were dressed in various fashions from Tommy Bahama florals to conservative solids. Brandy chose to wear a pink sundress in total defiance to Fizer's suggestion for black Capri pants.

Sitting alone at the farthest end of the bar, she ordered a glass of tonic water over ice, with a medicinal twist of lemon.

Down at the beach, the hotel staff had just finished setting up white, folding chairs facing out towards the gulf. A pre-fabricated stage had been anchored in place and a large, single spray of red roses stood in a metal stand, directly in front of a podium.

Only the sunset was left to finish out the arrangements, and only nature could deliver that.

Shields walked up behind Brandy, lightly tapping her on the shoulder. With the posture of a man displaying a strong determination to be noticed, he stood squarely in front of her and extended a 'hello' and a 'good to see you'.

All words of pleasantry were trapped in her throat and she could not utter an immediate response. She did, however, execute, without words, a quick reaction by giving him a visual once-over. Her eyes scanned up and down his body and he stood there allowing her that long look.

It triggered wonderful memories of why she had been attracted to him in the first place. His smile that was so genuine to her, coupled with the aroma of his after-shave had always tempted her to stroke his face.

With wanton temptation she slid her hands along her dress. It would be so pleasurable to reach up, to touch that face and, without regret, to release her blocked desire to be with him.

But she would not allow herself to do so.

In that moment of hesitation, it was as if she had fallen into a field of poison ivy. A hot, prickly rash popped out on the back of her neck; it crept up to her ear lobes and crawled down to the tender spot over her heart.

His heart thumped loudly when he saw this reaction. "I'm really glad I made this trip," he said. "No, it's more than just being glad; I came here determined to see you."

"We both look a little foolish wearing these silly flip-flops. I usually have on three-inch heels with a matching purse," she blurted out with jittery nerves.

"You always looked good to me in anything you wore. Today, you are more beautiful than I could have imagined," he said.

"You look pretty good yourself. With that tan I suspect that you've been out fishing." Her eyes darted away. Mentioning the boat was the very word that could lead to the unpleasant subject of Mildred.

But Shields cleverly ignored the opening or was, in his own way, trying to avoid the subject himself.

"I sold the boat and moved to Miami. I'm opening a school for bodyguards. I really think that there is a market for trained guards with all the drug wars and international kidnapping that goes on."

"Oh, I didn't know about the sale of the boat. I guess that's good if you were ready for a change. The piano is still my preoccupation. I've really been busy with my music and other things."

"Yea, time flies when I'm busy. Millie and I live in a small condo in Miami and she waits for me every afternoon. And when I'm late, she acts up," he responded, without thinking.

"Sounds cute and cozy," Brandy snapped back.

"Shit," he sputtered, knowing his comments had lit the fire. "Millie is a cat. When Mildred took off, she forgot about me and the cat. Listen, the thing with Mildred should never have happened."

"Yeah, that's right. It shouldn't have!"

"It was a crazy mid-life blunder, an infectious curse. I tried explaining it to you in an e-mail. But being here, face to face with you, makes it better. I can look into your eyes and promise that I never had any intentions of destroying your trust in me. I'm deeply sorry."

"PROMISE – I've had plenty! I'm in a PROMISE land! Your behavior may have been just a sexual release for you, but the aftermath of your actions left a bombshell in my life."

"Oh, Brandy, I wanted to honor your request that we stay apart for awhile. But the time grew longer and it all became harder for me."

"Hard. Now that's a play on words."

"Ouch! I deserved that," he laughingly replied.

The humor of the moment didn't change what Brandy was deeply feeling.

"After Hubert's death," she managed to say. "I wanted to be sure if I loved you or just needed you. Unfortunately, if it was ever love, it has since withered on the vine. Many things have recently happened for me, and now, I've adjusted and I'm doing fine."

He took her by the shoulders and turned her to face him. "That's not exactly what I had hoped to hear, but I am glad for you. Maybe in the future we can try again, only in a different way. We had something special once, surely we can restart as friends."

"Alright, friend, let's agree that we have reached a plateau of forgiveness. But the next steps can't be rushed, they need to slowly evolve."

"I'll agree to that," Shields said. "Come to Miami. You must come. I want you to see the building I've rented and to meet Millie the cat."

"Sure, one day," she replied. "That's the third invitation I've gotten for a trip. One was to Memphis and the other to Lexington. Maybe I'll do them all."

"Good. We are okay then," Shields responded, handing her his business card. "Be sure and call me; we need to talk."

He smiled and was turning to walk away, but she grabbed his arm and asked, "Where's Mildred now? I think that I would like to know."

"I don't know and that's the truth. She never contacted me. Frankly, I don't care where she went or what she is doing."

"I care; down deep inside, I care. I contributed to her escape from her strict family and that freedom completely changed her. So, maybe in a way, I was responsible for her loose behavior."

"No! Don't punish yourself with that thought. The blame lies exactly where it happened," he sternly responded. "Let's leave it at that."

The funeral wasn't really the place to discuss their sordid, love problems. But, for both of them, it had provided a cleansing forum; a place far removed from their Boston connection. They had arrived on neutral ground where the freedom to speak was uninhibited.

He lightly brushed a farewell kiss to her cheek and said his goodbye.

She watched him walk down the stairs. With a slight sigh, she zipped his business card inside the inner pouch of her purse.

Just in case, she thought.

Overhead, brown pelicans, wings spread wide in a v-formation, glided smoothly in quiet flight. One by one, they then broke free from their communal pattern and, with a direct plunge to the sea, scooped in a fresh dinner of small fish.

Off to the west, the sun was low in a crimson, cloudless sky. It was the signal for the final farewell to a man who had lived a long and productive life. His mourners took their places in the waiting chairs.

Two bearers carried Mrs. Steinberg in her wheelchair, down the wooden stairs and out across the sand to a small, wooden platform where there was a golden urn filled with her husband's ashes.

Her two daughters stood before the gathering and asked that everyone observe five minutes of silence, praying in their own beliefs or simply remembering in a special way their departed father.

So reverent was the pause that there was no disturbance to the sounds of the whispering roll of the calm sea and to the distinctive cries of the gulls, grouped like a singing choir at water's edge.

A robed man, whether rabbi, minister or guru, approached the podium, turned toward the setting sun and stood there without speaking. In moments, with glorious splendor, the sun appeared to float on the horizon of water and sky.

He spoke as it began to slowly disappear.

"That sun rises early with a glow; then it moves into a fullness of warmth. Finally, it descends into darkness. It is like our lives. We humans burst forth into newness. We grow and perform. We give warmth through love. Each of us follows the arc of our defined life and then, like that setting sun, each of us fades from view. Quickly, look at that sun! It has but one brilliant ray left for us to see. Look. It is gone."

No one moved or spoke. Almost instantly, the wind shifted, allowing a cool breeze to settle in. The robed man removed a single bud from the spray of roses and presented it to Mrs. Steinberg. He reached down and picked up the urn, placing it gently on her lap.

"We have hope if we believe that the sun will rise again," he said aloud. "Go then, all of you, and believe in life."

A few people got up, including Shields, and wandered along the beach. Other chose to gather in conversation within groups of three or four. The nine, lady friends, proud of their best behavior, began their retreat back to the bar.

Brandy walked up the stairs alone, carrying with her the words of hope and her own belief for a better tomorrow.

38

The sun did rise the next morning!

Brandy went back to the ordinary things like packing her suitcase and paying her hotel bill.

"Mrs. Berman," the cashier said, returning her credit card. "Ms Morningstar called down and asked that you wait for her."

"Thanks. If she shows up, tell her I'll be outside. A car is to pick me up very soon."

The trip, not counting Shields' apology, had not been a success, given that she had not learned the identity of the Society's new members. There had to be two more for there was no way she could handle it alone.

While she had dressed she had rehashed her various conversations, wondering that perhaps she had missed the signals. Shields had given her his business card and had asked her to call. Was she being too naïve in not considering him as a possible candidate? After all, he had said that they needed to talk.

Isaac Leftwich had done the same, telling her to contact his office. His hug had been respectable, almost business like. Perhaps she had missed that as a signal for he had never hugged her before?

Mrs. Steinberg had sent a note to her room, inviting her to New York. She had stated that as widows they should be cautious about becoming too active before it would be acceptable to society. Had she actually meant the Secret Society?

Brandy had barely begun to rethink these prospects before Mindy Morningstar came charging towards her.

"I was jolted upright this morning by a mental flash." she hurriedly said. "The number three hit me hard and by the time I was in the elevator, it had dropped to the number two. Now, seeing you, I know it to be one."

"It's too early for this, Mindy."

"It's important because it concerns you! A number has been the culprit that has continually disrupted the transference between us. I am attached to you by this number."

"If you are **attached**, explain it to me."

"I'm not sure, yet. I'm hoping for a clearer contact."

"I feel nothing. And, know nothing," Brandy stated just as the shuttle car pulled into the circular drive.

"The owl that was in the tree by your beach house was a villainous omen. It was the last symbol that a predator may attack and perhaps kill you."

This revelation by Mindy really startled Brandy. It quickly brought back the memory of the owl. But she never affirmed it and quickly grabbed the door handle, throwing her suitcase onto the backseat before the driver could offer to help.

As she jumped into the waiting car, Mindy made a final attempt.

"The end is not the end until everything is over. Then, and only then, is it ended. I can help, please let me."

"Get me out of here. Get me to the airport as quickly as you can," Brandy shouted to the startled driver!

"Lady, we'll get there soon enough," the innocent man replied, as he made the turn out the drive. "After the fiery crash I saw yesterday on Highway 98, I'm in no rush to visit hell."

All the way to the airport he couldn't stop talking about it. And when he took Brandy's tip, he offered her a parting piece of advice. "Ain't none of my business, lady, but you oughta calm down a bit. Your health's more important than your speed."

In the waiting area Brandy saw a newspaper article with a photo showing the very accident. The accompanying caption described how a speeding truck had slammed into a rental car driven by a tourist named Ox Moran.

The reporter had written about the gory details and how other motorists had pulled the victim from his car before it was engulfed in flames. The driver of the ill-fated car was, as of publication time, in a coma at Sacred Heart Hospital. The driver of the truck, a Buddy Lee, had no driver's license and no permanent address. He was being held at the local jail while investigations continued.

The names registered an absolute zero with Brandy. She quickly turned to the weather page and then, on page 3, she folded back the crossword puzzle, took out a pen, and let the rest of the sad world go by.

The waiting room, an open area with blue-padded chairs, was relatively quiet except for a few talkative workers. Two vending machines, one for cokes and one for crackers and candy, occupied one corner of the square room. A wall-mounted television set, near the other corner, was tuned to local news, but there was no sound.

"Hello, Brandy," Stanley Fizer called out, walking up to where she sat. "The funeral went well I've been told."

"Yes, it did. However, I don't remember seeing you there."

"Correct. But, of course, I planned everything for the Steinberg family, even to the design of the elaborate golden urn. Quite unique, don't you think?"

"With that brassy gold, I would agree that it was definitely your personal touch."

Nodding at her comments, a bit of amusement appeared on his face; a thing he rarely permitted.

Brief discussions of the funeral's activities followed, occupying the first few minutes of their meeting. As usual, Fizer kept the lead, capturing all the time, boasting of his talent for meticulous details.

"I've never really talked to you about your husband's death," he remarked, directing the subject back to Brandy.

He flashed an exaggerated and pretentious smile, took her arm and escorted her outside the waiting area, which was too public for the private conversation he had in mind.

Brandy offered no resistance, seriously doubting that this meeting was for words of sympathy, especially to her.

She had the wildest thought that this might be the very proclamation of his membership in the Society. But clearly, she had never seriously expected that he would be the one, given that Samuel Steinberg had labeled him no more than an assistant.

Yet, here he was, and if he proclaimed the Society's oath it was mandatory that she accept him.

Fizer looked over his shoulder, back through the glass door as if to ward off any intrusion before proceeding.

"The night of the Kentucky party," he began, "I was the first one to receive a phone call from Capalo. There was a rush about important things that I had to handle and he made sure that I knew about your husband's condition even before the ambulance was called."

"So what? Dr. Capalo alerted you to take care of errands for Hubert and the others."

"**Errands**, you say! That's not accurate. I was no errand boy. I was an important player. Capalo conferred with the medical staffs and Steinberg came from New York with some legal papers. I was the kingpin who stayed in close contact with the two of them and with Edwin Rothchild back in Boston."

"If you had not stepped in, I could have handled those calls about Hubert's condition. As I told you in Kentucky, it should have been my duty as his wife."

"Brandy, you are so far out of the loop," Fizer snickered. "There was a big money deal to sell the old man's share to a new partner named Roy Robinson. The legal papers had to be finalized before Rothchild or Robinson got wind of what was really happening in Kentucky."

"Sell his partnership? Hubert was retiring but he never said anything to me about completely selling out. I just assumed that he would be available as a support to the firm when we would be in Boston."

"Assumptions hold no water. And, it was not your place to know the details of his business. We're talking about the complete turnover of his share in a very profitable CPA firm. A whopping amount of money was on the table. It all required his signature."

"I may be from south Boston, but I'm not stupid as you constantly imply. I guess I do know that signatures would be needed."

"Good! You are finally showing some intelligence," he said with his usual condescending air. "All the credit is mine for the name Hubert Franz Berman appearing on those appropriate documents."

"If I don't act shocked about your devious involvement, I know you'll understand," she glared at him.

"My clever involvement goes to greater depths. At Presbyterian Hospital, on the Tuesday that Hubert died, I made sure that I was alone with him. I stopped any public exposure as to the exact time of his death."

"So now you are telling me that he died days before I was told."

"That's right. However, what you were told is of no importance."

"Thanks. You've just added another reason why I loathe you!"

"Your feelings don't bother me. And I am only interested in setting you straight that I am the one who now holds the cards. I am the only one who heard Hubert's babbling in his last hour."

Brandy had once called Fizer a yellow-bellied, sap-sucker. Now, he positioned himself before her more like a Doberman, crouched of body with bared fangs, ready to lunge forward into an attack.

But she stood rigid, squarely in front of him, waiting for the dreaded moment when she would have to accept him as a partner in the crimes of the Society.

"**OATH**," he spoke the word with theatrical drama! "Brandy, is that what you are looking for? Oh my, that archaic word is no longer appropriate. Because, you see, there is no substance to the Society anymore. Without the, what shall I call them? Yes, without the bursting-at-the-seams funds, there is nothing to have allegiance to."

Bordering on the edge of exploding, she lashed with heated breath. "Cut out the hog-wash and tell me, straight out, are you the new member?"

"Oh, dear Brandy, don't put the cart before the horse. Stay with me on this, little widow. You're dying to know what I have done."

"Move on with it before you are the one dying."

"You're such a testy listener," he said to further irritate her.

Her teeth clenched tighter!

She flashed a death-wish look!

"It's actually rather simple," he continued, ignoring her stiff posture. "The Capalo widow knew about the parade of women in her husband's life. She insisted on avoiding any publicity and wanted a very private service. I stepped in and handled everything. The doc might have been a great plastic surgeon, but he was very sloppy with his personal files. From there it was a hop, skip, and a jump right to Steinberg."

"Did you kill them? Are you that demented?"

"I'm a businessman. What transpired; transpired."

"I'm going straight to the police to tell them about your scheming involvement."

"Tell them what? Tell them some cock-eyed story about three teenagers who buried lots of money, many years ago. Tell them that **you** have been hiding some of the money in a safe place."

"I will. I tell you, I will!"

"Talking to the authorities would do nothing but put you on the defense, probably landing you in jail. Think more carefully before you make a big mistake."

"Don't be so damn condescending to me like I'm some kind of stupid, blond bimbo!"

Her 40 double-Ds nervously projected and her feminine constitution pushed her to the limits to bear his massive ego.

"Capalo hid account numbers, names, and little scribbled notes in a concealed, desk drawer. With his coded access to his computer, it was so easy to transfer his share of the money. He was weak for the women and he was a weak link to the Society."

"I don't believe that Samuel Steinberg was an easy target for you. What ghastly thing did you do to him?"

"He grabbed his chest when he learned of the transfer of Capalo's money. And, his racing heart stopped pumping when I showed him Capalo's handwritten note about you being Hubert's successor. The sweet Mrs. Steinberg, in her expensive wheelchair, was never the wiser."

"What about me, am I next? Do you have some lavish plan to make me tell you about my accounts?"

"That's not necessary. I followed all of the doc's mislaid notes and I have already been to the hidden safe. By the way, I like your photographs of sunsets. Nice arrangement there above your bed," he sneered, setting the worm bait, watching her squirm.

"You **were** in my home?"

"And, on your computer," he added.

"I don't believe this. You have a voracious appetite to destroy lives. You are the most…most arrogant, conniving……..absolutely…. **disgusting** person that I have ever met!"

"Thank you," Fizer replied, bowing to mock her outburst.

"It's all gone from my computer?"

"The whole kit and caboodle from all three computers," he boasted. "By the way, your computer is gone, too. I salvaged the hard drive for my needs and everything else went into a deep, watery grave."

"You go to great lengths in your madness," a stunned Brandy huffed!

"What can I say? I'm amazing aren't I?"

"No. You are far beyond any description of despicable behavior!"

"Come now, Brandy. No need for such an insulting display. After all, we do have some similarities."

"There is no way that I am anything like you!"

"Miss Jane Banks, you have been a thief, cheating the truth. I know many, many things about you. I read your e-mails and read the note on those flowers from the guy Garrett."

The black widow had bitten, had finally poisoned her thoughts.

"Did you send someone to spy on me?" she asked with disgust at herself, suddenly suspicious that Garrett Grayson may have snooped around to gather information for Fizer.

"Don't be absurd. I work alone. I'm too smart to use partners."

Those words were a soothing gel. Her disgust had turned into embarrassment that she had allowed this suspicion in the first place. Garrett was, as he had proclaimed, a loving suitor who deeply enjoyed her company and her music.

"Okay, Brandy, I'll confess. There was one person, though he was none the wiser. As an attendance prize just for you, I got Shields Mason to the funeral. It was my little joke."

"Shields had nothing what-so-ever to do with any of this!"

"I saw the looks and the touches between the two of you. I would say that he had a great deal of involvement in the old man's absence."

"You are killing me, inch by inch."

"Actually, I had planned to do away with you," he said, enjoying the mixture of anger and fear blanching across her face. "But, now, it's a waste of my time to see you as a threat. Besides, by tomorrow, Stanley

Fizer will no longer exist and I, with my new name and new millions, will disappear forever. And, you, pathetic little widow, will never know where."

"There is no way in hell that I would come looking for you!"

"I have no doubts about that. Yet, I'm almost sorry that our combat is over. It has been stimulating!"

"Someday, you will meet your match," she warned with contempt.

"Perhaps? But, I doubt it."

He walked away; suddenly stopped and walked the few paces back to where she stood.

"I'll leave you with one last statement of my profound wisdom," he boasted. "The best kept secret is the one that is never shared. Think on it, little widow."

With that, he left her outside the waiting room.

39

Stepping from the taxi onto the familiar walkway in front of Seahaven, Brandy paused momentarily to deeply inhale the sweet-scented air of the islands.

A steady stir of an ocean breeze parted her blond hair and rustled the hem of her cotton skirt. She glanced up to the small, widow's walk atop her mint-green bungalow. She smiled at the cuteness of its dainty placement that added height, but no real access for a lookout towards the sea.

Her eyes lowered to the view of her front porch, its long sweeping veranda reaching out to her. Welcome home was its message! Her heart leaped in thanksgiving for the uncomplicated beauty of her endearing retreat.

Oh, the potted plants may have needed water and the porch could use a good mopping; but those things could wait.

Instead, she placed her suitcase by the creamy-yellow door and walked over to the rocker where Garrett Grayson often sat. Stroking her hands across the smooth wood, memories flooded her mind with the fantastic replay of their endless conversations on that very porch.

She settled into the downy cushions of the swing, cuddling within the warmth of familiarity. With a light press of her left foot against the wooden floor, she pushed the swing into a steady rhythm, back and forth it floated.

What a joy to have these simple possessions! Sometimes taken for granted, they had gained prominence on this special day!

The dirty, secret money was gone, and with good riddance! The crisp, clean money from Hubert's life insurance and the five-million from her inheritance were at her disposal in legitimate, banking accounts.

She was solvent and anchored. And free!

Free from Fizer and from the overload of the stressful months that were now washed away into the past. Free to relax without hidden worries, to gaily ponder on easier days ahead.

Suddenly, a burst of thunderous music shattered all calm! Booming, booming louder and louder, it blared without mercy! There was no way to ignore it, save from cupping her palms to her ears. And, there was no way to label it into a category of quality music.

Stepping to the very edge of the porch, she determined that the deafening sounds were vibrating from the house next door. Strange, it seemed to her, why there would be any activity at that particular house, since no one had lived there for well over three months.

High, thick rows of hedges, separating the two lots, blocked her view. She wandered closer to the boundary of the two yards. There she found a gap among low branches. By crouching down in line with this opening, she had a good vantage point to see who and what was causing all the wild commotion.

What she saw was a young man on the front porch, his CD player wedged upright on the wooden railing. Void of a shirt, this yet unknown neighbor was flexing his muscles in a series of push-ups.

Without question he was Herculean, a man of brawny physique! Perfectly trim and physically fit, his muscles were well defined and glistening with the sweat of the strenuous workout that he performed to the erratic mania.

"YO," she shrieked!

This raw expression of delight spontaneously rolled from her tongue like that of a flirty schoolgirl on the streets of south Boston. Instantly, her hand flew up to silence her open mouth. Paralyzed by the thought that the young man may have heard her, she was locked in place. Gradually she managed to dig her feet deeper into the sandy soil as she crouched much lower, attempting to hide her inquisitive body.

Willfully watching! Nervously listening! And throw in perspiring, for that is what she was doing. She was, indeed, perspiring, quite profusely for a lady who had always shunned any type of outdoor exercises.

Boom…da-boom…da-boom! The music blasted forcefully; the ground was literally shaking beneath her feet. Yet the robust muscleman never stopped his pushups, never looked her way.

Brandy quivered with excitement and a few pleasurable sighs slipped out until that moment when embarrassment overpowered her actions. The wide, contented smile plastered on her face, drooped downward.

How absurd that a woman her age, could react in such a way! Yet, she could not deny it. The young man had innocently provided her with these unexpected moments of sneaky viewing.

In retreat, she crawled sideways like a crab, darting away from the opening. She stood up, pressing her hands to a new, sore spot in her lower back. Moaning, she reached down and brushed away the tell-tale sand from her dirty knees. Then, with hormones propelling her, she shot straight to her kitchen for a drink of water. She needed it!

As the cold water began to squelch the flames in her body, the pearly sweat beads, dewy fresh on her neck and forehead, gradually dried away. She refilled the glass and drank heavily to its last drop.

Rolling the chilly glass back and forth across her forehead, she regained her composure and reverted back to being a sensible woman with poise and maturity.

She retrieved her suitcase from the porch and, leaving the door open for air through the screen, she headed towards the bedroom to unpack. Passing her desk, she stopped cold-turkey. There sat a new laptop in the very spot of her old computer, the one that Fizer, in their tit-for-tat at the airport, had so boldly boasted of its destruction.

Gone, too, was the ugly conglomeration of electrical wiring that once hung off the side of the desk down to the floor. That ten-foot-long mixture of tangled wires had always gathered dust in an unruly maze. Now, a new assortment of black, gray, and creamed-colored ones lay in a straight line from the desk, down to a new surge protector.

Even if Brandy harbored pangs of animosity towards the devious Stanley Fizer, she could not deny that the man reeked of neatness. Damn it all, he was a perfectionist and deserved that one compliment though it fell hard from her lips.

She turned on the laptop to see what, if anything, he had set up on this new Dell. As the blue screen lit up, familiar icons popped on, including the one for her e-mails.

She quickly retrieved three: one each from Daisy, Scottie, and Patrick. Just as she had keyed in the name DAISY for a brief response, a rapid series of knocks pelted the front, screen door

"Hi," she said with a smile, surprised to see Hercules standing there.

"I'm Joey," he announced through the screen. "My grandmother bought the house next door and she sent me over to apologize for my loud music."

"Loud music?"

"Yea, you know, like she thought that I was bugging people because I had a CD on. When Grammy drove up, man did she yell! She said that it had to stop because the new neighbors might think that a hooligan had moved in."

"She said hooligan?"

"Yea. That's a word she always uses. It's an old word like Grammy. Man, you know, like it means I'm weird or something."

"Actually, Joey, it means a rowdy person," Brandy explained, thus without thought, casting herself into the pool of old folks, exactly as he had described his own grandmother.

"Whatever," he said, shrugging his shoulders.

"Will you be living next door?"

"Ain't no way, dude! Living with my parents is bad enough. Living with Grammy would be, like you know, just too many rules. Older women act that way, but I guess you know that."

"Sure," she chuckled at the truthfulness of his statement.

"Well, that's it. I did what Grammy told me to do."

"It has been nice meeting you, Joey. Please tell your grandmother that I wasn't disturbed by your music and that I think she has a great grandson who is really with-it."

"Cool," he remarked as he left the porch, jumping over her gate and disappearing beyond the broad-leaf bushes.

"Cool," she sighed, as if the word itself would cool her wicked thoughts.

* * * *

DAISY: My delay in replying is because my old computer has been put to rest. It's good that the weather has turned sunny in Boston; too bad, though, that your patrons are still complaining. Tell them to cool it and to enjoy the pleasures in life, like that sunshine or just simply looking at a cute, young man! It works!! ☺ Brandy

SCOTTIE: So sad to read your message about Mama Eve's death. She lived a good, long life and gave away a great deal of money. I bet she has her crown. I'm going to change my ways and smell the roses. Hope you get to smell the winning roses at the Kentucky Derby. Brandy.

PATRICK: Is your mother still delaying your wedding? Find her a boyfriend at Mac's Bar. (Ha!! Ha!!) Tell Father Murphy hello for me and that there will be a donation for the church. It will be in the mail soon. Keep the faith, Brandy

DEAR GARRETT: I attended a funeral and I came back home a changed person. Suddenly, I feel so FREE and ready to move on to better things. Say 'when' for my visit and I'll be there with a bottle full of our emerald sea and a bag of sugary sand. With you as my sunshine, we'll have our own little island up there in Tennessee. Have I pumped your interest or am I going too fast? What do you think? Love, Brandy

CPSIA information can be obtained at www.ICGtesting.com
Printed in the USA
LVOW11s0350090316

478342LV00001B/87/P